'My goodness what fruity language Fry uses! You can feel his enjoyment, and also the huge force of his desire to please you, as you read this'

Mail on Sunday

Also by Stephen Fry

FICTION

The Liar
The Hippopotamus
Making History

NON-FICTION

Paperweight
Moab is My Washpot
Rescuing the Spectacled Bear
The Ode Less Travelled
The Fry Chronicles

stephen fry

The Stars' Tennis Balls

arrow books

Reissued by Arrow Books 2011

13 15 17 19 20 18 16 14 12

First published in Great Britain in 2000 by Hutchinson
First published in paperback in Great Britain in 2001 by Arrow Books

Arrow Books
The Random House Group Limited
20 Vauxhall Bridge Road, London SW1V 2SA

Addresses for companies within The Random House Group Limited can be found at:
www.randomhouse.co.uk/offices.htm

The Random House Group Limited Reg. No. 954009

www.randomhouse.co.uk

A CIP catalogue record for this book
is available from the British Library

ISBN 9780099471554

Typeset by Palimpsest Book Production Limited, Falkirk, Stirlingshire

The Random House Group Limited supports The Forest Stewardship Council® (FSC®), the leading international forest-certification organisation. Our books carrying the FSC label are printed on FSC®-certified paper. FSC is the only forest-certification scheme supported by the leading environmental organisations, including Greenpeace. Our paper procurement policy can be found at
www.randomhouse.co.uk/environment

Printed and bound in Great Britain by Clays Ltd, St Ives plc

To M' Colleague

We are merely the stars' tennis balls, struck and banded

Which way please them

John Webster, *The Duchess of Malfi*, Act V Scene 3

1

It all began some time in the last century, in an age when lovers wrote letters to each other sealed up in envelopes. Sometimes they used coloured inks to show their love, or they perfumed their writing-paper with scent.

41 Plough Lane,
Hampstead,
London NW3

Monday, June 2nd 1980

Darling Ned –

I'm sorry about the smell. I hope you've opened this somewhere private, all on your own. You'll get teased to distraction otherwise. It's called *Rive Gauche*, so I'm feeling like Simone de Beauvoir and I hope you're feeling like Jean-Paul Sartre. Actually I hope you aren't because I think he was pretty horrid to her. I'm writing this upstairs after a row with Pete and Hillary. Ha, ha, ha! Pete and Hillary, Pete and Hillary, Pete and Hillary. You hate it when I call them that, don't you? I love you so much. If you saw my diary you'd *die*. I wrote a whole two pages this morning. I drew up a list of everything that's wonderful and glorious about you and one day when we're together for ever I might let you look at it and you'll die again.

I wrote that you're old-fashioned.

One: the first time we met you stood up when I entered the room, which was sweet, but it was the Hard Rock Café and I was coming out of the kitchen to take your order.

Two: every time I refer to my mum and dad as Peter and Hillary, you go pink and tighten your lips.

Three: when you first talked to Pete and – all right, I'll let you off – when you first talked to Mum and Dad, you let them go on and on about private education and private health and how terrible it was and how evil the government is and *you never said a word.* About your dad being a Tory MP, I mean. You talked beautifully about the weather and incomprehensibly about cricket. But you never let on.

That's what the row today was about, in fact. Your dad was on *Weekend World* at lunchtime, you prolly saw him. (I love you, by the way. God, I love you so much.)

'Where do they find them?' barked Pete, stabbing a finger at the television. 'Where *do* they find them?'

'Find who?' I said coldly, gearing up for a fight.

'*Whom,*' said Hillary.

'These tweed-jacketed throwbacks,' said Pete. 'Look at the old fart. What right has he got to talk about the miners? He wouldn't recognise a lump of coal if it fell into his bowl of Brown Windsor soup.'

'You remember the boy I brought home last week?' I said, with what I'm pretty sure any observer would call icy calm.

'Job security he says!' Peter yelled at the screen. 'When have *you* ever had to worry about job security, Mr Eton, Oxford and the Guards?' Then he turned to me. 'Hm? What boy? When?'

He *always* does that when you ask him a question – says something else first, completely off the subject, and *then* answers your question with one (or more) of his own. Drives me *mad*. (So do you, darling Neddy. But mad with deepest love.) If you were to say to my father, 'Pete, what year was the battle of Hastings?' he'd say, 'They're cutting back on unemployment benefit. In real terms it's gone down by five per cent in just two years. Five per cent. Bastards. Hastings? Why do you want to know? Why Hastings? Hastings was nothing but a clash between warlords and robber barons. The only battle worth knowing about is the battle between . . .' and he'd be off. He *knows* it drives me mad. I think it prolly drives Hillary mad too. Anyway, I persevered.

'The boy I brought home,' I said. 'His name was Ned. You remember him perfectly well. It was his half term. He came into the Hard Rock two weeks ago.'

'The Sloane Ranger in the cricket jumper, what about him?'

'He is *not* a Sloane Ranger!'

'Looked like one to me. Didn't he look like a Sloane Ranger to you, Hills?'

'He was certainly very polite,' Hillary said.

'Exactly.' Pete returned to the bloody TV where there was a shot of your dad trying to address a group of Yorkshire miners, which I have to admit *was* quite funny. 'Look at that! First time the old fascist has ever been north of Watford in his life, I guarantee you. Except when he's passing through on his way to Scotland to murder grouse. Unbelievable. *Unbelievable*.'

'Never mind Watford, when did you last go north of *Hampstead*?' I said. Well, shouted. Which was fair I think, because he was driving me mad and he can be *such* a hypocrite sometimes.

Hillary went all don't-you-talk-to-your-father-like-that-ish and then got back to her article. She's doing a new column now, for *Spare Rib*, and gets ratty very easily.

'You seem to have forgotten that I took my doctorate at Sheffield University,' Pete said, as if that qualified him for the Northerner of the Decade Award.

'Never mind that,' I went on. 'The point is Ned just happens to be that man's son.' And I pointed at the screen with a very exultant finger. Unfortunately the man on camera just at that moment was the presenter.

Pete turned to me with a look of awe. 'That boy is Brian Walden's son?' he said hoarsely. 'You're going out with Brian Walden's *son*?'

It seems that Brian Walden, the presenter, used to be a Labour MP. For one moment Pete had this picture of me stepping out with socialist royalty. I could see his brain rapidly trying to calculate the chances of his worming his way into Brian Walden's confidence (father-in-law to father-in-law) wangling a seat in the next election and progressing triumphantly from the dull grind of the Inner London Education Authority to the thrill and glamour of the House of Commons and national fame. Peter Fendeman, maverick firebrand and hero of the workers, I watched the whole fantasy pass through his greedy eyes. Disgusting.

'Not him!' I said. '*Him!*' Your father had appeared back on screen again, now striding towards the door of Number Ten with papers tucked under his arm.

I love you, Ned. I love you more than the tides love the moon. More than Mickey loves Minnie and Pooh loves honey. I love your big dark eyes and your sweet round bum. I love your mess of hair and your very red lips. They *are* very red in fact, I bet you didn't know that. Very few people have lips that really are red in the way that poets write about red. Yours are the reddest red, a redder red than ever I read of, and I want them all over me *right now* – but oh, no matter how red your lips, how round your bum, how big your eyes, it's *you* that I love. When I saw you standing there at Table Sixteen, smiling at me, it was as if you were entirely without a body at all. I had come out of the kitchen in a foul mood and there shining in front of me I saw this soul. This Ned. This you. A naked soul smiling at me like the sun and I knew I would die if I didn't spend the rest of my life with it.

But still, how I wished this afternoon that your father were a union leader, a teacher in a comprehensive school, the editor of the *Morning Star*, Brian Walden himself – anything but Charles Maddstone, war hero, retired Brigadier of the Guards, ex colonial administrator. Most of all, how I wish he was anything but a cabinet minister in a Conservative government.

That's not right though, is it? You wouldn't be you then, would you?

When Pete and Hillary both *got it*, they stared from me to the screen and back again. Hillary even looked at the chair you sat in the day you came round. Glared at the thing as if she wanted it disinfected and burned.

'Oh, Portia!' she said in what they used to call 'tragic accents'.

Pete, of course, after going as red as Lenin, swallowed his rage and his baffled pride and began to Talk to me. Solemnly. He Understood my adolescent revolt against everything I had been brought up to cherish and believe. No, more than that, he Respected it. 'Do you know, in a kind of way, I'm proud of you, Porsh? Proud of that fighting spirit. You're pushing against authority and isn't that what I've always taught you to do?'

'*What*?' I screeched. (I have to be honest. There's no other word. It was definitely a screech.)

He spread his hands and raised his shoulders with an infernal smugness that will haunt me till the day I die. 'Okay. You've dated the upper-class twit of the year and that's got your dad's attention. You've got Pete listening. Let's talk, yeah?'

I *mean* . . .

I arose calmly, left the room and went upstairs for a think.

Well that's what I *should* have done but I didn't.

In fact I absolutely yelled at him. 'Fuck you, Pete! I hate you! You're pathetic! And you know what else? You're a *snob*. You're a hideous, contemptible snob!' Then I stamped out of the room, slammed the door and ran upstairs for a cry. The President of the Immortals, in Aeschylean phrase, had finished his sport with Portia.

Poo. And more poo.

Anyway, at least they know now. Have you told your parents? I suppose they'll hit the roof as well. Their beloved son ensnared by the daughter of Jewish left-wing intellectuals. If you can call a part-time history lecturer at North East London Polytechnic an intellectual, which in my book you can't.

It wouldn't be love without opposition, would it? I mean, if Juliet's dad had fallen on Romeo's neck and said, 'I'm not losing a daughter, I'm gaining a son,' and Romeo's mum had beamed 'Welcome to the Montague family, Juliet my precious,' it would be a pretty short play.

Anyway, a couple of hours after this 'distressing scene', Pete knocked on my door with a cup of tea. Precision, Portia, precision – he knocked on my door with his knuckles, but you know what I mean. I thought he was going to give me grief, but in fact – well no in fact he *did* give me grief. That is exactly and literally what he gave me. He had just had a phone call from America. Apparently Pete's brother, my Uncle Leo, had a heart attack in New York last night and was dead by the time an ambulance arrived. Too grim. Uncle Leo's wife Rose died of ovarian cancer in January and now he's gone too. He was forty-eight. Forty-eight and dead from a heart attack. So my poor cousin Gordon is coming over to England to stay with us. He was the one who had to call the ambulance and everything. Imagine seeing your own father die in front of you. He's the only child too. He must be in a terrible state, poor thing. I hope he'll like it with us. I think he was brought up quite orthodox so what he'll make of family life here, I can't imagine. Our idea of kosher is a bacon bagel. I've never met him. I've always pictured him as having a black beard, which is insane of course, since he's about our age. Seventeen going on eighteen, that kind of thing.

The result of the day is that peace has broken out in the Fendeman home and next week I shall have a brother to talk to. I'll be able to talk about you.

Which, O Neddy mine, is *more than you ever do*. 'Won a match. Played pretty well I think. Revising hard. Thinking about you a great deal.' I quote the interesting bits.

I know you're busy with exams, but then so am I. Don't worry. *Any* letter that comes from you gives me a fever. I look at the writing and imagine your hand moving over the paper which is enough to make me wriggle like a love-sick eel. I picture your hair flopping down as you write, which is enough to make me writhe and froth like a . . . like a . . . er, I'll come back to you on that one. I think of your legs under the table and a million trillion cells sparkle and fizz inside me. The way you cross a 't' makes me breathless. I hold the back of my envelope to my lips and think of you licking it and my head swims. I'm a dotty dippy dozy dreadful delirious romantic and I love you to heaven.

But I wish wish *wish* you weren't going back to your school next term. Leave and be free like the rest of us. You don't have to go to Oxford, do you? I wouldn't go to *any* university that made me stay on through the winter term after I'd already done all my A levels and all my friends had left, just to sit some special entrance paper. How pompous can you get? Why can't they behave like a normal university? Come with me to Bristol. We'll have a much better time.

I shan't bully you about it though. You must do whatever you want to do.

I love you, I love you, I love you.

I've just had a thought. Suppose your History of Art teacher hadn't taken your class on a trip to the Royal Academy that Saturday? Suppose he had taken you to the Tate or the National Gallery instead? You wouldn't have been in Piccadilly and you wouldn't have gone to the Hard Rock Café for lunch and I wouldn't be the luckiest, happiest, most dementedly in-love girl in the world.

The world is very . . . um . . . (consults the Thomas Hardy textbook that she's supposed to be studying) . . . the world is very contingent.

So there.

I'm kissing the air around me.

Love and love and love and love and love

Your Portia X

Only one X, because a quintillion wouldn't be anything like enough.

7th June 1980

My darling Portia

Thank you for a wonderful letter. After your (completely justified) criticism of my terrible style of letter-writing, this is going to be completely tricky. It just seems to gush out of you like a geezer (spelling?) and I'm not too hot at that kind of thing. Also your handwriting is completely perfect (like everything else about you of course) and mine is completely illegible. I thought of responding to your little extra (which was fantastic, by the way) by spraying this envelope with eau de cologne or after-shave, but I haven't got any. I don't suppose the linseed oil I use for my cricket bat would entice you? Thought not.

I'm *so* sorry you had a row with your family. Would it help at all if you were to tell Peter (there, I said it!) that I am completely poor? We never go abroad for holidays, it's all my father can do to send me here and I know that it doesn't sound very left wing or anything but he spends all the rest on travelling between London and his constituency and trying to stop our house from falling down. If I had any brothers or sisters, I'd probably (by the way, where on *earth* did you get 'prolly' from?) have to wear their hand-me-downs, as it is, I wear *his*. I'm the only boy in the school who goes around in cavalry twills and old hacking jackets on days when we don't have to wear uniform. I even wear his old boater, which is almost orange with age, and the edge of the brim is chipped. When my mum was alive she genuinely used to darn socks for me, like some Victorian. So my father may be a fascist (which I honestly don't think he is) but he's a completely poor one. Also, I told him that I met a girl in London and he was very pleased. He didn't hit the roof at all when I said you had a Saturday job from school working as a waitress at a hamburger restaurant. In fact he said it sounded like you had some initiative. And as for the Jewish thing – he was very interested and wondered if your family were refugees from Hitler. He had something to do with the War Crimes in Nuremburg (berg?) and . . . oh, anyway I'm not trying to say my father is better than yours – I thought your parents were really nice actually – it's just that you don't have to worry about him disapproving or anything. He can't wait to meet you, and I can't wait for you to meet him. Most people assume he's my grandfather, because he's older than most parents, if you know what I mean. He is a very *good* man I think, but I know I'm completely biased. Anyway, he's all I have. My mother died when I was born. Didn't I tell you before? My fault really. I was her first one and she was nearly fifty.

What terrible news about your uncle in America. I'm so sorry. I hope Gordon turns out to be a nice bloke. It'll be great for you to have a brother at last. All *my* cousins are completely scary.

I just cannot wait for term to end. Thank God the last exam is over. I've been revising so hard that my head is bleeding, but I still don't think I've done as well as I need to.

Boring school gossip, Number One: I've been made Head Boy.

Ta-ra!

We call it 'Captain of School' actually. Just for next term but I'll be too busy revising for Oxford entrance for it to mean much. (More on that subject in a bit.) Anyway, by the time you get to my age all the glamour goes out of authority. It just becomes hard work and endless meetings with the headmaster and school monitors – we call prefects Monitors here, don't ask me why.

Number Two: the Sailing Club is going to the west coast of Scotland this August. The master in charge has invited me along. For two weeks: the very same two weeks you and your family are going to Italy, so it's the same two weeks we would have been away from each other anyway. For the rest of the time I'll be staying in my father's flat in Victoria and you'll be there with me as much as possible I hope! Are you going to get a job at the Hard Rock again?

Anyway. Oxford. I can't bear either that I've got to come back here in September while you'll be as free as a bird. For two pins I'd forget the whole thing and apply to Bristol and be with you. It's not that I'm really so stuck on Oxford, it's just that I know it would break my father's heart if I didn't go. His great-great-grandfather was at St Mark's and every Maddstone since. There's even a quad named after us. You might think that would make it easier for me to get in, but actually it doesn't work like that any more. I'll actually have to do better in my entrance exam than virtually anyone, just to prove that I've got in on merit not on family name and connections. It would mean so much to him. I hope that doesn't sound chronically pathetic. I'm his only son and I just know how much he'd love coming to visit me and walking round the colleges and pointing out his old haunts and so on.

I wish you could come and visit me *here*. Suppose next term I smuggle you in as a new boy? All you've got to do is squeak and look pretty, and you're very good at that. No, not pretty – you're beautiful of course. The most beautiful thing I've ever seen or ever will see. (You are very good at squeaking though.)

I *love* your letters. I still can't believe all this is true. Has it really happened to us? Other boys here have girlfriends too but I'm certain it's not the same for them. They show their letters around and make a great show of drooling publicly over them. That must be a sign that it's really no more than a joke to them. And it isn't a joke for us, is it?

You mention that strange thing about Fate and how it was that our school group was at the Royal Academy and how, if we hadn't been, we probably wouldn't have gone into the Hard Rock Café. That is such a completely *weird* thought. But then, when you came up to our table there were I think seven of us and why was it you looked twice at me? Apart from the fact that I'm such a moron that I was standing up. I really hate to disillusion you on that, by the way, but it wasn't politeness that made me stand up. I saw you and I stood up. It was like a sort of instinct. This must sound completely crazy – it was as if I had known you for ever. What's more, if I think about it, I could swear that I *knew* you were going to come out of that swing door. I had been feeling funny all day. Feeling *different* if you know what I mean, and by the time we got into the restaurant after sweating around the gallery for two hours and walking half a mile down Piccadilly I just knew something was going to happen to me. And when you started coming towards us (you patted the front of your apron and checked your ear for a pencil in the *funniest* way – I can remember every detail of it) I just leap to my feet. I nearly shouted out, 'At last!' and then you looked up into my eyes and we smiled at each other and that was it.

But you must have noticed the other boys there. Most of them surely taller and better looking than me? Ashley Barson-Garland was there, who's twenty times funnier and twenty times brainier.

That reminds me . . . I did something *completely* awful this morning, in Biology. It's a bit complicated to describe and I feel awful about it. It's not something for you to worry about, but it was odd. I read Barson-Garland's diary. Part of it. I've never done anything like that before and I just don't know what came over me. I'll tell you all about it when we meet.

When we meet.
When we meet.
When we meet.

I just CANNOT stop thinking about you. All kinds of wicked things start happening to me.

Before I was born my father was a District Commissioner in the Sudan. I remember him telling me once that young men arriving from Britain used to go about in ironed khaki shorts and sometimes, if they happened across one of the beautiful Nubian women who went around bare-topped, or often entirely bare, they would have to turn and face the wall or just sit down on the ground there and then, where they were, to cover the fact, as my father puts it, 'that they had become a little excited downstairs.' Well, just imagining you reading this letter, just knowing that these words will soon be in your eyes, that gets *me* a little excited downstairs. A *lot* excited downstairs.

So when I say that I'm thinking of you and thinking *hard*, you'll know what I mean. Well, I've gone and made myself blush now. I adore you so much that I hardly know what to do with myself except laugh.

I love you to the power of everything, plus one.

Ned X

Ned never knew why he had done such a sly and terrible thing. Perhaps it was Fate, perhaps it was the Devil, in whom he believed sincerely.

He had slipped the book from Ashley Barson-Garland's bag, dropped it onto his knees and opened the first page before he was even aware of what he was doing. His right hand lay on the desk and pretended every now and then to slide backwards and forwards through Advanced Cell Biology.

Lowering his eyes to his lap, he began to read.

It was a diary. He did not know what else he had imagined it might be. It looked at least four years old. He believed that it was its age that had first attracted him to it when he had seen it peeping from the bag. He had seen Ashley carry this book with him everywhere and that had intrigued him.

None the less it was very strange that he should have done such a thing. Ned did not like to think of himself as the kind of person who was interested in other people's diaries.

It was difficult to read. Not the handwriting, which was very small, but clear and strong: Barson-Garland's style was – how should one put it? – *opaque*. Yes, that was an intellectual's word. The style was opaque.

With each line that Ned absorbed, the drowsy buzz of the classroom fell further and further away into the background, until he was entirely alone with the words and a vein that throbbed quick and guilty in his neck.

3rd May 1978
Didsbury

Firstly, it has to be the *accent*. If you get that right, you're close to them. You're halfway there. Not just the accent, mind, the whole delivery. Note the way the voice comes out of the mouth, note too the mouth's limited aperture, the line of the lips, the angle of the head, the dipping of the head, the tilting of the head, the movement of the hands (hands, not arms, they are not Italians after all) and the direction of gaze.

Remember how there used to come a hot buzz of blood to your face on the bus every time you heard your name spoken by them? You believed for one heart-jump of a moment as they repeated and repeated your name that they were talking about you. You truly believed that inexplicably they must *know* you. They had recognised you as one of their own, displaced by some tragic turn of fate. The very first time on the bus, do you remember, they kept mentioning your name? Maybe you were going to be *friends*. How excited you were! They saw it in you. That *thing* you have. They spotted it. That indefinable quality of difference.

Then you twigged. It wasn't you they were talking about. They had no idea you existed. Theirs was another Ashley altogether. An *amusing* Ashley . . .

That's SAY funny, Ashley.
Ashley, that's a RAIL hoot.

Despite the initial bump of disappointment that had jolted you like an electric shock when you realised it wasn't you they were talking about, it still gave you a little glow of pride and connection. Made you walk with a bit of a swing for a day or so, didn't it? Maybe your name, the name you hated so much, the name that shamed you, that you had believed to be so *middle class*, maybe, if one of *them* shared it with you, maybe it was an all right name after all. Could it be that 'Ashley' was, in fact, upper middle class, or even – you never know – *aristocratic*?

Which one of them was Ashley, though? It was absurd, but you caught the name bandied so often that for a shining day or two you wondered whether they could *all* be Ashleys. Then you considered the possibility that Ashley might be a general name they used for 'friend', *their* counterpart of the ugly 'mate' that you heard every day in your concrete playground, just streets away from their stone quadrangle? But then you twigged again.

There was no Ashley. Ashley did not exist. There was only an *actually*.

That's so funny, actually. Actually, that's a real hoot.

Can you actually, can you actually, Ashley, have ever really believed that they might have been talking about *you*? Did you seriously think that their lazy glances might actually, Ashley, have so much as taken you in? Sometimes your face may have been in the way of the arc of their gaze, but could you have truly believed that your identity, or even your face, ever actually, Ashley, *registered*?

Yet they registered on you. Oh, how they registered. You looked at their skin and their hair and wondered how it could be so different from *our* skin and hair. From ordinary people's skin and hair. Was it a genetic gift? You noted the signature patch of flush on their cheeks, a hot scarlet, brighter by far than the dusty crimson bruise that stained the cheeks of the boys at *your* school. You noted too, on some, such pallor and translucence of complexion that you wondered if it might be their diet. Or the diets of their mothers while they still swam in the womb.

What burned into your mind most deeply of all of course, was the Flag. The Flag of the Blest. *Their* Flag. The flop. The flopping fringe. The fringe that flopped. The Flop Fringe Flag. And how it made you ache. What a great hole grew inside you when you gazed upon the Flag. Like a Frenchman, far from home, catching a whiff of Gauloise. Like an Englishman lost in Asia to whose ears there suddenly floats the opening music of *The Archers*. Because always, deep down, you did feel that *their* flag was really *your* flag too. If it weren't for the terrible mistake. And the hole that grew in you, the great ache you felt was not envy, or covetousness. Actually, Ashley, it was *loss*, it was *exile*. You had been banished from your own, all on account of the Terrible Mistake.

And you only ever shared a bus with them, what, five times? Six at most. You watched them climbing aboard and swinging themselves to the back seat, sometimes a hand would push down on *your* head-rest and the proximity of that hand to your head would send you dizzy and you would try to eat the air around you, so deep was your hunger for what they were. For what they had. Breaking rules, probably. Skipping into London out of school uniform. The beautiful, the ridiculous uniform of tailcoats and striped trousers discarded in favour of sweaters and cords. The Flag flying, free to flop without constriction from boaters and top hats.

On the last day, the day before the Move North, you retrieved a boater from under the seat, didn't you? He didn't realise at first that he had come onto the bus wearing it. They teased him and laughing he had skimmed it down towards the driver in mock self-disgust. You *nearly* opened your mouth to tell him it was lodged under the seat in front of you as he passed on his way out, but you kept silent. Ashamed of your North London vowels. You retrieved the boater and you kept it. A shallow straw hat with a ribbon of blue. And afterwards you wore it, didn't you? In your bedroom. You're wearing it now. You are wearing it now, aren't you, you *cheap*, you *creepy*, you *sad* . . . And it *doesn't work*, does it? Your hair is too coarse to flop like a wild Tay salmon or a swatch of Savile Row suiting, your hair *bristles*, like a bog brush, like a suburban doormat. In fact, you aren't *wearing* J. H. G. Etheridge's boater (note the three initials . . . *class*), J. H. G. Etheridge's boater just happens to be On Your Head. Just as this diary is On The Table and this table is On The Floor. The floor isn't wearing the table, the table isn't wearing the diary. There's a gulf, a great gaping gulf of difference. And it is this gulf, this gulf that . . . that's why so often you jerk off into this straw hat, isn't it? Isn't it, you miserable lump of nothing?

*

How did the Terrible Mistake happen? The terrible *series* of mistakes.

How could *your* consciousness be the issue of *his* commonplace seed and *her* dull egg? Birth was the first terrible mistake. The transmigration of souls might explain such a mix-up on such a vast scale. In a previous incarnation you were one of them and now a trace memory lingers to torture you. You are a foundling perhaps, or the bastard by-blow of a ducal indiscretion, farmed off on these woeful people you are obliged to call your parents.

Firstly the name. Ashley. <u>Ashley</u>. <u>ASHLEY</u>. Write it and say it how you like, it just won't do. There's a beery, panatella reek of travelling salesmen in tinted glasses and sheepskin car coats. Ashley is a PE teacher: Ashley says 'Cheers, mate' and 'Wotcher, sunshine'. Ashley drives a Vauxhall. Ashley wears nylon shirts and cotton/polyester mix trousers that are sold as 'leisure slacks'. Ashley eats dinner at lunchtime and supper at dinnertime. Ashley says 'toilet'. Ashley hangs fairy lights around the double-glazed window frames at Christmas. Ashley's wife reads the *Daily Mail* and puts ornaments on the television. Ashley dreams of tarmac driveways. Ashley will never do anything in the world. Ashley is cursed.

Mum and Dad gave you that name.

Don't say Mum and Dad.

Mama and Papa, with the emphasis on the final syllable. Mam*ah* and Pap*ah*. Well, perhaps not. That might over-egg the pudding. (*Note: Always pudding, never 'dessert' or, heaven help us, 'sweet'* . . .) 'Mother' and 'Father' is better.

Mother and Father gave you that name. And the criminal part of it is that, as a name, it's only *just* off. Roy or Lee or Kevin or Dean or Wayne, they're the real thing. *Echt Lumpenproletariat*. Dennis and Desmond and Leonard and Norman and Colin and Neville and Eric are revolting, but they are honest. *Ashley*, though. It's a Howard or a Lindsay or a Leslie kind of a name. It's *nearly* there. It seems to be trying to be there. And that, surely, is the saddest thing of all.

Americans don't have this trouble do they? With

names and the implications of names. The one Ashley, in fact, who might be said to have had a touch of class was American. Ashley in *Gone With the Wind.* So classy that they called him Eshley. In the film, Leslie Howard never even *tried* to give him an American accent. Leslie *and* Howard. Two disgusting names for the price of one. But then Leslie Howard wasn't English. He was Hungarian and to him no doubt, fresh off the boat, Leslie and Howard seemed posh.

The word 'posh' is right out. Unsayable.

But *seemed*. Seemed posh. There's the rub. What people *think* is smart is so far from what actually, Ashley, is. You might think silver fish knives would be pretty bloody pukka, but fish knives of any kind are an absolute no. You might as well put doilies round them and abandon all hope of social pretension.

But it isn't *about* social pretension. It's about the *ache*.

Look, some males grow up with a feeling that they're in the wrong body, don't they? A woman trapped inside a man.

Isn't it possible then that some people might grow up, as it were patricians imprisoned within plebeian bodies? Knowing, *just knowing* that they have been born into the wrong class?

But it isn't *about* class. It's about the *hunger*.

Oh but Ashley, you poor sap, can you actually believe that you're supposed to be of their world?

Don't you know that it's a world you can only be born into?

But that's so *unfair*. If he wanted, a man can become American. He can become Jewish. He can, like Leslie Howard, make himself not just English but a symbol of all that England ever stood for. He can become a Londoner, a Muslim, a woman, a man or a Russian. But he can't become a . . . a . . . nearly said *gentleman* there, didn't you, but what is the word? An aristo, a nob, a public school toff . . . a *one of them*. You can't become one of them, even if you feel yourself to be one of them in the deepest pit of you, even if you know in your innermost knowing self that it is your right, your destiny, your need and your duty. *Even if you know that you could do it better*. And that's the truth. You would carry it off with so much more style. Carry off the ease that belies any sense of anything at all *having* to be carried off, if that isn't too baroque. Carry off that natural, effortless taking-it-all-for-granted air. But the opportunity has been denied you because of the terrible mistake of your birth.

*

The Move North, that was another nail in the coffin. Another element of the Terrible Mistake. Your dad died and Mum got a job teaching at a deaf school in Manchester. Dad had been an officer. In the RAF, it grieves you to admit, not in a smart army regiment.

He never flew, so there was no romance to him. But at least he had been an officer. Be honest now, he was compelled to enter the service as a humble Aircraftsman. He wasn't ever officer class. He had to work his way up through the ranks and Lord that burns you up, doesn't it? Then he died of complications from diabetes, a rather bourgeois, not to say proletarian disease, and you, your mum and your sister Carina moved north. (Carina! Carina, for God's sake! What kind of name is *that*? All very well to say that the Duke of Norfolk has a daughter called Carina. There's a world of difference between saying, 'Have you met the Lady Carina Fitzalan-Howard?' and 'This is Carina Garland.') You moved away from Old Harrow and the proximity of them, their tail-coats, top hats, blazers and boaters. You were twelve years old. Slowly you have become infected by a northern accent. Not obvious, just a trace, but to your sensitive, highly attuned ears as glaring as a cleft palate. You began to pronounce 'One' and 'None' to rhyme with 'Shone' and 'Gone' instead of 'Shun' and 'Gun', you gently sounded the 'g's in 'Ringing' and 'Singing'. At school you even rhyme 'Mud' with 'Good' and 'Grass' with 'Lass'. Fair enough, you would be beaten up as a southern poof otherwise, but you have trailed some of that linguistic mud into the house with you. Not that your mum noticed.

And then this afternoon happened.

She brought some of her deaf kids home for tea

this afternoon. After they had gone you said that good God, they even *signed* in a Mancunian accent. You thought it a good joke. Mum bridled and called you a snob. That was the first time the word was ever said openly. It hung in the air like a fart in a teashop. I pretended not to hear, but we knew that something deep was up because we both blushed and swallowed. I made a fuss of doing up my shoelaces, she became fascinated by the teapot lid.

And I came up and started to write this and . . . ah. I've gone into the first person. I have said 'I'.

Never mind, all this will be past history soon. Watch out, I am about to join them. I am on my way in. And there's nothing they can do to stop me. I'm smarter than they are and braver and better too. I am prepared for every paper and they will not be able to refuse me.

But I must be prepared for the wider scholarship. The scholarship that counts. The scholarship of life, if I may be so sententious. I shall add my mother's maiden name of Barson. Why not? *They* have been doing it for years. I shall be Barson-Garland. It has a ring, I think. Damn it, I could triple-barrel myself. Barson-Barson-Garland, how would that be? A *little* too much, I think. But Barson-Garland I like. It palliates the Ashley, makes it almost tolerable.

But firstly, there must come the accent. When I arrive, the accent will be in place and they will never know. I have my exercises all written out:

Don't say good, say gid.
Don't say post, say paste
Don't say real, say rail
Don't say go, say gay
Don't say –

The outer door to the biology room banged and Ned looked up to see the top of Ashley's head in the window of the inner door. He slammed the diary shut, pushed it hurriedly back into the bag and hunched himself quickly over his Advanced Cell Biology, both fists pressed hard against his cheeks, hair flopping down like a thick silk curtain.

He was in this attitude of intense study when Barson-Garland resumed his place next to him. Ned looked up and smiled. He hoped that the pressure from his fists would explain any heightened flush.

'What was all that about?' he whispered.

'Nothing of great interest,' said Barson-Garland. 'The headmaster wants me to make the Speech Day Oration.'

'Bloody hell, Ash! That's completely brilliant.'

'It's nothing . . . nothing.'

Barson-Garland had rhymed the first 'nothing' with 'frothing' and then quickly corrected himself. Ned tried hard to look as if he hadn't noticed. Half an hour ago he *wouldn't* have noticed. His hand moved to Ashley's shoulder in a sudden surge of warmth and friendship.

'Bloody proud of you, Ash. Always knew you were a genius.'

Dr Sewell's high croak intruded. 'If you have absorbed all that information and have nothing better to do than gossip, Maddstone, then no doubt you will be able to come forward to the blackboard and label this chloroplast for me.'

'Righto, sir.' Ned sighed cheerfully and sent Barson-Garland a rueful smile over his shoulder as he went up.

Barson-Garland was not smiling. He was staring at a dried, pressed four-leaf clover on Ned Maddstone's stool. The same four-leafed clover that had lain undisturbed between the pages of his private journal for three years.

A heavy knock came on the door of Rufus Cade's study. After twenty seconds of oath and panic, Cade hurled himself into his armchair, gave a frenzied look about the room and, satisfied that all was clear, shouted a 'Come in!' that he hoped mingled relaxedness with boredom.

The sardonic face of Ashley Barson-Garland appeared around the door.

'Oh, it's you.'

'None other.' Ashley sat himself down and watched with amused disdain as Cade thrust half his body out of the window and spat mints from his mouth like a passenger heaving over the side of a ferry.

'A charming lavender fragrance seems to be pervading the room,' said Ashley, picking up an aerosol room spray from the desk and inspecting it with benevolent amusement.

Cade, still leaning over the sill, had started to scrabble at the flower-bed beneath his window. 'You might have said it was you.'

'And deny myself the pleasure of this pantomime?'

'Very fucking funny . . .' Cade straightened himself up holding a battered but expertly rolled joint, from which he began gently to flick away fragments of leaf-mould.

Ashley watched with pleasure. 'So delicate. Like an archaeologist brushing soil from a freshly unearthed Etruscan vase.'

'I've got a bottle of Gordon's too,' said Cade. 'Maddstone paid back the five quid he owed me, would you believe?'

'Yes I would believe. I happened to see his proud daddy slipping him a tenner just before the match this afternoon.'

Cade took a Zippo from his pocket. 'What, reward for being made Head Pig next term?'

'Such, I would imagine, is the case. Reward too for being captain of cricket and for breaking the school batting record. For being winsome and good and sweet and kind. For being –'

'You don't like him, do you?' Cade drew in a huge lungful of smoke and offered the joint to Ashley.

'Thank you. It is my belief that you don't like him either, Rufus.'

'Yeah. Well, you're right. I don't.'

'Nothing to do with the fact that he didn't select you for the first eleven?'

'Fuck that,' said Cade. 'Couldn't give a toss about that. He's just . . . he's a prick, that's all. Thinks he's God almighty. Arrogant.'

'So few would agree with you there. I fancy it is the general view of the school that our Nedlet is unflaggingly and endearingly modest.'

'Yeah. Well. He doesn't fool me. He acts like he's got everything.'

'Which he has.'

'Apart from money,' said Cade with relish. 'His father is dirt poor.'

'Yes,' said Ashley, quietly. 'Dirt poor.'

'Not that there's anything wrong with that,' Cade added with tactless haste. 'I didn't mean to say . . . I mean, money isn't . . . you know . . .'

'Isn't everything? I often wonder about that.' Ashley spoke clearly and coolly, as he always did when angry, which was often. Anger fed him and clothed him and he owed it much. Cade's clumsiness had pricked him hard, but he used the rage to let his mind fly. 'Shall we formulate it this way? Money is to Everything, as an Aeroplane is to Australia. The aeroplane isn't Australia, but it remains the only practical way we know of reaching it. So perhaps, metonymically, the aeroplane *is* Australia after all.'

'Gin then?'

'Why not?' From vexation to amusement, at speed. Ashley found it very hard to stay angry with a species as low down the evolutionary ladder as a Cade.

'Your oration was . . . it was amazing,' Cade said, handing Ashley a bottle and a glass tumbler. Ashley noticed that the bottle was half empty while Cade already appeared to be more than half full.

'You liked it?'

'Well it was in Latin, wasn't it? But, yeah. Sounded good.'

'We aim to please.'

'Want to stick some music on?'

'Some music?' Ashley scrutinised Cade's proudly filed stack of records with a fastidious and entirely self-conscious disgust. 'But you don't appear to have any. I mean what, for example, is a Honky Château? A castle filled with geese? A claret that makes you vomit?'

'Elton John. It's years old. You must have heard of it – *shit*!'

A gentle, loose-knuckled knock on the door brought Cade bolt upright. Before he had time to embark once more upon his Colditz routine, Ned Maddstone had entered the room.

'Oh gosh, sorry. Didn't mean to . . . Hey, for goodness' sake, don't worry. I'm not . . . I mean bloody hell, it's almost the end of term. Carry on please. I just . . .'

'Come in, Ned, we're just, you know, having a bit of a celebration,' said Cade, standing up.

'Wow, that's really kind, but actually . . . well, I'm going off to have dinner with my father. He's staying at the George. Thought you might be here, B-G, and I wondered if you wanted to come along? Er, *both* of you. Obviously. You know, last night of term and everything.'

Ashley smiled to himself at the awkward inclusion of Rufus.

'That's really kind,' Rufus was saying, 'but you know. I'm a bit hammered actually. Don't think I'd be much use. Probably embarrass you, as a matter of fact.'

Ned turned anxiously to Ashley. 'Unless you're doing anything else, Ash?'

'I should be honoured, Ned. Truly honoured. Will you

let me go upstairs and change into something a little more vespertine?' He pointed mournfully at his speech day garb. 'You go on ahead. I shall join you at the George if I may.'

'Great. Great. That's great,' said Ned grinning happily. 'Okay then. And Rufus, till August, then?'

'I'm sorry?'

'You *are* coming on Paddy's school trip?'

'Oh. Yeah,' said Cade. 'Sure. Absolutely.'

'I'll see you in Oban, then. Can't wait. Right. Okay then. Good.'

There was a silence in Cade's study after Ned had backed himself out of the room. As if the sun had been blotted out, thought Ashley with great bitterness.

That he, Ashley Barson-Garland, should be *patronised* by this brainless, floppy-haired, goody-two-shoed, squeaky-clean, doe-eyed, prefect-perfect, juicy-fruity piece of –

He saw it, of course, Ashley saw it quite clearly in Ned's eyes. The sorrowful apology. The friendly sympathy. Ned was too stupid to know that he knew. If anyone else, anyone else in the school had read his diary, they would have teased him, mobbed him to hell, spread it all over the school. Ashley wasn't popular, he was fully aware of that. He wasn't *one of them.* He sounded right, but he wasn't one of them. He sounded *too* right. These cretinous sons of upper-class broodmares and high-pedigreed stallions, they were loutish and graceless, entirely undeserving of the privilege accorded them. He, Ashley Barson-Garland, stood apart because he wasn't enough of an oik.

Such splendid irony. But, since it was Ned who had stolen a look into his diary, Ashley's secrets were safe.

Yet, no secret is ever safe when another has possession of it, Ashley told himself. It was intolerable to imagine his life, any part of his life, having a separate existence inside another person's head.

His mind considered the possibility that he had left his bag open beside Ned deliberately. When the message had come that the Headmaster wanted to see him, why had he not taken the bag with him? He was certain that he had never been so lax with his diary before. In the first place he almost never carried it around the school. It was always safely locked up inside the desk in his study. It must be noted too that Biology was the only lesson he took in which he sat next to Ned. Did he therefore *want* Ned to read it? Ashley shook himself out of this spurious cul-de-sac. Cheap psychological guesswork would get him nowhere. More to the point was this question: which pages had Maddstone read? Ned being Ned, Ashley reasoned, he would have started at the beginning. It was impossible that he had got very far. Speed-reading was not one of his accomplishments.

What would Ned have done next? *Prayed* probably. Ashley wanted to snort at the very idea of it. Yes, Ned would have gone to the chapel, fallen to his knees and prayed for guidance. And what manner of guidance would have been offered by Ned's shining auburn-haired shampoo-commercial Christ? 'Go thou and hold Ashley to you as a brother. My son Ashley is frightened and filled with self-hatred. Go thou then and may the kindness and love of God shine upon his countenance and make him whole.'

Sympathy. Ashley's whole body tightened. He wanted to bite Ned's throat open. Wanted to pull the veins and nerves out with his teeth and spit them over the floor. No, that was wrong. That wasn't it at all. He didn't want that. That was a scenario that only ended in Ned's martyrdom. Ashley wanted something far more perfect. He was feeling a new anger that he had some difficulty in identifying at first. It was hatred.

Cade had finished up the gin. 'You're not really going to have dinner with his parents are you?' he asked.

'Going? Certainly I am going,' said Ashley sweetly.

'Don't think he wanted to invite me,' said Cade. 'Cunt.' He banged a fist into the arm of his chair, sending up a puff of dust. 'I mean, what the *fuck* did I stand up for? Like he's a master or something. He acts so fucking *straight*. What a typocritical turd.'

'Typocritical?' said Ashley. 'I like that. Typocritical. You surprise me sometimes, Rufus.'

'Another toke?' Cade proffered a half inch of joint. 'I meant hypocritical.'

'No, you didn't. You may *think* you did, but your brain knew better. You can't have failed to read *The Psychopathology of Everyday Speech*, surely?'

'Bollocks,' said Cade.

Ashley rose. 'Well, I had better be going up to change. What a joy to get out of this confining nonsense.'

This was a lie. Ashley rarely felt more joy than when dressed in the Sunday uniform of striped trousers, tailcoat and top hat.

'Arsehole,' said Cade. 'Fucking fucking arsehole.'

'Why thank you, dear.'

'No, not you. Maddstone. Who the fuck does he think he is?'

'Quite,' said Ashley, leaving. 'Sweet dreams.'

'Mind you,' Rufus Cade rumbled to himself, leaning back in his armchair as the door closed. 'You're an arsehole too, Ashley Bastard-Garland. Let's face it, we're all arseholes. Ow!' He had burnt his bottom lip on the last thin quarter inch of joint. 'All arseholes, except Ned fucking Maddstone. Which makes him,' he reasoned to himself, 'the biggest arsehole of all.'

Pete and Hillary were wearing the insufferably smug look they always assumed when they had made love the previous night. Portia tried to cancel out its atmosphere by moving around the kitchen with extra noise and impatience, banging drawers so loudly that the cutlery inside resonated and jingled like a gamalan. Fierce Tuscan sunlight streamed through the window and lit the big central table where Pete was slitting large batons of bread.

'This morning,' he said, 'we shall feast on prosciutto and buffalo mozzarella. There's cherry jam, there's apricot jam and Hills is brewing up some coffee.'

'We have feasted on exactly the same things every morning since we got here,' said Portia sitting herself down with a glass of orange juice.

'I know. Isn't it wonderful? Hills and I were up early this morning and we went into the village for fresh bread. Smell that. Go on. No, go on.'

'Pete!' Portia pushed the proffered loaf away.

'Someone got out of bed the wrong side this morning . . .'

Portia looked at her father. He wore an unbuttoned batique shirt, an elephant hair bracelet, wooden sandals and, she saw with a shudder, tight maroon swimming trunks that emphasised every bulge and curve of his genitals.

'For God's sake –' she began, but was interrupted by the sleepy, shuffling entrance of her cousin.

'Aha!' said Pete cheerfully. 'It's awake. It's awake and needs feeding.'

'Well *hi* there!' said Hillary who had developed the strange habit of going slightly American whenever she spoke to Gordon. This also drove Portia mad.

'So what's up?' Gordon said, moving a shopping bag from the seat next to Portia and sitting down.

'Well now,' said Hillary brightly, as she set down a coffee jug between them, 'Pete and I were thinking of maybe checking out the palio.'

'It's been and gone, Hillary,' said Portia with the exasperated air of one addressing a child. 'We met that family who'd seen it last week, remember? A rider fell off his horse right in front of them and there was a bone sticking out of his leg. Even you can't have forgotten that.'

'Ah, but there's more than one palio in Italy, precious,' said Pete. 'Lucca has its very own palio this evening. Not as spectacular or dangerous as Siena, but rather fun they tell me.'

'Lucca?' said Gordon through a mouthful of bread. 'Where's Lucca?'

'Not too far,' Pete replied, pouring coffee into a large bowl to which he added hot milk. Fragments of skin floated to the top. Looking at them made Portia want to retch. 'I wanted to go there anyway. It's the olive oil capital of the world, they say. You can watch it being pressed. I thought we might swim and read this morning, then make our way slowly there, driving by the local roads and lunching somewhere in the hills. How's that for a plan?' Skin from the coffee clung to his moustache. Portia had never felt so ashamed of him. How Hillary could suffer such a thing on top of her had always been something of a puzzle. Now that she knew there was such a man as Ned in the world, it took on the qualities of an eternal cosmic mystery.

'Sounds good to me,' said Gordon. 'Sound good to you, Porsh?'

'Completely.'

Portia stopped herself from shrugging moodily. She didn't mind behaving like a spoiled adolescent in front of her parents, but in front of Gordon she preferred to look more sophisticated. What she really wanted to say was, 'So we're going to arrive at Lucca in time to find all the shops and cafés shut, are we? And as usual we're going to have to wander around a completely empty and deserted town for five hours until everyone else has woken from their siestas. That's a great plan, Pete.'

Instead she contented herself with remarking, 'Arnolfini was from Lucca.'

'How's that?' said Gordon.

'There's a painting by van Eyck,' said Portia, 'called *The Arnolfini Marriage*. Arnolfini, the man in the painting, was from Lucca. He was a merchant.'

'Yeah? How d'you know something like that?'

'I don't know, I must have read it somewhere.'

'I never studied art history.'

Portia realised that saying 'Neither did I, you don't have to "study" something to know about it,' would sound arrogant, so once again, she curbed her tongue. Really, she was becoming insufferably intolerant these days. And she liked Gordon. She liked his quiet acceptance of the terrible things that had happened to him. He seemed to like her too and it is very easy, she thought, to like someone who likes you. That wasn't vanity, that was practical common sense.

'Aha, methinks I hear the musical rattle of a Fiat,' said Pete, head cocked in the direction of the driveway, 'bearing, perchance, dispatches from England.'

Portia jumped up. She forgave herself her moodiness. As a junkie needs a fix, so had she been needing a letter. 'I'll go,' she said. 'I need to practise my Italian on him.'

Hillary called after her. 'Porsh, you know your results won't be coming through for at least another week! Besides, Mrs Worrell said she would telephone us here if anything arrived that looked like it might be from the examination board . . .'

But Portia was already out of the house and stepping into the harsh whiteness of day. Never mind exam results. Never mind anything. A letter from Ned, let there be a letter from Ned.

'Buongiorno, Signor Postino!'

'Buongiorno, ragazza mia.'

'Come va, questo giorno?'

'Bene, grazie, bene. E lei?'

'Anche molto bene, mille grazie. Um . . . *una lettera per mi?'*

'Momento, momentino, Signorina. Eccola! Ma solamente una carta. Mi dispiace, cara mia.'

A postcard, only a postcard. She fought back her disappointment and took it with trembling hands. He was sailing, she told herself. A letter would be difficult. Besides, looking at the postcard with a growing sense of delight, she saw that he had covered it in the tiniest script he could manage and even put the address of the villa in bright red ink so that it stood out against the minuscule blue handwriting which wormed around almost every square millimetre of the card. He had even managed to weave narrow threads of words between the lines of the address, she saw. It was better than a letter. To see how much care he had taken. A thousand times better. She was so full of delight and love that she almost broke into sobs.

'Ciao, bella!'

'Ciao, Signor Postino!'

She turned the card over and looked at the photograph on the front, shielding her eyes from the reflective dazzle. A small fishing port glittered in a softer sunlight than the one that glared down on her now. 'The Harbour, Tobermorey' the caption read in old-fashioned yellow cursive letters. The photograph looked as if it might have been taken in the nineteen-fifties. There was a small Morris Minor van parked on the quayside. Then Portia noticed that amongst the jostling crowd of fishing boats there was a little yacht there, hand drawn in red ink. A nervous smile and eyes had been sketched in on its hull, giving it the frightened look that Thomas the Tank Engine adopted when he was squeezed between the big scowling locomotives. An arrow pointed down to the boat from the sky and across the top was written, 'The pirate ship "Nedlet" lies pining at anchor.'

'News from lover boy?' Gordon had come out into the sunshine with *The World According to Garp* and a cup of coffee. He sat himself on a lounger in front of the terrace that ran round the front of the villa and looked up at Portia through dark sunglasses.

She nodded, not trying to disguise her happiness. Gordon crossed his right arm over his chest and scratched his left shoulder-blade. The compressed skin in the V of his elbow, cradled in his chin as he scratched, looked tanned almost to black. When he straightened out his arm again the effect was gone.

'He's sailing, right?'

'In Scotland.'

'I never been on a sailboat.'

'Nor me. I'm sure I'd be completely sick.' Portia had started using the word 'completely' a lot recently. Ned peppered his letters with it, and she thought of it as his word. Saying it was like wearing an old shirt of his and made her comfortable and proud.

'Uh-huh,' Gordon nodded seriously as if she had said a profound and interesting thing. Then he picked up a bottle of Hawaiian Tropic tanning oil. 'You want to rub some of this on me?'

'Okay . . .'

Portia put down the postcard and took the bottle.

'I'll turn around here and you can do my back.'

A wave of coconut arose from the palms of her hands as she rubbed them together. She noticed, smoothing oil over his skin, that Gordon had silvery filaments of hair growing in the small of his back, feathered and whorled like a wheat field after a storm, while darker hairs snaked along his shoulders from the base of the neck. She could feel their slight roughness under her hands. His chest was already dense with tight curly black hairs and his beard line heavier than Pete's who was more than twice his age. She wondered why this might be. It wasn't an ethnic thing. Pete was no less Jewish than Gordon. Perhaps it was something to do with the English climate. She thought of Ned and how proudly he had announced that he was 'going to have a bash' at growing a moustache over the summer.

Portia poured a small puddle of oil into the hollow at the base of Gordon's back. Ned was strong, but she did not think he had muscles that were packed as hard and tight under the skin as Gordon's. Every afternoon Gordon had gone into a routine of press-ups, pull-ups and sit-ups in the shade of the paved courtyard behind the villa, to Pete's apparent amusement and Hillary's poorly feigned lack of interest. Portia had watched Hillary watching from the kitchen and Pete had watched Portia watch Hillary watching and Portia knew that Pete had been thinking about his own drooping flab and evolving a socio-political explanation that would justify and ennoble it.

In New York Gordon played regularly on his school's tennis and lacrosse teams. He had been outraged to learn that in England lacrosse was a game played almost exclusively by girls in private schools. 'He's quite right,' Ned had told Portia in a letter. 'Lacrosse is a very hard, tough and physical game. It would scare me stiff. That's why I think it is much better left to you girls.'

Portia smiled as she contemplated the future. She pictured the days when she would be able to rub sun tan lotion on Ned's back on holidays yet to come in places yet to be imagined. It was strange, she thought, that she didn't yet know his body. She had never seen him in shorts or swimming trunks. She had never seen him naked. Once, when they had kissed, she had felt something push against her thigh. A hot rush of blood spread across her face at this memory and she giggled inside herself as she recalled the naivety with which she had originally supposed him to have had something in his pocket. Perhaps next week, in his father's flat they would go upstairs together. Perhaps –

'Where is "The Harbor, Tobermorey"?'

'Hey!' Portia snatched the card from Gordon's hands. 'That's private! Oh *no*!'

Portia looked down in horror. Her oily thumb had smeared across the card obliterating a whole trail of Ned's careful writing.

'No!' she wailed. 'It's ruined! Ruined! How *could* you! You, you *fucker*!'

'Hey, I'm sorry. I was only –'

Portia ran into the house, tears springing from her eyes. Gordon watched her go, shrugged and rearranged his khaki shorts to alleviate the discomfort of a pressing erection.

*

Gordon wondered if it was the fact of her being in love that awoke such a flood of desire within him. He considered that he might be just as much in love himself, only where he came from the phrase 'got the hots for' was more acceptable. Even most British kids, he had noticed, would rather say 'I fancy her' than 'I love her'.

The way Portia confided in him so instantly on his arrival in London had done more to disorient him than the strange food, incomprehensible accents and bewildering geography of the place. He had expected from the British Fendemans more of the chilly reticence and uptight reserve that his father used to talk about when explaining the irrefutable logic of his leaving England for America. Portia's directness not only confused Gordon, it needled him too. It was as if her emotions were more profound than anyone else's. Her very ability to describe them so freely and expressively stopped him from being able to say anything open and honest about himself and he hated that. He had feelings too and right now he felt like he wanted to take this virgin, lay her in a bed and fuck her till her eyes popped out.

That was the crazy injustice of it. She had painted him so far into a corner that the only territory left him was that of a predatory animal. It was so totally unfair. He wasn't like that. He was a good man, a feeling man with a feeling man's heart. He could be charming. He could be romantic. But she gave him no chance to be. Mr Wonderful, Mr Perfect absorbed her whole being. Gordon could see in her eyes that whenever she responded warmly to him she was really responding to Ned. By talking about him so much she had planted the faggoty English goy asshole right inside his head. It was like he was the host to a parasite, and the parasite's name was Ned Maddstone.

If his mother and father had died a year earlier, Gordon would have met Portia just at the moment she was ready to give her whole being to someone. But he had been just too late. By the time he arrived the door was already closed to him. That's why now he felt like he wanted to batter it down and splinter it into pieces. All he had needed was to have been given a *chance*. The chance to knock gently and have her open up, but instead the door was locked against him and the key had been turned by Ned Maddstone.

Ned fucking Maddstone.

Gordon did not think of himself as a bad man, but he knew that lately he had been having bad thoughts. He had stopped being able to think of the shock of seeing his father tumble in a heap to the ground in front of him, roaring in pain and clutching at his throat. He had lost any sense of his mother, retaining only the memory of his suffocating desire to get out of the hospital and into the open air, away from that thin, yellow-skinned woman with a tube up her nose and a frightened look in her eyes.

He had considered his new situation on the flight over.

'One, these guys are atheists,' he had said to himself. 'Saturdays, I won't have to go to synagogue. Two, they're anti-Zionist. I won't be forced to go on kibbutz August. Three, they're British, I won't have to talk about my "feelings" like I did after Mom died. Four, these guys are obscenely rich. Aunt Hillary's family were multi-millionaire retailers or something, so I won't be in that shotgun shit-hole in Brooklyn. I'll have a car. We'll vacation twice a year. Barbados and Hawaii.'

But oh no . . .

'This will be your bicycle. We don't believe in cars.'

'E. P. Thompson is delivering a lecture on Cultural Imperialism to the Fabian Society, we've forty-five minutes to get there.'

'We booked a villa in the Tuscan hills. Porsh wants to see the Duccios in Siena and Hills is collecting material for her next novel.'

'Gordon, let's consider how you feel about Rose and Leo's death, yeah?'

'You'll enjoy it! CND marches are always good fun. And they're making a difference too.'

What a fucking joke. But worst of all was . . .

'I've got this boyfriend . . .'

'His name is Ned . . .'

'There! That's him, sitting in the middle, holding a cricket ball . . .'

'Look, Gordon! He's done a drawing of himself bored in the middle of a French lesson . . .'

'Look at that smile . . .'

'Look, another letter already . . .'

'Look . . .'

Ned fucking Maddstone.

Ned leant over the *Orphana*'s gunwale and felt the spray fly up into his face. The sea glistened like wet coal under a sky heavy with stars. It was Ned's private ocean tonight.

Below, the school sailing instructor Paddy Leclare and the five other boys on the trip were asleep in their berths. When it had become clear that, because of the extra hours spent in the Giant's Causeway, they were going to have to sail back to Scotland through the night, Ned had offered himself at once for this watch. In the past he might have done so out of duty or good citizenship, but Ned knew that he had volunteered on this occasion because he so relished time alone with himself, time to think about Portia and time simply to take pleasure in being. On nights like these, in a good boat running free, a person could imagine himself the king of the world. On land, it seemed to Ned, man was always inferior to the animals and disconnected from nature. Cars and machines might be clever, but they bullied the natural world. At sea, man was using nature, but not using nature *up*. He would put this point in his next letter to Portia. Love was turning him into something of a philosopher. The clever ones, Ashley Barson-Garland for instance, would think him immeasurably stupid, but then Ashley might not understand that Ned liked being a little stupid. It was sometimes a comfortable thing to be. After all, Ashley's cleverness was no kind of solace to him. In fact it seemed to make him deeply unhappy. Unhappiness to Ned, especially in his present condition of unassailable elation, was an incomprehensible and alien thing to afflict a fellow human, like acne or bad hand-eye co-ordination. He knew there were people who suffered from these plights, but he could only wonder why they didn't snap themselves out of it and have more fun.

To be a lover was to be part of a group singled out by fate for special attention. Ned had never imagined that he might have possessed such pleasure in simply being himself. His skill at sport, his good looks, his easy-going nature, his popularity – he would never for a moment think of those with satisfaction – if anything they were sources of embarrassment. His being a Lover though, a Lover with the most capital of Ls, made him burst with so much pride he could scarcely recognise himself. He wondered for the millionth time if Portia really felt the same. Perhaps her feelings were stronger. Perhaps his were stronger. Perhaps she imagined that hers were stronger and would never believe how strong –

A sudden sound from below made him turn in surprise.

'Maddstone!'

Peering astern Ned made out the shape of a head appearing in the hatchway.

'Hello?' he called into the darkness. 'Who is it?'

'Maddstone, you've got to come below.'

'Rufus? Is that you?'

'There's something wrong with Paddy. He's been making weird noises.'

Ned leapt to the hatch and scrambled down into the galley.

Lit by nothing more than a single tile-lamp and the glow of the radio set, Paddy Leclare's body was slumped forward in his chair, face down over the charts.

Ned approached him softly. 'Skipper?'

'Is he dead?' whispered Cade.

'I can't tell,' said Ned, stretching out a hand to Leclare's neck. 'Skipper! Paddy! Are you all right?' He felt a bumping pulse beneath his fingertips and breathed a sigh of relief.

Leclare suddenly gave a great cough and started to struggle upright. Ned was shocked to see a long trail of bloody saliva suspended between his mouth and the chart table.

'Is that you Ned? Is it you?'

'Yes, Skipper, it's me. Is everything all right?'

'Ah, well now, I wouldn't say that . . . who's that with you?' Leclare stared over Ned's shoulder, a look of fright in his eyes.

'Sir, it's only Rufus, sir.'

'Rufus, that you there?'

'Yes, Skipper.'

Leclare's breath came in short shallow bursts and his skin gleamed with sweat.

'Well then,' he panted. 'I want you to do me a favour, young Rufus. I want you to go astern to the starboard locker.'

Rufus nodded, white-faced.

'You remember when I showed you the locker where the flares are stowed? Good lad. The locker beside it is padlocked. Here's the key . . .' Leclare pushed a keyring across the table. 'It's the bright gold one. I want you to open it up and fetch me out a bottle of Jameson's . . .'

'Skipper are you sure?' said Ned. 'If you're not well . . .'

'I know what I need, so I do,' said Leclare. 'You stay with me, young Ned. Off you go, Rufus. Quick as you like.'

Rufus turned and clambered noisily up the ladder to the main deck.

'What a lump,' said Leclare. 'He'll never make a sailor, that one.'

Ned put a hand on his shoulder. 'Paddy, please don't be angry with me, but I really don't think you should be drinking. Whatever it is that's wrong with you, I'm sure it won't be made any better by –'

'Calm down, Ned. There's no whisky in that locker, and I told him the wrong key too. It gives us a little time.' Laughter at the neatness of his strategy set Leclare off into a renewed fit of coughing that sprayed blood and spittle into Ned's face.

'Oh Jesus, Skipper. Look, I'm going to radio for a helicopter.'

'Pass me that bag over there,' said Leclare, as if he hadn't heard.

'This one?'

'That's the feller, hand it to me. Now Ned, look into my eyes.'

Ned looked into eyes that he recalled as being merrily blue. They were bloodshot now and leaking tears from the effort of coughing.

'I can trust you, can't I, Ned?'

'Of course, Skipper.'

'Tell me the thing in your life that you hold most holy.'

'Skipper . . .'

'For fuck's sake will you answer me, boy!' Leclare grabbed Ned's wrist and squeezed it hard. 'What is the thing that matters to you most in all the world? Are you thinking of it, is it in your head right now?'

Ned nodded as a vision of a laughing Portia arose before him.

'Good. Now I want you to swear on that most holy thing that what I ask you to do you will do without telling a soul. Do you understand? Not a soul.'

Ned nodded once more.

'Out loud! Swear it out loud.'

'I swear it, Paddy, I swear it.'

'Good . . . good. I trust you. Now then . . .' Leclare scrabbled inside his bag. 'Take this envelope here. It is sealed. If I don't make it back and healthy to land I want you to deliver it for me. Personally. It must go direct into the hands of . . .' Leclare beckoned for Ned to come close and leaned up to whisper a name and address, his hot breath panting into Ned's ear. 'There! You've got that?'

'Yes, I think so.'

'Say it back to me. Whisper it to me now.'

Ned cupped his mouth round Leclare's ear and

breathed, 'Philip R. Blackrow, 13 Heron Square, London SW1.'

'You've got it. And you'll not forget?'

'No, never. I promise.'

'That's that then. Tuck the envelope away, let no one see it and we'll say not one word more about it. And don't you forget that name and address. There. Not such a difficult or dreadful thing to ask, after all, was it now?'

Leclare let go of Ned's wrist and leaned back, gasping for breath. Ned watched the little remaining colour drain from his face.

'Can I radio for help now, Skipper?'

'We'll be ashore in five or six hours. Make no difference either way.'

'But what is it? What's wrong?'

'It's no more than a touch of illness,' Leclare said quietly, smiling and closing his eyes. 'A little kiss of cancer, so it is. No more than that.'

Rufus Cade arrived back in time to witness Ned, with great tenderness, laying a sleeping-bag over the dying man's shoulders and gently stroking his head.

Ashley Barson-Garland had written seventy letters that morning. Seventy calm, placating and – though he said it himself – beautifully expressed letters. Letters to old ladies unable to understand the changes to the law on pensions, letters to unemployed layabouts who chose to blame the government for their lack of self-respect, letters from delirious fascists who thought Sir Charles Maddstone was Soft On Crime and letters from transcendently sad individuals who were determined to tell the MP about Christ.

So much noise from the populace. So much clamouring for attention. So much inadequacy and resentment. The life of a politician was indeed one of lying, lying and lying. Not the lying that people supposed, not the trail of broken promises and cynical denials complained about by newspaper and bar-stool sceptics, another kind of lying altogether. Allowing people to believe that their bitter and ignorant opinions were of use or importance, this to Ashley was the great lie. There seemed to be millions out there who could not understand that their problem was not this or that injustice or social ill, but the diminished sense of self that caused them to blame anything other than their own bitterness and rage: to bolster this delusion, that was the supreme dishonesty. There were people who believed that their opportunities to live a fulfilled life were hampered by the number of Asians in England, by the existence of a royal family, by the volume of traffic that passed by their house, by the malice of trade unions, by the power of callous employers, by the refusal of the health service to take their condition seriously, by communism, by capitalism, by atheism, by anything, in fact, but their own futile, weak-minded failure to get a fucking grip. Ashley understood Caligula's disappointment that the people of Rome had between them more than one neck. If only the British, he thought, had one backside. What a kick he would love to give it.

To his right on the desk lay the letters, open flat in their envelopes awaiting signature. They were elegantly typed on parliamentary writing paper, the green House of Commons portcullis above Sir Charles's name, each letter clean, unblemished and perfect. Ashley moved the four piles to the left of the blotter, a more convenient position for signing for when Sir Charles arrived. Ashley prided himself on these touches. He was the perfect servant, intelligent, thoughtful, thorough and discreet and for the moment, this contented him.

From the briefcase at his feet he pulled his diary. Only five and a half pages to fill before he would need a second volume. He wondered if he would be able to find the same book again. The shop in St Anne's Square where he bought the first had closed two years ago. Another colour would be ideal, but it must be the same book. If he found a source he would buy at least ten, a lifetime's supply. Would ten be enough, however? He made a rapid calculation. Twenty would be safer. 'The Invicta' it called itself grandly, the kind of Empire name that used to be bestowed upon everything from urinals to pocketknives. He riffled through, observing with pleasure the growth in confidence and style of his handwriting. The last entry had been made five weeks ago. There was much to squeeze into the final pages. He should pick up from his last sentence: 'For the moment I must put this obscene invasion out of my mind, for I have the School Address to concern myself with.'

July 30th

Can it really be only five weeks since the end of term? The Oration, of course, was a triumph of wit, knowledge, flair and – as you might say – address. As such, it was understood by no one in the hall, not even by those who could decipher the Latin. The assembled parents, staff and boys knew just enough to imagine that it was clever and treated me afterwards to the embarrassed, sympathetic and bravely smiling looks which the British habitually save up for those afflicted with terminal cancer or with brains, brains being by far the more unfortunate condition in their eyes. Most people, after all, can imagine having terminal cancer, they can't begin to imagine having brains. Ned introduced me to his father who came as near to bowing as one can these days.

'Your own parents not here today, Mr Barson-Garland?'

'My mother teaches, sir,' I said, liking the 'sir' and liking the fact that Sir Charles liked it. I liked too Ned's discomfiture and watched him trying to think of something to say which wouldn't draw attention to the idea of my mother or my family.

'Ah well,' his father said. 'She must be very proud of you.'

Ned delivered a feeble matey punch to my arm as they passed on. He knew of course what kind of teaching it is my mother does. He probably even guessed that I had told her to stay away.

'Very few parents come to Speech Day,' I had written to her. 'You'll find it a bore.'

What I had meant was, 'You dare turn up and disgrace me in a bright print dress, cheap scent and a loathsome hat and I shall disown you.'

I dare say Mother read all that between the lines because mothers do and I dare say that I had meant her to because sons do.

Having endured the sickly congratulations and sherry of the Headmaster ('Ah, here comes our pocket Demosthenes!'), I escaped after lunch to the cricket match, only to find myself forced to witness the spectacle of Ned Maddstone distinguishing himself with unquestionable style against the Old Boys. Every time someone talked to me, they kept half an eye on him at the wicket and I could smell their minds weighing his tallness, blondness and smiliness against my squat, dark seriousness. The stench of that drove me back to the house where I looked up Rufus Cade whom I found in his study weltering in his own mephitic fug – cannabis, gin and resentment. Now here's an interesting thing. Whether to please me or not he professed a severe dislike of Maddstone. No, it cannot have been to please me, I had already sensed the fact and asked him outright. It had been instinct. And I was right. He *loathes* Ned. He is ashamed of loathing Ned, which makes him loathe Ned all the more. A treadmill of disgust and resentment I am all too familiar with.

Who should then turn up, flushed and triumphant in scarlet and green stained flannels, hot from glory in the field, but Maddstone himself? He invited me to dine with his father at the George. The transparent guilt in his eyes was almost hilarious. 'You may think of yourself as an outsider,' his eyes said, 'but I think of you as one of us.'

Balls. If he had thought of me as One Of Us he would have said, 'Ashley, bloody bore, but how d'you fancy joining me and my father at the George?' instead of which he got all flustered and asked Rufus to come too while managing to make it painfully obvious that he only asked out of politeness. Rufus declined on the grounds of intoxication, which I think embarrassed him into hating Ned all the more. I accepted with entirely sincere pleasure.

I wore my one suit.

'Very good of you to join us, Mr Barson-Garland,' said Sir Charles, shaking my hand in courtly style. 'How absurd of me, I can't keep calling you that. Ned hasn't told me your Christian name.'

'Ashley, sir,' I said, as Ned buried himself in confusion and the menu.

I talked a lot over dinner. Not so much or so greedily as to appear to monopolise the conversation or to boast, but enough to impress.

'You seem to know a great deal about politics,' said Sir Charles over the cheese.

I shrugged with open hands as if to suggest that, while I may have picked up the odd pebble of interest on the shore, like Newton I was all too aware of the great ocean of knowledge that lay undiscovered before me.

'I don't suppose this would interest you . . .'

There and then he offered me a summer job as his political researcher.

'A great deal of it is really not much more than a kind of secretarial work,' he warned. 'But it is, I think, an unrivalled opportunity to find out how the system operates. If it works out over the summer, I'll be happy to keep the place open for when you leave here in late autumn. Ned tells me that you are sitting Oxford entrance next term too.'

'Father, that's a brilliant idea,' Ned gasped admiringly (as if it hadn't been his idea in the first place!

How big a fool can he possibly take me for?). 'I'm Pa's biggest disappointment,' he added, turning to me. 'Never could summon up much interest in politics.'

'Sir Charles,' I said, 'I don't know how to begin to thank you . . .'

'Tshush, tshush,' said Sir Charles, waving a hand. 'If you're as good at the job as I suspect you might be, then the thanks will be mine. Do I take it you accept?'

'Well, sir. I live in Lancashire. I don't have any . . .' Lancashire, indeed. I was used to saying that. Any 'shire' sounded better than Manchester.

'I'm hoping you will consider staying in Catherine Street. It's a small house, but has been a political one for over a hundred years. It has its own Division Bell, not that you will hear it ring much at first. The House doesn't sit over the summer. If you're still with us next year however, you'll get so used to its ringing that you'll want to sabotage the damned thing. Isn't that right Ned?' He waggled an eyebrow at his son in a way that suggested some private joke.

'When I was a boy I used to get really hacked off by that bell,' Ned explained in answer to my questioning look. 'The House sits at the weirdest times and it was always waking me up at two or three in the morning. So one night I wedged a piece of cardboard between the bell and the clapper. Pa missed a vote and got into a bucket load of trouble.'

'I passed a quarter hour in the Whips' Office that I shall never forget,' said Sir Charles.

Ned added to me in a pretend whisper, 'He still says that nothing the Gestapo did to him in the war came close.'

'It's true I tell you, absolutely true.'

Ned was letting me into his life. A life in which casual mention of Division Bells and sticky moments with the Gestapo came as easily as references to buses and episodes of *Dallas* came to my family. Had I not seen that little four-leafed clover flutter from my diary, such generosity should have warmed and enchanted me. Since I knew exactly where it came from I was not fooled for a second.

They found me a flat in Kensington which I share with a researcher from Conservative Central Office. Flats in Kensington seem to be a staple currency of this world. There is a lazy sense of –

Between the two sounds of the front door opening and the front door closing Ashley had swiftly returned the diary to his briefcase, opened a copy of Hansard and begun copying one of Sir Charles's speeches into a notebook.

He heard the sounds of people moving up the stairs and wondered if his not coming halfway to greet them would look strange. Could he pretend not to have heard their arrival? He decided not.

'Ned?' he called over his shoulder from his desk. 'Ned, is that you?'

'*Ash*!'

Ashley was standing shyly at the desk with a look of pleased surprise on his face as Ned entered the room in the company of a girl and boy of about the same age, both darkly handsome and deeply tanned.

'This is Portia. Actually you've met.'

'How do you do?' said Ashley, with becoming gravity. 'We have indeed met. The Hard Rock Café, although you won't remember me – your eyes I think were elsewhere.'

'Of course I remember. Hi!'

Portia shook his hand. Ashley had not had time to wipe it against his trousers and he looked at her closely to see if she reacted to what he knew was the unusually moist clamminess of his palms.

'And this is Gordon, Portia's cousin.'

'How do you do?' said Gordon. Ashley registered with amusement the fact that English Portia had made do with 'Hi' while American Gordon preferred a formal 'How do you do?' It always amused him when people presented themselves as the opposite of what they were.

'Surprised?' said Ned, biffing Ashley clumsily on the shoulder. He too was tanned, but in that lightly golden style of the fair-skinned, as if anything more would be foreign and in poor taste.

'Well, your father did say that you wouldn't be back until tomorrow.'

'The trip, er, ended early in fact,' Ned's face looked troubled for a moment. 'We all decided to take the night train from Glasgow.'

'Really?' said Ashley, who knew this perfectly well.

'Anyway,' said Ned brightening. 'I was in London in time to meet the Fendemans off their plane at Heathrow. Not bad, eh?'

'What a pleasant surprise for them,' said Ashley.

Gordon was looking awkwardly around the room. Ashley had the feeling that he felt out of place. Indeed, the electrical sparks that crackled between Ned and Portia were little short of embarrassing even for Ashley.

'The old man been keeping you busy?' said Ned tearing himself away with an effort from Portia's smile.

'It's been fascinating. Truly fascinating.'

'You work for Ned's dad, right?' said Gordon.

'That's right. In fact I ought really . . . well, actually, here's an idea . . . I don't suppose you'd like to come with me? I've got to go over to the House now. Maybe I could show you round?'

'The House?'

'Of Commons. Parliament. Of course, only if it would interest you . . .'

'Sure. That sounds great.'

'What a brilliant idea!' Ned grinned with pleasure. 'Ash, that's completely decent of you. I bet Gordon would love to see where it all goes on. The cradle of democracy and all that.'

'Very well then. I'll just get my briefcase,' said Ashley, prickling with annoyance at Ned's fatuous remark. 'Cradle of democracy' indeed. Did he not know that Americans regard Washington as the cradle of democracy, just as the

French did Paris and the Greeks Athens, and no doubt the Icelanders Reykjavik, each with as much reason? Such typically casual arrogance.

'Er, we'll stay here, if that's okay,' Ned was saying. 'Portia has to be at a job interview at four. The Knightsbridge College. Thought I'd . . . you know, take her there.'

'Something good?'

'It sounds grand but it just means teaching foreigners how to say "This tomato is too expensive",' Portia said. 'It does pay better than the Hard Rock Café, though.'

She and Ned were holding hands now. It was apparent that every second out of each other's arms was agony to them. Ashley supposed that much of the agony came from a traditional lovers' quandary that they were too dull-witted to interpret. They wanted to conceal their passion but they couldn't understand why they also wanted desperately to show it off.

Ashley felt an intense desire to be violently sick.

*

'Thought it best to leave them to it,' he said, closing the front door and looking up at the top-floor window with what he trusted was a reasonable approximation of laddish worldliness. 'They'll be at it like knives before we've taken two steps.'

Gordon did not respond, but looked down at the ground with pursed lips. Ashley watched him curiously, was this American puritanism or something deeper?

Good God! The instant the possibility struck Ashley he

knew it to be right. He could have laughed aloud at his perception. Cousin Gordon is in love with Portia, he told himself with absolute assurance.

The essential truth that people always failed to understand about intelligence, Ashley believed, was that it allowed its possessor deeper intuition and keener instincts than those granted to others. Stupid people liked to delude themselves that while they may not be clever, they were at least able to compensate with *feelings* and *insights* denied to the intellectual. Drivel, Ashley thought. It was precisely this kind of false belief that made stupid people so stupid. The truth was that clever people had infinitely more resources from which to make the leaps of connection that the world called intuition. What was 'intelligence' after all, but the ability to read into things? The Romans, as so often, knew better than the Britons.

They turned and walked along Catherine Street towards Westminster. Perhaps feeling that his silence was brutish, Gordon began to talk. He confided to Ashley that at the airport his aunt and uncle had more or less forced him onto Ned and Portia.

'Why don't you guys take the bus into town together?' Hillary had said. 'Have a bite to eat somewhere. Maybe take in a movie. We'll take care of the luggage.'

Pete had slipped Gordon ten pounds and patted him on the shoulder while Portia bit her lip petulantly and Ned had done his best to look pleased.

'Just as well we did the tactful thing, then,' said Ashley. 'You really don't have to come to the House of Commons if you don't feel like it, by the way. It's most people's idea of hell. I'd quite understand.'

'Will they let an American in?'

'I just have to wave this,' said Ashley, flourishing his pass and trying not to look proud about it.

'You gonna be a politician?'

'Maybe. Maybe.'

'Like Ned?'

'I'm sorry?'

'Ned's gonna follow his father, right?'

'I hardly think so,' said Ashley, amused. An image came to him of Ned Maddstone in grass-stained cricket whites, flicking the golden flop out of his eyes and rising to speak from the government benches on the subject of currency fluctuations and interest rates. 'Politics and Ned don't quite go together.'

'Really? Only that's not what Portia said to me.'

'What do you mean exactly?'

'She said Ned had told her he was going to follow his father into Parliament one day.'

'Well, maybe he will,' Ashley said casually, while something inside him snapped with a familiar fury. Did Ned seriously imagine political seats could be passed on from father to son, like writing-desks and shooting-sticks? Well, perhaps they could, he reflected bitterly; this is, after all, *England*. Meanwhile of course, Ned's summer was too precious to him for it to be wasted on politics: too much fucking and cricket and fucking and sailing and fucking and fucking to be done, so why not let Ashley the

Manchester carthorse do the secretarial work this year, eh, Pa old thing? Plenty of time for catching up after Oxford, don't you think, Daddy darling? And one day, when I'm 'ready to settle down' I could send for good old Ashley and have him for a political assistant. Poor Ashley would be so grateful . . . in fact, why not get him in training for it now? Give him a bit of experience? Just the thing! We'll invite him along for dinner and put it to him, he'll be so grateful. It'll get that nasty business of reading his embarrassing diary off my conscience, too. We'll give him the old oil and have him typing letters and licking envelopes before you can say Arrogant Cunting Upper Fucking Class Arseholes . . .

'You all right?'

'Mm? Yes, fine, fine . . . miles away,' Ashley smiled vaguely at Gordon as if emerging from a gently eccentric daydream. 'So,' he said brightly. 'First time you've met the great Ned then?'

Gordon nodded cautiously. 'The Great Ned?'

'Forgive the promptings of a sarcastic heart,' said Ashley. 'He's very popular of course: Very talented, but . . . oh, you don't want to listen to me. None of my business.'

'Hey, if he's dating my cousin, I want to know everything there is to know,' said Gordon. 'Portia thinks his shit don't stink. But you're in school with the guy. You've known him longer than she has.'

'Well, let's just say I wouldn't like *my* cousin going out with him,' said Ashley. 'It's hard to define. Most people think he's charming and honest and everything that could ever be appealing in a man. Personally, I find him cold and arrogant and deceitful. Ah . . .' Ashley looked up as Big Ben began to chime the half hour. 'Twelve-thirty. If it's all right with you, we might stop off at that pub round the corner. Said I would meet a friend there for lunch. If we feel like it we can go on to the House afterwards.'

'Hey, look, if I'm in the way . . .'

'Not at all. You'll like Rufus. And he'll like you. Well, he'll like your ten pounds. You can buy a lot to drink with ten pounds.'

'Oh well, if . . .'

'I'm joking. He's as rich as God. And I'm sure you'll find that you have a great deal in common.'

Ned lay in bed gazing up at the ceiling. With a fist clenched over her cheek, Portia slept tightly curled like a kitten beside him.

He hadn't yet told her about the nightmare of watching Paddy Leclare dying on board the *Orphana*. On the bus from Heathrow they had talked almost like strangers, Ned concerned not to make Gordon feel left out and Portia strangely shy in her cousin's presence too. He wasn't going to worry her, but the experience had shaken him. He had never confronted death, responsibility and fear before and to meet them all in one go was unsettling.

Sailing back to Scotland with a dead man below had not been pleasant for him. Rufus Cade had behaved oddly too. It seemed natural that Ned should skipper the boat back to Oban and everyone but Cade agreed that it was right and sensible. Ned, without vanity he knew it to be true, was the best sailor amongst them, and surely Leclare's last bestowal of trust in him proved his right to command? Not that he was able to repeat that secret to Cade or anyone else. For five hours, as dawn broke and they made their miserable way back to harbour, Cade had sullenly criticised all Ned's decisions and gone out of his way to undermine his authority at every turn. This had never happened to Ned before and had left him feeling hurt and puzzled.

It was only as they were making their way through Oban harbour towards the quayside and the flashing blue lights of the ambulance and police cars awaiting them that he had understood.

Cade had approached him shyly. 'Look, I'm sorry, Maddstone,' he said, staring down at the decking. 'I suppose I was a bit upset by it all. Didn't mean to criticise you. It's right for you to be in charge.'

Ned had laid a hand on Cade's arm. 'Bloody hell, Rufus, don't give it another thought. Under the circumstances you've been amazing.'

The rest of the day had passed in a confused dream of witness statements, telephone calls and interminable waiting before Ned had finally been allowed to lead the party off to Glasgow to catch the night train to Euston. Leadership was exhausting.

Portia's head stirred on his chest and he found himself looking into her eyes.

'Hello,' he said.

'Hello.'

And they laughed.

Ashley watched as Gordon drained his second Guinness.

'You seen her, Ashley,' he said, belching as he wiped the froth from his mouth. 'She's beautiful. Wouldn't you say she's beautiful?'

'Very beautiful indeed, Gordon,' said Ashley who possessed several very old Greek textbooks that he considered infinitely more exciting.

'Sides,' Gordon continued. 'Where I come from you don't marry out. You just don't do that. It's wrong.'

Rufus was glowering into a pint of Director's that he had already chased with three triple whiskies. 'Marry out? What's that mean when it's at home?'

'Gordon and Portia are Jewish,' Ashley explained. 'It isn't done to marry outside the faith.'

'I'm a Catholic,' said Rufus. 'It's the same with us.'

'And she won't look at me,' said Gordon. 'She won't fucking look at me. You know what I'm saying?'

'You're saying she won't look at you?' said Rufus.

'Right. You got it. Won't look at me.'

'I see. That must piss you right off.'

'Piss me off is right.'

'It would piss me off too, I can tell you.'

Ashley was pleased to see Gordon and Rufus relaxed

with each other, but he dreaded having to cope with two drunks. Although he was in the process of teaching himself everything there was to be known about wine, Ashley took little pleasure in alcohol, and none at all in drunkenness in himself or others. He knew enough not to show it, however and could nurse a drink through several rounds without looking like a prude.

'So what exactly happened, Rufus? You say Leclare was dead when you returned?'

'Jesus, Ash, I told you. He sent me off looking for a bottle of fucking Jameson's that wasn't there and by the time I got back, there was Saint Ned cradling him in his arms, cooing like a fucking pigeon. Next thing you know he'd helped himself to the command. Treated me like dirt too. Then had the fucking nerve to tell me that "under the circumstances" I'd been brilliant. Meaning of course, that under the circumstances *he* had been brilliant. Tosser. Still, *he* was the one who had to deal with the police and the ambulance and all the paperwork. Ha! Bet that hadn't occurred to him.' Rufus struggled to his feet. 'Anyway. Fuck him. Who wants another drink?'

'Why not?' said Ashley. 'Same again please. Gin and tonic, ice but no lemon.'

'This stuff really gets to your gut,' said Gordon handing his empty glass to Rufus. 'Maybe just a half pint this time.'

'A half of gin and a pint of Guinness and lemon. No ice, but tonic. I've got you.' Rufus began weaving his way to the bar.

'He's not half as drunk as he appears,' said Ashley. 'His father's an alcoholic and he's trying it on for size.'

Gordon watched Rufus's retreating form and then turned to Ashley. 'You like to see through people, don't you?'

'Well,' said Ashley, in some surprise. 'Judging from that remark, so do you.'

'Right. Touché. So tell me, who was this guy, anyway?'

'The school used him as some sort of sailing instructor,' Ashley said with a dismissive wave, as if describing the local cesspit operative. 'Those who sailed were very fond of him in that insufferably matey way that the yachting fraternity adopts. He was endlessly organising trips in the holidays for boys who could afford it – or cared to busy themselves with an occupation so imponderably tedious,' Ashley added quickly.

'I heard of cases in the States where these guys are perverts,' said Gordon. 'You know, sailing round the Caribbean with schoolkids. Kind of weird thing to do.'

'Yes, but I hardly think so in this case. Whatever you may have read about English public schools that kind of thing is pretty rare.'

'Where'd they go?'

'From the west of Scotland round to the Giant's Causeway apparently and then back again. The year before that it was . . . where did you go last year, Rufus?' Rufus had returned, and was setting drinks on the table, a bag of peanuts between his teeth.

'Hng?'

'Last year. Where did the Sailing Club go?'

'Hooker Horror.'

'Excuse me?'

'The Hook of Holland,' said Rufus, tearing open the packet with his teeth and pushing it towards Gordon. 'From Southwold across the North Sea to Flushing. Then up the inland waterways to Amsterdam and all the way back.'

'And I take it Leclare never molested you in any way? Never threatened the delicate flower of your virginity?'

'Fuck off!'

'Just a thought we had.'

'As a matter of fact, I've been thinking of going back,' said Rufus. 'Amsterdam that is. They have naked girls in the windows and more dope than you've ever seen in your life.'

'You smoke?' Gordon asked Rufus.

'Does the Pope shit in the woods?' Ashley murmured, helping himself to a single peanut.

Gordon lowered his voice excitedly. 'You couldn't put me on to someone, could you?' he asked. 'I haven't had a smoke since I got here. I mentioned it to Portia one time and she looked at me like I was shit.'

'Be a pleasure,' said Rufus genially waving a hand. 'You a grass man or a hash man?'

'Grass,' said Gordon.

'No problem. As a matter of fact, I just happen to have on me the most seriously . . .'

Ashley's heart sank at the prospect of the conversation

descending into drug talk. It was so much more amusing to hear Rufus and Gordon swapping complaints about Ned. Ned and drugs, unfortunately, did not mix in conversation. Mind you, of course . . .

'Wouldn't it be fun,' said Ashley, sipping his gin and tonic primly, 'to watch Maddstone being busted by the Drug Squad? Bit of a scandal, bit of a disgrace, bit of a come down for the holy one and his father, don't you think? And just *imagine* how shocked dear Portia would be.'

Rufus giggled and Gordon's mouth fell open.

'He's going to be taking her to – what was it called? Something absurdly pretentious – the Knightsbridge College, that was it,' Ashley continued dreamily. 'Suppose the police were told that a wicked drug dealer had been seen hanging around outside the college most afternoons, distributing illegal substances to the students. Imagine witnessing the golden boy being led away in handcuffs.'

'Yeah, but how . . .'

'His jacket's at the bottom of the stairs. All we have to do, surely, is use a little intelligence.'

Ned stood naked at the window of his bedroom looking out over London. In an hour or so he might go down and scramble some eggs. Otherwise why would he ever want to leave this room for the rest of his life? They could stay here for ever. Only Portia had to be ready for her job interview. But they'd come back from that and run straight back up here again. Of course tomorrow morning his father was coming down from the country and they must be presentable then, but tomorrow was a world away. He couldn't wait for Portia to meet his father, he felt they would become instant friends. A vista of their future years together appeared before him. Portia and Pa at Christmas, in the maternity ward, on holiday together. The smiling, the laughing, the affection, the love . . . he wanted to weep with ecstasy.

A movement in the street below caught his eye. Ashley and Gordon were returning to the house, a third person between them. Ned smiled when he recognised the lumbering gait of Rufus Cade. How on earth had they bumped into him? Any other time it would be fun to welcome them in, but . . .

Never usually unsociable or selfish, Ned crept to the door and gently turned the key in the lock. The very delicacy of the sound woke Portia.

'Did you just lock the door?'

''Fraid so,' whispered Ned. 'The others are coming back. Thought we might pretend to have gone out.'

Portia watched Ned crossing the room towards her and an intense happiness rushed through her like wind through grasses and she shivered and rippled with so much pleasure that she almost believed it was pain.

'Don't ever leave me.'

'No fear,' Ned whispered, climbing back into bed.

They heard Ashley's voice calling up the stairs.

'We won't disturb you both. Something I had to fetch. You young people enjoy yourselves!'

The smothered laughter of Gordon and Rufus delighted them. How wonderful it was to be giggled about.

Ned sighed with the completest fulfilment and joy. Where in all the universe was anyone so unfathomably lucky? He was young, healthy and happy and without a care or an enemy in the world.

2

Ned shivered and pulled the blanket closer around his shoulders.

'Excuse me,' he said. 'Do you think it would be possible for someone to bring me my clothes?'

The policeman at the door shifted his eyes from the ceiling to Ned.

'Not cold is it?'

'No, but you see I'm only wearing . . .'

'Middle of summer, isn't it?'

'Yes, yes it is, but . . .'

'Well then.'

Ned stared at the foil ashtray in front of him on the table and tried to force his mind to concentrate on what had happened.

At four o'clock he had seen Portia into the College, which is to say they had rung the bell for the fifth floor of a disappointingly ordinary doorway in a narrow street behind the Scotch House.

'I'll be outside,' he promised, kissing her goodbye as if for the longest parting. 'And when you come out we'll go into Harrods for an ice-cream soda to celebrate.'

He had been waiting there on the pavement for nearly half an hour, trying to work out, in a cheerful sort of way, whether or not Portia taking such a time up there was a good sign. Being an optimist, he had naturally decided that it was.

A group of young Spaniards or Italians (he couldn't really tell which) had come up to the door. They had been in the act of producing a key when Ned had decided, on an impulse, to be let in with them. The sight of a respectably dressed boyfriend might just tip the balance in Portia's favour.

'Excuse me,' he had said. 'Would it be all right if I came in with you?'

They had looked at him in bewilderment. If this was the average standard of English here, then Portia was going to have a lot to do.

'I . . . JUST . . . WONDER . . . IF . . . YOU . . .' he had started to say, but before the words were out of his mouth it had all happened. Appearing it seemed from nowhere, two men had each seized an arm and bundled Ned towards a car. Too surprised to speak, the last thing he heard before a hand pushed him down into the back seat was the raucous laughter of a small group of people standing in the dimly lit doorway of the nearby pub.

'W-what's going on?' he had asked. 'What are you doing?'

'You'd better ask yourself what *you've* been doing,' one of the men had said drawing a foil package from Ned's jacket pocket, as the car accelerated away with a squeal of tyres.

At the police station he had been more thoroughly

searched. They had taken away for examination everything but his underpants and he had been sitting in this room now for over half an hour, wondering what could possibly be going on. The next time the door opened and someone came in, he decided, he would insist on being allowed to telephone his father. The police had no idea they were dealing with a cabinet minister's son. Sir Charles was a gentle and scrupulously polite man, but he had commanded a brigade in the war and run a small pocket of Empire for six years. In the Sudan he had pronounced sentences of death and seen them carried out. As Secretary of State for Northern Ireland he had extended the limits of internment without trial and authorised all kinds of extreme measures – 'strong medicine for a strong infection' he had said to Ned once, without revealing details. This was not a man to be messed with. Ned almost felt sorry for the police. He would assure his father that he had been kindly treated and that he held no grudge.

At last, the door to the interview room opened.

'Right then, son.'

'Hello, sir.'

'My name is Detective Sergeant Floyd.'

'If it's all right, I'd like to ring . . .'

'Cigarette?'

Floyd dropped a packet of Benson and Hedges and a lighter onto the table as he drew up a chair opposite Ned and sat down.

'No thanks. I don't smoke.'

'You don't smoke?'

'No.'

'Half an ounce of hash and you don't smoke?'

'I'm sorry?'

'Bit late for "sorry" isn't it? One thing to have it for your own use. But selling to foreign students. Magistrates don't like that.'

'I don't understand.'

'Of course you don't. How old are you?'

'Seventeen and a half.'

'Seventeen and a half? *And a half*!'

The policeman at the door joined in the laughter.

'Well, I am,' said Ned, tears beginning to form in his eyes. What was wrong with saying that, when it was true?

Floyd frowned and bit his lip. 'Let's forget about the drugs, shall we? Tell me what "Interior, interior, interior" means to you.'

Ned looked at him helplessly. 'I'm sorry?'

'Not a difficult question is it? *Interior, interior, interior*. Tell me about it.'

'I don't know what you mean.' Ned felt as though he was drowning. 'Please, I want to ring my father.'

'Let's start at the beginning, shall we? Name?'

'Do be quiet, there's a good fellow.'

Ned and the Detective Sergeant turned together. A neatly dressed man in his mid-twenties was standing in the doorway, a gentle smile on his face.

'And just who the hell might you be?' said Floyd, outraged.

'A word, Sergeant,' said the young man, beckoning with his finger.

Floyd opened his mouth to speak, but something in the young man's bland expression made him change his mind.

The door closed on Ned once more. He could hear Detective Sergeant Floyd's voice raised in barely controlled anger in the corridor outside. 'With respect, sir, I do not see the need . . .'

'With respect, that's the ticket, Floyd. Respect. Just what's needed. Now I'll take those if you please. Thank you . . . paperwork will follow.'

The door opened again and the young man popped his head in, smiling. 'Would you like to come with me, old chap?'

Ned jumped to his feet and followed the young man along a passageway, past an angry Detective Sergeant Floyd.

'Can I use the telephone?' Ned asked.

'Ridiculous of them,' said the young man, as if he hadn't heard, 'to strip you like that. Ah, here's Mr Gaine!' He indicated a broad-shouldered man in a denim jacket who was leaning against a fire door at the end of the passage bearing in his arms a pile of clothes, neatly folded with the shoes lying upside-down on top.

'Those are mine!' said Ned.

'That's right. We shan't have time to put them on just now, I'm afraid, we must be off. All set, Mr Gaine?'

The broad-shouldered man nodded and pushed against the bars of the door. The young man escorted Ned down some steps into a courtyard and towards a green Rover parked in the corner, where the sunlight beat down on its roof.

'You just hop in the back with me. We'll let Mr Gaine drive shall we?'

Ned winced when his bare thighs touched the upholstery.

'Scorched you a bit? Sorry about that,' said the young man cheerfully. 'Should've thought to park in the shade, shouldn't we, Mr Gaine? All righty, then, cabin doors to automatic. Let's not hang about.'

'Where are we going?' Ned asked, adjusting the blanket around himself to protect his legs and his modesty.

'My name's Delft,' was the reply. 'Like those ghastly blue and white tiles. Oliver Delft.' He put out a hand for Ned to shake. 'And you are . . . ?'

'Edward Maddstone.'

'Edward? They do call you Edward, do they? Or are you an Ed, Eddie, Ted or Teddy?'

'Ned, usually.'

'Ned. Fair enough. I'll call you Ned then, and you can call me Oliver.'

'Where are we going?'

'Well, there's lots to talk about, isn't there? I thought perhaps we might go somewhere nice and quiet.'

'Only, my girlfriend, you see . . . she doesn't know where I am. And my father . . .'

'We've a fair drive ahead of us, I'm afraid. I'd try and get a bit of shut-eye if I were you. I know I shall.' Delft settled against the headrest.

'She'll be worried . . .'

But Delft, apparently asleep in an instant, said nothing.

Since the sleepless night of his watch on the *Orphana* and the anxious day that followed it, Ned had lain awake on a bumpy train from Glasgow to London. The next day, today – could that really be *today*? – he had travelled out to the airport and then back again to Catherine Street. There he did, it was true, spend time in bed, but he had not slept. Portia had dozed a little, but Ned had been too happy to think of sleep.

But now, in spite of the strangeness of his circumstances, he found himself starting to yawn. The last thing he saw before he fell asleep was the rearview mirror and Mr Gaine's cold eyes watching him.

'You'll have to forgive my brutal way with an egg,' said Oliver Delft. 'It started life as an omelette *aux fines herbes* but now I'm afraid it's just scrambled eggs speckled with green. Non-stick! It's just a phrase if you ask me.' He pushed a plate towards Ned and smiled.

'Thanks.' Ned began to shovel the eggs into his mouth, amazed at how hungry he was. 'Very good.'

'You honour me. While you eat, we can talk.'

'Is this your house?'

'It's a place I come to sometimes,' said Delft. He was leaning against the Aga rail, a glass of wine in his hand.

'Are you a policeman?'

'A policeman? No, no. Nothing as thrilling as that, I'm afraid. Just a humble toiler in the lower realms of government. All very dull. Here to get to the bottom of one or two things.'

'If it's about the drugs the police found, I *swear* to you I don't know anything about them.'

Delft smiled again. The smile was an effort. Inside, he was very bored and extremely annoyed to be there. The pleasurable long weekend he had been looking forward to for ages had already been ruined.

Five minutes . . . five blasted minutes were all that had

come between Oliver and freedom. He had already locked his desk and had been in the very act of signing the duty log when Maureen had bustled in, twittering about a flash from West End Central.

'Isn't Stapleton here yet? I'm about to go off watch.'

'No, Mr Delft. Captain Stapleton hasn't signed in. There's no one else.'

'Bugger,' Oliver had said, meaning it. 'All right then, let's have a look.'

He had taken Maureen's typed slip and read it through carefully. 'Hum. Who's in the Heavy Pool?'

'Mr Gaine, sir.'

'Get him to warm the car up. I'll be out in three.'

That had been something at least. Mr Gaine was Oliver's man and could be trusted not to make life more difficult by ruffling feathers and stamping on sensibilities.

Whatever Oliver had expected when he arrived at Savile Row police station, it certainly hadn't been a worried schoolboy. The whole thing seemed ripely absurd. Undoubtedly a mistake, he had said to himself the moment he laid eyes on the floppy haired teenager jiggling his knee up and down under the interview-room table, a forlorn and bewildered look on his face. Delft may have been only twenty-six himself, but he had seen enough to be sure that Ned Maddstone was as innocent as a day-old chick. A day-old *carrier pigeon* chick, he thought to himself. He was pleased with the image and made a note to include it in his report. His masters were old-fashioned enough to enjoy a pert turn of phrase.

He looked across at the child now.

Ned was sitting at the kitchen table, still jogging his leg on the ball of his foot, with an earnest pleading look on his innocent face.

'Honestly,' he was saying. 'I absolutely swear. On the Holy Bible!'

'Calm down,' said Oliver. 'I really don't think a Bible will be necessary. Not that we'd be able to find one in a place of sin like this,' he added, looking round the room as if it were less a country kitchen and more a Louisiana brothel. 'You can swear on Marguerite Patten's *Cookery in Colour* if it gives you pleasure, but there's no need.'

'You do believe me then?'

'Well, of course I believe you, you daft young onion. All some silly mistake. Still, as we're here, you might as well tell me what the words "Interior, interior, interior" mean.'

'I don't know!' said Ned. 'The policeman asked me the same thing, but I've never heard them. I mean, I've heard the word "interior" before, obviously, but . . .'

'You see, this is what we have to try and understand,' said Oliver. 'And when we've got to the bottom of it we can let you go and you can get on with your life and I can get on with mine, which I'm sure we'd both like.'

Ned nodded vigorously. 'Absolutely! But . . .'

'All right then. Now let's have a look at this shall we?'

Oliver came forward and laid on the table a single sheet of paper.

Ned stared at it mystified. It was a typed list of names

and addresses. He recognised at once the names of the Home Secretary, the Lord Chancellor, the Secretary of State for Defence followed by others, vaguely familiar to Ned. Last of all came his father's name, *Sir Charles Maddstone*. At the bottom, in handwritten large black block capitals were the words –

INTERIOR INTERIOR INTERIOR

'What does it mean?' he asked.

'It belongs to you,' said Oliver. 'You tell me.'

'My piece of paper? But I've never seen it before.'

'Then what was it doing in the inside pocket of your jacket?'

'In the . . . oh!' The truth began to dawn. 'Was it . . . was it originally in an envelope?'

'It *was* in an envelope!' said Oliver. 'You're absolutely right! It was in *this* envelope!' He held up a white envelope, an envelope that to his annoyance the police had torn open without a single thought. Oliver had immediately spotted a tiny hair behind the flap, a little security measure sealed there to warn the recipient of any tampering. It might be possible to find a duplicate envelope and put the letter back in play, but one never knew what other safeguards the police might have blundered through. Not really their fault of course, he conceded. The search had been routine. They had imagined they were dealing with nothing more than a spoilt kid's drug stash.

'But why is it important?' Ned asked. 'What does it mean?'

'Well now, you've just admitted that it's yours, so I should've thought you'd be the one to tell *me*.'

Ned shifted uncomfortably. 'But you see I was . . . I was given it.'

'Yes, I'm afraid I'm going to need a bit more than that.'

'By a man.'

'Well that eliminates two billion or so, but it's still not quite enough, is it? We're going to have to narrow it down a little more than that.'

'He's dead.'

'A dead man gave it to you.'

'He only died yesterday.'

'Don't arse around with me, Ned, there's a good fellow. Who was he and how did he come to give it to you?'

Tell me the thing in your life that you hold most holy.

Ned could have wept with frustration. He was desperate to do the right thing. He wanted to please this nice man, but he wanted to keep his word too. Would it bring him the most terrible luck to break so mighty an oath?

What is the thing that matters to you most in all the world?

What would *Portia* want him to do?

'Is it very important that I tell you? Important enough to make me break a solemn oath?'

'Well now, young scout,' said Oliver. 'I'll tell you a thing. A thing you shouldn't know, but that I trust you to keep to yourself. Glass of wine?'

'Do you have any milk?'

'Milk? Let me see.' Oliver went over to the fridge and peered suspiciously inside as if it were the first fridge he had ever inspected. 'Milk, milk, milk . . . ah yes. Now my job, Ned, such as it is,' he went on, 'involves, amongst other things, doing my best to stop people letting off bombs in this country. Only UHT I'm afraid – semi-skimmed. Do you mind?'

'That's perfect, thank you.'

'Can't bear the stuff myself. Makes me snotty. Letting off bombs, Ned, is a thing some scallywags do, as you must have read in the papers. They'll do it in pubs, clubs, offices, railway stations and shops, killing and crippling ordinary people who have no quarrel with anyone but their bank managers, bosses and spouses. Drink it from the carton, there's a lamb. Now, some of these bombers, they like to call up a police station or a newspaper office to claim the credit, if credit is the right word, or – if they've a spark of humanity and it's only property they want to destroy – to warn the police to evacuate the area. Making sense so far?'

Ned nodded, wiping a white moustache from his lips with the back of his hand.

'Well then. To prevent any old deranged freak from calling up and leaving hoax warnings or taking credit just for fun, a more or less workable arrangement has been arrived at between us – the government, and them – the *bona fide* terrorists. When a bomber calls up a newspaper or a police station he gives a code word, to show that he is the real thing. Not going too fast for you?'

'No.'

'Good. Well now, it so happens that the Provisional IRA's latest coded warning for a bomb, just a few days old, is the word "Interior" repeated three times.'

'But . . .'

'So perhaps now you can see why Detective Sergeant Floyd, whom God preserve, got a little excited when he found this piece of paper in your jacket. And perhaps now you can see why he gave my department a call and why I am asking you now to tell me how you got hold of it. The man who gave you that envelope was an IRA terrorist, Ned. The worst and darkest kind of man. The kind of man whose idea of political protest is to blow the arms and legs off young children. Whatever oath of secrecy he may have sworn you to is meaningless. So let's have his name.'

'Paddy Leclare,' said Ned. 'His name was Paddy Leclare. He was a sailing instructor. We were at sea and he suddenly became terribly ill. He gave it to me just before he died.'

'Well now you see. There we have it,' Oliver said, patting Ned on the back. 'That wasn't so difficult, was it?'

'I had . . . I had absolutely no idea. I mean he was employed by the school and everything. If I'd thought for a *minute* . . .'

'Of course not, you daft young kipper.'

'Do you think it was because of my father?'

'Your father? Why should . . . oh, you're *that* kind of a Maddstone, are you? As in Sir Charles? What, he's your granddad is he?'

'He's my father,' said Ned defensively. 'I was a . . . a late arrival.'

'I had rooms in Maddstone Quad during my second year at St Mark's,' said Oliver. 'I had a perfect view from my window of a great big stone statue of John Maddstone, the founder of the college. You don't look a bit like him. We used to paint it dark blue during Eights Week, you know. Well, well. I expect it gave your friend Paddy Leclare quite a kick entrusting his letter to you. Sort of thing that appeals to his kind.'

'He wasn't my friend!' said Ned indignantly. 'He was just the school's sailing instructor.'

'Forgive me.'

Ned looked down at the piece of paper. 'So these are all people that the IRA wants to kill?'

'That's how things look on the face of it, certainly,' Oliver conceded. 'But how things are and how things look aren't always the same.'

Ned examined the list of names. 'I don't see what else it *could* mean,' he said. 'These are all politicians and generals and things, aren't they?'

'Well, maybe we are *supposed* to think that they're targets. Maybe your friend Leclare believed that you would open the letter out of curiosity, get suspicious and show it to your father. Maybe the whole idea is to make us run around wasting a lot of time, effort and manpower laying on extra protection while their real targets lie elsewhere. Or maybe the envelope has been impregnated with some deadly bug and the plan was for you to pass the infection on to your father who in turn would pass it on to the entire cabinet. Maybe that's why Leclare fell ill and died – maybe he'd been a bit careless with the old microbes.'

'Oh my God! But . . .'

'Or there's another maybe. Maybe they planted that cannabis on you and then tipped off the police just in order to winkle me out and follow us here. Maybe they're in a van outside now with a mortar trained on this very room. Maybe a thousand things. We don't know. There are as many maybes as there are seconds in a century. But this one thing I can tell you for certain,' Oliver said, drawing up a chair opposite Ned. 'We won't know anything until you've told me the whole story from start to finish. I hope you can agree with that?'

'Of course. Absolutely.'

'Good. I have been very frank with you and now you can repay the compliment. You give me everything you've got, and before you know it, Mr Gaine will be driving us back to London. You'll be home and in the bosom of your family before the *News at Ten*, that's a promise. You don't mind a tape-recorder, I suppose?'

'No,' said Ned. 'Not at all.'

'Excellent. Sit you there and drink your milk. Be back in a tick.'

Hoo-bloody-rah. Oliver's mind raced ahead as he went through into the sitting-room. If he got back to town, sketched out a preliminary report and left Stapleton to make the security calls, he could be heading out to the country by midnight. Maybe his weekend could be salvaged after all.

'As you were, Gaine. Where's the Revox?'

'Cupboard under the bookshelf, sir. I'll fetch it.'

Oliver picked up the *Evening Standard* Quick Crossword against which Mr Gaine had been pitting his mighty wits.

'There's your problem. Eft.'

'Sir?'

'Four across, "Newt". You've put Rat, should be Eft.'

'Ah.'

'Why Rat, incidentally?'

'Well, Mr Delft, sir,' said Mr Gaine, handing Oliver the tape-recorder. 'Pissed as a rat, pissed as a newt.'

'How silly of me,' said Oliver, marvelling once more at Gaine's unusual thought processes. 'Well, we shouldn't be much more than an hour. Oh, be a hero and fill the Rover up with petrol, will you? There should be some jerrycans in the garage.'

'Have done, sir.'

'Good man. Oh and Gaine?'

'Sir?'

'You're sure we weren't tailed on the way up?'

'Sir!' Mr Gaine was deeply reproachful.

'Thought not. Just checking.'

*

'So. To begin at the beginning. When did you first meet this Paddy Leclare?'

On and on came the questions, one after another. Ned had been talking for over an hour now, and still they hadn't come to the last night on board the *Orphana*. Oliver had wanted to know not just every detail of every previous trip abroad, but of every term-time meeting of the Sailing Club too.

'You're doing well, Ned, very well. Not too far to go now. Where were we? Ah, yes. Ireland. The Giant's Causeway. Two hours he was away while you boys played on the beach and gasped with pleasure at the rock formations. Two hours exactly?'

'One and half hours perhaps, two at the most.'

'And when he came back, he was on his own?'

'I definitely didn't see anyone with him.'

'And then you set off for Oban again, sailing through the night? What time was that?'

'Eight thirty-five. I helped with the log. I told you.'

'Just making sure, just making sure. Now, describe the conditions to me. There's a new moon rising just now isn't there? You can see it through the window. So two nights ago it must have been pretty dark. There you were, out to sea, hugging a barren coast. Pitch black, I should think, but only for an hour or so at the most, this time of year. Am I right?'

And on and on came the questions. Oliver was naturally thorough because he was trained to be, but he was covering the ground with especial care now because he had no wish to have to haul Ned back at some later date to go over any questions that he might have missed. There would be enough work in the coming weeks, interviewing the boy's headmaster, other members of the school bloody sailing club as well as witnesses in Oban and Tobermorey and Holland and a dozen other places besides.

'. . . I could tell at once he was very seriously ill . . . sent Cade off to find a bottle of whisky . . . no, Jameson's . . . seemed to find it funny . . . made me swear . . . whatever was most holy to me . . .'

Oliver drained his wine glass.

'Excellent, excellent. And the envelope came from where?'

'Well, a shop I suppose. A stationer's. He never said.'

'No, no. He *produced* it from where? His pocket? A safe? What?'

'Oh I see. From a small bag. It was on the chart table.'

'Colour?'

'Red. It was red nylon.'

'Any maker's name? Adidas, Fila, that sort of thing?'

'N-no . . . pretty sure not.'

'Good, good. Your chum Rufus Cade still out of earshot, was he?'

'Oh yes, definitely.'

'You're sure of that? You could see the hatchway from where you were?'

'No, but Paddy could and he would have seen if Rufus had come back.'

'Fair point. On we go.'

'Well, that's when he told me to deliver the letter.'

'There's nothing on the envelope. Not written in invisible ink is it?'

'No.' Ned grinned at the idea. 'He made me memorise the name and address.'

'Which were . . . ?'

'I was to deliver it to Philip R. Blackrow, 13 Heron Square, London SW1.'

It was as if a bolt of electricity had shot through Oliver Delft's body. Every nerve end tingled, his heart gave a great leap and for a second blackness crowded in on his vision.

Ned looked at him with concern. 'Are you all right?'

'It's cramp. Cramp that's all. Nothing to worry about.'

Oliver stood up, turned off the tape-recorder and walked away from the table, pushing hard down on the toes of his right foot, as if trying to stretch out a muscle spasm. It was absolutely essential that he remain calm now, completely calm and completely in control.

'Um listen,' he said. 'I won't be a moment. Wait here, would you? Make some toast or something. There's more of that milk in the fridge. I need to do a few things. Put in a call. Find you some clothes, that kind of thing. You'll be all right?'

Ned nodded happily.

Mr Gaine was still wrestling with the crossword.

'Everything all right, Mr Delft, sir?'

'He's a plausible little bastard,' Oliver said. 'We're going to need to do a D16 on him. I'll go up and clear it. Thank Christ we're only half an hour away.'

Mr Gaine's eyebrows shot up. 'A D16? Are you sure, sir?'

'Of course I'm bloody sure. This is ultra, Gaine. Absolutely ultra. Whistle up a couple of your own, the tougher and dumber the better. You can use their car when they get here. I'll be needing yours straight away. I'll meet you at D16 tomorrow morning with the paperwork. Go on, go and call them up. Use the clean phone. Go now, *now*! What the fuck are you waiting for?'

Gaine headed for the door, alarmed at his first sight in four years of his master looking anything less than in total control.

Oliver stood in the middle of the room thinking furiously.

It was unbelievable, unbelievable! The name and address, spoken clearly out loud into a live microphone – well, that tape was going to have to be wiped, for a start. No, *not* wiped. London would need something. The flash from West End Central had been logged, there was Maureen, there was that Detective Sergeant.

Christ, the boy was a cabinet minister's son. There'd be hell to pay if he played this wrong.

Oliver forced himself to take a mental step back and focus his thoughts. The Detective Sergeant and the arresting officers could be dealt with easily. They'd be signing the Official Secrets Act and swearing eternal silence by midnight, he would see to that personally. Besides, they didn't even know Ned Maddstone's name. Oliver had come into the interview room just as Floyd was asking Ned to reveal it.

The long weekend was shot to pieces now, no doubt

about it. Oliver wasn't even going to have a short one. And there was the problem of the tape. He needed a tape with a name and address spoken on it, that was certain, but not the name of Philip R. Blackrow and not that address.

It had been a horrible shock to hear that name, but when you came down to it, thought Oliver, it could be looked upon as a kind of gift from God. If the flash had come through just five minutes later, it would have been Stapleton here now, not Oliver. And if Stapleton had been given the name Blackrow . . .

No – all in all, God had been abundantly good. The boy had been picked up on the street. No one knew. *No one knew*. That simple fact gave him almost limitless power over the matter. From now on it was merely a question of finesse.

Oliver's first instinct, almost before the name and address were out of Ned's mouth, had been to undertake immediate terminal action, but he discarded any such thoughts now. In his world, whatever the contrary assumptions of newspapers and writers of fiction, death was always a very final resort – so final indeed, as to be almost beyond consideration. This was less a question of scruples than of options. An enemy might one day be turned into a friend and a friend into an enemy, a lie might be made true and a truth rendered false, but the dead could never, not ever, be transformed into the living. Flexibility was everything.

Besides, death had a way of loosening tongues. Dead

men may not talk, but living men do and Oliver had great need of living men if he was to survive this crisis. He was confident, of course, that Gaine was as trustworthy as they made them, but the long view had to be taken. There were many bleak scenarios that Oliver could project, and many more, he knew, that he could never even guess at, life being life. There was always the threat of the development of a conscience in Gaine, or of a sudden religious conversion that might bring with it a flood of remorse and confession. Old-fashioned guilt-sodden liberalism was a dangerous prospect too, come to that. There was a descent into the bottle to consider, bringing with it threats of indiscretion or blackmail. Oliver had seen Gaine drunk – pissed as an eft, as it were – and while he knew that the man's head was as strong as the rest of him, he could not possibly be sure how he would be in ten, twenty, thirty years' time. Given the impermanence and uncertainty of everything, the permanence and certainty of death could prove the most disastrous choice of all. It was paradoxical but true.

Oliver was the kind of man who had never understood the status accorded to *Hamlet*. For him, thought and action were one and the same thing. Even as he went upstairs to search the bedroom cupboards for clothes, the beautiful idea was forming itself in his mind to the last detail.

Gordon had arrived back in time to witness Portia's blazing row with her parents.

'He is *not* like all men!' she yelled at Hillary. 'Don't you dare say that!'

'Probably saw some of his friends going to Harrods and forgot all about you,' Peter offered. 'His type are like that. No sense of loyalty. Look at how they behaved in Palestine. Look at Ireland. Well rid of the chinless ass if you ask me.'

'Palestine? *Ireland?* What has Palestine got to do with anything?'

'Hey, hey, hey!' Gordon cooed as Portia flung herself onto his chest. 'Cool it, Pete. Can't you see that she's upset? What's up, Porsh? You and Ned have a fight?'

'Of course not,' she sobbed. 'Oh, Gordon, he's disappeared!'

'Disappeared? How do you mean?'

'I mean *disappeared*. Vanished. I . . . I went for that job interview. He was supposed to be down in the street waiting for me when I came out, but he wasn't. And he wasn't at his father's house in Catherine Street either. I hung around outside for hours but there was no sign of him. And then I thought perhaps he might have phoned here, so I came home as fast as I could, but there was no message, nothing. And anyway,' she said, rounding on Peter. 'What do you mean *chinless*? Ned's got a wonderful chin. What's more, he doesn't have to hide it under a scraggy moth-eaten beard like some people.'

'Well we won't know that for sure,' said Peter, folding open the *Morning Star* with a flourish, 'until he's old enough to *grow* a beard, will we, pet?'

'An appalling way to treat someone,' sniffed Hillary. 'As a matter of fact, it's a kind of emotional rape. It is. It's rape pure and simple. Rape.'

Portia turned towards her mother and snarled.

'Okay, okay,' said Gordon, laying a placating hand on Portia's shoulder and pulling her round to face him. 'Let's stay with it. Did you call yet?'

'Call? Call where?'

'Ned's house. His father's house. In . . . Catherine Street, was it?'

'Of *course* I called. I rang the moment I got back here.'

'Nobody home?'

'It just rang and rang,' said Portia going over to the telephone, 'I'll try again now.'

'Seems kinda strange.'

'I know it does. That's what I've been trying to tell these two, but they won't listen.'

'What about his dad?'

'I don't have his number. He's down at his constituency.'

'Yes, chasing after innocent foxes, no doubt.'

'It's *July*, Peter!' Portia shouted. 'They don't hunt in July!'

'Well, please excuse me, your highness. I'm sorry I'm so shockingly unfamiliar with the delicate nuances of the social calendar. I'm afraid my time these days is taken up with trivial things like history and social justice. There just never seems to be enough left over to devote to the really important issues, like how the upper classes organise their year. I really must get round to it one day.'

Much of this fine speech was wasted on Portia, as she had stuck a finger in one ear while the other was pressed hard against the telephone receiver.

'No answer,' she said, 'he's not there.'

'Or not picking up . . .' said Hillary.

Gordon was itching to turn on the TV to see if there was anything yet on the news, but he knew that for the moment he would have to concentrate on behaving in his most tender, brotherly and concerned manner. This crisis for Portia, and the public scandal that was certain to break, would draw her closer and closer to him. He needed to play it slow, not rush things.

'Would it help if I maybe went over?' he asked. 'To Catherine Street? You could stay by the phone in case he calls.'

'Oh, Gordon, would you?'

'Sure, no problem.'

'But suppose he phones after you've gone?' Portia wanted to know. 'How can I get in touch with you?'

'I'll find a call-box somewhere and check in every hour,' said Gordon.

'Be back by midnight,' Hillary called after him. 'If he

hasn't turned up then you'll have to decide what to do in the morning. I'm not having you hanging around the street all night.'

'Sure,' said Gordon. 'No problem.'

He wheeled his bicycle from the garage and set off towards Highgate, and Rufus Cade's parents' house, a pleasant evening of smoking grass and giggling at the news ahead of him.

Ned was tired, but strangely elated. There is no pain in talking to someone who is fascinated by every word you say. Once he had made the decision to tell Oliver everything, he had actually enjoyed the experience of examining his memory so minutely. He was rather proud of the accuracy and the detail of his recall.

And what a story! He couldn't wait to tell Portia all about it, if he was allowed to. He would tell his father for certain. And Rufus perhaps, who had been right there that very night. Oliver would probably have to question Rufus anyway, and the whole of the Sailing Club too. What a scandal for the school!

The cannabis in his pocket however, that remained a total mystery. Ned wondered if perhaps those Spanish students he had spoken to outside the college had seen the policemen coming up behind him and dropped the package into his pocket as a way of saving their own skins.

Oliver came back into the room holding a supermarket carrier bag. 'Details, details,' he said. 'My department, it grieves me to say, is an absolute bugger for details. Here you go, you can put these on in a second. I'm afraid yours got oil all over them in the boot of the car.'

Ned took the bag and looked inside. He could see a

pair of Dunlop tennis shoes, grey trousers, a pullover and a tweed jacket.

'Brilliant!' he said. 'Thanks so much.'

Oliver had set the tape-recorder running again.

'Think nothing of it. Now then, you have a girlfriend I think you said?'

'Yes. Portia. She doesn't know anything about this. In fact, I've been wanting to ring her.'

'All in good time. What does her father do, I wonder?'

'Well, he's a history lecturer at the North East London Polytechnic.'

Oliver could have hugged himself with delight. It was almost too much. A history lecturer! At the NELP, if you please . . .

'I see,' he said, 'and just for the record, I wonder if you could give me his full name and address?'

'Um, Peter Fendeman, 14, no 41 sorry, 41 Plough Lane, Hampstead, London NW3. But why . . . ?'

'Say that again for me, would you? Just the name and address.'

'Peter Fendeman, 41 Plough Lane, Hampstead, London NW3.'

'Excellent.'

Jewish too, by the sound of it. Oh frabjous day. When things fall into place like this, Oliver told himself, it doesn't do to become arrogant. It is God's work.

'Ned you've been fantastic! I can't tell you how sorry I am that we had to hoik you out here and put you through this nonsense. Look, I've got to hare up the motorway in the other direction from you, check out a few things in Scotland, so I'll say goodbye. Mr Gaine can look after you from now on.'

Ned took the outstretched hand and shook it warmly. 'Thank you, Mr Delft. Thank you so much.'

'It's Oliver. And thank *you*, Ned. It'll make a real difference you know. You should be very proud of yourself.'

'But what about the drugs?'

'Drugs, what drugs?' said Oliver, lifting the spools of tape from the recorder. 'The whole incident is forgotten, Ned. No, better than forgotten – *it never happened*. The police never picked you up, in fact they've never heard of you. They don't know your name, they don't even know what you look like. I promise you this, by tomorrow morning every record of your arrest will have disappeared for ever.'

And oh, if only you knew how true that was, Oliver said to himself. How wonderfully, wonderfully true.

'Phew!' Ned smiled as relief flooded through him. 'If the press had heard about it, my father would have been . . . well, devastated.'

Oliver checked his watch.

'I'm afraid it may be a little while before you can leave. I'm taking the only car. We've sent for another though, and it shouldn't be too long before it gets here. I'd get into those clothes now if I were you. Have a safe journey home and if you need anything, just ask Mr Gaine.'

*

The pullover fitted. There was that to be said. It smelled of rotten onions, but at least it fitted him perfectly. The jacket and tennis shoes were too tight by miles and the trousers seem to have been made for a five foot man with a forty-eight inch waist. Oliver hadn't thought to include a belt, so Ned hunted around the kitchen looking for string. He found some in a drawer and drew it five times around his middle. He was picking up a knife to cut the string when he heard the door open.

'Oh, hello, Mr Gaine,' he said, turning with relief. 'I was hoping you might . . .'

Gaine stepped forward. Before Ned knew what was happening his right arm had been twisted behind his back so high that the bone was wrenched from its socket. Ned screamed as much from the sound of the crack and pop as from the pain. He screamed again when Gaine's enormous fist slammed into the side of his head, dropping him to his knees. But when Gaine followed up with a blow of incredible force to the back of his neck, Ned was already incapable of screaming any more.

Mr Delft had been right as usual, thought Gaine, returning the knife to the drawer. Nasty piece of work. Weak though, he said to himself, looking down at Ned's unconscious body. Very weak. Like wrenching a wing from a chicken. Where's the challenge in that? He heard the sound of a van in the driveway and, pausing only to deliver a heavy and pleasingly crunchy kick to Ned's ribs, Mr Gaine made his way out into the hallway.

'Oliver, my dear, what a delightful surprise. I do wish you'd let me know. I can't offer you a scrap to eat.'

'I've not come for lunch, Mother,' said Delft, side-stepping her embrace. 'I've come for a talk.'

'Oh dear, that sounds positively horrid. Well, we'd better go up to the drawing-room. Maria is in the kitchen cleaning out the oven, poor thing. I had the most *spectacular* disaster last night, you wouldn't *believe*. Two boys from Australia who do dinner parties. The *highest* recommendation and shatteringly good-looking, as so many queers are these days, but their soufflés exploded and Maria had to run out and buy that new American ice-cream that comes in fifty-seven varieties. Monsignor Collins was here and some *frighteningly* rich people whom I wanted to soften up before digging into them for the Oratory Fund. Heavens, there's a terrible fug, isn't there? Jeremy's cigars I suppose. Shall I open a window?'

'No, Mother, just sit down.'

'Very well, darling. There!'

'Where is Jeremy, by the way?'

'At the *office*, of course. He's been working like a Trojan lately. So long as he doesn't overdo it like your poor father. Or like you, come to that. You're looking awfully tired, darling. Positively hagged. *Any*way, I think there's something rather good in the air, so if you know anyone who can buy shares for you, I would scoop them up as fast as you can.'

'Mother, how many times have I told you? It's against the law.'

'Oh, I know I was a bit naughty with Colin's airline, but this is family and surely that doesn't count. Besides, Father Hendry told me in confession once that insider dealing as you call it isn't the least bit of a mortal sin, it's only a manmade one, so I really don't think it can be said to matter very much.'

'I tell you what, Mother,' said Oliver taking up a position in front of the fireplace, 'let's cut all this dizzy Belgravia hostess nonsense, shall we?'

'Oh, do move away from there, Oliver. You look like a Victorian patriarch. It's *too* lowering. It reminds me of how Daddy used to stand when I'd been naughty. That's better! Come and sit down beside me and don't be so pompous. Tell me what's eating you.'

'Well, since you mentioned him, let's talk about your father.'

'Darling, what an odd idea!'

'Not Great-Uncle Bobby but your *real* father. We've never discussed him, you and I, have we?'

'Is there something to "discuss", as you put it?'

'Of course there is. I've always known, you know.'

'Always known what, dear?'

'How you felt about him. How proud of him you've

always been. I've seen it in your face the handful of times you've ever mentioned him to me.'

'Daddy was a very great man. A very great man. If you'd known him, you would have *adored* him. You'd have been as proud of him as I am. You are strangely alike in some ways.'

'I damned well hope not. The man was a traitor.'

'You're not to use that word. To die for your country isn't treachery, it is heroism.'

'But he didn't die for his country, did he? He was *English*. One hundred per cent hearts of oak, village green, maypole and mutton *English*. There wasn't a single drop of Irish blood in his veins.'

'He loved Ireland and Ireland loved him! Loyalty to your country of birth is vapid and unremarkable. Only loyalty to an idea has meaning. You don't understand the first thing about it. You wouldn't recognise a principle if it stared you in the face. You would stamp it with your dull civil service stamp, push it onto a spike and send it off to be filed.'

'I do recognise murder when I see it, however.'

'Murder? What are you talking about? Daddy never murdered anyone in his life.'

Oliver took a white envelope from his pocket. 'For you, I believe.'

'Goodness!' exclaimed his mother, reverting a little to her former manner. 'How wildly exciting. What is it, an invitation?'

'I believe everything is in place. You'll note the little hair protruding from the flap. Open it, Mother.'

'It doesn't *say* that it's for me . . .'

'I have it on the best authority that it is to be delivered into the hands of Philippa Blackrow of 13 Heron Square and none other. Those were the exact words – well, exact enough at any rate. Believe me, Mother, it is for you all right, the gift of a dead man.'

'Dead?'

'I'm afraid so. Paddy Leclare died two days ago. It was his last request that you should have this. Who am I to stand in the way of a dying wish?'

'It ate into my heart when you applied to the Home Office,' his mother said, looking sadly down at the envelope and twisting it in her hands. 'I remember how excited you were when they accepted you, and I thought how ashamed I was that a son of mine could be so unambitious as to choose such a career for himself. It turns out I misjudged you. You are like your grandfather after all, only a mirror image, fighting on the wrong side and with every good quality reversed. Do you have a knife?'

Oliver passed over a penknife and watched his mother carefully slit the envelope open.

'Ah, you've made a mistake there, darling,' she said, with something like triumph. 'The letter should be tucked in with the folded side up, how silly of you not to have noticed.'

'As it happens I was not present when they opened it.'

'When who opened it?'

'Never mind.'

'Well, thank you so much for delivering it, Oliver dear. What happens now? Am I to be arrested? Interned without trial? Shot out of hand? Escorted to one of your secret lunatic asylums and pumped full of thorazine perhaps?'

'We don't do that kind of thing, Mother.'

'Of course you don't, darling. It's just awful gossip and rumour. You don't shoot to kill, you don't torture, you don't lie, spy, bug and blackmail either, do you?'

Oliver turned his head at the sound of a sudden creak on the stair. He strode quickly across the room and opened the door.

'Ah, Maria, how can we help?'

'Good mooring, Mister Oliver. I'm sorry, distrubbing you. I woss wunnering if you or Mrs Blaggro like maybe some cop of coffee? Or some bisskiss? I have bake many bisskiss.'

'Thank you, Maria, no. If we need anything, we will come down,' said Oliver, closing the door.

'But such a sweet thought!' his mother called over her shoulder. 'Thank you, Maria, dear.'

Oliver closed the door, crossed over to the window and looked out over Heron Square. Through the balusters of the first floor balcony he could see a sparklingly clean turquoise Bentley manoeuvring into a parking space. In the central garden a game of tennis was in progress on one of three courts set aside for the use of residents. From most of the stucco façades that overlooked the square, national flags drooped from cream-painted poles. The houses here were so large and opulent that few were still in use as private residences, the majority served as embassies or grand offices.

'I just want to know one thing,' Oliver said. 'Why? That's the question isn't it. Why? You have more than most people ever dream of. A rich husband who adores you, health, friends, luxury, status . . . *why?*'

For Philippa Blackrow who had lived with her passion since almost before she could remember, the answer to that question was so clear in her mind that it seemed almost impossible to express. She lit a cigarette and looked up at her son, whose face was dark against the window.

'After the British shot your grandfather,' she said at length, 'Mummy and I went to live in Canada to avoid the fuss. She died there when I was fourteen. The doctors never explained what it was, but I knew that it was what they used to call a broken heart. We seem to have lost that capacity of late, don't we? Doctors have told us not to be so silly. Animals still die that way, but what do animals know? To this day I am sure that she would never have been taken ill if Daddy had still been alive. The British killed both my parents. Well, Mummy's brother, my Uncle Bobby, adopted me and so I came back to England and became his daughter. He never let me talk about Daddy. If I so much as mentioned his name I would be sent to my bedroom. Uncle Bobby was to be called Daddy and Aunt Elizabeth was to be Mummy. It was as if my real parents never existed. Daddy was the wicked brother-in-law that Uncle Bobby's poor sister had been tricked into marrying and his name was to be struck from family history. I suppose they thought I would forget him, but I never did. The less he was mentioned, the more proud of him I grew and the more determined to have my revenge on the unjust, cruel and gutless regime that destroyed him. You think I have more than most people dream of? What other people dream of doesn't matter. I always had less than *I* ever dreamt of. All I ever dreamt of was a family. A father and a mother. Most people don't even need to dream of such luxuries, they take them for granted. That is what I used to dwell on, alone in my bedroom. I dwelt as all children do, on the injustice. Injustice is the most terrible thing in the world, Oliver. Everything that is evil springs from it and only a cheap soul can abide it without anger. You were named, you know, after the great Irish patriot, Saint Oliver Plunkett, who was betrayed on the lying word of Protestant perjurers and condemned to be hanged, drawn and quartered on Tyburn hill just there, at the top end of Park Lane.'

'And there's me,' said Oliver, looking out over the rooftops towards Marble Arch, 'thinking I was named after Oliver Cromwell, the very man who had him hunted down. You paint a very sweet, a very sentimental, a very *Irish* portrait, if I may say so, Mother, of dignified suffering and noble ideals, but I seem to remember that the Blessed Oliver Plunkett, as he was known when I was at school, by the way . . .'

'The Holy Father canonised him not long ago . . .'

'Did he now? I must have missed the headlines. Be that

as it may, my memory tells me that he died thanking God for giving him the grace to suffer and praying for the forgiveness for his enemies. I don't remember reading that he shrieked down curses and swore bloody revenge on all the English. Would the sight of British children blasted into little pieces have made his heart rejoice, do you think?'

'I do not expect you to understand. In fact, I would prefer not to discuss it further.'

'I'm sure you would,' said Oliver, turning from the window. 'I can at least be grateful for one part of your childhood.'

'And what might that be?'

'Great-Uncle Bobby's adoption of you allowed my real ancestry to slip through the net, didn't it? He buried your father so deep that it was never picked up when they vetted me for the service. Do you seriously imagine that the government would have given me a job if they had known I was the grandson of a Fenian traitor and spy, a friend of Casement and Childers and a proven enemy of the Crown?'

'And now you will tell them, I suppose.'

'I'll do no such thing, Mother. You were wrong when you described me as unambitious. You and I are the only people on God's earth who know the truth and that is how it will stay. I have been busy making arrangements and you are one of them.'

'Really, Oliver? I'm one of your arrangements? But that's too tremendously intriguing. Have you worked it all out?'

'You'll send a message to your friends to tell them that

Leclare's last message to you was intercepted. You fear that you are being watched and have decided to lie low in the country.'

'Have I decided that, darling?'

'You have. From time to time I will visit you and you will furnish me with the names of every member of every bomb-making factory, every cell, every Active Service Unit, every safe house, every weapons cache and every recruiting officer, money-raiser and sympathiser you have ever heard of. The smallest shred of intelligence, rumour or gossip you have ever picked up in your long years of crime and betrayal you will pass to me. This will advance my career enormously and should fill your remaining years in the country with maternal pride.'

'My bowels opened as you were being born,' said Philippa. 'For many years I used to wonder if perhaps in all the confusion the midwife accidentally disposed of the child and wrapped the shit in a blanket for me to feed. Now I know.'

'A charming sentiment.'

'And supposing I refuse?'

'You really don't want to do that, Mother. I am in a position to make life very difficult for you, for Jeremy, for your step-children and most especially, for the young man who was assigned to deliver that letter to you.'

'Who is he?'

'You don't know him, but you would adore him, I promise you. He's suffering eternal torment like Christ on a crucifix, and all for your sins. I'll give you a week, to explain to Jeremy that you have tired of the city and yearn for the rural peace of Wiltshire. And if you think you can feed me useless information Mother, think again. I will take my chances and hand you in. You will spend the rest of your life as a prisoner in the hardest jail in Europe.'

Oliver walked across the square, humming 'Lillibulero'. The sun was shining and the roads were giving off a pleasant smell of softened tarmac. Poor Mother, he thought to himself, how she will miss London.

He stopped off at the Berkeley Hotel to use the telephone.

'News desk.'

'This is the Provisional IRA. We have the son of the British war criminal Charles Maddstone. His clothes will be sent you as proof. The code is "Interior Interior Interior". Good afternoon to you.'

Handcuffed to a wooden upright, Ned sat on the floor of the van opposite two of the ugliest men he had ever seen in his life.

At the age of fifteen his collarbone had snapped during a game of rugby and he had supposed at the time that this was as far as pain could ever go. He knew better now. Every turn and bump that Mr Gaine negotiated, driving in the cabin up front, sent through him blinding surges of a pain so intense that at each wave of it, orange and yellow light flashed in his eyes, the blood roared in his ears and the very guts within him seemed to explode in shock. The pain grew from his shoulder, where a grinding background ache radiated outwards into violent raging fires that scorched and spat into every corner of his body. The effort of holding still without tightening his frame as he breathed had prevented him from even trying to talk, but he could feel now that the van had joined a motorway and the smoother progress encouraged him to try a few words.

'Mr Delft . . .' he began. The men opposite turned their eyes towards him, 'Mr Delft said I was to go home . . . he said I was . . .'

Mr Gaine swung the van out to overtake a lorry and

Ned's body slid forward, detonating an explosion in his shoulder that sent sheets of pain flashing and screaming through his body.

Five minutes later he tried again. 'I'm supposed . . . supposed to go home . . .' The words came out in a whisper.

The men regarded him with silent interest for a moment or two, then looked away.

Ned had lost almost all sense of time and space. He did not know whether he had been left to lie for five minutes on the kitchen floor or for five hours. He could not tell how long they had been travelling or in which direction. The van was closed and windowless, and his only clue as to time was a feeling that the number of cars and lorries around them was increasing, which suggested the build-up of morning traffic.

He attempted speech again. 'My shoulder . . . it's . . . I think it's dis . . . dis . . . I think it's dislocated.'

Curiously, through the uncomprehending fog of his senses, Ned was still careful to be polite. He could have said that his shoulder *had been* dislocated, or even that Mr Gaine had dislocated it.

The men turned to each other.

'You know how to put a shoulder back?' one of them asked.

'I'm not bleeding touching him,' said the other. 'The cunt's cacked his fucking pants. Fucking stinks.'

Ned's smashed nose, bubbling with blood, had not detected the stench that surrounded him, but he understood now why he felt a soft squash and slide between his buttocks.

'I'm sorry . . .' he said, tears dropping down his face. 'I didn't know. I'm so sorry, only . . .'

'Give it a fucking rest, can't you?'

'Mr Delft said . . . he said I was to go home. He'll be angry . . . and my father . . . my father is an important man . . . please, *please*!'

To stop the unpleasant whimpering, they took it in turns to kick him into unconsciousness.

It is not often that I confess to being baffled, but for a short while today the disappearance of Ned Maddstone struck me as the most complete mystery imaginable. It was as if he had been simply scooped off the surface of the earth. I am pleased, however, that I was able to work out the truth for myself.

I spent a frustrating night, raging against the system that had covered up his arrest. How typical, I thought, as each succeeding bulletin on the television, and subsequently on the wireless through the early hours, failed to disgorge so much as a scrap of news, how supremely typical. The police had been got to, it was clear to me. Some squalid Central Office lackey had swung into action and initiated a cover-up. I was tempted to ask Tom, in whose house I have my basement flat, if he knew anything. Tom works at party headquarters in Smith Square and is privy to all the gossip. I should know, I regularly read his paperwork when he's upstairs drunk in his bed. I tamped down the desire, preferring not to have to answer questions. But it was frustrating to me that nothing of Ned's arrest had yet emerged.

Rufus and I should have tipped off the press as

well as the police, I told myself furiously, it was naïve of me not to have thought of it. I made a mental note to myself. One day, I resolved, I will put a sign over my desk –

This is, after all, *England*

– and I shall make no important decisions without referring to it. Although it seems now that I may have done the police and the establishment an injustice, the sign over the desk is still a good idea.

In the normal course of events, Sir Charles had been due to arrive at Catherine Street at midday for a diary meeting. It seemed obvious to me however, given the lack of any news, that he must have come down the previous night to bail out his son and establish some kind of media blackout. None the less, I was determined to ensure the full involvement of the press somehow, even if it meant another anonymous call from a phone-box. First, however, I would have to see precisely how events had unravelled at Catherine Street. The prospect of Ned's embarrassed explanations and confused protestations of innocence to his father filled me with delicious anticipation. Would he have been sent up to bed without any supper? Would he have been believed? I had decided to offer him exactly the same spaniel-eyed tactlessness and clumsy sympathy that he so crassly meted out to me.

Despite a great eagerness to be there as soon as possible, I took the tube to Victoria at my usual time of half past nine. While I would have loved to be there earlier, it was important not to show that I expected today to be anything more than a perfectly normal Friday.

As I turned into Catherine Street I was delighted to see a police car parked outside the house. Things were looking up. Such a sight argued against any concerted or coherent cover-up: at the most it suggested a very incompetent one. If the police had been got at they would hardly be there now, with an unmarked car outside the front door. Perhaps the Drug Squad were searching the place from top to bottom, I thought, hoping to enter and see floor-boards up and books scattered all over the Bokhara. What an agreeable prospect. I looked up at the façade and fancied I saw a face pressed against the window of the first floor study.

I let myself into the house and mounted the stairs, preparing an expression in which I hoped that mild curiosity and impassive preparedness were nicely blended.

Sir Charles was at his desk in conversation with two policemen. I saw that Ned's girlfriend, Portia, had been the face at the window. She stood at it now, restlessly turning her head one way and the other to look up and down the street, her breath misting the pane.

'Ashley, thank heaven!' cried Sir Charles, rising excitedly to his feet as I came in.

'Sir Charles, what is it? Is there something wrong?'

'Have you seen Ned?'

'Ned? Not since yesterday, sir, no. Why? Has he gone missing?'

'He hasn't been seen since four o'clock yesterday afternoon!'

'Good lord!' I said. 'But that's bizarre . . .'

The policemen were eyeing me with curiosity and I bowed my head respectfully in their direction.

'Gentlemen, this is Mr Barson-Garland, my researcher,' said Sir Charles with a wave of the hand in my direction.

The two policemen half rose from their seats and nodded grave good mornings to me.

'These kind officers are being very helpful, Ashley. But so far the thing seems to be a complete mystery.'

Very helpful? The Metropolitan Police should look to its policies on interdepartmental co-operation, I thought. The buffoons of the drug squad haven't yet bothered to tell these poor flatfoots that *they* were holding Ned.

I had to confess that I hadn't imagined that a minor offence like the possession of cannabis could warrant an overnight stay in the cells. But it struck me that on arrest, to save his father embarrassment, Ned might have refused to give his name. Perhaps such a lack of co-operation, allied to the arrogant Maddstone manner, had so annoyed the arresting officers that they had thrown him in a cell simply in order to teach him a lesson.

'Have you tried calling the hospitals?' I suggested. 'Or police stations, even. If he was mugged perhaps, or . . .'

'Yes, yes,' said Sir Charles, sitting down again. He had taken up the natural position of authority at his desk, with the policemen sitting respectfully across from him, caps on lap and notebooks in hand, like secretaries about to take dictation. 'We have tried everything. A missing persons alert has been put out, every police station and hospital in London has been contacted. Officers from Special Branch will be here soon. There is always the possibility you see, given my position,' he said, lowering his voice, 'that the security angle may have to be considered.'

There was something in the way he said 'given my position' that reminded me forcibly of Ned. The same Maddstone-maddening apologetic ruefulness – as if status, authority and birth were embarrassing solecisms to be understood and pardoned.

One of the policemen turned to me. 'When did you last see Mr Maddstone, sir?'

I considered the question. 'Um, about midday, I should say. Let me see. I spent the morning working on correspondence . . .' My eye travelled to Sir Charles's desk, where the pile of post still lay, unsigned. 'Those letters there, in fact. Then I left at . . . what time did we leave, Portia?'

Portia turned from the window with a blank stare. I could see that she hadn't slept all night and that the question hadn't penetrated, only my calling her name.

'I went off with your cousin Gordon,' I reminded her. 'To show him round Parliament. Do you remember? When was that, would you say?'

'Lunchtime,' she said in a dull voice. 'You went off at lunchtime. And then you came back.'

'Came back?' I said, raising an eyebrow. 'I don't think . . . oh yes, you're quite right, though. I let myself in to pick up my briefcase at . . . I suppose it was around three o'clock, but I didn't see Ned then. You were both up . . . you were both – otherwise engaged,' I amended with care, winning the ghost of a smile from one of the policemen. 'And then you were off to a job interview somewhere, weren't you? What happened?'

The story tumbled from her. I could tell that she had told it many times, to others and over and over again to herself and that in the telling of it she hoped somehow for a meaning or clue to emerge. Ned had not been there when she emerged from her interview. She had waited around Catherine Street, gone home, phoned and phoned and then at seven in the morning she had finally managed to persuade a House of Commons official to telephone Sir Charles in the country. He had driven up and called the police, who had so far discovered nothing.

'You'll forgive me, miss,' one of them said now. 'But there were no bad words between you and Mr Maddstone, were there? No quarrel or anything of that nature?'

Portia stared at him. 'Quarrel? Me and Ned? No, that was impossible. We have never . . . we *could* never . . . We were like . . .'

Sir Charles went over to her with a handkerchief and put an arm round her shoulder. The policemen exchanged glances, then saw me looking at them and transferred their gazes down to their notebooks. All deeply affecting.

'Is there anything that you think I could be doing?' I said. 'Anyone I should call?'

'That's very kind, Ashley, but I don't think . . .' Sir Charles began.

'There is the question of the media, sir,' said one of the policemen. 'They can be very useful. Maybe Mr Barson-Garland here could call someone you know in the newspaper world.'

Sir Charles stiffened. The press were not his favourite institution. They liked to mock him for being 'out of touch' and for possessing an accent that made the Duke of Edinburgh sound like a filing clerk. They habitually referred to him as Barkingstone, Loonystone and Sir Charles the Mad.

'Do we really think that's necessary?' he said worriedly. 'Surely they would only –'

Any further consideration of the role of the press was put aside by a loud pealing on the doorbell. Portia gasped and, wriggling from Sir Charles's grip, went to the window and looked down.

'Oh. It's just three men,' she said dully.

'That'll be Special Branch, sir.'

Sir Charles stood alone on the carpet, suddenly looking every month his age. It occurred to me that he had put his arm round Portia to support himself as much as her.

'I'll let them in,' I said.

*

And so the morning wore on. One nugget of news finally came through just before lunchtime and it puzzled me greatly. I relayed it to Rufus and Gordon over another pub lunch in the shadow of Big Ben.

'It seems that the police paid a visit to the Knightsbridge College,' I told them. 'Apparently four Spanish students saw a blond English youth being picked up and driven off in a car. They can't agree on whether it was a Vauxhall or a Ford and have been taken off somewhere to look at pictures of Ned.'

'Bloody hell,' said Rufus. 'They'll recognise him straight away.'

'I don't get it,' said Gordon. 'The cops already

know it's him. They're the ones who picked him up, for Christ's sake.'

'The more time that passes and the more policemen that get involved, the less likely it appears that they ever picked him up at all,' I murmured, but Gordon was listening to Rufus.

'That car was definitely a Vauxhall,' he was saying with conviction. 'No doubt about that. A T-reg Cavalier. And they looked like Drug Squad to me. Unshaven, leather-jackets, tattered 501s, Adidas trainers. Classic DS. It's their idea of undercover. Pathetic, really.'

'Christ, what a screw-up. You mean the Drug Squad are holding the guy and they don't realise that he's been reported missing? Maybe we should make another call.'

'Gordon, that is a disastrous idea,' I said. 'Listen to me. You have to get it into your head that whatever kind of jeans and whatever kind of footwear favoured by those men we saw yesterday, they were in fact *not* the Drug Squad, nor any other kind of squad.'

I spent a very fervent quarter of an hour persuading the pair of them that for us to confess to any part in the business would only confuse matters.

'It has to be a coincidence,' I explained. 'Ned has been *kidnapped*. That is the obvious and the only explanation. It just so happens that the kidnappers chose that particular time and place. If you think about it, it's not as illogical as it seems. Yesterday would have been the first proper opportunity they'd've had for a long time. He's been at school for months and then away sailing. But yesterday, yesterday they could have followed him and Portia from the house all the way to Knightsbridge, seen him left alone on the pavement and nabbed him. We saw the whole thing and of course assumed it was an arrest. In fact the police probably didn't think our tip-off worth bothering with. Or,' I added, 'they heard Rufus giggling in the background and recognised it for what it was, a schoolboy hoax. In any case, it's just a coincidence. Nothing more.'

It sounded pretty thin to me, but they bought it and chewed on it for a while. Gordon, as I thought he would be, was the first to see the flaw.

'If he's been kidnapped, why hasn't there been some kind of ransom demand?'

I was ready for that. 'There are kidnappers and kidnappers,' I said darkly. 'For two years Ned's father was Secretary of State for Northern Ireland.'

Their mouths dropped as they took in the significance of this.

'So now you see,' I continued, 'why we must lie low and not say a word. None of it has anything to do with us.'

'Except that we witnessed it,' said Gordon. 'We might be needed for evidence . . .'

'Those Spanish students were right there, they can

give plenty of descriptions. We were the other side of a busy street. No, believe me, there's nothing we can add but confusion.'

I left the pub confident that I could trust them not to do or say anything indiscreet. I arrived back at Catherine Street and found that to gain admittance I now had to show my House of Commons pass to a policeman posted by the front door.

There is a chaise-longue in Maddstone's office, all plush and gilt, the kind on which exotic princesses used to pose with panthers. I went upstairs to find Sir Charles slumped on it, the colour drained from his face. Portia was leaning against him, or he against her, and the tears were pouring down her face. It was clear that news of great import had broken while I had been away.

A man in his middle to late twenties sat on the desk, talking into the telephone. His eyes had taken me in as I entered the room and I had the unpleasant feeling that, lazy and pleasant as his inspection seemed to be, he had seen right through to the back of my soul and been unimpressed with what he had found there. An intelligence operative of some kind, I told myself, trying to shake the feeling off. No doubt a course of training in the perfection of that kind of look goes along with instruction in the use of code books, microfilms and cyanide capsules.

'What's going on?' I asked.

Sir Charles opened his eyes and tried to speak.

The man was completely in pieces. If this is the quality of our political leaders, I thought, then no wonder the country has gone to the dogs. You won't find me cracking like that when I'm in power.

When I'm in power . . .

How strange. That's the first time I've ever articulated such a thought. I have always told myself that I was going to become a teacher. How very strange. Now that I've written it down I feel pleasantly relieved. Perhaps I knew it all along. Well, well.

'And you might be?' said the man on the desk, gently replacing the receiver and smiling across at me.

'Ashley Barson-Garland, I'm Sir Charles's personal assistant.'

'Ashley Barson-Garland, Ashley Barson-Garland . . .' he picked up two black notebooks that lay by the telephone. 'What frightful handwriting our friends in blue have . . . ah, yes, here we are. Ashley Barson-Garland. Says here you're a researcher for Sir Charles and a schoolfriend of Edward's. But surely you must be at least twenty-two? Twenty-three perhaps?'

'I shall be eighteen in two weeks,' I said, flushing slightly. It has not been uncommon for new boys at school to take me for a member of staff and I dislike being reminded that I look older than my years.

'My mistake. My name is Smith.'

Smith indeed. A deliberate insult. I went forward

to shake his hand and he had the cheek to look into his palm afterwards and then to my face, causing me to flush again.

'Well, Mr Barson-Garland,' he said, and I would have found open revulsion infinitely less offensive than the expressionless way he now took a handkerchief from his sleeve and wiped it against his hand. 'I'm afraid that while you were at luncheon some rather bad news came in . . .'

The tone of 'While you were at luncheon' seemed to suggest that I had been guilty of some terrible, sybaritic dereliction of duty. In fact, Sir Charles had insisted that I get something to eat and the policemen with him had agreed there was nothing further I could do.

'Bad news?' I said, resisting the temptation to explain this and open myself to further humiliation.

'. . . it seems that a call was made to the offices of *The Times* newspaper an hour ago claiming responsibility for kidnapping Edward Maddstone. We are working on the assumption that the call was genuine.'

'But who? Why?'

'The claim was made by a man purporting to represent the IRA. As for why . . .'

Sir Charles made a kind of moaning noise and Portia hugged him close to her.

'Oh Jesus,' I whispered. 'I was right.'

'You were right?' 'Smith' raised his eyebrows in mild astonishment.

'Well, the thought had crossed my mind,' I said.

'I mean it seemed a possible explanation, you know. Given, given . . . everything,' I completed, lamely.

'What a sharp fellow you are, Mr Barson-Garland. Well, perhaps you might employ some of that sharpness in making yourself useful, if you've a mind to?'

I nodded vigorously. 'Of course. Anything.'

'*The Times* will give us a little time to check out the information before they act upon it, but act upon it they surely will. I think perhaps Sir Charles and the young lady here should leave before the media circus arrives and all hell breaks loose. Perhaps you can think of a suitable bolt-hole. Where do you live, yourself?'

'Tredway Gardens,' I said. 'It's just a flat.'

'And do you ah, *share* it with anyone?' He put the question innocently enough, but again I had the impression that he had detected something in me that amused him.

'Tom Grove. He works in party headquarters, it's his house, I have the basement. Sir Charles's PPS made the arrangement,' I said, annoyed at myself for feeling the need to elaborate.

'I see,' said Smith. 'Well, let us repair thither and that right speedily.'

'I can't drive a car I'm afraid . . .'

'My dear old periwinkle, leave all that to me.'

As I write this, Sir Charles is upstairs in Tom's bedroom, asleep. The man Smith arranged for a doctor to come and pump him full of tranquillisers.

Poor Tom Grove has been warned away. Portia was driven off for further questioning half an hour ago, still hysterical with grief. Seems a little hard on her, but I dare say the authorities know what they're doing. Smith himself has disappeared to 'rattle a few trays' somewhere, whatever that means, but said that he would 'pop his head round the door' some time tomorrow, would I mind meanwhile 'commanding the support trench' – he really is insufferably pleased with himself.

The flat is now pleasantly calm, however, with no sign of the press anywhere. A part of me feels a little sorry for Ned, but another part tells me that, wherever he is and whatever is happening to him, it will do him a great deal of good.

Enough for the moment. I think I shall watch the six o'clock news now.

No matter how strongly she fought it, Portia's evenings at home had fallen into a routine. She had tried for a long time to prolong a state of perpetual crisis by arguing with Pete and Hillary over everything and nothing, but over the weeks the outbursts subsided and life began to assume a normality that she was not able to resist, however much of a betrayal the very assumption of ordinariness in life might signify.

Were it not for Gordon, she felt she would have gone mad. With tremendous tact and psychological understanding, he had suggested that instead of waiting for news or continuing to sit by Sir Charles's bedside looking in vain for signs of recovery, she could do Gordon a great favour by showing him the sights of London. All the crazy tourist shit, he meant. Stupid stuff that would take her mind off Maddstone Junior and Maddstone Senior at least for a few hours every day. He'd really appreciate it, he was starting to feel homesick and he still couldn't find his way round the city.

Pete conceded that it would be cruel to hold her to any promise of working through the summer holidays and had provided enough pocket money for the two of them to buy summer travel passes and spend long days trailing around galleries, churches, museums and royal palaces.

'I want you both to keep a notebook,' Peter had said. 'The architecture and building in London is a discourse on the movement of power and money. You'll find it's a kind of economic geology. From the church to the kings to the aristocracy to the merchant classes to the banks and finally to the multinationals. It's like reading rock strata.'

Gordon and Portia took no notice of this and pressed the buttons at the Science Museum, giggled at the Yeomen of the Guard and tried to get the sentries in their boxes outside St James's Palace to flinch or move their eyes, just like the other adolescent tourists they accompanied around London. Portia found that taking Gordon around her favourite art galleries and explaining the pictures to him was as close as she had come to pleasure for many weeks. It was something to be able to answer questions, to be needed and useful.

Pete never asked to see the notebook he had insisted on. His own time was taken up by his summer students at the polytechnic. One of them had flattered him into forming a discussion group for the analysis of British colonialism in Northern Ireland and Peter had bullied the Inner London Educational Authority into funding a visit to Belfast so that they could see for themselves what was happening 'on the ground', as Pete liked to say. Hillary, busy with her novel was happy enough in the belief that Portia was in the hands of a sensible cousin.

Twice a week Portia still went to visit Sir Charles. It was a relief to her that the press were no longer keeping up a vigil outside the hospital gates, but it was a sign too of waning public interest and that worried her. Events had moved on and the disappearance of the cabinet minister's son had slipped from the front pages to smaller paragraphs inside until quietly dropping from the agenda entirely. At the height of the public fever, when the Prime Minister, cutting short her holiday in the south of France, had stood at the hospital entrance assuring the cameras that steps would be taken and revenge exacted, Ned's kidnapping had been the sensation of the summer period known in journalistic circles – Portia discovered with distaste – as 'the silly season'. But, as sightings of Ned dwindled and reports emerged that the IRA were now denying any part in the affair, the papers began to suggest that the whole thing had never been anything more than a family row, a teenage tantrum of the kind that went on every day. They resumed with relish the usual August parade of fifty-stone women, two-tailed dogs and string beans that spelled out 'armageddon' in Hebrew. The senior newsmen left Britain for their summer holidays, and the deputies minding the shop preferred not to mess with tradition. Besides, the only person worth interviewing would have been Charles Maddstone, and he wasn't saying a word. To anybody.

The two massive strokes that had felled him during the week following his son's disappearance had been so severe that doctors doubted he would ever walk or talk again. The first had completely incapacitated the left side of his body and the second had reduced him to a state of motionless coma. Portia found that her time at his bedside gave her an opportunity to talk without any fear of being misunderstood.

'No news, Daddy,' she would say, closing the door of the private room, drawing up a chair and offering the latest scrap of news. Calling him 'Daddy' gave her a secret and almost erotic thrill. 'Someone was seen in Scarborough, but it was another false alarm.'

She would talk on, pouring out whatever came into her mind, every now and again finding opportunities to emphasise Ned's name in a sentence and glancing across to see if that one mention might be the lowered rope to pull Sir Charles from the well of his unconsciousness.

One day, as she repeated to him for the thousandth time the story of the afternoon Ned had come into the Hard Rock Café with his friends, there was a knock on the door. A doctor Portia had never seen before told her that he had spoken to Sir Charles's sister, Georgina.

'It may be time to consider switching off the life-support,' he said, 'and let the old fellow slip away.'

'But *Ned* is the next-of-kin,' protested Portia, outraged. 'It's his decision.'

'It's been over a month. We must face up to the fact that there is no chance of any change. Miss Maddstone has said that she will think about it for a week before coming to any decision. I do not believe,' the doctor added, 'that you are a member of the family?'

Back home at Hampstead, Pete explained that any

decision of this kind in a private hospital would be based on financial rather than clinical considerations.

'It'll be the insurance company, believe me,' he said. 'That kind of twenty-four hour intensive care is expensive. The money men will be the ones clamouring for the machines to be switched off.'

Gordon was surprised to hear this. 'I thought England had a public health system.'

'A public health system?' Pete snorted. 'That'll be the day . . .'

Oh, God, here we go, thought Portia. Gordon should have known better than to walk into that one. There'll be no stopping Pete now.

In fact, Peter was only warming up when Hillary came downstairs demanding to know what clothes he wanted to take on what he had been rather grandly calling his 'Northern Ireland Fact Finding Trip'.

It always amazed Portia that her mother, such an ardent and devoted feminist on paper and in conversation, should spend so much time, when it came to the realities of everyday life, looking after Pete's every need. From childhood on, Portia had never seen her father so much as pick up a sock, let alone wash one. Hillary cooked for him, shopped for him, washed his clothes and packed his bags, and not once had Portia heard her complain. If all men truly were, as Hillary had written so many times, rapists, it seemed odd to Portia that they should be waited on like Maharajahs.

As they discussed the wardrobe that would most

make Pete look assured, supportive and at home on the streets of West Belfast, Gordon came up to Portia and suggested they leave Pete and Hillary and go for a walk somewhere.

'All right then,' she said. 'Let's go to the Flask. You'll like it.'

'What is that, some kind of park?'

'It's a pub. You'll like it.'

Gordon knew perfectly well what the Flask Inn was, since he had already been there twice in the company of Rufus Cade. He wanted Portia to have the pleasure of introducing him to it, however. He discovered early on that the more helpless and ignorant he appeared, the more she liked it. Gordon was used to that. Most of the girls he had known back home had been the same.

'You guys make sure you're back before eleven,' Hillary insisted. 'In time to say goodbye to Pete.'

A loud pealing came on the doorbell as they left the room and Portia's heart gave a little jump. She had learned not to get too excited by the sound of the door or the telephone, but one day soon a call would come and it would be *the* call. You never knew . . .

'And see who that is,' Pete shouted after them. 'If it's not important, we're out.'

As they went downstairs, a huge bang shook the front door as if a car had slammed into it. An even louder one followed and the whole hallway shuddered. At the third bang, the front door splintered off its hinges and fell inwards with a crash, shattering the floor tiles and rocking the staircase. Three men in gasmasks and body armour stepped through.

At precisely the same time, to the very second, there came a delicate tinkle of broken glass in the sitting room above, followed by the thumping hiss of tear gas canisters and the shrill terrified screams of Hillary and Pete.

Dr Mallo was a very simple man. He approached life rationally, not empirically. The horizons of his world were narrowly confined and this afforded him, he believed, more happiness than that granted to the majority of his fellow creatures. The young Englishman in front of him now, for example, was of no interest to him at all. The trained psychiatrist in him recognised the submerged tension, emotional sublimation and signs of erotic shame in him as a matter of course, but only the paperwork and money being laid on the desk were worthy of scrutiny and serious attention. Where the man came from, the source of his money, the authority behind the documents he produced and the reasons for his neuroses were questions that only an empiricist or – worse still – a psychologist, would ask. The only questions Dr Mallo considered worth asking were questions of authenticity, quantity, reliability and seriousness of purpose.

'This money,' said Dr Mallo, 'is good for one year of treatment. Also, with the current weakness of the pound, what you have given me is, I regret, too little by approximately one and one quarter per cent.'

Oliver Delft took a thick wad of twenty pound notes from his pocket. 'The case is a severe one,' he said. 'Regular sums will be paid into a bank of your choice, annually or quarterly. I believe this procedure is agreeable to you? Unluckily, as you know, this is not the first time my family has had occasion to avail itself of your services.'

'Sometimes these problems lie deep within genetic inheritance,' said Mallo, watching the money being counted onto the table. 'Enough, one hundred and forty is fifteen pounds too much. Be pleased to sign here and here. I can offer change for you in dollars US or francs Swiss.'

Oliver replaced the roll of money and took the proffered pen.

'Dollars, if you'd be so kind.'

'I note,' said Dr Mallo, 'that your unfortunate brother has no name.'

'I'm afraid you will discover that he has many,' said Oliver with a rueful smile. 'Last year he was the rightful heir to the Getty fortune. He kept that one up for over six months, almost a record. In his time he has been . . . let me see, Margaret Thatcher's secret lover, he has been an abused orphan, a Palestinian gunrunner, a member of the Danish royal family – frankly, you name it, he's tried it.'

'You don't say?' murmured the doctor. 'And at the present time?'

'It's back to politics. Thinks he's the son of an English cabinet minister called Maddstone. Won't answer to any name but Ed. Or is it Ned? No saying how long it'll last. He gets it all from the newspapers, of course. The real

Maddstone boy was snatched by terrorists two days ago. Dare say you've read about it in the papers?'

Mallo gave no answer.

'Anyway,' Oliver continued, 'that's the current delusion. It's sad to have to give up on the lad, but we just can't cope with him any more I'm afraid. He's young, extremely fit and capable of terrible violence. He's done some appalling things to the family. Quite *unforgivable* things. You wouldn't credit it to look at him, but then I believe that's often the way.'

'Indeed so.'

'I understand also that this kind of mania is generally somewhat intractable. *Permanent* often, I believe.'

'Sometimes it is regretfully true, patients seldom respond quickly. If, however, some improvement were noted . . . ?'

'I think it very unlikely,' said Oliver. 'But if the family's circumstances *were* to change in any way and we found ourselves willing to give him another chance we would of course be in touch with you in the usual manner. Otherwise . . .'

'Otherwise, sir, you may trust that he will receive the highest quality of care. In the event of demise . . . ?'

'He is very dear to me, I trust that you and your staff will ensure that he lives a long and, in so far as he is able, happy life. My father and uncles assure me that you are to be relied upon in this respect.'

'Naturally we are to be relied upon,' the doctor assured him. 'Our diet and exercise regimes here are of the highest standard. You will be pleased also by the seriousness with which we regard issues of hygiene, safety and general health. Besides, we are subject to rigorous inspection from the authorities. There are patients who have lived happily amongst us for more than thirty years. Indeed we have three men who were placed here by your . . . grandfather.'

'You'll find that the company and conversation of other people excites him,' said Oliver, rising. 'They feed his delusions. You may find it best to keep him on his own until he is a great deal calmer. Let the memory of his old life fade away.'

'Of course, of course, you may depend upon it. And when shall we expect the pleasure of receiving him?'

'My friends will arrive here with him some time later this afternoon. I wish I could stay to see him settled in, but pressure of work I'm afraid . . .'

'Really, I quite understand. If there's nothing more you wish to see, a car will take you to the airport directly.'

Ned awoke from a dream of rivers of gore and spittle pouring from Paddy Leclare's mouth and knew at once that the movement under him was of a sea in full swell. He tried to open his eyes. For a moment it felt that they had become glued tight by blood and sweat, before he realised that they were indeed wide open. It was simply that there was nothing to see. Either he was in a place where no light shone – not the smallest reflection of anything – or he had become stone blind. Some instinct told him that he was not blind but enclosed in a vacuum of absolute darkness.

While the grinding ache in his shoulder socket hung like a black cloud over his every conscious moment, he found that he could foreground each of his other torments. He could concentrate separately on the hot pain of the torn skin around his wrists for example, on the nauseating throb of his smashed nose or on the stabs of a broken rib that pierced his lungs with each breath or movement. These tortures feasted on him like a swarm of angry wasps, yet behind them all, the shoulder, nagging like an evil memory, rasped and grated against its socket with relentless cruelty. But behind even the sick torment of his ruined shoulder, terrible as it was, other agonies raged that were harder yet to bear, the agonies of bewilderment, loneliness and naked fear.

Ned's mind was so closed in by terror and confusion that he became less and less able to make sense of any past or present identity. In delirium and over the course of hours that might have been minutes or days, he reached out with his mind to every image that had ever been sacred to him, his father, cricket, a yacht skiffing in the wind, his best woollen blazer, hot porridge lightly salted, the sound of the school bell at evening – the images came randomly – a pair of silver hair-brushes he had found in a jumble sale and polished to perfect brightness, the gear wheels on his first bicycle, the sharp sour stink of National Geographic magazines, cold milk, freshly sharpened pencils, his naked body in the mirror, gingerbread, the clatter of hockey-sticks at bully-off, the smell of a record-duster . . . yet each picture that he fixed upon flew from his mental grip, and, like soap from a closing fist, the harder he tried to force them the further they leapt away.

The image above all others that he had saved from bringing into the open could at last be denied no longer, and he conjured up Portia to be with him. But she would not come. Her handwriting, her laugh, the shining warmth of her skin, the grin of animal wickedness in her eyes – they had all gone.

Now only Christ was left. Christ would come to him and lift him from this empty despair. Ned's torn lips could barely close on the words of his prayers. He asked for pity and hope and love. He asked for a sign that he had been heard. And then, all at once, Jesus rose and floated before him, glowing with light. Ned looked into the gentle, loving eyes of his saviour and leaned up to be taken into his arms and away from this terrible place. With a snarl of fury, Satan sprang forward and opened his huge mouth. He tore the Son of God into bloody pieces and turning towards Ned with a roar of triumph, he closed his black jaws around him.

*

Ned awoke again in darkness to the sound of the van's engine and the swift hum of passing traffic. Perhaps he had imagined the sea.

All that he had to connect him to reality now were his pain and the rhythmic flip of tyres on tarmac road. It was as if he had been reborn, reborn into a churning waste of unending isolation and pain. Every instant seemed to contain an eternity of suffering that flung him further away from what he had been and further towards a new existence in which friendship, family, future and love could never have a part.

Later he imagined that he had been inside a white room. He recalled a glare of fluorescent light and the rising stench from him as a scalpel cut the string from around his waist and his trousers fell to the floor. He thought he had felt a sharp sting in his arm, a quite new slam of pain and a jarring thump in his shoulder, streams of warm water washing over him and strong arms bearing him away.

He awoke once more to find himself on a bed in a small

room whose every surface had been painted cream. The door, walls and ceiling, the tubular steel at the end of the bed, the bars on the single window and the clouds in the sky beyond – all were cream. He couldn't tell the colour of the floor because the room was small and something was pinning him tight to the bed. When he raised his head, stretching the nape, he could see two thick belts of black webbing strapped across his chest and legs, each fastened by what appeared to be seat-belt buckles. But when he raised his head, the muscles in the back of his neck burned and the broken ribs shifted and clicked inside his chest, so instead he lay back and let the general ache of his body comfort and console him. He was calmer now and almost frivolously cheerful. The black torrent of his nightmares had subsided and the stupidity of his situation was starting to entertain him.

He dozed for a while and awoke with the bedroom still washed by the same creamy daylight. The skin in the arm below his good shoulder itched and a memory surfaced of the first of the straps having at some time been unbuckled, hands forcing him to sit upright and a needle pricking his skin. He believed that he had woozily murmured 'Good morning' and 'Thank you' before falling asleep again. He stared at the cream ceiling and attempted to assemble his thoughts. Before he could do so he heard the sound of footsteps squeaking on a shiny surface. Ned raised his head an inch from the pillow as they approached. A door close by opened and closed, and Ned sank down again.

Keys rattled in the lock and Ned started awake, annoyed with himself for having slipped off again.

'Hello there, young sir! Feeling much better now, I am sure.'

A plump little man in a white dentist's tunic came into the room, smiling and twinkling. He had spoken with an accent that Ned could not place. A very tall and elegant younger man with white-blond hair and pale blue eyes stayed in the doorway, holding in his hands a steel bowl.

'You have been most unwell, my chap, and we are here to see that you may become better and stronger.'

Ned started to speak, but the plump little man raised a hand.

'No, no. There will be time for us to talk a little later on. My name is Dr Mallo and we will have many good chats, I promise you. But now I want you to know that Rolf will be looking after you. You have done a great amount of harm to yourself and we must give your body some time to be healed. Rolf can help you with your pain . . .' he gestured to the tall man who came forward, holding out the steel bowl with outstretched arms like a communion server offering the paten, '. . . and in gratitude for this, I hope you will be very calm and not disturb yourself, yes?'

Ned nodded and watched as Dr Mallo took a syringe and a glass phial from the bowl.

'Excellent, this is excellent. You are a good fellow.'

Rolf stooped down to loosen the strap around Ned's chest. Ned forced himself upright and watched the doctor push the needle into the cork top of the phial.

'But this is very fine! Already you sit up on your own!' Dr Mallo beaming with approval, raised the loose sleeve of Ned's gown and rubbed cotton wool on the upper arm. 'That is cold, I know. Now, Rolf is more in practice with needles than I, but I am hoping this will not hurt . . . So! It was nothing.'

Ned lay back again and immediately a warm surge of calm flooded his brain. He smiled up at the doctor and at Rolf, who was bending over the bed and buckling the straps.

'S'nice . . . s'very nice. Z'lovely . . .'

Dr Mallo beamed again and moved round to the other side of the bed. 'And your shoulder is not so hurtful?'

'It's fine,' murmured Ned, his mind floating happily. 'I can't feel a thing.'

'We have strapped him tightly for you. You are young and he will mend very nicely, I think. So. Sleep now and stay at peace.'

Ned could not remember either of them leaving the room and when he next awoke, it was nearly dark.

*

Over the next few days Ned tried his best to exchange even the smallest number of words with Rolf, who visited at regular intervals with his steel bowl and syringe, sometimes bringing with him fresh dressings, a plastic bottle to urinate into and flasks of soup which Ned was only allowed to drink through a shiny steel tube.

Rolf proved entirely uncommunicative. Ned decided

that he couldn't speak English. Dr Mallo, whom he had not seen since, had spoken with an accent that might have been German or Scandinavian, so it seemed logical that Rolf too was foreign.

No, Ned was the foreigner. Wherever he might be, it was far from England. The black nightmare of his day or days in the pain and dark was proof of that. Distant seagull cries gave Ned the impression that he was close to the sea, perhaps even on an island. Some instinct told him that he was somewhere *north*. Perhaps it was the nature of the light that made him so sure, perhaps it was his interpretation of Dr Mallo's accent, which he now believed may have been Scandinavian. That would accord too with the sharp blue of Rolf's eyes and the silver blondness of his hair.

Ned began to use the periods of physical pain and mental clarity that attended him for the hour or so before each injection to consider his circumstances. He decided after a while that it was not the *nature* of the light that told him he was in a northern country, it was its steadiness, its constancy. No matter at what time Ned awoke, the sky outside his window was always bright, or at the most in a state of gentle twilight. At this time of year, Ned knew, the farther North you travelled, the shorter the hours of darkness. The night he had sailed on the *Orphana* for Oban, the night Paddy died, it had been dark only for the briefest time.

Ned was sure that Oliver Delft's colleague, Mr Gaine, was mad or criminal. He had beaten and broken Ned and taken him away with two evil, ugly, violent and malevolent psychopaths whose dead and brutal eyes would haunt Ned for ever. He had arrived here, where he was being treated kindly and with consideration, yet kept tied to his bed in a locked room with bars on its window. What could that mean?

Somewhere, Oliver Delft and Ned's father would be looking for him. Perhaps Mr Gaine was demanding a ransom. Ned was sure enough of Delft's skill and his father's influence to feel confident that he would not get away with it.

But meanwhile, what could his father be thinking? And Portia, what of her?

He was puzzled that it should be so, but it was his father, not Portia, who visited him in the loud and vivid dreams that filled his sleeping hours. In his waking moments, when he pictured what he would do when he got back, when he thought of home and school and the places and people that he knew, Portia's image was never there. Ned was not worried that he had to force her to his mind. He supposed that he was frightened she would have been angry at his disappearance. She might have believed that he had run away from her. Perhaps she even feared that she had disappointed him somehow during their afternoon in his bedroom and that he had escaped like a coward at the first opportunity. When this whole nonsense had been cleared up Ned would take her away to a country inn and they would get to know each other all over again.

For the moment, Ned hoped that Rolf might at least bring him something to read. When his straps were loosened, he could sit up easily now and he believed he could move his right shoulder and the muscles of his upper body well enough to handle books. Reading would help pass the time, which was beginning to hang more and more heavily as the pain receded and the drugs began to have less and less hold over his mind. Besides, the school had given him a reading list at the end of the summer term and Ned didn't want to be left behind.

He started to ask Rolf each time he came.

'Morning, Rolf. I was thinking . . . Are there any books here, by any chance?'

'Rolf, I can definitely move well enough to read now . . .'

'It doesn't matter what kind of books, really, but if you could find some on European history . . .'

'Perhaps you could ask Dr Mallo what he thinks, but I really believe it might help me to get better . . .'

'Did you ask Dr Mallo? What did he say?'

'Rolf, *please*! If you can understand me, can I have something to read? *Anything* . . .'

'Rolf, I want to see Dr Mallo. Understand? You . . . tell . . . Dr Mallo . . . come to me, yes? *Soon*. I see Dr Mallo. It's *very important* . . .'

Anger began to boil up inside Ned and anger forced him into a terrible mistake. It was impossible, he decided angrily during his endless hours of isolation, that Rolf could have failed to understand him. He was being deliberately cruel.

One morning, he could take it no longer.

'What has Dr Mallo said about my books? Tell me.'

Rolf continued his methodical routine of loosening the straps and preparing for Ned's injection.

'I want to know what Dr Mallo has said. *Tell me.*'

Rolf handed him an empty urine bottle without a word.

Ned, seething with the bitter injustice of it all, passed the bottle under his bedclothes and began to fill it, anger rising and rising within him.

Rolf leaned forward with the syringe and Ned, maddened as much by the calm routine as by the silence, pulled the bottle up and threw the contents into Rolf's face.

For at least five seconds, Rolf stood completely still and allowed the urine to drip down his face and off his chin.

Ned's temper subsided in an instant, and he tried unsuccessfully to smother a laugh. Rolf bent slowly down and replaced the syringe on the trolley, picked up a towel, folded it carefully into four and started to pad his face. There was something in the cold impassivity of his demeanour that turned Ned's laughter to fear and he started to babble apology like a three-year-old.

'Please don't tell Dr Mallo!' he pleaded. 'I'm sorry, Rolf, I'm sorry! But, I just wanted to . . . I'm so sorry, I didn't know what I was doing . . .'

Rolf replaced the towel on the trolley and straightened up. He looked at Ned speculatively, without a trace of visible anger or concern.

'I don't know what came over me, Rolf. Please forgive me!'

Rolf beckoned with his hands for Ned to lie down, the usual gesture he made to show that he was ready to fasten the straps.

'But what about my injection? My injection, Rolf . . .'

Rolf snapped the buckles and looked down at Ned, his head cocked to one side.

'Rolf, I'm *really* sorry, I promise . . .'

Rolf placed both hands, one on top of the other, flat on Ned's shoulder and pushed down, his whole weight behind it, like a baker pressing dough. The ball gave a crack as it jumped from its socket.

Rolf gave a little nod, then turned and wheeled the trolley from the room. Within a few hours Ned had lost his voice. The screaming had torn his throat to shreds.

Over the eternal days that followed he lay alone and whimpering. Unvisited, undrugged and soaked in his own sweat and urine, he had nothing to turn his mind to but two terrible facts and one impossible question.

Firstly, Rolf had not lost his temper. If he had done what he did in the heat of the moment, while Ned was laughing right in his piss-streaming face, there might be some possibility of reconciliation or appeal. The violence would have been terrible, but human.

Secondly, and Ned wept and wept at the cruelty of this, Rolf had quite deliberately set to work on Ned's *good* shoulder, the left. The right shoulder, still recovering from its earlier mauling, he had left alone. Such implacable, methodical malice offered no hope at all.

Thirdly came the question: a question that grew and grew inside him as he whispered it to himself over and over again.

Why? What had been his offence? In the name of Jesus . . . *why?*

3

Finally, finally, finally, finally.

*

Paper.

*

Two pens.

*

Felt-tipped, to stop myself doing damage to myself. To stop myself doing damage to somebody else.

*

It is very difficult to describe how they feel in the hand. I have not held a pen for a long time. I am taking an age to complete each word. I put myself off by watching my hand so closely that it becomes self-conscious and forgets how to shape the simplest letters.

*

I have been having the same trouble with my voice. Sometimes days go by and I do not say a word. I am afraid of talking to myself. Sometimes I hear other voices shuffling past and they sound like mad voices. I do not want to sound like this.

*

When I do decide to talk to myself I make sure that what I say is ordered and sensible. 'Today I shall do three hundred press-ups before lunch and five hundred press-ups after lunch,' I might tell myself. Or, 'This morning I shall run through the Lord's Prayer, the General Confession, all the hymns I know and every capital city I can remember.' And I remind myself out loud that I must not despair if I forget. Frustration and disappointment are the enemy, I have found. Some time ago I forgot the capital of India. It seems stupid, but for the longest time I was weeping and screaming, punching myself on the chest and wrenching at my hair so violently that it came out in bloody knots, and all because I could not remember the capital of India. Then, for no reason I can be sure of, I woke up one morning with 'New Delhi' on my lips. It had caused me such misery and pain, its absence, that I was almost angry to have remembered it, and for it to be such a simple place-name too. I know that the forgetting, even for a few days, had done more than make me miserable: it had given me spots and constipation and utter despair. I decided that in the future I would laugh and smile when I forgot even the simplest thing.

*

There was a time, for example, perhaps a year ago, when I forgot the name of my biology master at school. I laughed with pleasure. I actually made myself laugh with pleasure at the idea that my brain had buried Dr Sewell below the surface. Why should New Delhi or Dr Sewell be instantly available to me here? This way of dealing with memory has actually helped. Now that I am not forcing myself to remember, or judging myself by my ability to remember, all kinds of things actually stand out more clearly. I could sit down tomorrow, I think, and pass all my exams with ease. Mind you, looking up at the first two pages I have covered, I would have to admit that any examiner would disqualify me on the grounds of the illegibility of my handwriting. And of course, I know now that Dr Sewell was *not* my biology master at school. He and my school were imagined.

*

It is very interesting to look back up at what I have written. I notice that I keep trying to double letters. I even started to spell 'disqualify' with two Qs. I wonder what that means. I have a sense that it is something to do with a fear of finishing things too quickly. I have learned to eke everything out here. Each spoonful of food, each push-up, press-up, sit-up or organised room-walk that I undertake is very rigorously planned and very thoroughly thought through. Oh! Doesn't that look wonderful! Thoroughly thought through!

. . . thoroughly thought through . . .

Oh goodness, the *beauty* of it! I never noticed how language looked on the page before. To foreign eyes that phrase must *reek* of English. I have spent huge epochs of time rolling words around in my tongue and throat for the pleasure of their sounds, but never, never before has it occurred to me that words might, even in my dreadful handwriting, look so beautiful and so eternally fine.

*

'Thoroughly thought through' *sounds* beautiful too, by the way. At least, said out loud in a lonely room it does.

*

I think what it *means* is beautiful as well, to one in my condition.

*

Well, I am looking at the paper I have covered and putting off the moment of writing coherently and consequently about myself and my situation for fear that I will do it too quickly and that the day might come when I find that my writing has caught up with my present and that I will have nothing more to report.

*

Consequently? Is that what I mean? I mean 'in historical sequence', but surely 'consequently' isn't the word.

*

Chronologically is what I mean. They do come back to me when I relax.

*

Writing it all down chronologically will make me confront everything in a very different way I think. In my head and my mind, alone in this room, my life has become nothing more than a peculiar sort of game. Like any game it can be amusing and it can be deeply upsetting. On paper I suspect that it will take on the quality of a *report*. It will all become true and I cannot be certain what it will do to me when I know that it is all true. Perhaps it will send me truly mad, perhaps it will set me free. It is worth taking the risk to find out.

*

I will begin with time. I have taken, I think, five hours to write this much. I base all my calculations on shadows and food and counting. I have assumed that breakfast comes at eight o'clock. It doesn't really matter if it is eight o'clock or seven or nine, all that matters is the *passing* of the hours, not what they are named. When I was in the school choir for a short time before my voice broke, we were taught to read music by interval. It didn't matter whether the first note you sang was called a C or an F, it was all about the jump between the first and the next one, the *interval*. That's what Julie Andrews taught the children, the . . . I'm not going to get cross if I can't remember their names . . . the girls and boys she taught to sing 'Doh Re Mi' to. It is more or less the same with me and time. There's a word for it. *Tonic* something . . .

*

So, let us say that breakfast is eight. If that is true then lunch is half past twelve. I know this, for I have counted the whole stretch of time between breakfast and lunch many times. One Mississippi, two Mississippi, three Mississippi, four Mississippi and so on. That was a very dark period: over the course of many many days and weeks I would lose count somewhere and the failure would set me weeping for the rest of the day. I began to believe that I was losing count deliberately because I did not want to be a master of time again. The day did come, however, when I had perfected the art of counting without *dropping a stitch*, as I called it, and I could be sure that four and a half hours passed between breakfast and lunch, I discovered that the count (when I was sure of it) was always between sixteen thousand and sixteen thousand five hundred Mississippis. Sixteen thousand two hundred seconds is four and a half hours, though you would be ashamed of me if you knew how long it took me to be absolutely certain of that simple calculation. Dividing by sixty and then by sixty again ought to be easy, but my brain found it hard to contain all the numbers at once.

*

16,200. It doesn't really seem like that much when I write it down. Sixteen thousand two hundred. Does it seem more written in words or figures? Believe me, when you count them out, one by one, it seems to take hours. Well, it does take hours of course. Four and a half of them.

*

There is a single high window in this room and on the other side of it (I have jumped up when trampolining on the bed) there is a tree which I call my larch. I never really knew a larch from an oak at any time, but I think larches are tall and my tree is tall, so therefore it may as well be a larch. On winter days when the sun is low I can see its shadow move across the ceiling. I ought to be able to calculate a great deal from this, but I don't know enough about the sun and the earth. I do know that when I start to see the shadows summer is over and the long winter is about to begin and that when the shadows fade away it is spring and the endless summer is close at hand.

*

I have attempted, as you might imagine, to count the days and weeks, but something is stopping me. I tried once to mark them off against the wall, using my fingernails but the act of it soon filed them down and I wasn't able to continue. They always take back the plastic cutlery and I am sure that if I were to mark the walls with my felt-tipped pens they would be permanently confiscated. I could start now on the paper, with the prisoner's traditional rows of soldiers and a line through them to mark the week, but the truth is, I don't want to know how much time has passed. I cannot tell you how many winters and summers there have been. Sometimes I think it is three, sometimes as many as five.

*

There was a time when I thought I could detect when it was Sunday. There would be a brightness outside and an atmosphere inside that made me sure of it. The echo of footsteps seemed to ring differently in the corridors, which I suppose sounds mad. I would say to whoever brought in the food, usually Rolf or Martin, 'Happy Sunday!' but there was never any response. Once Martin, who for a short time I had decided was nicer than Rolf, said, 'It is Wednesday today,' and that upset me greatly for some reason.

*

I was moved into this room when my shoulders had mended. I have almost forgotten the first room, which might be a kind of mercy. I had been strapped to the bed there and was at almost my lowest point. Rolf would not speak to me. Dr Mallo would not come. My memories tormented me more than the pain. I still believed that it was all soon to end, you see. I thought that the father of my dreams would come and set me free, that the terrible misunderstanding was shortly to come to an end. I know better now. Dr Mallo has explained that this is my home and that I have no other. I have been ill. My mind has been full of false memories which only time can dispel. If I am slow with myself and patient I will be able to see things more clearly.

*

I am a very sick young man. I am a fantasist who has chosen to invent a history for himself which does not belong to him. A feeling of personal inadequacy has led me to believe that I once possessed a life of ease and affection and respect. I imagined that I was a happy, adjusted and popular boy with a famous and important father and a contented existence at a well-known public school. This is, apparently, very common. Many unfortunate children choose to inhabit a world like this rather than confront the reality of their lives. It is difficult for me because the fantasy was so real that I have burned out of my memory the real life into which I was actually born. I just cannot recapture or imagine it, no matter how hard I try. My assumed identity is so strong a part of me that even now, knowing the truth, I cannot fully let go of it. Dr Mallo tells me that mine is almost the strongest and most intractable case he has dealt with in all his professional life and this helps. It is hard not to feel a little proud.

*

The more able I am to accept the truth the easier my life here becomes. The paper and felt-tipped pens are a result of a 'breakthrough' that occurred some time ago. I see Dr Mallo every now and then. Perhaps these sessions are regular, once a fortnight, or once every ten days, it is hard to tell. Eight or nine visits ago I broke down and admitted to him that I knew I was not called Ned and that everything I thought had been my memory was indeed false, as he had been telling me for so long. Perhaps he thought I was saying this to please him, for at first nothing changed. In fact he was quite severe with me, accusing me of pretending to agree with him just to make life easier for myself. After a few visits however, he told me that I had made a genuine breakthrough and that this meant I could be trusted with a few privileges. I asked if that meant I might be allowed to read some books. Books will come later, he told me, for they can be dangerous to those with a frail grip on reality. Firstly, it would be a good idea for me to have some paper and pens and to write down everything I felt. If Dr Mallo trusted that I was really coming to grips with my situation, I might then start to visit the library.

*

What about other patients? Would it be possible for me to join in with them? I had noted evening and afternoon periods marked by an electric bell and always connected with the distant sounds of doors opening and closing, feet shuffling and sometimes a little laughter.

*

Dr Mallo congratulated me on my observation and held out the hope that one day I would be balanced and strong enough to associate with others without danger to myself. In the meantime, it was important for me to grow healthier in my mind. He is pleased that I have the self-respect that keeps me physically fit and hopes I will be able to set myself mental exercises that are the equivalent of the bench-presses and sit-ups with which I test my physical self.

*

So now I shall take everything very slowly and not allow myself to become too excited. I must not exaggerate any apparent improvement, for if I am honest, I have to confess that in my sleeping moments, and even sometimes when I am awake, the echoes of the old false memories still fill my mind like seductive ghosts. It will be of no use to me at all if I am over-optimistic about my condition. There is still a very long way to go.

*

I hear the squeak of the trolley outside. It will soon be time for my medication and supper. I must set down my pens, square the paper neatly on the table and sit up straight. I would not want Dr Mallo to hear that I have been overheated or undisciplined.

*

Von Trapp! Those were the children in *The Sound of Music*. You see! Things really do come back when you relax. The Von Trapp Family Singers . . .

*

This has been a wonderful and encouraging day.

'So now, Ned my friend, how are you today?'

'I'm very well, Dr Mallo, but I wonder if I can ask you something?'

'Of course. You know that you can ask me anything you please.'

'I think it's wrong that you still call me Ned.'

'We have talked of this before. I am very happy to call you what pleases you. Have you perhaps another name for me? A remembered name?'

Ned wrinkled his brow at this. 'Well, sometimes I think I might be Ashley.'

'You would like me to call you Ashley?'

'I don't think so. It isn't quite right. I'm sure that I do remember an Ashley and that I think of him with someone like me. I associate the name Ashley with pretending to be something you aren't, but it's all a little confused. I don't think Ashley is me. I was hoping you might think up a name. My real name may come back to me soon, but in the meantime, anything you give me is better than Ned. The name Ned is beginning to annoy me.'

'Very well. I shall call you . . .' Dr Mallo looked around the room as if expecting to light upon an object that would offer a connection to a suitable name. 'I shall call you

Thomas,' he said, after gazing for a while at a picture on the wall behind Ned. 'How is Thomas? An English name I think, for you are an English young man. This we know.'

'Thomas . . .' Ned repeated the name with pleasure. 'Thomas . . .' he said again, with the delight of a child unwrapping a present. 'Thomas is very good, Doctor. Thank you. I like that very much.'

'So we shall call you Thomas,' said Dr Mallo, 'but I need to believe that you understand the name. It is an escape from Ned, a symbol, we shall say, of a new beginning. It is important you are realistic with this name and do not imagine that Thomas has a past into which you may retreat. It is a name we have conjured up together here for convenience and to mark your progress. Nothing more.'

'Absolutely!'

'So now, Thomas my young friend. How have you been?'

'I think I've been well,' said Ned. 'I've been very happy lately.'

The sound of the new name in his ears was wonderful, it released a feeling to be hoarded and treasured in his room later. 'Hello there, Thomas.' 'Thomas, good to see you.' 'Oh look, there's Thomas!' 'Good old Thomas . . .'

'And at last,' said Dr Mallo, looking at a tall sheaf of paper in front of him, the trace of a smile on his lips, 'I am beginning to be able to read your writing without great effort.'

'It *is* better, isn't it?' Ned agreed enthusiastically. 'I find I can shape the letters so much more easily now.'

'And more *slowly* I hope? With less excitement?'

'Completely.'

'You are growing quite a beard now. Does it bother you?'

'Well,' Ned's hand went to his face. 'It has taken some getting used to. It itches and it must look very odd, I suppose.'

'No, no. Why should it look odd? A beard is a most natural thing.'

'Well . . .'

'You would like to see yourself in your beard?'

'May I? May I really?' Ned's legs started to jog up and down on the balls of his feet.

'I do not see why not.'

Dr Mallo opened a drawer in his desk and brought out a small hand-mirror which he passed across to Ned, who took it and held it on his jiggling knees, face turned away.

'You are afraid to look?'

'I'm – I'm not sure . . .'

'Set your heels to the floor and take some deep breaths. One-two-three, one-two-three.'

Ned's knees stopped their jogging and he moved his head. He lifted the mirror from his lap, swallowed twice and slowly opened his eyes.

'What do you think?'

Ned was looking at a face that he did not know. The face stared back at him in equal surprise and horror. It was a gaunt face, a face of hard cheekbones and deep-set eyes. The straw-coloured hair on its head was long, hanging lankly over the ears, the beard hair seemed coarser and tinged with a suggestion of red. Ned put a hand to his own face, and saw a bony hand rubbing the beard line of the face in the mirror and pulling at its moustache.

'You like this face?'

Ned tried to avoid meeting the eyes in the mirror. They were resentful and coldly blue. They seemed to dislike him.

'Who is he?' Ned cried. 'Who is this man? I don't know him!'

The face in the mirror had tears streaking its beard. It licked its cracked lips. Its mouth pursed in disgust at the face of Thomas looking in.

'That is enough. Give me the mirror now.'

'Who is he? He hates me! Who is he? Who is he? That isn't me! Is it Thomas? It isn't Ned. Who is it?'

Dr Mallo pressed a buzzer on the underside of his desk and sighed. Foolish of him to have tried such an experiment. A distasteful display, yet fascinating also. Such pitiable distress, such complete dislocation of subject. Mallo's student dissertation on the work of Piaget came back to him. If he were still a man of academic energy there could be a paper in this. But Mallo's days of professional ambition were behind him. He watched Rolf come into the room, wrestle the mirror away and snap bracelets on the boy's wrists with the methodical efficiency that never deserted him.

'Calm yourself, Thomas. You see now I hope that there is still a long way for you to go. We will allow you a period of calm for a while. No more writing for the time being, just peaceful reflection. Chlorpromazine,' he added to Rolf, '75 milligrams, I think.'

Ned's eyes were fixed on the hand-mirror which lay face down on the desk. He was not aware of Rolf pulling up his sleeve. His mind was filled only with a desire to see that haggard face once more and to tear its malevolent eyes from their sockets.

There were special days that came very rarely, days when the food was piled high on Ned's tray and flower vases and bowls filled with fresh fruit were placed on his table. In the mornings Martin and Rolf would lead him out of the room and stand him under a shower at the end of the corridor. They would hold him there and sponge him clean. Then, still under the shower-head, but with the flow of water turned off, they would cut his hair and shave his beard. His room too, when he returned to it, would have been scrubbed clean and washed. The chamberpot would have gone and the sweet scent of pine room-freshener would hang in the air.

In the afternoons of these extraordinary days Dr Mallo would visit him, together with two others, a man and a woman who did not wear white coats and who brought the atmosphere of the outside world into the room with them. The woman's handbag and the man's briefcase fascinated Ned. They bore flavours and smells that were intriguing, enchanting and frightening too.

They all spoke to each other in a language that Ned could not understand, the same language that Rolf and Martin spoke and that he had decided long ago was Scandinavian. He heard his name mentioned in those conversations, always as Thomas now, they never used the name Ned any more.

The woman liked to talk to him sometimes.

'Do you remember me?' she would ask, in thickly accented English.

'Yes, how are you?' Ned would reply.

'But how are *you*?'

'Oh, I am much better thank you. Much better.'

'Are you happy here?'

'Very happy thank you. Yes. Very happy indeed.'

One day in summer they came again, but this time there were three of them. The same couple as before but with another woman, younger than the other, and a great deal more inquisitive. Ned picked up Dr Mallo's tension at her questions and did his best to say what he thought the doctor expected and wanted of him.

'How long have you been here, Thomas?' This new woman's English was better even than Dr Mallo's and she spoke to Ned very directly. The others used to ask him questions politely, but never with the impression that they were especially interested in his answers. This woman seemed very curious about Ned and paid great attention to the way he replied.

'How long?' Ned looked towards Dr Mallo. 'I'm not sure how long . . .'

'Don't look at the doctor,' said the woman, 'I want to know how long *you* think you've been here.'

'It's a little hard to tell. Perhaps three or four years. Maybe a bit longer?'

The woman nodded. 'I see. And your name is Thomas, I believe?'

Ned nodded enthusiastically. 'Absolutely.'

'But when you first came here, your name was Ned.'

Ned found that he did not like to hear that name. 'I was in a bit of a state then,' he said. 'I needed to clear up a lot of the ideas in my head. I had been imagining all kinds of things.'

'Have you made friends with the other patients?'

Dr Mallo started to speak to the young woman, she listened for a while and spoke back at him rapidly. Ned imagined that he heard some words that were a little like the English words 'Better' and 'Hysteria'.

It was strange to see how small Dr Mallo looked, and how afraid he was of this young woman. His head was on one side as he listened to her, and he nodded and smiled, passing his tongue quickly over his lips and making notes on the clipboard he carried with him. It was something more than the woman's height that made him look so small beside her Ned thought, even though she was nearly a foot taller than him. His whole demeanour reminded Ned of how he tried to look when he was doing his best to please Rolf or even Dr Mallo himself.

The woman turned to Ned. 'The doctor tells me that you have chosen not to associate with any other patients since you have been here?'

'I . . . I don't think I have been ready.'

The woman raised her eyebrows. 'Why not?'

Ned knew that he must not look to Dr Mallo for

prompting or encouragement. It would please him more if he showed that he could think for himself.

'I wanted to be more confident in myself, if you see what I mean. I didn't want to lie to anyone about who I was. Also,' he added, 'I only speak English and I've not wanted to have the problem of being misunderstood.' That last idea came to him from nowhere and he hoped that Dr Mallo would be pleased at his inventiveness.

There followed another flurry of conversation in which the other woman and her companion joined. Dr Mallo nodded his head decisively and made some more notes. Ned could see that he was trying hard to appear pleased.

'I will see you again soon, Thomas,' said the young woman. 'I hope that the company of some English speaking people will be helpful for you. Will you promise me to try and talk to other patients? Just one or two to start with. Under supervision in case you become nervous. I think you will enjoy it.'

Ned nodded and did his best to look brave and resolute.

'Good.' She looked around the room. 'You do not have any books here, I see.'

'I have been writing again,' said Ned almost defensively. 'I have written some poems actually.'

'No doubt you will write better poems if you have the chance to read. Books are always healthy. Goodbye, Thomas. I will see you on my next visit and I expect to see you with books in here. We will talk about what you have read and what friends you have made.'

That evening, when Martin came with his supper and

to take away the fruit bowl and the vase of flowers, Ned almost whined at him.

'That woman said I had to talk to other people. Is it true? I don't want to. I want to be left on my own. Tell Dr Mallo that I don't want to meet anyone. Especially not English people.'

'You do as Doctor tells. If Doctor wants you meet other people, you are meeting other people,' Martin replied. 'Not matter if English or not English. Not your choosing. For Doctor to choosing. And here, look.' Martin dropped an enormous English encyclopaedia onto the floor beside the bed. 'You will read.'

Ned smiled himself to sleep that night. The lost memory came to him of a kind old man reading the *Tales of Uncle Remus*. Something about Brer Rabbit, the Tar Baby and the briar patch. He did not quite know why the story was relevant but he knew that it was.

Babe glanced up from the chessboard as Martin led a reluctant patient through the glazed partition and into the sun-room.

Smooth-shaven from yesterday's official visit, Babe noticed. Another bloody Scandiwegian by the look of the blue eyes and flaxen hair. Frightened eyes they are. Mind you, fake-frightened perhaps. Wary and alert under the guise of compliance and the fog of Thorazine. I know that look well enough. Our man has been here a while and a day, I can see that. Knows how to play it safe. Now why have they kept him from us? What will be *his* big secret, we wonder? Been keeping himself fit all on his ownsome, that I can see. The full range of physical jerks. And talking of physical jerks, Martin will have tried it on with him, the lardy beast. Not got too far either, by the angry claw of his grip on the boy's shoulder. Well, well. This is all something new to put the mind to.

Babe dropped his eyes to the chessboard and set up a high-droned mumble over the pieces.

'Ah, and you'd try a semi-Slav on me, would you, you whore-master dog? I know a few ways to beat *that* . . .' What a master of the slurred babble, you are, Babe, he added to himself.

'You sit here,' Martin said to the young man.

Speaks to him in *English*, by Christ! In God's own blessed English tongue. Martin's tortured approximation of it, I allow, but English none the less.

Babe almost gave away his interest by sitting up and looking across in their direction.

Calm down there, the Babe. There's many a reason for Martin to be speaking in English. The boy may yet be Finn, Flem or Hollander. No certainty that he's a Brit from Britland. It don't pay to go leaping to conclusions. The lingua franca of all ritzy international institutions is English. Spoken in every high class bank, brothel and lunatic asylum from here to the Balkans.

The young man had sat down and was now trying to stand.

'I say *sit*,' said Martin, angrily pushing him down. 'You sit, you stay.'

Why don't you *speak*, boy?

Babe's eyes were flicking from one chessman to another, his fingers pulling at his loose lips. No one would suppose that he knew that any world existed outside the sixty-four squares in front of him, certainly it would be impossible to guess that all his attention was on this awkward new arrival into the world of the sun-room.

Martin moved about, looking at the other patients while his patient fretted on his plastic chair.

'May I go now please?' the young man whined at last.

Angels and ministers of Grace defend us! More than a Brit. *English!* English as a maypole! English as torture!

English as hypocrisy, pederasty and the Parliament of Fowles! Five wee words, but I can parse them and strip them of their code as easy as all thank you.

May I go now, please? Privately educated. A *good* school too, none of your minor drosses. Top drawer top three or I'm a fool, and I have never been that, as God is my whiteness.

F3, bishop-g2, castle short . . .

Winchester, Eton or Harrow?

Advance the c pawn, sacrifice him later for space on the queen's side . . .

Not Winchester, I believe. Too polite.

Exchange the bish for his knight and the black squares are mine . . .

Eton? I think not. Doesn't quite have the carriage. That would never quit an Etonian, not even here. That leaves us Harrow. Semper floreat herga.

'Babe, I've got someone for you to meet.'

Martin stood over the board and spoke in Swedish.

'Don't want to meet anyone,' Babe muttered in the same language, clumsily enacting an exchange over the board and letting the pieces topple over. 'Leave me alone.'

'Never mind what you want, old man. His name is Thomas. You can teach him to play chess.'

Ned bent down and picked up a black bishop from the floor. Babe snatched it back and banged it on the board without looking at him.

'Sit down and play at chess,' Martin ordered Ned. 'This

is Babe. He is our oldest guest. Here before Dr Mallo even, is that right, Babe?'

'Here before you were a watery drop of seed down your sinful father's leg, you miserable perverted gobshite cunt,' murmured Babe resetting the white queen with great care.

'What's that? What he saying?'

'He says that he has indeed been here a long time,' said Ned. 'Look, Martin, do I have to talk to him? Can't I please go back to my room? Or be on my own at least?'

'You talk,' said Martin. 'I come back lunchtime. Sit down. You talk. You play chess. Be nice on each other.'

There was silence at the table for almost a minute as Babe set up the pieces and Ned sat down and concentrated on looking miserable.

Over Babe's shoulder he could see a lawn that sloped down from the sun-room. At the bottom was a line of trees, whose thickness suggested the possibility of a river. There were other patients outside, sitting on benches and walking. That all this was possible amazed him.

The brightness of the room and the smell of other people mingled with the sour odour of sunlight on vinyl were intoxicating to Ned. He could feel Martin's distrustful eyes upon him somewhere so he did not allow himself to appear eager for conversation, instead he slouched sulkily and glared down at the chessmen as if they were enemies.

What the old man, Babe, if Ned had heard right, had said right under Martin's nose had thrilled him beyond imagining. He had called him a miserable perverted gobshite cunt and trusted to the slur in his voice and speed in his delivery to obscure the meaning. He might be a mad and ugly old man, but he was certain to be more entertaining than a lonely room.

'That's the ticket, old son,' said the old man suddenly. His eyes were down on the table and he spoke in a mumble, but the words came clear to Ned's ears. 'You've worked Martin out. The more browned off you look, the better he likes it. Don't talk back to me right off, rest a hand on your chin to hide your lips and keep that spoilt, petulant look going. You do it to a turn.'

Ned's heart began to beat more quickly. He put his elbow on the table and pushed his mouth into the upturned cup of his palm.

'Are you English?'

'Devil a bit I am.'

'Is Martin looking?'

'Standing there with a cup of coffee in his hand gazing at the back of your head with a frown on him like an angry turd-wasp. Turned down his bedroom advances, did you, lad? No, no. There's no call to go pink. He tries it on with all the new patients. Are you going to make a move? You're not going to tell me they didn't teach you chess at Harrow?'

Ned gasped and could not stop himself from looking up.

Babe was plucking his lips and staring down at the chessboard as if nothing had been said. He mumbled through his dribble in a sing-song. 'It was wrong of me to spring it onto you like that. I'm a devil of a show-off and you'll have to forgive me. But if Professor Higgins can do it, why not the Babe? Eyes down and make a move, you pampered Asiatic jade.'

Ned pushed forward a pawn and resumed his previous position, hand concealing mouth. 'How could you possibly know? I mean . . . not that I *am*, not that I *did* go there. Have you been looking at Dr Mallo's records? You've overheard me speaking to him?'

'Calm yourself right down, young Thomas. Let's not be rushing like a bull at the gate of a china shop. Or any kind of bull at all, whether at a gate, in a shop, or rising from the sea to rapine and lust. You'll get used to my mad ways with metaphor and allusion in time. Just remember this, if we manage ourselves aright here today and for the next few days as well, then Martin there will leave us be and happy enough in himself to do so. He knows me for a mad old, strange old, harmless old, comic old, disgusting old man, but you he does not trust or like. He and Rolfie, they see it as their job to protect this institution from the foolish liberal credulity of the good Dr Mallo. If you have been allowed out to socialise, it's because of the new girl who came visiting yesterday, or am I wrong?'

'No, that's right!' Ned breathed.

'Well now – dear God, you've a lot to learn about chess, young monkey. Have you never heard of a fork? – well now, I thought that must be so. She had reformer and new broom stitched into her milken breasts. Mallo and the staff will be madder than the maddest amongst us to have her interfere. If you've not been out to talk to us yet, there'll be a reason and they won't like being overruled by a liberal doxy with modern doctrines about her. Who put you away in this place?'

Ned was silent.

'You not want to talk about it? I'll never force you, boy.'

'No, it's not that. It's just that I don't know.'

'Well, how long have you been here?'

'I . . .' Ned did not know what to say.

'Easy to lose time. Do you have an inkling of the date it was when you were last a free man?'

'It was July the thirtieth. But I was ill . . . I thought all kinds of things. I shouldn't really be thinking of that time. It holds me back. Dr Mallo told me that I had to forget all those associations, they are delusions . . .'

'Delusions are the one things you may trust in here. July thirtieth, eh? And what year?'

'Nineteen eighty,' said Ned, excitement beginning to build in him, 'and what's more Thomas isn't my name. My real name is . . .'

'I don't want to know. Not just yet. If they've changed your name, you don't want to be heard telling me the old one. Make a move, go on. Make a move now. Try and get that poor bishop out of the shit, if you can.'

Ned looked down at the chess pieces swimming beneath him.

'I can call you Babe?'

'Certainly you can call me Babe, and what pleasure it will give me to answer to the name spoken in a voice so fine and so true. And the first thing that Babe will do for Thomas, when we have convinced our keepers that it was their idea to force us together, is he will teach him to play a proper game of schach, écheques, shachmatyin, chess, scacchi . . . call it what you will, for you've a dismal idea of it at the moment, you young lummock. Checkmate with knobs on.'

'I never really knew much more than the rules, I'm afraid.'

'I shall set the pieces up again, and you will turn away. Droop all languid like a listless lily in Lent. You're bored with me and you find me osmically offensive, which is to say you think I stink like the stinkiest stinkweed that was. But before you turn away, answer me something.'

'What?'

'How long is it that you believe you've been here?'

'Well, I don't know the year now, but it must be . . . I don't know. Three years? Four?'

'It is ten, Thomas my friend. Ten years next month.'

'What?'

'Not so loud! And keep your eyes ever cast downwards. Today is, by the Grace of God, the eighteenth of June in the year nineteen ninety.'

'But it can't be anything *like* . . . it *can't* be that long! That would make me twenty-seven years old. That's impossible!'

'I hate to be the one to tell you, Thomas, but you look

nearer thirty-seven or forty-seven. There's grey mixed in your hair by the temples and those eyes of yours do not contain at all the look of youth. Ah now, he's glaring over at us. Turn and look away.'

Martin came towards Ned, a meanly sarcastic smile on his face. 'This was quick game. You no good for chess? You letting mad old man beat you?'

Ned shook his head.

'I don't like him,' he said, gesturing towards the mumbling Babe. 'He smells.'

'You come and play and talk with Babe every day. Every day one hour longer. Is good for you each.'

'But . . .'

'No but. No but. You make complaint and I have you two together all the time. Share room maybe? You like that? You like share your room with smelling old man?'

'I won't,' said Ned, outraged. 'I won't! You can't make me!'

*

Over the next eight weeks Ned went to his room with small scraps of paper hidden about him. On them were written all the chess theory, attacks, defences, gambits, combinations and endgame strategies that Babe knew. His course of instruction began with games played by Phillidor and Morphy and masterpieces of the romantic age, games that, like paintings, had titles: titles like The Evergreen, the Two Dukes and the Immortal. Ned was moved from these towards the age of Steinitz and the modern style, then to an understanding of a positional theory called the Hypermodern that made his head ache. Next came an induction into opening play and counterplay whose language made Ned laugh. The Caro Kann and the Queen's Indian, the Sicilian and the French Defences, the Gioco Piano and the Ruy Lopez. The Dragon variation, the Tartakower and the Nimzowitch. The Queen's Gambit Declined and the Queen's Gambit Accepted. The Marshall Attack. The Maroczy Bind. The Poisoned Pawn.

'We shan't be friends until we can play a game of chess together. You have it in you to play a decent game. Everyone has it in them to play a decent game. It's nothing but memory and a refusal to think of yourself as a mental rabbit. If a soul can read and write, a soul can play a game of chess.'

There was so much Ned wanted to ask Babe, but any questions were waved aside over the board.

'Chess lad. Pressing lidless eyes, we will play a game of chess. Your move, and watch your back rank.'

Dr Mallo had paid a visit to the sun-room during Ned's first week there and ordered Babe away for a turn on the lawn.

'I want to talk to my friend Thomas. I shall not move the pieces,' the doctor had assured Babe, who shuffled away mumbling oaths into his beard.

'So, how are you finding it, Thomas?'

'It's a little strange,' said Ned uncertainly. 'He's a very peculiar man and I don't really understand much he says. He can be very rude, but as long as I don't talk too much he doesn't seem to mind me.'

'Have you talked to any other patients, I wonder?'

'I try to sometimes,' said Ned. 'I don't know which of them speak English. I upset that man over there yesterday by taking a chair that was next to him and he swore at me in English.'

'Yes, that is Dr Michaels, a very unhappy man. You will never derive much sense from him I fear. Unstable, but not dangerous. I am pleased, Thomas, that you are able to sit out here. And Babe is not –' Dr Mallo looked down at the chessboard with what Ned could instinctively tell were uncomprehending eyes, '– Babe is not *curious* about you? He does not load your mind with questions?'

'He doesn't ask me anything,' said Ned in a disappointed voice, 'except when I'm going to make a move or why I bounce my knees up and down under the table.'

'Ha! I ask, you understand, because it is so important that you are not encouraged into more fantasy concerning yourself. If anyone were to ask who you were and what is the nature of your illness . . . ?'

'I don't know what I would say, Doctor. I would tell them that my name is Thomas and that I am getting better. I prefer not to talk about myself.'

'Quite so. He plays a good game of chess, Babe?'

Ned shrugged.

'I think not, you have a checkmate in four moves if you look closely,' said Dr Mallo rising and taking his leave with a brisk and satisfied nod of his head.

'Mate in four moves, my arse and the arse of every man here!' Babe had hissed under his breath when Ned reported the conversation to him. 'The bullshit of the man, the fraud and fakery of him. If you don't move up your h-pawn you'll be the one to be mated and in one move, never mind four.'

'When can we talk of anything except chess, Babe?'

'When you have beaten me.'

'But that's never!'

'Don't you believe it. I've written out the Nimzo-Indian for you today. You'll love it.'

As the weeks passed, Ned found himself becoming more and more obsessed by their games. He fell asleep each night with the diagonal tensions and energetic force-fields exerted by each piece pressing against his mind. Chess and the power of each man on the board dominated his inner life. He began to replay positions easily in his head, without having to picture the whole board. His questions, now solely confined to chess, began to please Babe.

'Ah now. You're confusing strategy with tactics there. That's a thing that reminds me of my old lessons in military training. The strategy, you see, is the battleplan, the Big Idea. We will win the battle by taking that hill. There's your strategy, to take the hill. *How* do we take the hill? Ah now, there's your tactics. We might soften her up with artillery and follow through with an assault by armoured troops. We might bombard her from the air. Perhaps we will pretend to deploy around another target altogether and fool the enemy into thinking that we don't care a damn about the hill. By night we send in our special forces, knives in their teeth and boot-black on their faces, to take our hill by stealth. There's any amount of tactics and all at the service of the one strategic idea. You follow me?'

It was only later that Ned, all absorbed in the detail of chess, turned his mind to the remark 'my old lessons in military training'. A man of Babe's age had probably fought in the war. The Second World War. When Ned had first asked him if he was English, Babe had replied 'Devil a bit I am,' which Ned took to mean an emphatic negative. Babe's voice however, in accent and delivery, was very English indeed, a rich fruity and deliciously old-fashioned sounding English that reminded Ned of old wireless broadcasts. The *way* he spoke, though, his choice of words and the strange spin he put on familiar phrases, that was somehow not very English at all. It had a stage Irish, or Hollywood pirate quality to it. One day he would discover more about him.

Meanwhile, two months into his training, Ned had an exciting week ahead of him. He had, for the first time, *drawn* a game. Babe had been the one to extend his hand across the board to make the offer which Ned, in his excitement and with the scent of victory in his nostrils, had turned down. Babe then forced an exchange of queens and rooks and the game petered out into the draw which it was always destined to be. But Ned had been playing black and to draw as black was always a positive result. The game of chess is so delicately balanced, Babe had explained, that the advantage of the first move is enough, in tournament play, to ensure that the majority of victories go to the player with the white pieces. Ned knew that this result with black was therefore a turning point.

The following day, Babe playing black had won easily and Ned, furious with himself, made assiduous plans that night to do something magnificent the next day.

He fell asleep with an idea in his mind that he should try the Winawer variation of the French Defence, which some instinct told him Babe did not enjoy playing. He awoke with a fully formed sense of how to win implanted in his mind. The plan involved not only the absolute chess of the game but psychology too and when Rolf, whose duty day it was, led him out to the sun-porch, he was already looking grouchy and underslept.

'I shouldn't have lost like that yesterday,' he said, without offering any of his usual polite greetings. 'You trapped me. It was pathetic.'

'Dear me,' said Babe straightening the white pieces in front of him. 'Did we get out of bed the wrong side this morning?'

'Let's just play,' said Ned moodily, inwardly praying that Babe's king pawn would advance but staring instead at the c-pawn, as if hoping for an English opening or deferred Queen's Indian.

With a shrug, Babe played e-4 and Ned instantly replied by pushing his own king's pawn forward to meet it. Babe moved his knight out to f-3 and Ned moved a hand to his queen's knight, as if resigned to an Italian or Spanish game. Then he dropped the hand back with a resentful tut and started to think. He took five minutes over his second move, the dull, seemingly ultra-defensive and amateurish d-6 that marks the French Defence. Babe continued to rattle out his pieces in the standard way and Ned haltingly replied. His heart beat faster and faster as each move repeated the pattern that he had planned the night before, developing into the very line of the Winawer that he had prepared. A moment came when Babe had to play with extreme accuracy to avoid a trap that Ned knew would cost him the loss of an active pawn. Babe stopped himself from playing the quick and obvious move and Ned, his head down, could sense in his field of peripheral vision, that Babe's head had turned up to look at him. Ned did not shift, but continued to frown over the board, not revealing anything when Babe, avoiding the mistake, played the only correct move possible. Ned had not banked everything on a cheap tactical trap as he might have done two weeks earlier. In fact, he would have been disappointed if Babe had fallen for it. He knew that his position was good, and that was all that counted.

After an hour of fraught and completely silent play, Babe found himself a pawn down and having to marshal unconnected pieces to avoid all manner of tactical horrors. When a position is won, dozens of attacking combinations, traps and spellbinding sacrifices present themselves to the player on the winning side. Ned was busy considering a spectacular sacrifice of his queen that he believed would force a checkmate in five or six moves, when Babe knocked over his king and gave a rich, low chuckle.

'Outplayed from pillar to post, you devious son of a mountain whore.'

'You resign?'

'Of course I resign, you dastardly bog and vice versa. My position is so full of holes it's a wonder the board doesn't fall to the floor. You planned this, didn't you, boy? From the first petulant pout of the lip to the last maddening stutter. Oh, you're wicked. Wicked as whisky.'

Ned looked up anxiously. 'But the chess, it wasn't all tricks and psychology was it? I mean, the pure chess was good too.'

'Lad, there is no such thing as pure chess. There's good chess and there's bad. Good chess takes in the breath of your opponent and the dip of his head as much as depth of his mind and the placing of his knights. Good chess cares about the way you move a piece just as much as the square you move it to. Did you know you played a Smyslov Screw just now? You did, you know. A real life Smyslov Screw.'

'A what?'

'Vasilly Smyslov, world champion from the Soviet Union. I saw him play, as it happens. A master of the endgame and as wily a fox as you'd care to be matched against. He had a way of setting a piece when he made a move and *screwing* it into the square, pressing down on it and slowly twisting it as though to fix it there for ever. Put the fear of God into his opponents, that simple little trick. You did the same just now when you moved your rook to the seventh. But more than that, you understand the greatest chess secret of all. The best move you can ever play in chess is not the best move. No, the best move you can ever play is the move your opponent least wants you to play. And that you did time after time. You *knew* that I hate the turgid tactical hell of the French, didn't you? I never told you, but you sensed it. Oh my God boy, I could hug you I'm so proud.'

Ned saw that tears were falling down Babe's face.

'It's all thanks to you,' he said.

'Fuff to that! What is it, nine . . . no, eight and a half weeks since you first pushed a pawn in my direction. Look at you, look at what you can do with those sixteen pieces of cheap wood. Did you ever know your mind could think so deep and play so mean? Did you? Did you? Tell the Babe you've amazed yourself!'

'Babe, I've amazed myself,' said Ned. 'I don't know how I did it. I can't believe it. I just can't believe it. It's you. You did it for me.'

'I did nothing. Nothing at all, but let you understand the power of your own mind. There isn't a player in the world who could call you a patzer or a rabbit now. The great ones will beat you, for sure, but you'll never disgrace yourself over a checkerboard, not if you live as long as me. This calls for a marvellous toast to be drunk.'

Ned laughed. 'I'll whistle for Rolf, shall I?'

'You think I'm joking. Reach into your mind and draw out your favourite drink. What is it? Are you a whisky man like myself, or does your Harrovian favour the great deep wines of Bordeaux? Is it maybe the gossiping fizz of champagnes fit only for tarts and scoundrels that pleases you? Myself, I'm hankering for the salt oil of a Bunnahabhain, that mysterious Other of the Islay malts. I've its queer squat bottle in my hand now and I'm snagging my nails on the lead about its bung . . . hey now! What have I said to upset you?'

Tears were dropping from Ned's chin onto the chessboard.

'It's nothing, nothing . . . only you see I've never really had a chance to drink anything. My favourite drink is . . . used to be . . . just a glass of cold milk.'

A memory of Oliver Delft opening the refrigerator door crashed into Ned's mind and he gave a gulping sob.

'Tss!' Babe hushed him urgently. 'Don't let your distress be seen. I'm sorry Thomas, truly sorry. I had no idea in the world. My stupid tongue, it fancies itself to have a pleasing way with it. The women used to think me a seducer with words and sometimes I play up to the memory of that. It's my one last vanity in this place of ruined minds and in my vulgar haste I took you to a place you have forgotten to visit. But never mind that now. The day will come when you'll be pleased to go back there.'

'No!' said Ned forcefully. 'I mustn't. I absolutely mustn't. There are things in my past that I still don't understand properly and Dr Mallo says . . .'

'Dr Mallo says! Take comfort in knowing that this is a man who is capable of saying, "It's checkmate in four unless I'm much mistaken." Dr Mallo, he don't know shit from sugar and you can't pretend it isn't so. He has a soul of pus and the mind of a rotted turd. He is a failure and not a word he says can come near to you.'

'*He's* a failure? Then what does that make us?' choked Ned. 'What on earth does that make us?'

'Well that's something we must decide for ourselves, Thomas. Now, Rolf is walking by, heave a giant sneeze into your handkerchief as if you'd caught a mote of dust in the sunlight.'

The last words that Ned said to Babe that afternoon were, 'Will you teach me, Babe? Teach me everything you know. Just as you did with chess. Teach me all the science and poetry and philosophy you can. Teach me history and geography. Teach me music and art and mathematics. Will you? You know so much and I know so little. I was supposed to have gone to Oxford, but . . .'

'Well, you were saved that at least,' Babe had replied, 'so there's hope yet. Yes, I'll teach you, Thomas. We shall tread the wide path of philosophy as we trod the narrow path of chess and who knows what we shall discover about ourselves as we go along the way?'

*

Babe, who was allowed to spend as much time as he liked in the sun-room or out on the lawn, watched Ned being led back through the glazed partition and smiled to himself.

A wickedly enchanting game of chess the lad played there.

Babe was not quite possessed of a God complex, but the mind he had kept so assiduously alive was yearning to do something, to mould and to create. He had always known that he was born to teach: the life of action and ideals had done nothing for him but lead him to this place. In the outside world he had denied his real vocation and was being offered now a chance to redeem himself in one last act of dedication. Dedication this time not to the poor, the dispossessed, the conquered and the subjugated masses, but dedication to the life of the mind and the power of human will.

Before Ned had walked into the sun-room two months earlier Babe had been almost ready to give up his tenacious grip on the world, almost ready to quit the inner fortress he had so carefully constructed and so faithfully inhabited all those years. Ned was not to know it, but the games of chess they had played together had been Babe's salvation. Whatever they might have done for Ned, they had done more for Babe.

Babe's brain was a freak of God's and God deserved better than to have that freak die with the old man that housed it. His prodigious and flawlessly complete memory was the gift that had first marked him out. A memory without energy, will and purpose is of no value however, and those qualities Babe had too and in terrifying superabundance. Without them, his brain, no matter what its speed and power, could never have survived the appalling regime of drugs, isolation and electric convulsions to which it had been subjected for so many years.

Babe's brain and memory were, after all, a simple matter of genetic fortune and he took no pride in them whatsoever: he had come to discover that it was his will and his will alone that marked him out from common men and will – unlike cerebral proficiency – could be taught, passed on and made to live for ever.

With the exception of the *Universal British Cyclopaedia* (Ed. F. S. Dorrington) the only books to which the staff allowed Ned access were in Swedish, German and Danish. While Dorrington's work on everything from Aahhotep to Zwingler seemed perfectly acceptable to Ned, Babe had other ideas. He had taken the book from Ned, opened a page at random and snorted with contempt.

'Look at that,' he said, stabbing down an angry finger. 'Will you just look at the two Grays?'

Ned peered over Babe's shoulder and saw that there were two entries under the name Gray, the first for a George Gray which began 'Professional champion player of Queensland who, at only 17 years of age created a sensation in the billiard world with his exceptional hazard play . . .' and a second shorter entry for a Thomas Gray, 'English poet buried in Stoke Poges.'

'And here's this,' Babe continued, flipping back a page, '"Grappa, Mountain of Italy, scene of fierce fighting between the Italians and the Austro-Germans in the Great War." Not a mention of that heavenly and disgusting drink that makes the place immortal! No, no, no, this won't do. I'm taking it off your hands. We start you on Swedish and German books right away.'

'But, Babe, I can't read Swedish or German . . .'

'Can you name me a great book that you know well? We'll see if they have it in either language.'

Ned shuffled uncomfortably. 'A great book?'

'A novel, tell me at least that you've read a novel before now.'

'We did *The Mayor of Casterbridge* at school. And *Lord of the Flies*.'

'Of course you did, you poor lamb. *Treasure Island*, did you ever read that? I know for a fact they have it here in German.'

'Oh yes!' said Ned enthusiastically. 'I must have read it at least six times.'

'Only six times? And what was wrong with it? The book's a masterpiece.'

'But, how will I understand a word of it? The only German I know is *Sprechen Sie Englisch* and *Achtung, Schweinhund*.'

'We shall read it together. You'll amaze yourself.'

*

The weeks passed and, with painful slowness at first, they passed through the pages of *Treasure Island*. After *A Christmas Carol*, *The Scarlet Letter* and *The Count of Monte Cristo*, Ned found himself able to absorb at a faster rate and shape more sentences of his own. After a while he began reading by himself, getting through German books in his room faster than he had read in his own language when a boy. Swedish followed, then Latin, French, Spanish and Italian.

'Fluency equals necessity times confidence over time,' Babe liked to say. 'If a five-year-old can speak a language, it cannot be beyond a fifty-year-old.'

'But a five-year-old can run around for hours, tumbling and falling over without getting tired,' Ned might often complain, 'it doesn't follow that a fifty-year-old can do the same.'

'Bolshy talk. I'll have none of it.'

Sometimes, in the summer months, Babe and Ned walked on the lawn together, speaking low in Swedish (it was a game they enjoyed, not letting any of the staff know that Ned had learnt the language of the place and could now understand the staff when they spoke in front of him) and Babe would encourage Ned to talk of his past.

'Charlie Maddstone. You don't say? Never served under him myself, but I had friends who did. And he turned to politics? Now that was a mistake for a man like that. He was born a hundred years too late that one.'

The relief for Ned to be able to talk about his life was enormous and he felt himself thriving. His appetite for knowledge grew and it was not long before he and Babe were talking about ideas that Ned had never considered in all his life.

'We're conquering time, do you see, Ned?' Babe called him by his real name now, when they were beyond the ears of the staff. 'What do all people in the real world, the world outside this wicked island, regard as the most precious commodity known to them? Time. Time, the old enemy, they call it. What do you hear again and again? "If only I had more time." "Had we but world enough and time." "There's never enough time." "I never had the time to learn music, to enjoy life, to find out the names of the stars in the sky, the plants of the earth, the birds of the air. I never had time to teach myself Italian." "There's no time to think." "How can I possibly find the time to do that?" "I never found the time to tell her how much I loved her."

'And all we have, you and I, is that very thing, time, and if we look on this as the most magnificent gift afforded to mankind, then we can see that in this place we are one with Augustine in his cell and Montaigne in his tower. We are the chosen, the privileged. We have what the richest man on earth most covets and can never buy. We have what Henri Bergson saw as God's chief instrument of torture and madness. Time. Oceans of time in which to be and to become.'

There were days when Ned, remembering this speech, endorsed it and praised Fate for his captivity and the freedom over time it gave him. At other moments, the more he knew, the more he balked and fretted.

'Do you understand why you are here, Babe?' he asked once.

'Pooh, Ned, it's so simple. I am here because I am mad. We are all here because we are mad. Was that not explained to you when you arrived?'

'No, seriously. You're not mad and I know that I am not, although that is entirely thanks to you. Don't you trust me enough yet to tell me about yourself? You've never even told me your real name.'

They had been walking around the lawn and Babe stopped now and tugged at his beard. 'I sprang from an impoverished branch of the grand and ancient Scottish family of Fraser and was christened Simon. As the youngest of six the nickname of Babe has always stayed with me. I was hired fresh from university because of this memory of mine,' he said, staring out over the lawn and towards the bald and distant hills. 'Things stick in the deep brain-pan with which God saw fit to curse me. In those days they stuck even faster and firmer. Intelligence and purpose had nothing to do with it. I remembered the time of every Derby winner as well as I remembered the postulates of Spinoza or the categorical imperatives of Kant. There was a cold war on and a man like me was a useful asset. But I had a conscience, Ned and the day came when I went to see a writer friend of mine. I told him I wanted to collaborate on a book. A great book, to be published in America, for they would never have let it see the light of day in Britain. A book that would blow the whistle on every dirty trick, every hypocritical evasion and every filthy lie that ever came out of the west in its squalid battle for supremacy over its perceived enemy. I'm not a traitor, Ned, nor never would be. I loved England. I loved it too well to let it sink lower than the level of a dung-beetle in its pursuit of lost grandeur. Well, it turned out that the writer friend was no friend at all and the long and the short of it is that I found myself here. This is a place they use if it suits them. When someone is a threat, you understand. The Soviets have their psychiatric prisons and so, as you have found, do we. Ours are a better kept secret, that is the only difference that I have ever been able to make out.'

Ned thought for a while. 'I suppose I had imagined something like that,' he said at length. 'That's why I wanted to hear it from you. If you are here for that reason then it follows that I must be here for that reason too. Only, you know why you are here and I do not. Some – I don't know – some *conspiracy* brought me here and I need to understand what it was.'

'We are merely the stars' tennis balls, Ned, struck and banded which way please them.'

'You don't believe that. You believe in will. You told me so.'

'Like anyone with a sliver of honesty in them I believe what I find I believe when I wake up each morning. Sometimes I can only think we are determined by the writing in our genes, sometimes it seems to me that we are made or unmade by our upbringings. On better days, it is true that I hope with some conviction that we and we alone make ourselves everything that we are.'

'Nature, Nurture or Nietzsche in fact.'

'Ha!' Babe clapped Ned in the back. 'It's coming on, the creature is coming on,' he boomed to the wide uncomprehending lawn. 'Listen,' he said, tucking his arm in Ned's, 'if you want to understand your own situation, can you not apply some of the logic it has cost me so much brain blood to teach you? Take out Occam's Razor and cut away the irrelevant and the obfuscatory. Set down only what you know. Did I never tell you about Zeno?'

'His paradox of how Achilles could never reach the winning line? Yes, you told me.'

'Ah, but he had another lesson to teach us. I will show you.'

Babe led Ned towards a tall pine that leaned away from the slope and towards the high fence at the bottom of the lawn.

'We shall sit under the tree. Great thinkers have always sat under trees. It is an academic thing to do. The word itself derives from the Academia, the grove where Plato taught his pupils. Even the French *lycée* is named after the Lyceum garden where Aristotle held his classes. Enlightenment came to Buddha and Newton under trees they say, and it shall come to Ned Maddstone there too. Now, watch. I pick up a fir cone, an immobile strobile, and I put it in front of you and ask this question. Is it a heap?'

'I'm sorry?'

'Is that a heap?'

'No, of course not.'

Babe added another. 'How about that, do we have a heap now? Of course not, we have nothing more than two fir cones. Incidentally did it ever strike you as suspicious that fir cone is an anagram of conifer? More dirty work from God, you might think. Look at the arrangement too. A band of three, then five, then eight, then thirteen and so on. A Fibonacci series. Beyond coincidence, surely? Mr God giving himself away again. But that is a side issue. Here we have two cones. All right then, I add another. Is it now a heap?'

'No.'

'I'll add another.'

Ned leant back against the soft warm bark of the pine tree and watched as Babe scrabbled about fetching fir cones, each time adding another.

'Yes,' he said at last, as much out of pity for Babe as because he thought so, 'I'd say that is definitely a heap.'

'We have a heap!' Babe clapped his hands. 'A heap of fir cones! Seventeen of the darlings. So Ned Maddstone is telling the world that seventeen is officially a heap?'

'Well . . .'

'Seventeen fir cones constitute a heap, but sixteen do not?'

'No, I'm not saying that exactly . . .'

'There we have the problem. The world is full of heaps like this, Ned. This is good, this is not good. This is bad luck, but this is a towering injustice. This is mass murder and this genocide. This is child-killing, this abortion. This is lawful intercourse, this statutory rape. There is nothing but a single fir cone's difference between them, sometimes just the one lonely only little cone telling us that it represents the difference between heaven and hell.'

'I don't quite see the connection . . .'

'You yourself, Ned, you say a conspiracy brought you here. That is like saying a heap brought you here. Who is a conspiracy? Why? How many exactly? For what purpose?

Don't tell me it was a heap, just a heap, no more no less. Tell me it was seventeen, or four, or five hundred. See the thing as it is in all its quiddity, all its whatness, all its particularity and deep nature. Otherwise you will never understand the blindest thing about what happened to you, not if you were here for a thousand years and spoke a thousand languages.'

It was deep midwinter and the whole island glowed crystalline white under its eternal shroud of winter darkness. The chairs had been moved from the sun-room into a salon deeper inside the building. In one of the arches Babe and Ned sat playing backgammon over a formica table.

The stone arches that ran along the side of the salon were one of the few detectable remnants of the original monastery around which the hospital had been built and its Romanesque structure of blank arcading had once allowed for a rare practical lesson in architectural elements. Only the sun and clouds by day, the stars at night and the rounded hills visible through the windows in summer had offered like chances for Ned to use more than his mind's eye when taking instruction.

The backgammon they played was of an unusual kind. Since the hospital did not have a set, they played using five paper dice and nothing else. The board and thirty men existed only in their minds. The eccentricity of their games amused the staff. Two of the patients had grown upset however and attempted to pull the imaginary board from the table and trample it – presumably, Ned had suggested, because it played hell with their own sense of the real and the invisible. Their pride, as lunatics, in being able to see what others could not was inflamed when they could not see what others apparently could. By reason of the strong effect their playing had on others, Ned and Babe were allowed to sit in that vaulted arch, away from the central area of tables where the others sat.

It was easy for Ned and Babe to see the pieces laid out in front of them. They played for a hundred pounds a point and at this time Babe owed Ned forty-two million pounds. They had no need for concentration to remember their positions and were able to carry on conversations of some complexity in languages of their choosing, without ever challenging the other's sense of where the pieces were, or quibbling over how many men were left to be borne off in the ending. Sometimes, as on this evening, Ned flicked a flat stone around the fingers of one hand. Babe had taught him coin and card magic and he liked to keep in practice, French dropping, palming, stealing and manipulating as he talked.

For the last week, Ned had been able to do a little teaching of his own on the subject of cricket, a game of which Babe was ignorant.

Babe was talking now of the writings of C. L. R. James, a historian and social commentator he greatly admired.

'It's a pity I shall never read him again, Thomas,' he said with a sigh. 'I always skipped those passages where he waxed lyrical about cricket. He connected it to West Indian life, to colonialism, Shakespeare, Hegel and every other bebuggered thing. I interpreted it as sentimental hogwash, such was the puritanical ignorance of my youth.'

'I was a fine player, you know,' Ned said. 'I think I might have played for Oxford and maybe even for a county if things had turned out differently. God, it sounds absurd to talk about cricket in Italian. Can't we switch?'

'Certainly,' said Babe in Dutch. 'This is much more appropriate, don't you think? They do play a little in Holland.'

'I suppose so. My father's hero was Prince Ranjitsinji. I told you about him, didn't I? From the golden age of cricket. Men said that watching his leg-glide was like seeing the Taj Mahal by moonlight.'

'I did see the Taj Mahal by moonlight once,' said Babe. 'Very disappointing it was too, the . . .'

'I know,' said Ned, with a hint of impatience, 'you told me. I couldn't sleep last night, my father visited me in my dreams again.'

'Your mind always harks on the past in the middle of these long winters,' said Babe, accepting a double from Ned and placing the cube close by him. 'The bones in your shoulders ache and you fret. The spring is not so far away. You'll be more cheerful then.' Babe softly whistled a tune under his breath.

'*Die Walküre,*' Ned said, absently. 'Act One, Scene Three. "*Siehe, der Lenz lacht in den Saal*" . . . look, spring smiles into the room.'

'Ten out of ten. And this?' Babe whistled again.

'Never mind all that,' Ned reverted to English. 'I'm not in the mood for testing tonight. I still want to *know*, you see. I still *need* to know.'

'What is there that you do not know?'

'You must be aware by now, Babe, that I am not a fool. This is a private lunatic asylum, or as Mallo prefers to call it "élite international clinic". Nobody comes here for free. Someone has paid for you to be here and for me to be here. And they have gone on paying.'

'The art of good intelligence work is nothing to do with spying, Ned. The art is to manipulate the civil servants and ministers who operate the Secret Fund. The world follows money with a keener nose than it follows anything. If you can hide your bank accounts and your standing orders, if you can siphon and launder and divert streams of government money, then, and only then, can you truly call yourself a spy.'

'All right. So there is no great mystery about the how. But in my case there is still the why. That is what makes no sense. When I first arrived I thought I'd been kidnapped. But kidnappers don't keep shelling out money for their captives. So after a few years I began to believe what Mallo told me, that I was a fantasist whose real life was buried so deep that no memory of it remained. I know that isn't true and I suppose I always did. I know that I was taken here quite deliberately. But by whom and why? That is what still eludes me. No one can have thought for a moment that I was an IRA collaborator, and if they had they certainly would not bring me here, to the same place they bring people like you.'

'As you have seen, Ned, the genuinely insane come here too. You and I are the only inmates to flatter ourselves that we are political prisoners. You keep denying the possibility, but have you not stopped to think that perhaps those who put us in this place knew what they were doing? Perhaps I was admitted here because I truly am mad? Quite terribly mad.'

'Yes,' Ned admitted with a smile, 'naturally I've considered that. And of course you *are* mad, if by a madman we mean one who possesses a mind that questions and rejects every civilised norm. And, whatever your condition on admittance, you have certainly become mad. The solipsistic hoarding of your own self and the hubristic munification of your will against the potent authority of the institution, these are textbook psychopathologies. Psychopathologies that privilege the artist, the revolutionary and the lover quite as much as the lunatic, however. You may acquit yourself of insanity on that account.'

'Dear God, Thomas, acquit me too that I ever taught you to speak like that.'

'I choose this style of discourse to provoke you, and well you know it. I return to the same problem again and again. I have somehow got on the wrong side of the British secret service, or whatever one chooses to call it. Can you not at least agree with me on that?'

Babe bowed his head in assent.

'You remember that time you sat under the *picea abies* and went through Zeno's paradox of the heap?'

'I do.'

'The idea being to encourage me to look at facts clearly?

To separate the concrete from the abstract, the actual from the perceived?'

'I don't believe I put it quite like that, but yes, I do remember.'

'Well, every night I go over what I am sure are the five salient points in my history and try to be sure that I have seen them clearly. They yield nothing.'

'Tell me what you mean by the salient points.'

'They are obvious. One, I unwittingly agreed to deliver a letter that was given me by an IRA courier. Two, I was arrested for the possession of drugs which had been planted on me. Three, because that letter was also still on my person, I was removed from a police station and taken to what I may assume was a British intelligence safe house where I was interrogated. Four, at the end of the interrogation I was told that I would be taken home. Five, I was not taken home, I was cruelly beaten and transported here, where I have stayed ever since. I don't believe I'm wrong in identifying those as the important facts, surely?'

'If you say so.'

'What do you mean "if I say so"? I've beaten my head against the wall of those facts for years and years.'

'Which might suggest,' said Babe gently, 'that they are of no use to you. Perhaps you have still not been approaching matters in the right way. The right way would not endlessly lead to an immovable wall of facts, it would disclose a pattern of events. A pattern that could be unlocked. By labelling your facts one, two, three and so on, you are implying a causal sequential relation between them that may obscure that pattern.'

'But there *is* no pattern! That's what I'm saying.'

'Don't ask yourself what happened to you. Ask yourself what happened to *you*.'

'And what on earth is that supposed to mean?'

'Did you have enemies, for example? You never talk about that possibility.'

'I never had an enemy in the world!' said Ned with some heat. 'I was the most popular boy in the school. I was about to be made Captain of School. I was captain of the cricket team. I was in love. I was ready to go to Oxford. How could anybody hate me?'

Babe laughed.

'And what's so funny?'

'I'm sorry. Let me try and explain. You have just summarised the situation of a person who might have good cause to be happy, but how does it answer my question? It is a description of someone for whom the classic response "Don't you just hate him?" was invented.'

'I don't follow.'

'Don't tell me you haven't heard that kind of cliché banter before? "What, he's good at sport *and* work? *And* he's good-looking? Don't tell me he's *nice* as well, or I'll *really* hate him." That's how real people in the real world talk, Ned and you must know it.'

'But I *was* nice . . .'

'Nice is a heap word. You pile up enough "nice" actions and you think that makes you a whole heap of nice? What were you really? What did you *do*? It is your actions that define you, not your qualities.'

'I did nothing.'

'Your *inactions* then.'

'You're saying some people hated me?'

'Not hated necessarily. It might be worth separating a number of these salient facts of yours. Let's forget the big one, your arrival here and concentrate on the initiating fact. Let us suppose the dope was planted on you to disgrace you. Now who might benefit from that?'

'No one. How could anybody benefit from such a stupid thing? It would just upset those who loved me that's all.'

'Ah, well. Maybe that was the very benefit sought. But perhaps too there was a more tangible advantage for someone. Captain of School, captain of cricket and in love with a beautiful girl. There are plenty of hot youths who might covet any one or all three of those things to distraction. Who would become Captain of School, for example, if you were expelled for the possession of drugs?'

'How can I know that?'

'You must have some idea.'

'Well, Ashley Barson-Garland probably.'

'Ashley Barson-Garland. Tell me about him. Everything you can think of. Talk in numbers, not in heaps.'

So Ned told Babe all about Ashley, concluding his description with '. . . but he liked me, I'm sure of it . . .' which sounded a little lame, even to his own ears.

'You don't think he suspected that you had looked through those five private pages of his innermost thoughts?'

'I was incredibly careful not to show it. No, he couldn't possibly have known.'

'Oh Ned. Poor Ned. Think back on yourself. Think back on the pretty, smiling lad you were. How much did you know then? How well were you able to hide anything? What guile did you possess? Don't you see that a sophisticated, prickly, bitter and self-aware creature like this self-styled Barson-Garland could have read you more easily than you read his diary? Snobs see social slights wherever they go and frauds can read exposure in every glance. Even if he did not know, can you not believe that he might have *suspected*?'

Ned chewed his bottom lip in irritation. 'All right, but even if he did, why would he hate me?'

'Use your imagination.'

'I thought you told me to examine everything dispassionately. If I use imagination I can dream up anything, what help is that?'

'Don't confuse imagination with fantasy. Imagination is the ability to project yourself into the mind of others. It is the most hard-headed and clear-eyed faculty we have. If you use your imagination, you can see that from Ashley's point of view you were every single thing that he was not. My own instinct, I must tell you, is that he was also in love with you but unable to see it.'

'Oh for God's sake!'

'Think back what you read. Masturbating with all that fury into the boater he kept. I won't labour the point, it's just a theory.'

'That's all *any* of this is, just theory.'

'Then why does it upset you so much?'

'It doesn't upset me . . .' Ned's knee began to bounce up and down, a thing that had not happened for a long time. He stopped himself. 'All right, perhaps it does. Because it's so useless. Because it doesn't get us anywhere.'

'It upsets you because it is *not* useless, because it might get us closer to the truth. The truth that others may not have seen you as you believed they did. Maybe they saw you as arrogant, thoughtless, obnoxious and vain, as so self-assured that even your politeness and charm were like daggers in their poor fucked up adolescent hearts. But you're a grown man now, and you should be able to see all that without hurting yourself.'

'Well even so,' said Ned irritably, 'you can't tell me that Ashley Barson-Garland would go so far as getting hold of drugs deliberately to have me thrown out of school. He didn't know the first thing about . . . *Cade*!' Ned brought his fist down on the table, crushing the paper doubling cube. 'Oh Jesus, *Rufus Cade*.'

'Never mind that,' said Babe, as Ned tried to reassemble the cube. 'Rufus Cade. That's not a name you've mentioned before.'

'He wasn't anyone. I did drop him from the First Eleven . . . but that's ridiculous. No one, I mean no one could be so vindictive and petty-minded as to . . . he smoked cannabis though, I do know that. All the time.'

'Well now, suddenly we have two boys with motives,

however trivial. And one of them even has access to what we might call the murder weapon.'

'Do you know,' said Ned, only half-listening. 'I think deep down I always had a feeling that Rufus didn't really like me. I can't quite explain it. There was something in the way his eyes slid away from mine when we talked. He was never exactly rude, but I do remember the time I had to skipper the *Orphana* back to Oban, after Paddy died. Rufus was on board then and he was horrid to me. I think he resented my taking command. It really puzzled and upset me. Maybe I *was* arrogant. But you're asking me to believe that he and Ashley were like insane Iago figures plotting to bring Othello down. I wasn't Othello for God's sake, I was just a schoolboy.'

'What was Othello's crime? He was big, handsome and successful. And he had Desdemona.'

'But Rufus had never even set *eyes* on Portia. Ashley met her the same day that I did, but *Ashley* . . . I mean, there were always rumours that he might be, you know, queer . . . *not* that that means I agree with you when you said that he might be in love with me,' Ned added quickly. 'After all, he can't have loved me and hated me at the same time.'

'Don't tell me you've forgotten all that Catullus I once tried to ram into your head,' said Babe sorrowfully.

'*Odi et amo*, yes I know. And if you're trying to tell me that Portia hated me too then I'll just walk away and never talk to you again. I *know* that isn't true. But if . . .' Ned's voice trailed away and he stared down at the table, thinking furiously.

'An idea taking shape, is it?' Babe asked after a long pause. 'If there were an art to find the mind's construction in the face, then I would say you were thinking imponderable thoughts and that light was beginning to break.'

'*Gordon*. Gordon Fendeman.' Ned drew the name out slowly. 'Portia's cousin. If I think very hard . . . the way they were when I met them at the airport. They'd been on holiday together and it irritated me the way he stood next to her. I wasn't jealous exactly, but I remember that I didn't like it. It made me uncomfortable. And Portia told me she had never read my last postcard to her because Gordon had ruined it. Accidentally, she said, but maybe not.'

Babe listened carefully to everything Ned had to say about Gordon.

'Let's see if I've got this clear,' he said. 'Ashley and Gordon went off together to look at the House of Commons the day you got back from Scotland and Portia and Gordon got back from Italy?'

'That's right, I remember thinking that it would be nice for Gordon to see the Mother of Parliaments.'

'Dear me, I hope you didn't actually *say* that?' Babe smothered a smile.

'And just what exactly would be wrong with that?'

'Just a *tiny* bit pompous perhaps?'

'Well, perhaps . . .' Ned smiled too. 'Anyway, the point is that later, when Portia and I were still . . . when we were still upstairs making love, they came back.' Ned struck the table again. 'God, that must be it! That *must be it!*'

'Gordon and Ashley came back?'

'Yes, but *with Rufus*. Don't you see? Ashley must always have been going to meet up with him in a pub somewhere. He and Rufus were thick as thieves. Rufus came down to London from Scotland on the same train as me. Ashley took Gordon off to meet Rufus in a pub and they all came back while Portia and I were still upstairs.'

'What did they say?'

'It was only for a moment. Ashley said . . . what did he say? Said there was something he had to fetch. He called up to me. "You young people enjoy yourselves . . ." those were his exact words. And Babe, listen to this! *My jacket was hanging on the banister in the hallway downstairs*. Jesus, they must have sat there in the pub and planned it all. They even knew where I was going! They knew I was going to Knightsbridge with Portia to . . .'

'Calm down, Ned. Calm down.'

'Can't you just picture them sitting there, getting tanked up around a pub table and moaning about Ned bloody Maddstone and how they'd like to see him come crashing down? That's when they decided to ruin my life. All they had to do was make an anonymous phone call to the police. And they laughed as they planted the stuff in my jacket. "You young people enjoy yourselves!" Those are the words that Ashley called up and I heard Rufus and Gordon smothering their giggles. I remember feeling touched and proud. I thought my friends were giggling like naughty schoolboys at the thought of me and Portia upstairs and I was proud. But they were laughing because they knew I was about to be destroyed. And I'll tell you something else! They *watched it all happen*!' Both Ned's legs were jogging up and down uncontrollably as revelation after revelation poured into his head. 'I distinctly remember laughter from the doorway opposite as the police pushed me into their car. They destroyed me and they *laughed*.'

Ned's face was white and spittle creamed at the corners of his mouth as it did on the lips of some of the real lunatics they saw every day. Babe leaned forward to touch his arm. 'It's all right, my friend. It's all right. Take it slowly. You *may* have landed on the truth here . . .'

'Of course I have! That's *it*! How in hell could I not have seen it before?'

'You *know* how you didn't see it before. I told you. You didn't see it before, because you were not looking clearly. Look clearly now. Four schoolboys, a stupid prank played on one them, that is what you are talking about. Nasty perhaps, certainly nasty, but don't allow yourself –'

'They *laughed*, Babe! They laughed at me.'

Martin's voice intruded on them. 'What exactly is going on here? You two having some kind of lover's quarrel?'

Ned almost betrayed his understanding of Swedish by leaping in with an angry retort, but Babe beat him to it.

'Not a quarrel, Martin . . . can't remember the numbers. Can't remember the numbers,' he said in a dazed mumble, staring down at the invisible backgammon board.

'You two,' said Martin in English, 'both crazy. Everyone here crazy,' he spread his arms to include the room, 'but you two most crazy of all. Is time now you go to rooms. Tomorrow shall be an inspection. Shave in the morning, be behaving well.'

Ned did not sleep that night. Around in his head revolved three laughing faces. Fendeman, Garland and Cade. The names repeated in his mind like the rhythm of a train or the thunder of hooves on a racetrack.

Fendeman, Garland and Cade. Fendeman, Garland and Cade. Fendeman, Garland and Cade. Fendeman, Garland and Cade.

*

Babe also lay awake that night, and for many subsequent nights. He had detected a change in Ned that worried him.

'I don't like to see you thrashing your engine like this,' he would say. 'There is nowhere to take it. It can only burn you up.'

Ned seemed to take no notice and retreated more and more into the past where he relived his final days in the world over and over, hearing again each syllable that had been spoken to him by Fendeman, Garland and Cade, seeing once more in his mind's eye every glance and gesture they made. He had built up a picture of himself through their eyes.

He saw from Rufus Cade's point of view an image of Ned the arrogant, Ned the cocky, Ned the careless and vain. Every sweet smile, every polite mumbled apology seemed to him now an obvious cause of resentment.

Ned understood how to Ashley he must have represented everything assured, everything attractive, everything unattainably privileged, perfect and graceful. Even the act of securing him summer employment as his father's assistant could appear patronising and offensive.

Gordon too, arriving in a foreign land, would naturally look upon Ned Maddstone as the living image of all that was remote, English, gentile and alien. To see his cousin Portia ignore him in her obsession with a boy so opposite to himself could certainly drive Gordon to hatred.

Everything Ned had and was he could now interpret as repugnant, ugly, oppressive and obscene. Everything in and of him – the V-neck cricket sweaters, the flopping fringe of hair, the rueful smiles and pretty eyes, the lazy athleticism, the delicate skin and peachy blush, the voice, accent, manner and gait – all of Ned Maddstone stood as a monument that those of spirit would cry out to despoil.

Yet how dared they? How dared they not see that Ned had been unaware of all this? How dared they not understand that he was blamelessly unimaginative, gentle and innocent? Whatever arrogance he may have displayed, Ned would never in those days have assumed that his feelings had primacy over those of others. That they could be so confident in their interpretation of him was an arrogance way beyond anything he had been capable of. They hid their rage. They pretended to like him. They coldly planned to disgrace him in the eyes of his father and his lover, as if he had no emotional life, no point of view and no right to happiness of his own. That they could treat him as a symbol without life or capacity for pain marked them down as evil beyond imagining. There did not exist the faintest possibility that Ned could ever forgive them.

Fendeman, Garland and Cade. Fendeman, Garland and Cade.

'I have been trying to apply the same thinking to what happened after my arrest,' he said to Babe one morning, while Babe sketched a circuit diagram.

'Let's just concentrate on what we're doing, shall we? Have you an idea what it is yet?'

'It's a hi-fi amplifier circuit.'

Babe shook his head. 'You're not trying. Count the capacitors.'

'An electronic calculator. A central heating thermostat. Controls for an automatic milking parlour. Who cares? Babe, we've got this far, we've got to go further. I'm right about everything that happened up to my arrival at the police station, I know it. Those three planned my arrest. But they knew nothing about the letter. I need to understand what happened next.'

Babe sighed and put down his pen. 'A burglar alarm, and such an elegant one too,' he said, folding the diagram in half. 'Here, you can study it later. I shall be asking you questions about it another time.'

Ned took it impatiently. 'Sure,' he said. 'Another time.'

'Tell me once more,' said Babe. 'You were taken by a man called Oliver Delft to a house in the country. You sat in the kitchen and explained to him how you came by the envelope and its incriminating code words. You are there again now. Picture it. Feel yourself there, Delft in front of you with a glass of wine, you at the table with your carton of milk.'

Ned closed his eyes and tried to recall the dialogue.

'. . . you'll be home before the *News at Ten* . . . Don't mind a tape-recorder do you? Tell me more about your friend Leclare . . . He wasn't my friend, he was just the school's sailing instructor . . . We went on lots of school trips . . . More questions. Endless questions.'

'Can you remember them all?'

'He asked me everything. Everything about the sailing trip. How long did we stay at the Giant's Causeway . . .' Ned screwed his eyes tighter. 'He was relaxed, bored almost. You're doing well, Ned, very well. Not too far to go now . . . was it a moonless night? . . . That's good, Ned. Excellent, excellent. And the envelope came from where? . . . Well, a shop I suppose, a stationer's . . . No, no, he *produced* it from where? His pocket? A safe? What? . . . Oh, from a small bag on the chart table . . . Any maker's name? Adidas, Fila, that sort of thing? . . . Good, good. Nearly there, old son. Your chum Rufus Cade still out of earshot, was he? I see. Nothing written on the envelope was there? . . . On and on came the questions.'

'And he's standing over you,' Babe's voice seemed to come from far away. 'He's questioning you, the tape is running and you say he looks almost bored?'

'He had a sudden twinge of cramp and that woke him up a bit,' said Ned.

'Cramp?' said Babe, frowning. 'What do you mean cramp?'

'Well, he leapt out of his seat and started walking up and down. I asked him if he was all right and he said it was just a touch of cramp. Then he went out of the room for a moment and came back with a bag of clothes . . .'

Babe leaned forward. 'What had you said?' he asked. 'What had you said just before he got cramp? What *exactly* were your words?'

'He had been asking me about the envelope, who Paddy wanted me to deliver it to, all the details . . .'

'But what exactly had *you* said?'

'Well, I told him what Paddy had asked me to do – I told him the envelope was to be delivered to a Mr Blackrow, Philip R. Blackrow in . . . what was the name of the street? It was a square, Heron Square, SW1. Number Thirteen, I'm pretty sure –' Ned broke off. Babe was staring across the table at him with a look of horror on his face. 'What? Babe, what on earth is the matter?'

Babe shook his head and made a noise that sounded like something between a groan and a laugh.

'Are you all right? What is it?'

'Oh, Ned, Ned, Ned.' Babe rocked backwards and forwards in his chair. 'Why did you never tell me that part of it before? You only told me Blackrow. But Paddy didn't say *Philip* Blackrow, that isn't the name he gave you.'

'Yes it was. I was the one there, for God's sake, not you!

The name was Philip R. Blackrow, 13 Heron Square. I heard it clear as anything.'

Babe had started to shake with laughter. 'Philip R. Blackrow! Oh, you poor young donkey, is that what you heard? Don't you see? It wasn't Philip *R.* anything, it was *Philippa. Philippa Blackrow.* That was the name. Philippa Blackrow.'

'Philippa? But how could you be so sure of that?' Ned stared at Babe in bewilderment. 'I mean it's possible, I suppose but – are you saying you *know* her?'

'I should have joined the dots earlier,' said Babe. 'You mentioned the name Blackrow and I never made the connection. What a fool you are, Babe.'

'What connection? Babe, if you know something, then tell me.'

'Delft and Blackrow, I can't believe I've been so slow. But there again, who but I would have remembered those names from just one glance at a file over thirty years ago? Oh, you're an unlucky man, Ned Maddstone, a most unlucky man.'

'Tell me, Babe. Tell me everything.'

'Did you ever hear of Jack Custance?'

Ned shook his head.

'Shot as a traitor during the Second World War. English as a china spaniel, but Fenian to his core. He left a wife and one child, a daughter called Philippa. The wife died in Canada, so her rich brother Robert Wheeler brought little Philippa back to live in England with his family. She grew up as Philippa Wheeler and in due course married one Peter Delft, bearing a child, unnamed, ungendered and undated in the file. Peter Delft died in September, nineteen sixty-one, if memory serves – which of course it does. In April nineteen sixty-three she remarried the merchant banker Jeremy Blackrow and by the time I came across the file in sixty-three no one had ever bothered to update it from that day forward. Thus Philippa Custance became Philippa Wheeler became Philippa Delft became Philippa Blackrow. I only read Jack Custance's file to research his early life. I had been given the tedious job of writing a paper on the profile of your typical British republican sympathiser, as if such a definable type ever existed.'

'Philippa Blackrow was Oliver Delft's mother?' Ned enunciated each word with extreme deliberation, as if afraid the meaning of what he said would totter and collapse. 'He was her son. He was the son of the very person Paddy wanted me to give the letter to?'

'No cross referencing,' said Babe with a disapproving purse of the lips. 'Her son applies to the service and they don't connect Oliver Delft with the daughter of a condemned traitor. Well, how can we expect an intelligence service that can't spot a full Colonel of the KGB in its ranks to notice a small thing like that? But no wonder Oliver had a touch of cramp when you mentioned her name out of the blue. Must have put the fear of God into him.'

'So he was a traitor too?'

'Perhaps, but not necessarily. He might have joined without knowing anything about his mother's true allegiances.'

'In either case,' said Ned, 'he couldn't allow me to wander about the world knowing her name.'

'Precisely. If he was any good at his job he would have to find a way to get rid of you and cover all your tracks. We know how he got rid of you. But I wonder how he hid the trail . . .' Babe's voice trailed off.

Ned grasped him by the sleeve. 'What are you thinking?'

'You have to think of it from Delft's point of view,' murmured Babe, more to himself than to Ned. 'He's on duty. A flash comes through that a youth has been picked up with a document that might interest the service. He interrogates you, all seems fine, you turn out to be nothing but an innocent. He discovers his own mother is implicated. What can he do? His section chief will ask all kinds of questions next day. "We see from the log, Oliver, that you were sent out to a police station. Who was this boy? What did he have on him?" What would I do if I were Delft?'

'I don't follow,' said Ned. 'What exactly . . . ?'

'Sh!' Babe put a finger to his lips, 'I would pretend to be *playing* you, that's what I'd do. "I've turned him, Chief. He's feeding me all kinds of gold. But hands off, he's mine and I don't want him compromised." But he would need to give something in return. There's the tape, of course, but that had his mother's name on it – he'd need another. Did he, Ned, did he by any chance get you to say anything specific on the tape? After his attack of cramp, that is?'

'I'm not sure . . . *yes*! Portia's family! He wanted to know about her father. I told him what I knew and he asked for the full address. He even asked me to say it twice. But why? I still don't understand.'

'Mine was a grubby trade,' said Babe. 'Let me tell you what Oliver did.'

*

That night, as Ned lay awake, another name joined the others pounding inside his head. Now it was *Delft*, Fendeman, Garland and Cade.

Delft, Fendeman, Garland and Cade. Delft, Fendeman, Garland and Cade. He banged the names with his fist against his thigh. He scratched them with his nails into the palm of his hand. He burned the names into his brain. Delft, Fendeman, Garland and Cade. Delft, Fendeman, Garland and Cade.

Spring on the island was a time when, in the past, Ned had always felt at his most imprisoned. As the long winter melted away and the days lengthened, birds would begin to arrive bringing thoughts of a world outside. As they built their nests and started to sing, Ned would feel the limits of his own mind. No amount of literature, science or philosophy could counter the absolute beauty of the daffodils and the birdsong, nor palliate the terrible achings they awoke in him.

One day in mid-April, just a week after the sun-room had been opened up for the year, Ned sat at the chess-board waiting for Babe. They rarely played these days. It embarrassed Ned that he could beat the older man so easily and it annoyed him that Babe seemed so devoid of will as not to care who won.

Martin came out into the sunlight, blinking. He approached Ned with a smile.

'You waiting for Babe, I suppose?'

'Of course,' replied Ned.

'You wait long time then. Babe had some heart attack last night. Babe is in his bed dying right now.'

Ned sprang to his feet and grabbed Martin by the coat.

'Hey, Thomas! You let go. You want to be strapped up in punishment cell?'

'Take me to him!' Ned yelled. 'Take me to him right now.'

'I don't take you to nobody,' Martin sneered. 'Who you think you are? You don't tell me orders. I tell *you* orders.'

Ned let go of Martin's collar and started to smoothe it down placatingly. 'Please, Martin,' he said. 'Try to understand. Babe is everything to me. He is my father, my brother and my only friend. We are like . . . we are like you and Henrik.' Ned gestured towards where a young newly-arrived Swede was sat trembling and hugging his knees in a basket-chair at the other end of the room. 'You and Henrik, how close you are. How wonderful it is. It is the same with Babe and me. You understand don't you? You do understand. I know Dr Mallo would understand. He would want me to be with Babe now, I am sure of it.'

Martin's eyes narrowed and then dropped. 'I let you see Babe, you don't go talking bad things about me to Dr Mallo?'

'Never, Martin. Never would I say bad things about you to Dr Mallo. You are my friend, Martin. My good friend.'

Ned allowed Martin to lead him to the hospital wing. It took him past Mallo's office and into a corridor down which he had never been before.

Babe was the only patient in the small four-bed ward. Lying on his back with a tube up his nose, he seemed shrunken and old. Ned knelt by his bed and looked at the face he loved so deeply.

'Babe,' he whispered, 'Babe, it's Thomas.'

'I come back half an hour,' said Martin, closing and locking the door. 'You go then. Not see Babe again.'

Ned could see the thick orbs of Babe's eyeballs rolling under the loosened skin of his eyelids.

'Ned?' The name came out in a whispered breath.

Ned took a hand. 'It's me,' he said, tears starting to roll down his face. 'Babe, you can't leave me. You mustn't leave me. Please . . . please . . . I'll go mad. I know I'll go mad.' His voice cracked and he gave a huge sob. 'Babe! Oh Christ, Babe! I will kill myself if you go. I swear to Christ I will.'

Babe pushed out his blackened tongue and passed it over dry and flaking lips. 'I am dying,' he said. 'They will pack me in a box in the room next to this. I heard them talking when I woke up an hour ago. They will seal me in a crate and take me to the mainland where I will be certified dead, nailed into a coffin and sent home. They will burn me in England.'

'Please don't talk like this,' the tears were dropping from Ned's face onto the bedsheets.

'We have half an hour, no more,' whispered Babe, 'so you must listen to me. In sixty-nine I was preparing to leave England. They caught me before I could leave and they brought me here, but they never guessed what I had been up to.'

'Babe, please! You're working yourself up . . .'

'If you don't listen,' Babe took Ned's hand and gripped it hard, 'I shall die here and now!' he hissed. 'Be silent for once and *listen*. They took me before I could escape. But I had taken money. I knew the account numbers, dozens of them. I remembered them all. I funnelled and finagled them, united them all into one grand account. Here, take it, take it!'

Babe opened the hand that had been grasping Ned's. A small fold of paper was clipped between his fingers. 'Take it. There is money there, perhaps after thirty years it is more than you can spend. The Cotter Bank, Geneva. When they found out that it was missing they came here to question me. I had hidden its trail and they were mad with rage. "Where is it? What have you done with it?" I had been here no more than a month, but Mallo had passed that month jolting my brain with electricity and filling me with drugs. The violence of my behaviour had given him no choice. I had known they would come you see, and I wanted to be ready. When they arrived, I dribbled, I giggled, I simpered, I slobbered and I wept. You would have been proud of me, Ned. I was the maddest of the mad. A ruin of a noble mind. They went away cursing, in the belief that they had destroyed the sanity of the only man that knew where all that money lay. I'd love to know how they explained it to their Minister. Now, read that piece of paper, learn it and destroy it. The Cotter Bank, Geneva. All the money will be yours when you leave here.'

'Why do you think I want money?' Ned's tears still flowed in an endless stream. 'I don't want money, I want you! If you die, I will die. You know I will never leave this place.'

'You *will* leave this place!' cried Babe with terrible urgency. 'You will leave in a coffin. Listen to me. There is a metal spoon by my bed, take it now. Take it!'

Ned, weeping at this inconsequential madness, took the spoon.

'Hide it on you, no not there. Not in a damned pocket! Suppose Martin searches you?'

'Where?' Ned looked down at Babe in bewilderment.

'Your anus, man! Push it deep in your anus. I don't care if it bleeds.'

'Oh Babe . . .'

'Do it, do it now or I swear by almighty Christ that I'll die cursing you. There! I don't care if it makes you scream. I don't care if you bleed like a pig, push it up, push it up! Now, can you stand? Can you sit? Good, good, you'll do.'

Babe leant back down on the pillow and slowed his breath. 'Now then,' he said at last. 'Now then, Ned. You've got the piece of paper. Look at it. The Cotter Bank, Geneva. I dared not write that down. See on the paper. There's a number, a password phrase and a counter phrase. Learn them. Repeat them to me . . . good, and again. Again . . . once more. Now swallow the paper. Chew it and swallow. Repeat the number . . . the passwords . . . the address again.'

'Why are you doing this, Babe? You're frightening me.'

'I owe you the money. Backgammon. You're a devil at the game. Not much more now, lad. Cast your mind back to last winter. The week before Christmas. The day we talked together about Philippa Blackrow. I had been drawing a circuit diagram for you, do you remember? You kept it, like I told you?'

'It's in my room, I suppose. With all my other papers. Why?'

'It's Thursday. Paul is on night duty. You get on all right with Paul. Hold him in conversation, ask him about football as he closes you in. You'll need your wits to time it. Use the teaspoon to catch the lock. There's so much for you to do. You'll need all your strength. I'll go on the morning boat to the mainland. Christ, what's that I can hear?'

A key rattled in the lock and the door swung open. Martin beckoned to Ned.

'You come with me now. Leave Babe, come with me.'

'You said half an hour!'

'The doctor, he comes to look at Babe. You come.'

Ned threw himself down on the bed, his tear-sodden face soaking Babe's beard.

'Goodbye, my boy. You have already saved my life. My mind will live forever in yours. Build great things in my memory and to my memory. We have loved each other. For my sake now, stop your howling. Go quietly and pass this last day in remembering. Remember everything. You take my love and memory with you for ever.'

'Come now! *Now*!' Martin strode to the bed and pulled Ned roughly away. 'Against the wall. I search you. Many bad things in the hospital ward.'

From the doorway, Ned cast one last look back into the room as Martin pushed him against the wall.

Babe's eyes were closed tight. All his concentration now was being spent on forcing his heart to beat faster and faster until it might burst in his chest.

*

An hour after lunch, Martin came to the sun-room with the news that Babe had died.

Ned, sitting alone at the chessboard, nodded. 'Was he in pain?'

'No pain,' Martin's voice was quiet and almost reverential. 'Very peaceful. He has quick heart attack once more and was dead fast. Dr Mallo say there was nothing nobody could do,' he added, with a hint of defensiveness. 'Not in any hospital in the world.'

'Would you mind,' Ned asked quietly, 'if I spent the rest of the day in my room? I would like to think and . . . and to pray.'

'Okay, I take you there.'

They walked in silence to Ned's room. Martin looked around at the piles of books and papers leaning up against the walls. 'Babe, he teached you many things, yes?'

'Yes, Martin. Many things.'

'Some books in my language here, but you are not speaking.'

'A little, I can read a little, but not speak very well,' Ned replied, in halting Swedish.

'Yes. Your accent is bad. Maybe, now Babe gone, we are better friends,' said Martin. 'You teach English, I teach Swedish. You teach music and the mathematics to me also.'

'That would be nice,' said Ned. 'I would like that.'

'I leave school early. I run from home where my father was beating me. The more you teach, the better friends.'

'All right.'

'It's not necessary you have to be nice with me,' Martin said, looking awkwardly at the floor. 'I understand this. Sometimes, I am bad. I have bad feelings in my heart. You must have me in your prayers now.'

'Of course,' Ned felt unwanted tears falling down his cheeks again.

'Okay, Thomas,' said Martin. 'I leave now.'

It took almost half an hour for Ned to find the circuit diagram that Babe had drawn and two hours for him to be sure that he had memorised and understood it properly.

Paul came on duty at suppertime and Ned practised without the teaspoon by engaging Paul in brief conversation just as he was pulling the door closed.

'Oh by the way,' he said, holding the door by the handle on the inside and talking through the gap. 'Before you lock up. You couldn't do me a favour could you? In return for me teaching you the nicknames of all the British football clubs. Just a small thing.'

'Favour?' Paul looked worried.

'You wouldn't have a piece of chewing gum, would you?'

Paul grinned. 'Maybe at suppertime. I'll see.'

'Thanks. Are Trondheim playing today?'

'Sure they are playing today.'

'Good luck then,' said Ned cheerfully, pushing the door closed himself. 'See you later.'

At nine o'clock Paul came in once more with a mug of hot chocolate and some pills.

'What's this?' Ned was alarmed. 'I'm not on medication.'

'Dr Mallo is worried that you are upset about Babe,' Paul explained. 'They are not strong. Just to help you sleep.'

'Okay then,' said Ned cheerfully, slapping them to his mouth and swallowing. 'Very thoughtful of the good doctor.'

'And here is some chewing gum for you.'

Ned took the stick of gum and beamed. 'Hollywood, how glamorous! Paul, you're a hero.'

'Good night, Thomas. Have a good sleep.'

'Oh tell me though,' said Ned, stopping Paul from closing the door again. 'How did Trondheim do?'

Ned held the spoon in his right hand, which he held casually against the side of the door. He leaned harder and harder, with only a gap of an inch through which he could talk to Paul, the handle of the spoon pressing against the sprung lock.

'Three goals to one? A great victory for you,' he said. 'Well, I'll see you in the morning perhaps. Goodnight.'

With one last push, Ned closed the door. The spoon handle projected into the room from the gap between the door and the jamb. As Paul's footsteps died away down the corridor, Ned pulled at the door, which gave. The spoon was holding back the lock spring. Almost sobbing with relief, Ned returned to his desk, spat out the sleeping pills and for the last time unfolded Babe's circuit diagram.

At what he judged to be a time somewhere between half past two and three in the morning, he went to his door and pulled it open. The spoon dropped to the floor with a metallic clatter and, cursing himself as the sound rang around the corridor, Ned stooped to pick it up.

No sound came from any part of the building as he walked past the empty sun-room, chewing on his Hollywood gum. Only the clicking of the bones in his bare feet and toes disturbed the huge vacuum of silence that hung over the building like a shroud.

When he reached the door to Mallo's office, he listened for a minute before entering. Once inside, he switched on the desk light and looked around, blinking at the sudden glare. The curtains were drawn, but there would be a line of light showing under the door. He knew there was very little time to lose. He went straight to a wooden box on the wall, opened it and took out a key. An impulse made him take out another, smaller key and try it in the lock of the small grey filing cabinet against the opposite wall. The key fitted and Ned searched quickly about the rest of the office until he found a plastic shopping bag into which he pushed sheaf after sheaf of papers and files. Tying the top of the carrier bag in a tight knot, he took out the chewing gum, swallowed the small key, popped the gum back in his mouth, switched off the desk light and crept back out into the corridor.

As he approached the staff quarters, rhythmically

chewing on his gum, he pressed the carrier bag under his arm hard against his body to diminish the rustle it made as he walked. He could hear music playing and saw an oblong fall of light in the passageway ahead. The room where Paul would be sitting had a window that looked over the passageway through which Ned had to pass. He crept slowly towards it and had just dropped to his knees ready to crawl along the floor under the line of view when the door opened and Paul walked out. Ned's heart jumped and his whole body froze. The carrier bag crackled, sounding in Ned's ears like a truck running over a thousand plastic egg-cartons.

Paul crossed straight over into the room opposite without looking in Ned's direction. The vigorous splash of a stream of urine tumbling into a lavatory bowl echoed around the corridor and trembling with relief, Ned rose and walked forward. As he passed the door he gave a quick glance to his left and saw Paul standing legs apart, his back to the corridor, shaking off and humming the Ode to Joy. He wore a tee-shirt and jeans and the unprecedented sight of such ordinary clothes awoke feelings of great excitement in Ned. They seemed to assure him that the outside world was real and within reach.

He rounded the corner and leant against the wall. The night was cool, but still he could feel trickles of cold sweat running from his temples onto the back of his neck. He stopped chewing and listened, his mouth open. He heard the sound of a flush, footsteps crossing the corridor and a door closing. Spearmint saliva was dribbling from his open mouth. He sucked it in and started to chew again.

On the wall opposite him he saw the winking green light of the alarm-box. Tip-toeing across, he examined it close up, mentally laying Babe's diagram of the control-box over the real thing. The circuit that controlled the hospital corridor was designated as Zone 4. Ned took the key he had taken from Mallo's office and tried to fit it into the master lock. It slipped out of the lock and for one heart-stopping moment he thought he might have swallowed the wrong key. He tried again and this time it slipped in easily. With a gulp of relief, he gave it a half turn to the right. The winking green light became a winking red light. Holding his breath, he flicked up the fourth in a row of dipswitches that ran the length of the control-box and moved the key another quarter turn to the right. He held it there for a second then switched it twice to the left, returning it to its original location. As the key passed from three o'clock on its way to the home position, the whole unit gave a quick blaring bleep of such intensity that Ned almost yelled in fright. Backing into the doorway opposite he waited, eyes fixed on the lights of the control-box. The green light was flashing again, but there was a new red light next to it which winked four times in succession, paused then winked four times again, revealing to anyone who knew the system that Zone 4 had been by-passed. No doors opened or closed in the staff room around the corner and no alteration came in the volume of the music emerging from Paul's radio. Only in Ned's ears had the bleep blasted like a cavalry bugle sounding in hell. Approaching the alarm-box once more, Ned gently pulled out the key. The lights flashed as before but all was quiet. He pulled a tiny wad of gum from his mouth and pressed it over the winking red beam, tamping it firmly so that no light leaked out from the sides. He stepped back to look.

It worried him that whoever disabled the alarm in the morning would spot the little plug of chewing gum. If they noticed it *after* switching off the alarm it might mean nothing, but if they removed the gum while the system was still active, the four flashes of light would tell them everything they needed to know and all hell would break loose. Ned pressed against the lump of gum with the end of the key, working it flat until he felt that it was flush with the surface of the control-box. By the small green glow that offered the only light to work by, Ned pressed and sculpted until he believed that the gum had become as good as invisible.

Satisfied finally that everything appeared normal, he put the key in his mouth and moved silently towards the doors that led to the hospital wing.

Babe was dead and he, Ned, had not felt more alive for over twenty years. The blood was singing in his ears, his heart thumped and banged in his chest like a slapping belt-driven engine and every nerve in his body vibrated with power and energy. No matter what happened to him now he knew he could never regret the return of so much intense excitement. If Dr Mallo and all the staff were to leap out from the next doorway, if Rolf were to pin him to the wall and dislocate his shoulders again and all privileges, books and papers were taken away for ever, if he were made to subsist on nothing from now on but a regime of chlorpromazine and electric shocks, still it would have been worth it just to have experienced this short burst of true living.

Dr Mallo and the staff did not leap out from the next doorway. The next doorway led to the room adjacent to the ward where Babe had died and the hospital wing remained as quiet as the tomb it was serving as. Ned put his hand to the doorknob and turned the handle. If he had made a mistake with the alarm-box he would discover it now. He pushed the door open. No bells jangled, no sirens wailed. All was silent. He closed the door behind him and felt for a light-switch.

He had found himself in a store room whose walls were lined with shelves filled with rows of medical supplies. In the centre of the room was a trestle-table on which stood a packing case about seven feet long and three feet wide with thick rope handles attached to the end sides. Ned approached the table and laid his hands on the lid of the packing case.

'Hello, Babe,' he whispered. 'So far so good.'

He laid down the carrier bag and looked about him. The teaspoon was still gripped in his left hand but he had hoped he might find something stronger. He searched the shelves and saw nothing that would help him. He had almost given up when he glimpsed the end side of a metallic blue toolbox under the table itself.

Helping himself to a heavy-handled chisel, Ned set to work on prising the lid free, being careful not to bend any of the nails. It took close to fifteen minutes and Ned was sweating profusely by the time he lifted the lid clear and laid it on the floor.

Inside the crate Babe's body was covered in a white sheet. Ned swallowed, gripped the fabric and plucked it away. He almost screamed in shock.

Babe was smiling. It was the smile that Ned had come to love over the last ten years. It was the wicked grin of complicity, excitement and pleasure that always preceded a new lesson in a new field.

Wait till you meet Joyce, old lad!
And next week, Faraday and magnets – prepare to be astounded!
The Battle of Lepanto tomorrow, Ned my boy!
Wagner. Richard Wagner! Once in your system, never out.
The Marshall attack. Not an opening for the faint-hearted.
Let's say Heil to Herr Schopenhauer, shall we?
Russian verbs of motion, Ned. They'll drive you mad.

Ned leaned down and stroked Babe's beard.

'Here we go,' he said.

Ned was prepared to find the body heavy and had planned in his mind all evening how he would set about lifting Babe out of the crate. In his mind he had imagined that he would put a hand under each of his arms, summon up all his strength and heave until Babe's body was draped face down over Ned's back in a kind of fireman's lift. What Ned had not foreseen was the enormous strain this would throw on his weak shoulders. As he strained at Babe's dead weight he could feel the socket of the left shoulder grinding in the old familiar way. He had not put one of them out for at least seven or eight years and while he knew perfectly well how to snap the socket back, tonight he could not allow anything to disable him. He decided to try letting his right shoulder take the weight instead. He drew in nine or ten sharp lungfuls of breath and pulled.

Staggering from the table with Babe over his shoulder, Ned sank down to the floor, sweat pouring from him and his right shoulder on fire with pain. Babe's head banged against the floor and his body tumbled to the ground with a crack of bone as the neck snapped like a dry twig.

Ned rose unsteadily to his feet and gently stretched out his arms. The right shoulder gave a small click but held in its socket. Inhaling and exhaling deeply, Ned forced his breathing to slow to a calmer rhythm and waited for the trembling in his arms and legs to stop. Stretching and inhaling deeply once more he switched off the lights, opened the door and listened. Satisfied that no sound other than the thumping of his heart pierced the deep black silence of the night, he bent down and hooked a hand under each of Babe's arms.

He pulled the body slowly along the corridor of the

hospital wing and reached the alarm-box. The radio around the corner was playing music. Ned recognised it to be Grieg's *Death of Åse* and instinctively looked down at Babe, as if to share the joke.

He dragged the body around the corner and laid it down face up. Crouching at Babe's feet, he pushed him forward along the ground and past the door to the staff room. If Paul came out for another pee, he could not help but trip over the corpse and all would be lost. Bent as low as possible without losing his purchase on the soles of Babe's feet, Ned pushed again. He was now directly below the window and he pushed faster and faster, wishing that the radio had programmed something louder and more percussive. If it was to be funereal, why not Siegfried's *Death*, Verdi's *Dies Ire* or the *March to the Scaffold*? The muted strings of Grieg whined on as Ned cleared the window, stood up and resumed the more comfortable grip under Babe's arms that allowed him to drag the body backwards over the linoleum that led to his own wing.

Back in his room, it took another shoulder-wrenching effort to heave Babe onto the bed. He did so without first pulling back the blankets and had to rock the body backwards and forwards on its side before he could loosen the bedsheets and cover Babe up, cursing himself for his stupidity. He imagined Babe too tutting at such a lack of foresight and common sense.

'Sorry,' he whispered. '*Mea culpa. Mea maxima culpa.*'

Ned arranged the head on the pillow, pulled up the blankets and bent down to lay a final kiss on Babe's head.

'Goodbye my best and dearest friend. Whatever happens, you have saved my life.'

On his way back to the store room Ned returned to Mallo's office and replaced the alarm-key, parking the residue of his gum under the doctor's grand leather chair. One day Dr Mallo would find it and wonder how it got there.

Ducking under the staff-room window, from which Rossini's overture to the *Barber of Seville* now blasted triumphantly, Ned passed by the alarm-box and made his way back to the store room, closing the door behind him and switching on the light.

He could not afford now to make the slightest mistake and he prepared everything he needed with meticulous care. He dropped the carrier bag into the crate and looked around the room. An idea had come to him as he had been dragging Babe's body along the corridors and he searched the shelves now until he came upon a box marked 'Diacetylmorphine EP'. He ripped it open and emptied its contents, dozens and dozens of polythene bags, into the crate, throwing in for good measure a polythene bag filled with syringes. He looked down and saw that there was room for another boxful too. And another. After a moment's thought he added a waste disposal sack, large enough to contain all the polythene bags and the carrier bag he had taken from Mallo's office too.

His initial plan had been to cannibalise screws from the hinge of the door and work them into the inside of the lid using the teaspoon as a screwdriver, but he discovered that the blue toolbox contained a small jar of wood-screws and even a brace and selection of drill bits. One thing he could not find however was rope, so he tore strips from the sheet that had covered Babe's body and plaited them tightly together. He held this home-made rope against the inside of the top of the crate and drilled with the brace, being careful not to break through to the other side of the lid. He screwed the plaited cloth tightly into the wood, with just enough give to offer a firm hand hold, which he tested by tugging on it with all his strength until he could be sure that the cloth would not rip and that the screws would hold fast.

Ned now laid the lid on top of the crate, lining up the nails with their original holes. He pushed down and saw that three of the nails, instead of finding their holes, jumped up proud. He readjusted each one and tried again. When he was reasonably sure that each nail would find home he pulled off the lid once more and laid it upside down crossways over the crate.

He gave a final look around the room, kicking the toolbox under the table into its original position. He glanced about the shelves and down at the floor. With the exception of the lid lying across the crate, everything was as it had been when he had first walked in.

Drawing in a deep breath, Ned switched off the light and moved slowly forward in the pitch darkness until he felt his leg bump against the table. He climbed onto it and stood slowly up, his head nearly brushing the ceiling. He picked up the lid and felt at it until his fingers closed on the loop of cloth. He lifted the lid by this handle and, holding it in front of him like a Norman shield, he stepped into the crate and lay back on his bed of polythene. Manoeuvring the lid into position and satisfying himself that, so long as he pulled down on his plaited handle, all was well, Ned concentrated so hard on staying awake that he fell asleep almost instantly.

The bang of the store-room door opening awoke Ned with a jolt. Tiny slivers of light pierced the darkness of the packing-crate and at first he was convinced that too much time had passed. Perhaps they had decided to keep the body longer and send it on an evening boat. Babe would already have been discovered in Ned's room and the hunt would be up. He cursed himself for sleeping. If he had stayed awake he might have realised that too much time had passed and managed to escape another way. Babe had assured him that the island was at least thirty miles from land, but attempting to swim for freedom would have been better than ignominious discovery here.

The sound of weary morning voices yawning and moaning reassured him. Working his hand into the cloth loop, Ned pulled down on the lid as hard as he could and waited, hardly daring to breathe.

Two male voices spoke in Danish.

'We'll take it on our shoulders.'

'What's the rope on the ends for?'

'Yah, but it will bite into our hands. Believe me, I've done this before. On our shoulders. You first, one, two . . . *three*.'

'I thought it was going to be an old man. Christ, he's heavy.'

'It'll be the wood mostly. Come on.'

'*Ow*!'

'What is it?'

'You were supposed to hammer the nails in. I just cut my finger!'

Ned lost all sense of direction as his body bumped back and forth inside the crate. He was dropped onto the floor twice when doors had to be unlocked and opened and each time Ned was fearful that the lid would bounce up and he would be discovered. He prepared in his mind the possibility of having to fight for it and run.

Finally, cold morning air seeped through the sides of the box and he heard the cry of gulls followed by the groaning creak of a sliding van door. The crate was pushed with bone-jarring carelessness onto a metal floor, the door slammed shut and an engine started.

Ned recalled the infernal torture of his last journey in a van. He saw again the two dead eyes of the men who had kicked him to unconsciousness and heard the rhythmical flipping of tyres over a ribbed causeway. He remembered Mr Gaine and he remembered every detail of those two brutal men. He could not, however, reassemble in his mind the identity of the Ned who had undergone those infernal torments of soul and body. That Ned had been as innocent, terrified and blinded by the world and its cruelty as a newborn puppy. He had been a particle, without will, direction or purpose. That Ned had been dead for almost twenty years: all the life had been snuffed out of him the day Rolf had dislocated his left shoulder and murdered his last remaining shreds of hope and faith. The Ned who travelled now was an entirely different being, a man of iron will, an avenging angel – an instrument of God.

Ned stood up on the rocks and turned to look at the ferry half a mile out to sea. When she put in, the crew would carry the wooden box, now weighed down with sea-chain and iron tackle, to the dock where, after a time, it would be opened and the deception discovered. Perhaps the island had already sent a message to shore and Ned was already a wanted man.

He shivered and unwound from his aching shoulders a large yellow oilskin bag that he had stolen from the captain's locker on board the ferry. In the locker he had also found clothing and a wallet containing two and a half thousand Danish kroner. He had no idea whether it was a fortune or barely enough for a small breakfast.

Half an hour later he walked into a crowded café on the Århus road. He had not been surprised to discover that he was in Denmark. Babe had told him that the hospital island lay in the Kattegat, somewhere between the Swedish coast and northern Jutland. Ned marched straight to the counter and ordered a cup of coffee and a plate of eggs and bacon. He took a seat and looked around him. He had seen five large lorries parked outside and decided that his best course was boldness and speed.

'Hey!' he called out above the noise of the juke box.

Everyone in the café looked up and stared at him. 'Anybody here going south? I need to be in Germany by tonight. I'll go halves on the fuel.'

Most of the men in Ned's eyeline shrugged and looked back down at their plates. One or two shook their heads regretfully, but no one responded. Damn, thought Ned, what do I do now?

A voice behind him spoke up in broken Danish. 'I have to be in Hamburg tonight. You are welcome to ride with me.'

'Fantastic!' cried Ned, in German. 'You've saved my life!'

'Oh, you're German,' said the other. 'Thank Christ for that. Danish is a nightmare.'

'I know,' said Ned with a sympathetic smile. 'Trying to speak it gives you a nosebleed. Let me buy you a cup of coffee, you don't mind waiting while I dive into a quick breakfast do you?'

'No problem,' said the other, coming round to join Ned at his table and extending his hand. 'Dieter, by the way.'

'Karl,' said Ned. 'Pleased to know you. Ah, *prachtvoll*!' He smiled up at the waitress as a plate was put in front of him. 'And a cup of coffee for my friend here,' he added in Danish.

Someone had left a newspaper on the table and Ned searched it for a currency table. With relief, he worked out that he was carrying over two hundred pounds. Unless inflation had gone entirely insane over the last twenty years, he reckoned it should be enough to get him where he wanted to go.

Ned rode up front with Dieter, who told him that he had picked up a consignment of paper pulp in Skagen fifty miles north of the roadside café they were leaving, which was just outside the port of Ålborg. Ned calculated that they still had a drive of a hundred and fifty miles south to the German border. The ferry would be putting in at the harbour in Ålborg now. It was all a question of whether or not Dr Mallo had decided to alert the police. He would have discovered that there were papers missing from his filing-cabinet and Ned was confident that this would prevent him from contacting anyone in authority. Perhaps Mallo would call Oliver Delft, probably he would not dare. In Mallo's position, Ned would fabricate a death certificate and try and forget that the troublesome Englishman had ever existed.

Dieter was not a demanding conversationalist. His world appeared to revolve around his wife Trude and their children, of whom there were photographs displayed all around the cabin, and football of which Ned knew little. What he did know was confined to what he had learned of the Scandinavian leagues from Paul. The doings of Trondheim held no interest for Dieter whatsoever.

'Not much traffic,' Ned remarked at one point.

'April sixteenth,' said Dieter. 'It's a public holiday here. The queen's birthday, so they tell me.'

'Ah, of course.'

They stopped for lunch outside Århus and here Ned made his first mistake. They were sitting at a table and

Ned picked up a small object that Dieter had brought with him into the café.

'What on *earth* is this?' he had asked, holding it in his hand and staring at it in bewilderment.

'You're joking!' Dieter smiled broadly. His eyes narrowed when he saw that Ned was completely serious. 'Are you telling me that you don't know what this is?'

Ned realised that he had blundered and tried to laugh it off. 'What I mean to say is,' he said, 'I've not seen one like this before . . .'

'Not seen one like this? Look around you, man!'

Ned glanced at the other tables and saw at least six almost identical objects.

'Well, it's the *colour* really . . .' he said, with an attempt at heartiness. 'Yours is red, the others are mostly black and grey.'

'Where have you been the last ten years?' Dieter asked. 'Where on God's earth is there a place without mobile phones?'

Phones! Mobile phones. Ned cursed himself for not working it out for himself. Now that he looked he could see two people speaking into them. 'I've . . . I've not been well,' he said. 'I've been in a hospital.'

'A prison more like.'

'No, no, a hospital. You must believe me, Dieter. I'm fine now. Totally well, but I have . . . you know, missed out on some things.'

Dieter let Ned back into the lorry, but he was more silent as they continued the journey south towards Åbenrå and the German border. Ned sat beside him, thinking furiously. He came to the conclusion that his best recourse was a kind of limited honesty. The last thing he wanted was for Dieter to flag down a police car. It would be hard to explain the quantity of drugs packed into his oilskin bag.

'I'll be straight with you, Dieter,' he said at last. 'I've escaped from a Danish hospital. My family put me there because of a drug problem, but I'm fine now. Really. Absolutely fine. I'm heading for Hanover to be with my girlfriend. I've messed up my life, but I'm better now. I just need help to get home.'

'How long were you there?' asked Dieter, his eyes firmly on the road.

'Nearly a year.'

'Nearly a year and you don't know what a mobile phone is?'

'They gave me electric shock therapy. I forget things sometimes. What can I say? I'm not a bad man, Dieter, I promise you that.'

'Sure,' said Dieter and he fell quiet again.

After an agonising silence which Ned did not dare break with pleadings or further justification, Dieter spoke again, shyly and with some embarrassment. 'Me, I had a drug problem too some years back. I am a trained engineer, you know? I had a very good job, lots of money. I got a little too fond of the heroin and I lost my job. With thanks to my marvellous wife Trude and the mercy and love of my saviour Jesus Christ I am now a clean and healthy person.

I shall take you to Hamburg and introduce you to my church. A church is better than any hospital. Only the Lord can help people like us.'

'Bless you,' whispered Ned. 'You are truly a Good Samaritan.'

'I suppose,' Dieter went on, after blushing slightly at the compliment, 'that you do not have a passport?'

'No,' replied Ned. 'I'm afraid I don't.'

'They do not always require them at the border, but even if they do not, the customs will certainly need to check my consignment papers. It is better they do not see you. We are ten miles away. I shall stop at the next filling station and you must hide amongst the cargo. They do not search.'

'Let me give you some money for the diesel.'

For a terrible moment Ned thought that he had said something wrong. Perhaps diesel was a thing of the past and lorries were now fuelled by methane, or hydrogen or God knew what else.

'Money? I do not want your money,' Dieter said. 'I do this for my Saviour. That is my reward.'

As they drove the ten miles to the filling station, Ned, as gently as he dared, probed Dieter about his drug habit and how much money it had cost him.

'Heroin is that expensive?' he said wonderingly.

'Sure, but it is cheaper if you smoke it,' Dieter said. 'You must know this, surely? What was your drug?'

'Cannabis.'

'Your family sent you to a hospital for *cannabis*? My God! My mother smokes a joint every evening.'

'My parents are very old-fashioned,' Ned said, uncomfortably aware that there was much about the world he had yet to learn.

*

Approaching the traffic-lights at the outskirts of Hamburg, Ned felt a pang of guilt as he grabbed his oilskin bag, opened the door and jumped down onto the street.

'Sorry, Dieter,' he called back into the cabin. 'But I really don't think your church can help me.'

Dieter shook his head sorrowfully and pulled away with a hiss of brakes and a big double honk from his horn. Ned skipped aside and waved and waved until the lorry disappeared around a corner. He hoped that Dieter could at least see this last gesture in his wing-mirrors and know that his help had been appreciated.

Which indeed it had been. Ned had been crammed amongst the bales of pulp for no more than an hour either side of the border. The doors at the back had not even been opened, though the side of the lorry right next to Ned's ear had been slapped twice as they had been waved through, causing him a ringing in the ears which was still with him. Dieter was amused and teased him about it all through Schleswig-Holstein.

'It was the Lord speaking to you, Karl. Take my word for it.'

Ned turned now and looked around him. It was getting late and there was much to do. At a small Sparkasse he changed his kroner into Deutschmarks, then crossed the street to the underground station and took a train to St Pauli. He had a strong feeling that Babe was watching him now and would disapprove violently of what he was about to do.

From St Pauli he crossed the street into the Reeperbahn. Sitting at a window in the Bar Bemmel, opposite the Lehmitz, he sat nursing a glass of milk as the street outside warmed up into a whirl of touristic Friday night frenzy. The lights, the colour, the noise, the music were all absolutely alien to him. He saw men and women with jewellery and metal bars affixed to their noses, ears and eyebrows. He saw black men with dyed blond hair, and orientals with orange hair. He saw men passing by holding hands. Once a woman with a shaved head poked her tongue out at him as she passed. There had been what looked like a metal stud in her tongue. Ned blinked and swallowed hard.

'Oh, brave new world, that has such creatures in it . . .' he murmured to himself and shook his head, like a dog that has just taken a bath.

At the U-Bahn station he had bought a map and three tourist information booklets which he had read twice through before a waitress approached him and told him that if he was going to stay here he would need to drink more than one single glass of milk over the course of two hours.

'Of course,' said Ned. 'Bring me one of those,' he commanded, pointing at a pink looking cocktail at the table next to his.

'All cocktails five marks,' said the waitress.

Ned supposed (indeed had seen) that his Danish fisherman's outfit of jeans, thick white pullover and donkey-jacket were not the usual habiliments favoured by the night people of Hamburg and he smiled understandingly as he produced a ten mark note.

'I have been fishing all day. Keep the change and have a drink yourself.'

The suspicious scowl was instantly replaced by a happy grin. 'Thank you, sir!'

'Er, I forgot to ask,' he said when the cocktail arrived. 'What's in it exactly?'

'Cranberry, grapefruit and vodka,' came the reply. 'It's called a Sea Breeze.'

'Good title,' said Ned, sipping cautiously. 'Mm . . . delicious.'

'You are a tourist in Hamburg?' The waitress pointed at the map and guides on the table in front of Ned.

'That's right. Just looking for a good time. Is this a dangerous area?'

'The Reeperbahn? No!' she laughed at the idea. 'Once maybe, perhaps yes, but today it is all just businessmen and tourists.'

'Ah,' said Ned, 'so there are no drug dealers or anything like that?' He put the question innocently enough, but held the waitress's eyes steadily.

She leaned forward to wipe down his table and whispered in his ear. 'You looking for something perhaps? You can pay?'

'I *am* looking for something,' Ned replied. 'Do you know anyone . . . er . . . *respectable*? I would be *extremely* grateful.' He looked meaningfully into his wallet and back again at the waitress.

'I'll call my friend. He knows people. Are you interested in going *uptown* or *downtown*?'

Ned pondered her strange use of these American English phrases before the meaning became apparent to him.

'Ah, I understand,' he said. '*Downtown*, please.'

'Okay.' She looked a little surprised. 'I'll see what I can do.'

'Thank you . . . er, I don't know your name.'

'Cosima.'

'Thank you, Cosima. Karl Freytag at your service.'

Ned watched as Cosima went behind the bar to make a phone call. After less than thirty seconds she put down the phone and nodded to him. He nodded back and raised his glass to her in salutation. Picking up his oilskin, he went to the gents to prepare for his meeting.

The man who came into the Bar Bemmel half an hour later was older than Ned, perhaps as old as fifty, which surprised him. He looked more like a successful publisher or prosperous advertising executive than the tattooed leather-jacketed gangster that Ned had imagined.

'Gunther. I understand that you are anxious to do business,' said the man sitting down without a handshake. 'How may I assist you, Herr Freytag?'

'I want you to take what I am holding under the table,' said Ned. 'It is a syringe . . . don't worry it's capped.'

'Hey listen,' said Gunther, starting to rise. 'I'm in the business of selling, not buying.'

'Then find me someone who *will* buy,' said Ned. 'What I have is pharmaceutical grade liquid diamorphine, the purest heroin in the world. Enough to make you a great deal of money.'

Gunther paused. 'How much?'

'I have half a million marks worth, which you can at least double if you cut it sensibly. I'll take four hundred thousand in cash, a usable credit card and any contact that will allow me to buy a passport.'

Gunther looked Ned right in the eyes for perhaps five seconds before reaching under the table and taking the syringe.

'Give me some more for testing.'

Ned was prepared for this. 'Leave two thousand marks as a deposit,' he said.

Gunther nodded and Ned passed a small vial under the table.

'I make a phone call,' Gunther stood up and took a small mobile phone from his pocket, moving away out of earshot. Ned watched him light a cigarette, dial and speak into the phone. He marvelled at the technology and wondered what the range of such telephones might be. Ned was too far away from Gunther to be able to pick up any of his conversation, but when he returned to the table everything seemed set up and he smiled a brief, tight smile.

'Your two thousand's in there,' he said dropping a

cigarette packet on the table. 'I shall return in one hour. If everything is satisfactory we will go together to a place where the rest of your goods will also be checked out. Cosima is watching you. If you leave with my two thousand marks before I return, you will be followed and dealt with. Dealt with very harshly. If all goes well a passport can be ready for you in two days, the credit card and cash you will have tonight. You understand and approve?'

'Perfectly,' Ned extended his hand and smiled. 'A bottle of champagne will await your return.'

'*Bis bald*,' said Gunther, shaking Ned's hand briefly and turning to go.

'*Tschüs*!' said Ned.

Five minutes after Gunther had gone, Ned called Cosima over to him.

'Thank you, Cosima,' he said handing her a hundred mark note. 'You have been very kind.'

Cosima smiled and tucked the note into her apron. 'You're welcome.'

'So Gunther is your boyfriend?'

She laughed at this. 'Oh no,' she said. 'He's my father.'

Ned tried not to look surprised. 'I see. Oh, tell me something, Cosima,' he said, a thought occurring to him. 'Which, in your opinion, is the best hotel in Hamburg?'

She looked at Ned through half closed eyes, like an artist sizing up a model. 'For you, I should say the Vier Jahreszeiten on Neuer Jungfernstieg. Very classy. Very old-fashioned. Just like you.'

'You flatter me. One more thing, before you bring me

a cup of coffee and a glass of milk.' The effect of the Sea Breeze was making him dizzy and light-headed. 'Will I find a decent clothes shop in the area still open in an hour or so? I need some luggage too.'

'This is Hamburg!' said Cosima. 'Nothing closes.'

'Good. Perhaps we can go shopping together. After I have concluded business with your father, naturally.'

Cosima smiled happily. 'My favourite occupation. Hugo Boss, I think. Something dark and elegant.'

*

The platinum American Express card that Gunther had found for Ned was in the name of Paul Kretschmer, and the blonde woman in black at the desk scarcely glanced at it as she slid it through the side of a machine she kept under the desk and passed it back to him with his room key. Ned supposed it was some kind of cash register, but it was unlike any he had seen before.

'Oh, by the way,' he said. 'I need to fly to Geneva on Monday morning.' He gave her a folded hundred mark note and his best smile. 'Be good enough to arrange it for me would you?'

'Certainly, Herr Kretschmer,' she beamed at him. 'With pleasure. Do you prefer Swiss Air or Lufthansa?'

'I tell you what,' said Ned, '*you* choose. First Class.'

'First Class?' she frowned slightly. 'I am not sure they have First Class on such a short flight.'

'Whatever . . .' Ned waved a hand airily. 'I'm sure you'll find me the best seat.'

'Of course, Herr Kretschmer. And may I help you with anything else this evening?'

'It's been a long day,' Ned replied. 'Nothing but a shower and bed. No calls please.'

He crossed over to the lifts, trying not to look impressed by the profusion of late nineteenth-century marble, mahogany and oak panelling all around him. No calls! He smiled at his own impudence.

The receptionist watched his firm athletic stride as he walked to the lifts and turned to the manager.

'Oh, my God,' she said with a sigh. 'I think I'm in love.'

'Me too,' said the manager.

Ned spent Saturday morning playing with the television remote control and reading the magazines in his suite. Gunther called him up at lunchtime and invited him to dinner at his flat, just around the corner from the hotel.

'I should be honoured and delighted,' Ned replied. 'I'm going to do some shopping this afternoon, I don't suppose your charming daughter would be kind enough to escort me around the town? I assure you my intentions are strictly honourable.'

Gunther chuckled down the telephone. 'That would disappoint her terribly,' he said. 'She was hoping they were anything but!'

With Cosima's help Ned bought a laptop, a printer and a large number of books on computing and the internet. The magazines in his room had seemed to be full of articles on this and he wanted to understand everything he could about a world that appeared to be so important.

He had asked Cosima shyly what the internet was and she had given an explanation that had left him more confused than before.

The shop that sold the computer had seemed to be nothing more nor less than an Aladdin's cave of incomprehensible magic. Ned had tried not to look astonished at the pictures on the screens, at the colour photographs printed out, at the scanners, video cameras, global positioning devices and handheld electronic diaries that were shown to him. Compact discs reminded him of an episode of *Star Trek* he had seen as a boy and the mobile phone he bought, which flipped out when he wanted to speak, put him even more firmly in mind of the Starship Enterprise. When he discovered that these telephones were more than walkie-talkies, but could actually be used to talk to any phone, mobile or otherwise in any country, he frankly gaped and Cosima and the shop assistant found it hard to suppress their giggles. He was Rip Van Winkle, awaking from a hundred-year sleep.

At the railway station overlooking the Alster, he sat in a photo-booth and had six passport photographs taken.

As he waited for the photographs to appear he murmured under his breath, 'Thank God not everything has changed. These machines, I remember well.'

It took the hotel porter two journeys to transfer all Ned's purchases from the taxi to his suite and he stood looking at the pile of shopping in the drawing-room with a look of such comical bewilderment on his face that Cosima reached up and kissed him.

'Where have you come from, Karl?'

'You mustn't call me Karl,' said Ned. 'Here I am Paul Kretschmer.'

'You have come from another planet. From heaven, perhaps?'

'From heaven?' Ned smiled. 'No, I don't think you could call it that.'

'Where then? You have never seen a computer, a mobile phone, a CD, a Palm Pilot, a video camera . . . where have you come from?'

She pulled him towards the bedroom, but he braced his legs like a mule.

'Cosima . . .'

'So. It follows that you are also probably a virgin. Don't be frightened.'

Frightened.

It struck Ned, given all that he had done in the last twenty-four hours, and the strange universe he had emerged into after eighteen years that he *should* be frightened. He should be scared by this baffling world of infra-red, satellite positioning and microwaves, scared by its gadgets and buttons and bleeps. He should be scared too by his friendless isolation in this world, scared by Gunther and, most of all, he should be terrified out of his wits by the very fearless ease with which he had been able to achieve everything he had thus far. He knew, however, that he had become someone who would never feel fear again. In the past he had been afraid because of what had happened to him. Now and in the future, he would never be a passive victim of events. Nothing would ever *happen* to him. He would make things happen to others and fear would have no place in him.

'All right,' he said following Cosima into the bedroom. 'Teach me, then. I'm a fast learner.'

The following afternoon Gunther paid a visit to the Vier Jahreszeiten and with a *ta-da* of triumph, produced from his jacket a gleaming German passport. Ned took it greedily, but before he had so much as turned the first page to look at his photograph, he had betrayed his ignorance once more.

'*Germany*? But it doesn't say which one . . .'

Gunther turned to his daughter with a look of astonishment. 'Which *one*?'

'There *is* only one Germany,' said Cosima. 'Since eighty-nine. Don't tell me you didn't know that?'

'Ah, yes . . . of course.' Ned smiled. 'I . . . er . . . I forgot for a moment.'

'Forgot?' Gunther stared at him in disbelief.

'And my last explanation of you,' sighed Cosima, 'was that you might be a lost Berliner from the East, tortured by the Stasi and only just returned to society. Now I am completely mystified.'

'Who are you?' Gunther asked. 'Who the hell are you? You're a German but you know nothing of Germany.'

'Let's just say I've been away. Does it matter? We have done business and we have helped each other. I am grateful to you both for everything.' Ned picked up a bottle of champagne. 'Tomorrow morning early, I fly to Switzerland, so let us drink to each other and part friends.'

'Here,' said Cosima, taking the bottle, 'it helps if you *twist* the cork, like so. When will you be back?'

'My plans are uncertain. Tell me, Gunther. Do you happen to have any contacts in Geneva who might be useful to me?'

'You have more to sell? If you do, believe me I would be happy to take any surplus off your hands.'

'No, no. I may need another passport, that's all.'

'You should see my friend Nikki,' said Gunther, scribbling a number on a card. 'He's a Russian, but nothing happens in Geneva without his permission.'

'Thank you.' Ned took the card and handed Gunther a glass. '*Prosit.*'

'*Prosit.*'

Cosima was inclined to be tearful as she left with her father. 'I will never see you again,' she sniffed, clinging to Ned's jacket.

'Nonsense. You have been a wonderful friend to me, of course we shall see each other again. I do not forget friends. I will call for you one day.'

'Come, my dear,' said Gunther from the doorway. 'Goodbye, Karl, Paul, whatever your name is. If you do happen across another consignment –'

'You will be the first to know,' Ned assured him.

He closed the door and leaned against it.

Outside in the corridor he heard Gunther hiss to his daughter. 'A mental patient, you mark my words.'

'Daddy, he's the sanest man either of us has ever met and you know it.'

'He can't even open a champagne bottle!'

'And what proof of lunacy is that? You can't open a pickle jar.'

'Who else could get hold of medical grade stuff like that? It all fits, I tell you.'

They continued arguing as they went around the corner towards the lifts.

Ned smiled and looked at the room and the parcels around it. He had a great deal of packing to do.

*

Ned walked into the hall of the Banque Cotter Cantonaise and smiled at the expensively pearled female cashier.

'I wonder if I might see the manager about my account?'

It was all very well for Babe to write down numbers and passwords, but how did one actually go about the business of withdrawing money from a Swiss bank? Ned was entirely prepared to be disappointed. He imagined a smooth-faced bank official staring at him with supercilious contempt.

'This account was opened thirty years ago, sir. It cannot be yours.'

'I . . . it was my father's.'

'We have no instructions from him. Do you have papers, sir? Accreditation of any kind?'

In his mind, the striped-trousered official would press a bell under his desk and Ned would be tossed onto the pavement or even sent to jail for attempted fraud. Or perhaps the British had got there first and left word with the bank.

'Sir, this account was closed down many years ago. Our security officer will now escort you to the British Consulate.'

Maybe the whole thing had all been a figment of Babe's imagination.

In the event things proved much simpler.

The cashier passed him a form and he filled in the account number. There was no space for passwords. She took the form, looked briefly down at it and, with the bang of an electric lock, disappeared into a room behind the guichet. Within a very short space of time a spruce young man, close enough to the striped-trousered official of Ned's imagination to make him smile, came through into the banking hall.

'How do you do, sir?' he said in English, extending a hand. 'Pierre Gossard. Would you like to come through?'

Ned found himself in an expensively furnished office whose main features were a Louis Quinze desk and two matching chairs. Gossard sat down behind the desk and pointed to one of the chairs.

'Just one or two formalities,' he said, tapping into the keyboard of a desktop computer which was perched incongruously on the heavily ornamented desk. 'Perhaps you would be good enough to write for me the opening password phrase?'

He passed over a compliment slip and Ned wrote down 'Simon Says' and handed the slip across the desk to Gossard who glanced at it briefly, looked at his computer screen and nodded. He passed the paper back to Ned.

'And the secondary phrase?'

Ned wrote 'This is a stick-up' and passed it over again.

Gossard smiled thinly and pushed the compliment slip into a small metal box.

'Security paper,' he explained. 'It is no more. Well, everything seems to be satisfactory, my dear sir. How may I help you?'

'Well, firstly I'd like to know how much is in my account.'

'Mm-hm . . .' Gossard typed at the computer. 'You understand that since the account is linked to leading share indices on the European bourses I can only give you the balance as from close of trading on Friday. Quite a substantial sum has accrued over the past thirty years.'

Ned nodded as if talk of share indices, bourses and substantial sums was a matter of everyday conversation to him. Gossard wrote a figure down on a fresh compliment slip and handed it to Ned who looked down.

'That's in Swiss Francs?' he said gulping slightly.

'Just so,' said Gossard.

Ned swallowed again and did a rapid calculation in his head. Roughly two and a half francs to a pound. Good heavens.

'As for what I would like to do with the account,' he said as naturally as he could manage. 'I should like a little time to think. Perhaps we can meet again on Friday? You don't need anything else from me, I take it?'

'No indeed, sir. Since your account is as old as it is, it does not fall under new disclosure rules. But it is not old enough to qualify for inspection under the recent Jewish reparation schemes.'

'Excellent,' said Ned. 'Friday morning, eleven o'clock?'

'I shall look forward to seeing you, sir.'

Ned was still trembling when he reached his suite at the Hotel D'Angleterre. He sat on the balcony sipping coffee and looking out over the lake. He watched a rainbow shimmering in the spray of the fountain.

Staring into the rainbow, Ned wept.

'Oh, Babe. Why aren't you here with me?'

He looked down at a hotel notepad on which he had jotted a set of numbers.

'It is indeed a substantial sum,' he whispered to himself, the tears dropping down onto the paper. 'Even with the price of a cup of coffee being what it is today, three hundred and twenty-four million pounds is still a substantial sum. Oh, Babe, there is such a thing as Justice. Truly there is.'

4

Simon Cotter arrived in England by private plane in the autumn of 1999. His reputation for financial adventuring preceded him.

There was not an ambitious young person in Europe who did not want to catch the attention of this remarkable buccaneer. No one rode the dot.com bubble harder, funding young, energetic and ambitious dreamers whose ventures, when floated on the European technology exchanges, made opening valuations that caused the eyes of seasoned traders to pop. Some said that the swollen, iridescent membrane of e-commerce would soon burst, but for the moment no one was soaring higher than Simon Cotter of CotterDotCom. The doomsayers insisted that the balloon was given its stratospheric lift by hot air and that the world was growing giddy with altitude sickness. The faithful maintained that the venture was fired by a true spirit of innovation and enterprise and would last beyond the lifetime of the sceptics.

Cotter was not yet forty, but the gossip had it that he owned twenty-five million for every year of his life. A website tracked his estimated fortune against the fluctuation of the markets, one day in October it showed him earning four million pounds sterling in just eight hours of trading. The Man of the Millennium had arrived and, to the excitement of the British press, he was about to make his home in England, the land – some claimed – of his birth.

He was unmarried and said to exude a magnetic appeal that had men and women alike gasping and moaning with admiration. Cynics asserted that a dead sea-slug with that kind of money and power would radiate charisma and sex-appeal. That isn't necessarily so, it was pointed out to them – look at Bill Gates. Not all that is gold, glitters.

That no one knew where Simon Cotter had come from with such indecent speed added greatly to his mystery. One moment the world was Cotter free, the next he was bigger than Harry Potter. Poems were written on that very subject, taking advantage of the happy accident of the rhyme.

The man was rumoured to be able to speak nine languages and play an unbeatable game of backgammon. The French believed that he was French, but the Germans, Italians and Austrians also claimed him for their own. The Swiss pointed to his head offices outside Geneva, not five kilometres from where the World Wide Web itself had been devised and declared Cotter to be Swisser than a yodel. Others tapped the sides of their noses and whispered gravely about the Russian mafia, Colombian cartels and other dark and dangerous corners of the world. Geneva might be the birthplace of the World Wide Web, they said, but it was also the world's financial laundromat. Where there's brass, there's muck, they said. It can't last, they said. It's brightest just before the dusk, they said.

Wiser heads were silent and disdained to take any notice of the mutter in the gutter. Talk it was that pushed prices up and talk that pulled them down again. Any fool could talk. Prattle and tattle were cheap and getting cheaper. What was this telephony revolution, with its faxes, pagers, cellular and satellite phones, email, intranets and real-time video-conferencing but a cheap and faster way to chatter and gossip and jabber? If it was more than that, then it could keep for the moment. Give us time to think, they said. We who wait on the platform may arrive later than those that jump aboard the speeding train, but we've a better chance of a good seat and a restful journey. We get there in the end, sounder in wind and limb. Only bandwagons are to be jumped upon, and bandwagons always crash at the first dangerous corner.

Cotter too kept his own counsel. His spokesmen would announce with great puff and pizzazz the latest bright young venture that CDC was funding and he might from time to time attend the launch of a favoured new dot.com enterprise in person, but the Robespierre of the Digital Revolution himself gave no interviews and threw out no theories for the world to chew over and tear apart. With his dark hair, his beard and the sunglasses that never left his face, the press had other nicknames for him too. The CyberSaviour they called him and the Jesus of Cool.

When he did, uncharacteristically, reveal to a London financial journalist at one of his company launches in

Lausanne that he would soon be coming home, England sighed with pleasure and pride. He was immediately offered tickets to the Dome for Millennial Eve, the membership of four clubs, accounts with a dozen tailors and the opportunity to be interviewed on Channel Four by Chris Evans. This last offer he turned down.

'I'm really so uninteresting,' he emailed to the producer. 'You'd be much better off with somebody else. Believe me, I'd only bore you.'

He was not believed and the crush of press waiting to meet him at Heathrow would have gratified a pop star.

Amongst the Britons who watched the footage and listened to the comment and analysis that spilled out in the media over the next few weeks were many who sat down immediately to compose letters to him, explaining their ideas for world-beating new internet sites or simply begging for money, employment or a charitable donation.

The reactions of three different individuals are of particular interest, however.

*

Ashley Barson-Garland MP, QC, had recently won the curious Commons lottery that gives the right to back-benchers to try and push their own Private Member's Bill through Parliament. Barson-Garland had been very keen to sponsor new legislation that would prove his party's commitment to the family. He knew that in the next election, whenever it came, each party would attempt to represent itself as the true champion of Family Values.

He believed that, since his party was almost certain to lose that election, he could do himself a great deal of good by making a name for himself as the Tories' most prominent spokesman for the Family Agenda. When the dust of defeat had settled and the present leader had gone, as go he must, the Tories would look to someone like Ashley to lead them to victory in 2005, which he had for so long marked down as the year that would see him installed in Downing Street.

The Bill he had drafted called for the strictest laws yet on the control of the internet. All British Service Providers would be held accountable in law for any unseemly traffic that passed through their pipelines. Barson-Garland called for an all-embracing firewall to be built around the island to keep the British family safe from the 'tide of filth' that threatened to 'engulf' the 'young and vulnerable' and other 'at-risk members of the community'. (He had long ago overcome any scruples about using clichés. They worked. For some extraordinary reason, they worked and only a fool would consider himself above their use.) Under the terms of his proposed Internet Service Providers Act, an independent agency would be set up and given the right to sweep all email randomly, much as police had the right to point speedguns at road traffic. Anyone who opposed such legislation might regard themselves as a friend of liberty, but Barson-Garland would demonstrate that in reality they were nothing less than enemies of the Family. Only those with suspect agendas or something to hide could possibly object to the purification of cyberspace.

Ordinary, decent, law-abiding citizens would welcome such a move.

He did not expect his Bill to be passed into law, Private Members' Bills almost always failed, but it was a way to plant a (patriotic) flag in the territory of family and to 'force the agenda'. The Labour government already attempted to prove its family credentials by talking of family tax credits, child income allowances and other mechanisms that provoked yawns even from those who benefited directly from them. With his Bill, Barson-Garland had staked a claim that would force New Labour to play or pay. If they opposed him, he could make great political capital of their folly.

The middle-class tabloids were already on his side. Ashley Barson-Garland's Great National Firewall appealed to the 'instincts' (as they preferred to call bigotry and prejudice) of the 'vast majority' who worried about 'bogus' asylum-seekers and 'rampant' Euro federalism. What was the internet after all, but backdoor cultural immigration of the most pernicious kind? Children (*children* for heaven's sake!) were at the mercy of homosexual propagandists, anti-capitalist rioters, drug dealers and perverts. Thank God a man like Ashley Barson-Garland was standing up to all this. His Internet Service Providers Bill, all in all, 'pressed the right buttons' and 'sent the right signals'.

This evening, this hero of ordinary decent law-abiding citizens was watching a BBC special on the 'Dot Com Phenomenon' chiefly in order to see how much of what he had said in an interview to the producers of the programme had been cut, mangled in meaning or entirely omitted. When footage of Simon Cotter appeared he laughed contemptuously at the accompanying hyperbolic journalese, but his ears pricked up at the reports that Cotter was coming home to England. He opened his laptop, keyed in his password and made an instant note in his journal.

Like Winston Churchill, I find that sometimes it is enough just to read or hear 'patriotism' 'England' or 'home' for tears to spring to my eyes. I believe that 'senile lability' is the phrase for it. In my case it seems to have come early. What a turnaround . . . as a teenager, my prick used to twitch and leak at the mere sight of words like 'youth' and 'boy'. In middle age 'family', 'hearth' and 'country' are the words that jump from the page and it is my eyes that do the twitching and leaking. Different symptoms of the same sickness, no doubt . . .

This Simon Cotter interests me. He has not nailed his colours to the mast. He thrives on enterprise and must perforce be a natural Tory, for all his hippy-happy appearance. Now that the glamour of New Labour is wearing thin he must be caught and cultivated. It is probable that he will instinctively see my bill as a threat. If I ask to see him however . . . suggest that I value his input, am anxious to consult all interested parties, canvas all views, hear all opinions, weigh all options, include not exclude, etc. etc., he may be flattered into some sort of co-operation. What a catch he would be . . .

Ashley closed the lid and looked up at the television screen once more. His Private Member's Bill was being discussed. Some lank-haired millionaire yob in a tee-shirt was accusing Barson-Garland of trying to create a sterilised intranet that would cut Britain off from the rest of the world.

'Cyberspace is like a giant city,' the scrofulous oaf insisted in vowels that made Ashley wince and an intonation that rose at the end of every sentence as if everything this poltroon said were a question. 'Along with the shopping centres, galleries, museums and libraries, it's got its slums and redlight districts. Sure. That's true in Amsterdam, New York, Paris, Berlin and London. It's not true in Riyadh, Saudi Arabia or Montgomery, Alabama. Where would we rather live, London or Riyadh? Amsterdam or Alabama? Think about it, yeah? Wherever there's freedom, you'll find sex, drugs and rock and roll. The internet's no different.'

Ashley snorted with derision. 'And wherever there are sex, drugs and rock and roll,' he said, 'you will find desolated communities, dysfunctional families and moral wastelands befouled by gibbering nonentities like you.'

He was pleased with that and added it to his diary entry for the day.

Rufus Cade let himself into the flat and flopped onto a sofa.

'I'm getting too fucking old for this,' he told himself with a heavy sigh.

He could see the answering machine light flashing and ignored it. Probably Jo, Jane or Julie moaning about money. Why couldn't he have married a girl whose name didn't begin with a J? Just for once in his life at least. Given it a try. Lucy at the office, she was a good girl. A good girl and a damned good shag and all. Zoë too. And Dawn. *They* didn't threaten him with court orders and solicitor's letters. They called him 'Roofy' and teased him about his weight. In his next life he'd run a mile before speaking to any Js. Whining bitches the lot of them. School fees, health insurance, holidays. Every child, he thought furiously as he tapped out the last of his coke onto the glass-topped coffee table, every last sodding child has to have work done on their fucking teeth. Some bastard in Soho has decided that braces are now cool and there isn't a teenager in the land without expensive multi-coloured metalwork wired across their front fucking snappers. Bollocks to the lot of them.

He picked up a newspaper. A new-laid pubescent

dot.com millionaire grinned out from the front page, acne flaring.

'Cunts,' muttered Rufus. 'How the fuck do they do it?'

Rufus had sent Michael Jackson, Madonna, Marilyn Monroe and the Prince of Wales to the launch of another new e-commerce company (e-tailers they called themselves now, ho, fucking ho) at the Business Design Centre just the week before. For some reason the people behind the launch – CotterDotCom, who bloody else? – had asked Rufus to turn up too, which had annoyed and puzzled him. He had better things to do than watch Madonna spilling wine and Michael Jackson having his hair pulled by drunken journalists. Why the hell did they want him there? He could hardly argue with them. Who pays the piper calls the tune and all that, and CDC paid better than anyone. Most people thought his agency was already over the hill (too eighties, sweetie, so *vieux chapeau*) which meant that the imprimatur of a hot shop like CDC took on special value. Rufus would have jumped naked through fiery hoops if they'd demanded it.

He had stood like a fat lemon watching his models move around the room with drinks and canapés. He listened to a presentation that bored and irritated him and he got drunk. Mind you, he did score, so it wasn't entirely a wasted morning. Come to think of it, he reminded himself, checking his watch, John should be here soon.

Weirdest thing. Just coming out of the cubicle after a nice toot and there's this big fat old guy combing his hair in the mirror.

—Got some more if you want it.

—More what? Unlikely he would be law, but better safe than sorry.

—If you're not interested, no worries. Very pure, very cheap. Try a line.

The guy hands me a wrap, just like that. Incredible. And fuck me, was it ever wild gear. Whooh! Nearly blows my fucking head off.

—How much? I ask, coming back out of the crapper, eyes watering, heart pumping like a locomotive.

—Fifty a gram.

Fifty. I mean, what? It was sixty fifteen years ago. *Fifty*. There's got to be a catch.

—Come on, man. What's the catch?

—Need you to take an ounce at a time. Got to get it off my hands.

—Look, I don't have much cash on me at the moment.

—Got a card?

—You're kidding. Thought for a second he meant a credit card. Oh, right. I give him my business card.

—*Faces?* What's that then?

—Model agency, the waiting staff out there. They're mine.

—The lookalikes?

—We call them featured stand-ins in the business.

—Yeah, right. Lookalikes. And there's me thinking that really was Prince Charles. The name's John. Give us a call.

And off he goes, leaving me with over two grams in the wrap which he doesn't even ask for back. Don't remember much more of that day, I can tell you. And next day a whole ounce for only five hundred and fifty quid. That soon went, twenty-eight grams in five days. *Thirty* grams if you include the initial freebie. You're burning the candle at both ends and the middle, Rufus.

The doorbell chimed and he got up from the sofa and went over to the entryphone.

'John.'

'Oh hi. Come on up.'

By the time John had got to the top of the stairs his face was streaked in sweat and he was wheezing like a perished accordion.

'Christ,' he gasped. 'Haven't you heard of lifts?'

'Mm, sorry about that, mate.'

The flat was on the second floor but even Rufus, flabby, overweight and unfit as he was, could usually manage it without heaving and panting like a dying walrus.

'Get you a voddie?'

'Nah, I'm driving.'

Rufus poured one for himself and watched, out of the corner of his eye, as John took a baggie from his pocket and dropped it on the coffee table.

'Chop one for yourself,' said Rufus.

'I'll love you and leave you, mate.'

Oh, such bliss. So many dealers liked to hang around. Worse still, so many stayed at home and forced you to visit. It was the part of drug life that Rufus most hated. The enforced pretence of matiness. If you want a pork chop, all you have to do is go into a butcher's shop, he reasoned. You order and walk out with the fucking thing in a bag. No chit-chat, no shit. No 'cheers mate'. Visit a dealer for a supply of charlie on the other hand, and you're in for an hour of droning views on music, sport, politics, genetically modified crops and the evils of the World Bank. A sensitive social dance had to be danced, to show that you didn't think of the guy as a servant or social inferior. You had to pretend that the whole transaction had something to do with friendship and mutual studenty Bohemian cool. It was a relief that he got none of that bullshit from John.

Still, he thought, it would be nice to see him take a line just once. Just to show that he did. Dealers who didn't use always made Rufus nervous and guilty.

'Can I ask you something?' John said as he stood in the doorway, ready to leave. He looked a little nervous.

'Sure. Ask away.'

'You don't fancy coming in with me on something bigger, do you?'

'Bigger?'

'It's my brother, see. He keeled over with a heart attack a couple of weeks ago . . .'

'Oh, bummer,' Rufus said. 'I am sorry.' And you'll soon be following him, he added to himself. Not so much a gene pool, more a lard pool.

'No, it's not that. He was a streak of fucking piss as it goes. Couldn't stand the sight of him. Only, fact is, he didn't have no family besides me and I've inherited five kilos of his bleeding gear and I don't know how to shift it. Found it in a cupboard when I was clearing his flat out.'

'John, I'd love it. Believe me, I'd love it, it's great gear but I don't deal. I wouldn't know where to begin.'

'No, what I'm saying is that I heard tell of some guys up in Stoke Newington who might be in the market. Turkish boys. Thought you could come up with me and help push it through. I'd go sixty-forty with you.'

'If you already know who these people are, why do you need me?'

'Well, I don't want to get ripped off. You, you're a businessman, you've got the public school accent and all that, touch of class. They wouldn't dare do the dirty on someone like you. Someone like me, they'd probably just take the stuff and dump me in an alley, you know what I mean?'

'Sixty-forty?'

'Yeah. Reckon that's fair.'

Rufus did some reckoning of his own. A kilo is a thousand grams. Fifty thousand quid. Five fives are twenty-five, so that's a quarter of a million. Forty per cent of quarter of a million is . . . one hundred thousand. A hundred grand. *A hundred grand.*

'You're on,' he said. 'What kind of people are they?'

'Well, they're not boy scouts. They're drug dealers, aren't they? But business is business, I reckon. How's Thursday night for you? I'll give 'em a bell and set it up. I can come and pick you up and we'll drive there together.'

They shook on the deal and, as John waddled slowly down the stairs, Rufus sat down on the sofa and breathed out long and slow. A hundred grand. A hundred fucking grand.

With a hundred grand he could set up an international agency on the web. Lookalikes, singing telegrams, party events. He could have girls and boys across the globe, hired electronically. They would pay a registration fee, he would get them work. With his hundred grand he could design a ritzy pitch, artwork, dummy website, financial projections – the works. He'd take it to CotterDotCom and blow their minds with it. Might even get to meet the great Messiah himself.

Rufus dipped the corner of a credit card into the bag and dug out the biggest bump he'd ever sniffed in his life.

Breakfast time at the Fendemans' was a confused affair that transcended age and gender expectations. Gordon ate nothing, but tried a different coffee or tea every day, Portia tucked into bacon, sausages and eggs and Albert, on the rare occasions he breakfasted at all, would eat nothing more than a slice of toast.

There were reasons for this. Albert rarely had appetite in the mornings. Anything that took him from his room and his computers he considered a waste of time. He had once spilled a cup of coffee over a USB hub and on another occasion the entire contents of a glass of orange juice had destroyed a printer. Portia, on the other hand, had discovered a new high protein diet. It was a regime that involved such a low intake of carbohydrates that she would check her urine each day with diabetic testing sticks to see how many ketones her body was leaking, much to the affectionate derision of her family. Gordon sampled different teas and coffees every day because tea and coffee constituted his trade. He usually spat the coffee out because he had inherited his father's weak heart and the specialist disapproved of him ingesting caffeine. Java the cat ate whatever was going, but preferred pilchards in tomato sauce because he was peculiar.

On this particular morning however, Gordon was making a terrific mess in the kitchen because he had decided to experiment with cocoa. The fine powder was being transferred from surface to surface and from fingertips to fingertips, which was causing panic.

'Where's my carbohydrate counter?' Portia wailed.

'Dad this stuff is getting *everywhere*,' complained Albert, coming into the kitchen and spreading his hands out in front of Gordon's face. 'Look at it. The more you try and dust it away, the more it gets ingrained into everything. I've got cocoa on my keyboard, cocoa on my screen and cocoa on my mouse.'

'Good lyrics,' said Gordon, approvingly. 'Come on, kiddo, it's only powder. Try this mocha, it's not bad.'

'Nineteen grams per hundred!' gasped Portia. 'I don't believe it.'

'No, hon,' said Gordon, peering over her shoulder and dripping mocha coffee onto the pages of her book. 'Those figures are for *sweetened* cocoa. Unsweetened is only three grams, see?'

'All the same,' said Portia crossly, pulling the book away from the drips, 'you might be more careful.'

'If you've ingested one hundredth of a milligram, I'd be amazed,' said Gordon. 'So, child of mine,' he turned to Albert, who was assiduously scrubbing his hands under the sink. 'How many hits yesterday?'

'A new record. Three hundred and twenty-eight. From seven different countries. Not bad, huh?'

'Not bad,' conceded Gordon.

'If only half of them, a *quarter* even, had placed orders, imagine how much that would be.'

'We're doing fine, Albie.'

'I'm getting emails all the time asking if we sell direct. Every time I have to say no, I feel like we're losing business.'

'Selling to the public is a nightmare,' said Gordon. 'We've got all the supermarkets, let them do the work.'

'Yeah but Dad, you've seen where they stack them. The lowest shelves, no special offers, no targeted advertising, no loyalty tie-ins, nothing.'

Portia went out to the hall to retrieve the newspapers and the post. This was an argument that she had heard a hundred times, ever since Gordon had first employed Albert to create his company website. She believed, with a wife and mother's loyalty, that they were both right. Maybe the business should embrace e-commerce, as Albert thought. But maybe Gordon had a point too when he argued against the trouble and expense of guaranteeing secure transactions on the net and the added burden of costs that accrued with advertising, shipping and the extra staff who would have to be hired to handle the whole enterprise.

Café Ethica, founded by Gordon five years ago with money inherited from Portia's mother Hillary, had become an enormous success. Gordon was the hero of students, eco-warriors, anti-capitalists and self-styled protectors of the Third World. Ethical Trading was the new big thing and Gordon's courage in leaving his well-paid job as a successful commodity broker and striking out on his own, dealing direct with peasant farmers and co-operatives from the world's poorest and most abjectly dependent cash-crop countries had transformed him into one of the country's favourite businessmen. He had appeared on *Question Time* and *Newsnight* and, if he were to become a full British subject, many believed that he would be in line for a knighthood. Portia stayed out of the business and continued to plough her own furrow in academia. Albert had once offered to write web pages for her too, but she had gracefully declined. She found it hard to believe that a site devoted to Sienese tempera would be of much service either to her or to her students.

'Pornography and a letter for you,' she said now to her son, returning with the post. 'Bills of course for us.'

Pornography was Portia's name for Albert's preferred reading matter. Almost every day a different computer or web publishing magazine would hit the doormat and he would disappear with it into his bedroom, emerging several hours later with flushed cheeks and a faraway look in his eyes. If only the magazines really were pornography, she sometimes thought, wistfully. At least sex was something that she understood. The free CDs that came with the magazines filled the house. Portia, who liked to turn her hand to anything artistic to remind herself that she wasn't just a dry professor and writer of obscure and expensive books, had created a number of amusing installations from them. There was a table whose top was constructed of nothing but America On Line give-away disks, sealed in with perspex. There were silvery mobiles and sculptures all over the house. On her desk she had a number of stacks all glued together which she used as pen holders. In the kitchen they did service as coasters and place mats.

Albert, standing by the toaster, gave a gasp when he opened his single letter.

'I don't fucking believe it,' he said, passing it to Gordon. 'No, hang on. You don't touch it till you've washed your hands. You read it first, Mum.'

Portia took the letter and held it to the window behind the sink. Presbyopia had come early to her. Too many slide shows and too much poring over too many documents in too many dark Tuscan libraries.

The letter was printed on expensive company stationery.

CotterDotCom

Dear Mr Fendeman,

Your name has come to our attention as the author and webmaster of The Café Ethica website. As you may know, our company has already acquired a unique name for excellence and innovation in the expanding world of electronic commerce. However, we are constantly looking for bright, imaginative and creative personnel to join us in our mission to continue to forge new businesses on the leading edge of the digital revolution. We believe that you may be just the kind of person we need.

If you are interested in visiting our London offices to discuss helping to set up and lead a new Ethical Trading Division, we would be delighted to talk to you about an employment package which we believe includes the most competitive share options, private health insurance, pension and bonus schemes in the field.

Your confidentiality in this matter would be appreciated.

Yours sincerely

Simon Cotter

Gordon took the letter from Portia.

'It's got to be a hoax,' he said. 'I mean, with the best will in the world, Albie, someone is pulling your bloody leg.'

'We'll see,' said Albert snatching the letter from his father's sudsy hands and going over to the telephone.

'But darling,' cried Portia. 'What about Oxford?'

Albert was too busy dialling to pay any attention.

They stood and watched as he talked nervously into the telephone. At one point he stood up straighter and Portia noticed that he was blushing slightly.

'Three o'clock?' he said. 'Absolutely. No problem. Three o'clock. I'll be there. Of course. Absolutely.'

He hung up, a dazed and ecstatic look on his face.

'Well?'

'I spoke to him! I actually spoke to him.'

'You aren't going to see him?'

'Are you insane?' Albert gave his mother a look of amazed disbelief. 'Of course I'm going to see him! You heard. Three o'clock this afternoon. In his office.'

'But you will tell him that you're going to Oxford next October, won't you? You will make it clear that you can't even think of long term employment for at least three years.'

'Bugger Oxford. I've just spoken to Simon Cotter, Mum. Simon Cotter.'

'And who's he? Mother Teresa and Albert Schweitzer all rolled into one? Your education comes first.'

'This will be my education.'

'Has he any idea how young you are?'

'Mum, there are people at CDC still awaiting their second set of teeth. There are millionaires working for Cotter with undescended testicles and training bras.'

'Well that sounds encouraging, I must say.'

'You know what I mean. I wouldn't be the youngest person there by a long way.'

'Gordon, tell him.'

Gordon had taken the letter back. Portia felt a wave of something coming from her husband that disturbed her. Was it irritation? Not *envy* surely? She was shocked to realise, once the thought had flashed across her mind, that there could be no doubt of it. It was *envy*. Something in the way his tongue flicked over his lips and his eyes darted so quickly over the letter, as if still looking for proof that it was a hoax, told her that he was, beyond question, jealous of his own son. He was annoyed, he was resentful, he was angry. No one but Portia could have detected it, but it made her stomach turn over to see it.

'Well now,' said Gordon, assuming the measured tones of a wise and objective man of the world. 'If you do go and see him, you make damned sure you don't agree to anything – *anything,* without talking it through with us first. If there's a contract we'll make sure the company lawyers see it before you even think of signing. These people can be very convincing, very plausible but none the less . . .'

'Sure Dad, sure. Jesus!' Albert flashed a smile at both his parents and skipped from the room, a slice of toast between his teeth.

Oliver Delft hated politicians. Most people profess a dislike that springs from distaste at what they perceive as the hypocrisy, double-dealing and populist vulgarity of the breed. Delft disliked them for almost opposite reasons. It was their grindingly slow moral probity and obsession with 'accountability' that maddened him. Accountability in a double sense. Their pettifogging fixation with audits, financial openness and Treasury Rules was as numbingly odious to him as their perpetual nervous glances over the shoulder towards Commons Ethical Committees, 'best practice guidelines' and investigative journalists. If a thing was to be done, then surely it should be done without qualms and scruples. Wavering and havering about morality was almost always, in Oliver's view, the least moral option. He had warned them about Kosovo, Chechnya, Nigeria, East Timor, Zimbabwe, Myanmar – he could name a dozen little local cancers that could have benefited from the quick kindness of invasive surgery but had instead swollen and flourished in the name of 'ethical foreign policy' or 'constructive engagement' – the politicians had failed to listen and paid the price.

The secret world's big secret was that it made a profit. This simple and surprising truth had saved Delft's department from even more ministerial interference than he already suffered. Secrets made money and Britain (especially now that there were no ideological factors to complicate the world and make martyrs and traitors out of intellectuals and fanatics) retained a healthy balance of payments surplus with the rest of the world when it came to her trade in the dark arts. So long as those figures stayed on the right side of the ledger, ministers could be relied upon to allow Delft a freer hand than that enjoyed by any of his successors since the Second World War. Nevertheless, as far as Oliver was concerned, any interference was too much. It is a melancholy fact that shareholders in a company that makes a fat profit are greedier in chasing down every penny than shareholders in a company that breaks even or reports a small loss. Delft had siphoned off over the years enough to guarantee him an opulent retirement, but there was always room for more. For the moment however, his rectitude was beyond question. Every pony for his daughters and every necklace for his wife was bought with honest money from his meagre public salary and dwindling inheritance. That he had made provision for a better life in the future, no one could possibly guess. He was covered. In the meantime however, his surface life continued on its dull and grinding course. Today, for example, was a day of meetings.

He weathered the fortnightly RAM committee with his usual show of patience. The Resource Allocation Module had been the bright idea of a twenty-three-year-old wunderkind from Treasury and Oliver's private contempt for the fashionable accountancy mechanisms dreamt up by such weird creatures knew no bounds. Old-fashioned double-entry book-keeping with quill and feint-margined foolscap was more secure and less easily manipulated. The RAM, however, used the latest 'input engines' and 'nominal ledgering' to model the department's financial behaviour and (more importantly) it boasted its own logo, departmental colour-coding and screensaver. This made it the darling of ministers and entirely proof of criticism.

In a moment of weakness, Oliver had agreed to lunch with Ashley Barson-Garland to talk about his wretched Private Member's Bill. They met at Mark's Club in Mayfair. The good taste of the décor and the discreet expertise of the staff ('Good afternoon, Sir Oliver.' How the hell did they know his name? He needed people like that on his payroll) settled him into a better mood and by the time he had absorbed the menu he was ready to enjoy himself despite the prospect of political company.

Ashley arrived at the upstairs bar two minutes late and spent more than five minutes apologising in what Oliver guessed with a revolted shudder was supposed to be a charming and self-deprecating manner.

Oliver found it reassuring to remind himself that he was actually some six or seven years older than the balding, jowly and unappetising creature blathering beside him. Oliver's secret vice was vanity. He had an interest in skin-care and male cosmetics that only his wife was aware of and no colleague or underling would ever have guessed at. Pomposity, ambition and bad soap had written themselves indelibly across Ashley's features, Oliver noticed, much as gin and tropical sun used to print themselves on the complexion in the grand old days of Empire. A course of humectants, exfoliating creams and cell refreshant night masks would go some way to improving general skin tone, but very little could be done to help the folds of double chin and the dull glaze over the eyes. Perhaps these are nature's way of warning us off, he thought.

'I see they've shown you a menu,' Barson-Garland said, when the tiresome story of his taxi ride from Westminster to Charles Street had finally wound to an end. 'As to wines. Shall we go Burgundian? What do you think? There's a mighty Corton Charlemagne to begin with and I happen to know they have recently added a La Tache that it would surely be madness to pass over.'

Oliver was well aware that the only La Tache on the list cost over four hundred pounds a bottle. He suspected that Barson-Garland knew that Oliver would know this. Hum, he thought to himself. Trying to impress me, are you? Trying to soften me up? You in your Old Harrovian tie and Christ Church cufflinks. Jesus God, what kind of man wears college cufflinks?

They moved downstairs from the bar to the dining-room. Barson-Garland had ordered a boiled egg crammed with Beluga caviar which he ate with repulsive elegance as he talked.

'Let me first of all assure you that I am not here to enlist your support for my Bill,' he said. 'That would be quite improper. Quite improper. However, as you may be aware, there remains a certain level of confusion about the implications of my proposals both within and without the House. There are those who cast doubt on the Bill's technical, legal and practical feasibility. It depends, as you know, upon the creation of a new body, something akin to America's National Security Agency. Our own GCHQ won't quite answer. I'm sure you agree with me there.'

Oliver moved his head in a manner that might have been interpreted as a nod.

'Quite so. My proposed agency would have considerable, even awe-inspiring powers. We already have satellites that scan the surface of our world, but I am suggesting an electronic capability that would allow us to scan, as it were, *beneath* the surface. We have the macrocosm, let us help ourselves to the microcosm. There are those who fear that I am taking, as the *Guardian* put it only this morning, one hell of a civil liberty.'

Oliver made another non-committal movement of the head. A nauseating vision arose in his head of Barson-Garland pasting his press reviews into an album and sending them to his mother.

'It seems to me,' Ashley went on, delicately pressing at the corners of his mouth with a napkin, 'that I need a trusted figure, someone of irreproachable integrity and proven expertise in the field of security, who is willing to shoulder the responsibility of building such an agency from the ground up. If it were known in the right quarters that a man of the reputation of Sir Oliver Delft might be prepared to take the job on . . .' Barson-Garland took a prim sip of wine and let the thought hang.

'I have not heard anything,' Oliver said, 'that leads me to believe that your Bill will meet with success.'

'Naturally not. The Bill will fail. That is axiomatic. We take it as read and move on. The issue will have been laid out, you see. That is the point. The possibility of government having such power within its grasp will have been propounded. The genie, as it were, will be out of the bottle. Such tedious niceties as open debate will have to, ah, take a powder.'

'I hate to remind you of this, B-G, but you are not in government. You are in opposition.'

'Oh, as to that,' Ashley waved his hand, 'while a week may be a long time in politics, a decade is but a passing breath. The Blessed Margaret already feels like a distant dream, does she not? His Toniness too will disappear into the vacuum history in a twinkling. I am sure you agree with me that it is in the interests of your service to take a longer, more strategic view. My suggestion is that you and I develop an informal relationship. Consider it as a wager on the future. I have no doubt that you have cultivated unpleasantly ambitious politicians like myself before now. You see? I have at least the virtue of self-knowledge.'

'If I were to suggest to my masters that I do favour the idea of an agency along the lines you have proposed, how would that benefit you?'

'It would benefit the *country*,' said Ashley. 'That may sound sententious, but I happen to believe it to be true.

It would also establish my credentials in the field. Opposition provides few opportunities to do more than talk. The popularity of my bill amongst some journalists and much of the public is one thing, but I need to demonstrate to my party that I am capable of treading my way around the dark and slippery corridors that people like you inhabit without coming an arser. You follow?'

'Mm,' said Oliver. 'I think I do.' Barson-Garland put him in mind of those poison toads whose heads were said to contain jewels. Ugly and dangerous, to be sure, but offering the possibility of great riches none the less if handled properly.

'There is nothing unethical about mutual advantage,' said Ashley, as if reading his thoughts. 'Quite the reverse, I should say.'

'Do you remember when we first met?' Oliver asked.

Ashley seemed a little taken aback by the question. 'Well now, let me see,' he said, twisting the stem of his wine glass and screwing up his piggy eyes. 'I pride myself on a fair memory. I fancy it may have been at the *Telegraph* Christmas party in Brooks's club. December nineteen eighty-nine.'

'No, no,' said Oliver. 'We met many years before that. You were still a schoolboy.'

A terrible image arose in Ashley's mind of furtive liaisons in Manchester public lavatories long ago. 'Really?' he said with a ghastly attempt at a smile. 'I'm not sure I quite understand. When and where might that have been?'

The dark crimson flooding Ashley's face and the flash

of fear leaping into his eyes had not escaped Oliver's attention. 'Catherine Street,' he said, watching carefully. 'You were working for Charles Maddstone. Private secretary, personal assistant, something like that.'

'Good Lord,' said Ashley. 'How clever of you to remember!'

Oliver noted the instant look of relief that replaced Ashley's initial expression of terror and wished, not for the first time, that he had the power of a J. Edgar Hoover to look more deeply into the lives of his political masters. It seemed that some dark secret lurked in Barson-Garland's childhood. Oliver wondered if he came from a background that shamed him. Those plummy patrician tones and fifteen hundred pound Savile Row pin stripes were clearly too good to be true. Of course, with a free and unfettered press the resources of an intelligence service were hardly needed. The further Barson-Garland advanced in his career the more the media would uncover for themselves.

'I am desolated that I do not recall the meeting,' Ashley said. 'Sir Charles had many political contacts of course, and I was young and inexperienced . . . wait a moment!' Ashley stared at Oliver as the truth dawned. 'I've got you now. You're Smith! Good God! Smith, you called yourself. Smith! Young as I was I never for a minute believed it was your real name, even then. I'm right, aren't I? You were Smith.'

Delft inclined his head. 'The same.'

'Dear me,' said Ashley. 'There's an odd thing. And what a bad business that was. I don't believe I've thought about it for the past – what – fifteen years? More perhaps. There wasn't anything . . .' he lowered his voice. 'There's nothing you can tell me about *l'affaire Maddstone* that didn't make the public domain, is there?'

Oliver shrugged. 'I dare say a river will be dredged one fine day and a skull dug up.'

Ashley nodded wisely. 'Poor old Ned.'

Their main courses were set down in front of them and the *sommelier* approached to offer Ashley a taste of the La Tache.

'The law is profitable, it would seem,' Oliver remarked drily. 'This poor public servant thanks you for such a heady glimpse of the high life.'

Ashley smiled. 'Tush,' he said. 'When it comes to spending money, I am a poor amateur. My wine merchant let slip last week that Simon Cotter has recently given him *carte blanche* to create the finest cellar in Europe. He has already spent over a million.'

'Lordy,' murmured Oliver.

'That's not the most amazing part of it. The man has never been seen drinking anything other than milk.'

'Milk?'

'Milk,' said Ashley. 'As a matter of fact, I am to be granted an audience with him tomorrow. If he offers *me* milk I think I may scream and go into spasm.'

'He has need of a lawyer?'

'No, no. I'm sounding him out. His political affiliations are unknown. In fact,' continued Ashley with a meaning look, 'his whole life seems to be shrouded in mystery.'

'I can't help you there, I'm afraid,' Oliver said, rightly interpreting the look as a plea for information. 'We don't have so much as his date of birth on file.'

'Ah, you've looked then?'

'Naturally we've looked. We know as much about him as you do. If anything comes up of course . . .'

Oliver was prepared to let Ashley believe that the intelligence services were at his disposal. It was, after all, perfectly possible that the Conservatives were just insane enough to elect him as their leader one day. Money would have to be spent on image consultancy, of course. Not to mention dermatological treatment. But wasn't Barson-Garland divorced? That wouldn't do. Spokesmen for the family should be happily married. No, it was nothing more than a separation, Oliver recalled, and not yet picked up on by the press. She was the daughter of an earl, if he remembered rightly. Not quite the populist touch that the Conservative Party craved these days. On the other hand, it would never do to underestimate the snobbery of the Great British Electorate. They preferred the public school and Oxford manners of a Blair to all that forced Yorkshire 'man of the people' nonsense that came from Hague. As for poor old John Major . . .

No, the tide of history had washed weirder flotsam than Barson-Garland into Downing Street and no doubt would do so again. If he succeeded in getting Simon Cotter to unbelt some of his millions and drop them in the Tory coffers Ashley would take a deal of stopping.

Oliver smiled his most charming and confiding smile.

'A superb lunch, Ashley. I don't know when I've had a better. We should do this more often.'

'Perhaps – what is today?' Ashley looked at his watch. 'Thursday. Perhaps we should meet here the first Thursday of every month? Chew things over and work our way through the wine list?'

'An admirable idea.'

'Would you like me to propose you for membership?'

Oliver put up his hands. 'Above my touch,' he said. 'Quite above my touch.'

They parted, each glowing with a warm sense of self-satisfaction and good wine.

The theme from *Mission Impossible* rang out in Jim and Micky Draper's cell. It was muffled by Micky's pillow, but loud and insistent enough to distract the brothers, who were watching *The Shawshank Redemption* and in no mood to be disturbed.

'Bollocks,' said Jim. 'Nobody calls on a Sunday afternoon. Leave it.'

The tune continued to play for a full minute before falling silent.

Tim Robbins and his fellow prisoners sipped beers on the roof of Shawshank Prison.

'Lucky bastards,' said Jim. 'I could do with a pint myself.'

'I could do with some of that sunshine,' said Micky.

Mission Impossible started up again.

'Who the fuck?'

'I'll see who it is.' Micky went to his bunk and moved the pillow aside. 'Doesn't say. Number withheld. Shall I answer the fucker?'

Jim paused the movie and Micky pressed a key on the mobile.

'Is that Mr Draper?'

'It's Micky Draper. Who wants to know?'

'Good afternoon, Micky,' said an unfamiliar male voice.

'Sorry to disturb your Sunday afternoon movie. Tim Robbins escapes and the prison governor commits suicide. Morgan Freeman finally gets his parole and joins Robbins in Mexico. Charming film. I thought you should know the outcome as I'm afraid you won't be able to watch the rest of it.'

'Who the *fuck* is this?'

'A well-wisher calling to let you know that all privileges are to be withdrawn from you and your brother as of right now.'

'Do what?'

'You and Jim are enjoying quite absurd levels of comfort and protection. It's a little unfair, don't you think?'

'Who is it?' Jim asked, turning from the screen.

'Some fucking posh nutter,' said Micky. 'Says we're going to lose our privileges.'

'Oh no,' said the voice. 'Not a nutter. Considering that I'm taking all this trouble to give you advance warning I think that's somewhat ungrateful. Prison officers will be arriving at any moment. They will take away your television, your toaster and kettle, your radio, your furniture – even the mobile phone we're having this nice little chat on. I'm afraid you're both going to have to start right at the bottom of the heap again.'

'Who is it?' repeated Jim.

'It's a fucking wind up merchant. Did Snow put you up to this?'

'It grieves me to relate that I do not have the honour of Mr Snow's acquaintance. This is all my own work. Stand by your bunk now, Micky. The screws are on their way. I have a melancholy feeling that they are in a rough mood. You and Jim have been getting a little soft and flabby lately, I do hope you can take it. Goodbye.'

Micky dropped the phone onto the bunk.

'What was all that about?'

'Some twat,' said Micky. 'His idea of a practical joke. When I find out who it was –' Micky turned towards the cell door, alarmed by the sound of metal tipped heels marching along the corridor towards their cell. 'Nah,' he said. 'That's impossible.'

'What?' repeated his brother, perplexed.

A voice shouted their names in a tone they had not heard for years and the cell door swung open.

'Draper, J., Draper, M. Stand by your bunks. *Inspection*!'

Five screws came into the cell, followed by the Senior Prison Officer, Martin Cardiff.

'Well, well. What have we here? A Babylonian orgy by the looks of it. A Babbi-fucking-lonian orgy. I have never seen such decadence in all my life. Not in all my life.' This was not strictly true, since SPO Cardiff liked nothing better of a morning than to join the brothers for a cup of coffee and a slice of toast in their cell. 'Look at this, lads. A sofa, books, magazines, a coffee machine. Even a little fridge. Highly cosy.'

'What the fuck's going on, Martin?'

Cardiff's eyes narrowed. 'Martin? *Martin*? Oh dear, oh dear. Whatever happened to courtesy? Whatever happened to respect?'

Cardiff nodded to a prison officer who stepped forward and threw a punch so deep into Jim Draper's stomach that he fell to the ground whooping for breath.

'It's *Mr* Cardiff to you, you fat cunt. You fat *disgusting* cunt,' he added with distaste, as Jim vomited over himself.

Micky started towards Cardiff. 'What did you do that for? What the fuck d'you do that for?'

This time Cardiff administered the blow himself, driving his fist into the side of Micky's neck. The iron frame of the bunk rang as Micky crashed into it head first.

'There's the bell for Round Two,' said Cardiff. 'Time for a bit of tag wrestling, lads.'

The prison officers laughed as they moved in on the brothers and set to work.

An hour later Jim and Micky were lying naked on the floor of their empty cell. The screws had taken everything, even the bunk-bed and mattresses. Before slamming the door on the brothers they had hosed the cell to wash away the blood and vomit.

For five years, Jim and Micky Draper had ruled the prison. Nothing had moved, nothing had worked and nothing had been traded without their say-so. The arrangement, as usual, had suited the governor and his staff admirably and they had repaid the Drapers in the usual way, by allowing them levels of comfort and autonomy that were denied the ordinary inmate. Now, suddenly and for no reason at all this had been taken away from them. The occupants of the neighbouring cells would have heard their weeping screams for mercy and their plight would already be known all over the prison. Power depends on strength and the appearance of impregnability. Many prisoners had cause to hate the Drapers and now that all support and protection had been withdrawn from them, their lives would be horribly different.

Jim raised his head. The posters had been taken from the wall and all he could see were smears of blood and buttons of blu-tak. His brother lay on the floor beside him.

'Micky?' he whispered, the effort shooting arrows of pain all around his body. 'On the phone. Who the fuck was it?'

But Micky was unconscious.

Jim's head dropped back to the floor and he tried to focus his thoughts. They would be out in a year, but it would be twelve months of fear and pain. From this moment on they were in hell. Jim consoled himself with one thought. The Drapers held one advantage over ordinary people, an edge that had helped them and given them strength throughout their troubled and violent lives. They had each other.

'I think they should be separated as soon as possible,' said Simon Cotter.

'Different cells, you mean?'

'Perhaps different wings. Would that be a possibility?'

'Consider it done, sir.'

Cotter put a hand over the phone and apologetically shrugged his shoulders at the boy who had just come into his office. 'With you in a moment,' he said. 'Just got to get this sorted out.'

Taking this to mean that he should leave, Albert turned towards the door.

'No, no. Stay. Sit down, sit down.'

'Sir?'

'Not you, Cardiff.'

'Is there a problem talking, sir?'

'No, no, not at all. How are our friends this morning?'

'Well, sir, Micky was out for eighteen hours, but he's conscious now. They'll both be taking food by straw for a month.'

'Oh that *is* good news. Well done.'

'Er . . .'

'Say on, Mr Cardiff.'

'I think you might have accidentally overpaid me, sir.'

'How very honest of you. Not an overpayment, Mr Cardiff. Appreciation of a job well done. Your email was most marvellously and entertainingly composed. Quite beyond the call of duty. You should consider a literary career, you know.'

'Well, thank you very much indeed, sir. Very kind indeed.'

'Goodbye then.' Cotter put down the phone and smiled across the desk. It had amused him to notice that the boy had been studying the carpet with great concentration, as if to imply that by not looking at the telephone he had not been listening. Quite illogical, but human and most charmingly polite. 'So sorry about that. What a pleasure to meet you. I'm Simon Cotter.'

Albert stood up to shake hands across the desk.

'No, no. I'll come round. We're not very desky here. They are tables to put computers and phones on, not for talking across.'

They shook hands and Simon led Albert to the corner of the office.

'Now then,' Simon sat down in an armchair and pointed Albert to the sofa opposite him. 'I said in my letter how much I admired the work you have done for your father's company. Quite brilliant. I nearly said "for an amateur", but we are all amateurs at this game and your work was brilliant I think by any standards.'

'Amateur is the French for "lover", after all,' said Albert, shyly. 'And it was very much a labour of love.'

'Good for you! What I didn't say in my letter was that

I think Café Ethica is one of the great achievements of the last few years. Your father must be a remarkable man.'

Albert's face lit up. 'He is, he really is! He used to work in commodities, trading tea and coffee futures in the City, but he went out there to Africa once and saw how the people lived and it completely changed his outlook. He now says, it's not about coffee futures, it's about human futures.'

'Human futures, yes . . . very good. Human futures. How does he feel, I wonder, about the possibility of you joining us here?'

'Well, since the website has been rather a success, I think he imagined that after university I would, you know . . .' Albert trailed off and looked towards Cotter, who nodded sympathetically.

'He thought you might go into the business with him? Look after the cyber side of life.'

Albert nodded. 'And my mother . . .'

Simon moved a hand down to his knee and pressed it down to stop a slight involuntary jogging motion that had started up. 'Your mother,' he said, lightly. 'She's the famous Professor Fendeman, is she not? I have read her books.'

'I think she's worried about me not getting a degree.'

'Naturally. Any mother would be. You're due to go up to Oxford – how very modest of you not to mention it by name, by the way – in October of next year, I believe. Which college?'

'St Mark's.'

'Any reason for that choice?'

'My mother always said it was the best.'

'Hm . . . St Mark's, that's the one with the famous Maddstone Quad, isn't it?'

'I think so, yes.'

'Very quaint as I remember.'

'My mother's always wanted me to go there. Doesn't like the idea of me missing out on an education.'

'I think she's absolutely right,' said Cotter. 'I agree with her completely.'

The disappointment in Albert's face was pitiful to behold. 'Oh . . .'

'But,' Cotter continued. 'I don't like the idea of missing out on *you*. There's ten months or so until October. Why don't we come to an arrangement? Join us now and if in that ten months you and your family still feel that Oxford is a good idea, you can go. We'll still be here when you emerge, all qualified and polished and graduated in your cap and gown. After all, you can carry on working for us in your vacations, and if you've done as well here as I think you will, we might even consider paying you a retainer, a kind of scholarship, if you like. As it happens we're looking at endowing a chair in IT at Oxford at the moment, so I think the university will be disposed to look favourably on anything we might suggest. Like all ancient and venerable English institutions Oxford will roll over backwards and do all kinds of undignified somersaults if there's a smell of money in the air. How does that sound to you?'

'It sounds . . . it sounds . . .' Albert searched hopelessly for a word. 'It sounds brilliant.'

'I'll talk to my legal department about drawing up a contract. I like doing things quickly, if you've no objection. Let's suppose a draft is delivered to you by five o'clock this evening. Your parents will want to show it to a lawyer. Perhaps you will have come to a decision by Friday? Come to me when it's all been thoroughly thought through.'

Albert looked behind Cotter's shoulder. A projector beamed the phrase 'Thoroughly thought through' onto the wall.

'Ah, you'd spotted it. My motto. You'll find it everywhere. On our screensavers and our desktop wallpaper.' Cotter rose from his armchair and Albert instantly leapt to his feet.

'Mr Cotter, I don't know what to say.'

'It's Simon. We're very informal here. No suits, no surnames.' Cotter put an arm round Albert's shoulder and walked him to the door. 'And by a happy coincidence, you'll find that we only serve Café Ethica coffees and teas. Now, you'll have to excuse me. Things are getting rather busy. I'm in the middle of trying to buy a newspaper. You've no idea how complicated a process it's turning out to be.'

'Really? I do it every day,' said Albert, surprised at his own daring. 'You just hand over money to the man in the shop and . . . *voilà*!'

'Ha!' Simon punched him playfully on the arm. 'All this and a sense of humour too!' How like his mother, he thought to himself. How absurdly like his mother. 'I wish it were really that simple,' he added. 'I almost find myself feeling sorry for the Murdochs of this world. It's nothing fancy, just the old *LEP*, but none the less, the regulations . . .'

'*LEP?*'

'*London Evening Press*. Way before you were born. But it's about time the *Standard* had a rival, don't you think? You never know, we might even start you on a column. Anyway, I look forward to hearing from you some time before Friday.'

Crossing Waterloo Bridge on his way to the restaurant where Gordon and Portia would be awaiting him, Albert looked back towards the great glass tower that he had just left. He was not a superstitious or a religious youth, but he could not help wondering what power or deity had blessed him with such outrageous good fortune. Like all seventeen-year-olds his sense of guilt was greater than his sense of pride and as a rule if he expected anything from fate it was more likely to be punishment than reward. Four and a half years ago, during his barmitzvah, he had mentally crossed his fingers and thought scabrous blasphemous thoughts throughout the ceremony. For weeks afterwards he had been in dread of God's revenge. None had come. God had expressed his wrath by giving him good friends, sound health and kindly parents. To crown it all he was now to become a favourite in the Court of King Cotter.

He strode up the stone stairs of Christopher's two at a time. Portia and Gordon, nervously sipping mineral water at their table, didn't see him enter. He stopped a passing waiter and smiled broadly.

'Could you bring a bottle of champagne to that table over there? The best you've got.'

'Certainly, sir.' The waiter bowed and hurried away.

'Darling!' Portia beckoned him over. 'How was it? How did it go?'

'Blimey, where do I start?'

Feeling absurdly adult, Albert sat down at the table and told them of Simon Cotter's plans.

'So you see, it's the best of both worlds,' he said. 'Is that brilliant or what?'

A waiter approached their table with an ice-bucket and a bottle of Cristal.

Gordon had been staring down at his cutlery with furrowed brows as if listening for a catch somewhere in Albert's breathless recitation. He looked up now at the waiter. 'What's this? I ordered no champagne.'

'Er, that was me actually, Dad. I'll pay you back for it soon, I promise.'

Portia squeezed Albert's hand. 'Quite right too,' she said, looking anxiously at Gordon. 'This definitely calls for a celebration, don't you think, darling?'

Albert caught the pleading note in his mother's voice and leaned forward to add his own encouragement.

'Dad, I know it's all moving very quickly, but it's just *great* don't you think? I mean, I can't lose either way.'

Gordon smiled suddenly and put a hand to Albert's shoulder. 'Of course it's great, Albie. My years in the City have made me cautious, that's all. I'm sure everything's fine. I'm proud of you. Truly.'

'He said . . .' Albert blushed slightly, 'he said that he thought you were a remarkable man, Dad.'

'Did he? Is that so? Well, he's a remarkable man himself.'

'He's buying a paper at the moment, did you know that? The *London Evening Press*.'

'Are you sure? There's been nothing about it in the financial pages.'

'Absolutely. He said it was a complicated business but it was time the *Standard* had some competition. He's endowing a chair at Oxford too.'

'Never mind about all that,' said Portia. 'Tell me what sort of man he is. Did he take his sunglasses off at any time? Do you think he's Jewish? From pictures he looks impossibly dark and handsome. Does he dye his hair, do you think?'

'For God's sake, Mum . . .' Gordon and Albert caught each other's eyes and laughed with male solidarity.

'Well, these things are important,' Portia said defensively. 'They tell you a lot about a person.'

'He's read all your books anyway. He said so. What does *that* tell you about him?'

Father and son laughed again at Portia's flustered reaction.

'Let us drink to this paragon of taste and judgement,' said Gordon, raising his glass.

'To Simon Cotter,' they chorused.

Rufus Cade sat in his flat and gazed lovingly at the money piled up in front of him. He had counted it twice and was considering counting it for a third time. Counting out a hundred thousand in used twenty pound notes is quite a task, but when the money is your own and wholly exempt from the ravenous clutches of tax men and ex-wives it is a pleasurable enough way to pass the time.

Rufus chopped a line on the small amount of free space on his coffee table. Finally, *finally*, things had taken a turn for the better. This evening was to be his last as a user. All those twenty pound notes were going to be put to good use. He would transform the business, settle down with a girl whose name didn't begin with J and move to the country. Clean air, healthy exercise and a good diet would transform him from the flabby, sweating, red-eyed pig he had got to know into someone he could truly love. He realised now, as he looked at the money, that throughout his wretched life he had never even so much as liked himself. He would start by thinking more of others. Wasn't that 'the road less travelled'? The true path to self love is to take baby steps towards others.

To be able to go early into the office, with a clear sober head, that would be something in itself. There would be a special buzz to be got from sobriety, an irreducible high that would never lead to a terrible low. His cheerfulness and humour would become a byword. He had the weekend to begin the business of cleaning himself up. He would start any minute by throwing away his shot glasses and his silver straw. He might even drive round to see his parents. He played out the scene. His mother's pleasure at seeing him, a bunch of flowers under his arm and a teasing joke on his lips, sprang to life within him and he smiled the broadest smile he had smiled for many years. He wasn't such a bad man. He had a dry humour and quiet companionability that had appealed enough to turn three women into wives and countless others into girlfriends.

The entryphone buzzer sounded on the wall behind him and his heart banged in his chest at such a violent intrusion of the rude world into his thoughts. He rose from the sofa and was surprised to hear his voice trembling as he picked up the receiver.

'Who is it?'

A voice he did not recognise spoke into the intercom with exaggerated intonation above the passing roar of traffic from the street. 'I am a friend of John's. It's very important that I speak to you.'

Rufus turned and looked at the money heaped on his table. 'It's not very convenient at the moment,' he said. 'I'm . . . I'm expecting some people.'

'I won't take more than five minutes. It's for your own security.'

'Okay then . . . second floor.'

Rufus pressed the buzzer and ran to the kitchen for a bin liner. He stuffed the money into the bag and threw it into the corner of the room behind an armchair. By the time a knock came on the door, sweat was running down his face and he was out of breath.

He ran a sleeve across his dripping forehead and opened the flat door. A tall, powerfully built man of indeterminate age stood there, smiling apologetically, his eyes hidden by mirror shades.

'I do apologise for calling so late.'

'No, no . . . come in. I was just . . . you know.'

The man came in and stood in the centre of the sitting-room. Rufus stared at him in disbelief.

'Wait a minute . . . don't I know you?'

'The name's Cotter. Simon Cotter.'

Rufus was already dizzy with the exertion of hiding his money. The presence of such a man as Simon Cotter on his doormat confused him completely. He could only imagine that there had been some problem with his looka-likes the day of that launch in Islington. But why on earth would Cotter himself come to visit him at home. On a Friday night, to boot. 'I don't quite follow. You said you were a friend of John's.'

'That's right,' said Cotter. 'I've come to warn you.'

'Warn me?'

'The Suleiman brothers are rather upset.'

Rufus blinked. 'I'm sorry. Suleiman brothers? I don't believe I know anyone of that name.'

'You sold them a consignment of cocaine for a great deal of money. Only a few ounces of it were genuine. The rest was sherbet, I'm afraid. They are not in the least bit happy. Sherbet retails in sweetshops for a pitifully low price, I believe. Pitifully low. They'll be wanting their money back. They may well want some pieces of your body to go with it. To be perfectly frank with you, they aren't very nice people.'

Rufus had trouble focusing. Sweat was stinging his eyes. 'I haven't the faintest idea what you're talking about,' he said in a voice that he recognised as absurdly tremulous and far too high in register to carry conviction.

'Really?' Cotter's eyebrows shot up. 'Then I'm wasting your time as well as my own. I thought you might want to understand what was going on.'

'Well, of course I want to know what's going on, but . . .'

'You've sold a dud and the vendor is coming for revenge. It's really as simple as that.'

'But it was *John's* gear! John set the whole thing up. I only went along as . . .'

'Ah, but John has been rather clever. I happen to know, you see, that he told them that all along *he* had been acting for *you*. As far as the Suleimans are concerned John is a nobody. A bagman, nothing more.'

'But that's a lie!' Rufus grabbed the lapels of Cotter's suit. 'You've got to tell them. Tell them I acted in good faith. They'll listen to you. In good faith.'

'*I?*' With the ease of a man brushing flies from his coat, Cotter took Rufus's hands by the wrists and pulled them down. 'Why in the name of God's green earth should I do the slightest thing to help you?'

'You know what happened! You can set them straight.'

Cotter looked at his watch. 'They will be here in no more than five minutes. I left the front door on the latch. It's a pity that you don't seem to be in any kind of shape. I believe they favour machetes.'

Rufus almost danced with terror and bewilderment. 'You can't be serious. This is England.'

Cotter looked at him in amusement. 'Yes,' he said. 'This is England. And you are English. Wipe your face, stop snivelling and put up a good show, that's my advice. They may spare your life, you never know. The sight of you snotty, sweaty, dribbling and whimpering will only bring out their fullest rage, you can be sure of that. Believe me. I know something about bullies.'

Rufus edged towards the corner of the room, possessed with the wild idea of grabbing the rubbish sack and making a run for it.

'Ah, you've stashed it over there, have you?' Cotter peered behind the armchair. 'Well at least they won't have to look very hard for it. That may count in your favour.'

'For pity's sake,' cried Rufus.

'For *pity's* sake?' Cotter's voice was hard and cold. 'Did you just use the word pity?'

'You can have the money. Take it all.'

'My dear Cade, I already have more money than I could possibly spend. Don't you read the newspapers?'

'Then let me go. Protect me. Pay them off, I'll do anything, anything you say.'

'Anything? Do you mean that?'

'I promise!' Something in Cotter's voice lent Rufus hope. 'Just tell me and I'll do it.'

'Very well. Sit down.'

Rufus obeyed instantly. Sweat and mucus dropped from his chin onto the sofa. It had been many years since Cotter had last seen a grown man tremble so violently. His face, his hands, his feet – every part of him quivered.

'What do you want me to do? Tell me and I'll do it.'

'I want you to build me a time machine.'

'*What?*'

'I want you to build me a time machine and to go back twenty years into the past.'

'I – I don't understand.'

'Really? Yet it's so simple,' said Cotter. 'And it's the only thing that will save you. All I want you to do is to go back to the day when you, Ashley Barson-Garland and Gordon Fendeman planned the destruction of my life. Go back and rewind the tape. Reverse your decision.'

Rufus turned dazed eyes on him. He was hallucinating. On the very day he had determined to give up coke, the drug had visited upon him some insane psychotic nightmare.

'You don't remember?' Cotter went on, removing his sunglasses and staring him in the face. 'You don't remember planting dope in the pocket of my sailing jacket? You don't remember standing in an alleyway in Knightsbridge giggling as they led me away? Go back and make it all unhappen. Do that for me and I'll pay off the Suleiman brothers and more. I will set you up in idle luxury for the rest of your pitiful and disgusting life.'

'*Ned*? Ned Maddstone?' Rufus leapt up from the sofa. 'Jesus, it *is*. It's you. I don't fucking believe it.'

'But somehow I don't think it can be done, can it? I know a little about physics and a little about technology. Something tells me that a time machine is wholly beyond your powers to invent.'

'Christ, man, where have you been? What *happened* to you?'

'Get away from me,' Cotter took a step backwards as Rufus once more clawed desperately at his jacket. 'How dare you even think of touching me?'

'This is a joke, right? You're winding me up. It's your idea of revenge. To get me shit scared. Fucking hell, man . . .'

'You'll find out about shit scared,' said Cotter. 'You'll discover that it's more than a phrase. You'll find out too that there's something worse than fear. Something called dread.'

'You're not serious,' Rufus almost laughed at the look on Cotter's face. 'I mean come on, we were *kids*! We didn't know what we were doing. Anyway, you were *kidnapped*, it was in all the papers. That was nothing to do with us. Jesus, man . . .'

'My father died. My *father*. He clung on for six months unable to speak or move. He died in an agony of fear and guilt, believing that his only son had been kidnapped and killed because of him and his work. An honourable, decent man who gave everything he had to his country. A man incomparably above you in quality and greatness. He died because of what you and your friends did to me.'

Rufus looked round in terror at the sound of car brakes squealing in the street below. Cotter moved towards the door and replaced his sunglasses.

'I just want you to think of me as they start work on you. I want you to think of a frightened and bewildered child who had everything taken away from him because of your spite and envy.'

Rufus had scrambled behind the armchair and stood now in the middle of the floor clutching his money.

'They know about the fire-escape,' said Cotter. 'They are certain to have it covered.'

'NED!' screamed Rufus.

Cotter let himself out of the door.

'MADDSTONE!'

Cotter went quickly up one flight of stairs and looked down the stairwell as three men came running up to the second floor. He saw a flash of bright silver as one of them transferred a gleaming metal knife from one hand to the other. Inside the flat he heard Rufus still screaming his name, over and over again.

The door slammed shut and all screaming stopped.

Five minutes later the door to the flat opened and the three men emerged. One carrying a black bin liner. They said nothing as they descended the staircase.

Simon waited for the sound of their car being driven away before he crept down and entered the flat.

Rufus was lying on the floor in a spreading pool of blood that had already reached the extreme edges of the carpet. On the coffee table ten feet away from him, his legs had been neatly laid, one beside the other, like bouquets recently delivered by a florist.

'Dear me,' said Simon. 'Legless again, Rufus.'

Rufus stared up at him. 'Fuck you,' he hissed. 'Fuck you to hell.'

Simon looked down and shook his head, 'Phew!' he said with distaste. 'I was right wasn't I? Now you *do* know the meaning of shit scared. I pity the person who finds you. Let's see, your cleaner comes on Monday, I believe. Maybe I should spare her sensibilities and warn the police. An anonymous tip-off perhaps . . . you're an expert in those, aren't you? As a matter of fact you're very lucky, do you know that? They say that it is quite pleasant to bleed to death. I dare say you won't be feeling much pain. The effects of shock can be merciful. Not a word I have much use for, of course.'

As he left, Rufus shouted after him. His voice came out huskily and over the next hour, as the life flowed out of him, he tried to console himself with the thought that Simon must have heard every word.

'I was right about you from the first, Ned fucking Maddstone,' he had called after him. 'You were always an arrogant fucker. I saw through you from the very beginning!

Fuck you, Ned. Fuck you. You deserved it. Whatever it was, you deserved it.'

Simon flicked out the latch and closed the door, leaning against it until the lock snicked home. Rufus's words had not, in fact, penetrated the hammering in his own ears. He went slowly downstairs and out into the cold air.

Ned, trembling with exhilaration, looked up at the night sky. The stars winked down at him.

'Four!' he whispered, and winked back.

The Barson-Garland Page was turning out to be something of a *succès d'estime*. Taking a cue from the regular columnists on the rival evening paper, Ashley found that he had a gift for tediously obvious opinions expressed in a formulaic polemical style that exactly suited the kind of brain-fagged commuter most ready to confuse polysyllabic misanthropy for intelligent thought. London's appetite for trenchant attacks on 'Political Correctness' seemed to know no bounds and Ashley was happy to feed it. He had in abundance that peculiar journalistic gift of stating all the prevailing bourgeois prejudices in a language that represented itself as 'maverick', 'daring' and 'unconventional'. Nor had the heroic failure of his Private Member's Bill done anything to harm his growing reputation as one who dared to speak up for 'Common Sense', 'Decency', 'Standards' and the deeper feelings of the 'Silent Majority' and his beloved 'Instincts of the British People'. Whispers were growing within the Party. Barson-Garland was achieving more for the Conservatives from the backbenches than leading figures were managing from the front. His name had been openly mentioned by the BBC's senior political correspondent as a contender in any future leadership election. Things were moving along well.

Simon Cotter had not been able to help him with his Bill, but had expressed his sympathy in an orotund style very like Ashley's own.

'I have no doubt that governmental access to net traffic is ultimately inevitable,' he had agreed. 'The imperatives of financial security, public morals and systemic virus protection will make the idea irresistible in time. I cannot be seen to endorse it, however. I'm sure you understand that for commercial reasons I must place myself on the side of the civil libertarians. When the time does come, I suspect that you will play some part in its implementation and I want to assure you that you will have our full co-operation here at CDC. In the meantime, I wonder if I can talk to you about something else? As you may know, we have recently acquired the *London Evening Press*. My editor is on the lookout for a good regular columnist. Does the idea appeal?'

The idea – and Cotter's elegant (to Ashley's mind) manner of phrasing it – had appealed greatly and Barson-Garland had waxed great. On the back of his new found success as a Common Sense Tribune of the People, he had recently embarked upon a series of live television debates. Armed with a microphone and a bank of experts, victims and unbelievers, he stalked the studio like a grand inquisitor, probing moral and ethical issues to their depths: a Great White Oprah, an intellectual Jerry Springer, a Moral Montel for the New Millennium.

The first programme, under the title of 'The Failure of Feminism' had gone exceptionally well and he was currently preparing the next. His producer had told him that it was essential, in television, to put your heaviest artillery in the second programme in a series.

'If the first is good,' she had said, 'the second must be better. Those who missed the opening episode will have been told about it by their friends or read reviews in the papers. They will tune in to number two in their droves, so let's make it a stormer.'

It was to be entitled 'The Threat of the Net' and a stormer it would certainly be. Parents whose children had run up impossible phone bills or had met unsavoury perverts through chat room friendships, musicians whose royalties had been threatened – all had been lined up and were ready to accuse the defenders of the net, the authors of software that allowed mass music copyright infringement, the service providers who failed to filter repulsive news groups, the credit card companies, the irresponsible online medical services, the whole internet establishment. One of the programme's researchers had built a bomb by using information readily available on the web, another had bought drugs and yet another – and this would surely constitute one of the most sensational exposés in television history – had been posing as a twelve-year-old for six months and was planning, live, to meet another apparent minor whom the programme had deduced (by linguistic analysis) to be an adult. A hidden camera would record the whole scene and police were standing by to make an arrest.

On the day of transmission, Ashley appeared to be the

only one with a cool head. A group of parents had found themselves having supper in the studio canteen next to a man whose laptop displayed repulsive photographs of dead bodies and mutilated limbs. The parents had screamed and accused the producers of insensitivity, stupidity and deliberate manipulative wickedness. Ruffled feathers were smoothed when it turned out that the offending laptop belonged to a reporter who was researching Angolan landmines for a completely unconnected programme. The reporter in question, who had gone off to join the supper queue, was severely reprimanded for leaving his computer unattended. The father of the child who had opened the laptop was persuaded against legal action and relative calm was restored.

By the time Ashley made his opening address, the studio was crackling with tension.

'Cyberspace, the final frontier . . .' he began, standing in the centre of the studio. 'We have sought out new worlds and new civilisations. We have boldly gone where no man has gone before and what has been our reward? An explosion in crime, gambling, pornography, exploitation, video-gaming and vice – a good old-fashioned word for a bad old-fashioned evil. No laws stand between a seven-year-old child and the corruption of his innocence. We are told nothing can be done about this. Is that true? Is there no such thing as political will? Are we already victims of the machine? Or is it just possible that humanity, as it always has, still retains the power to say No? Is it too late to decide simply to walk away?

'Against the anarchy and degradation represented by the slimier corners of the net stands one institution: ancient, kindly, wise, noble, but apparently powerless in the face of man's lust for technology . . . we call this institution The Family. What a pitifully small thing it seems when ranged against the colossal vested interests and unquenchable greed of e-commerce and the great e-future. Is it possible that the still, small voice of the Family can stand up to such howling din? Can the British Family truly resist . . . The Threat of The Net?'

Music. Applause. Titles. A collage of images showing Ashley Barson-Garland, bald, unprepossessing, ugly even, but somehow made glorious by his very ordinariness. He stands, he swoops, he glides, he bobs his way through ranks of admiring studio guests. There are stand-up rows and tearful reconciliations. The face of Barson-Garland stands above them all. The final image: his summing-up, directly into camera, his eyes holding yours as he weaves together the threads of the week's debate. End music. End titles. End applause.

A double-sided plasma wide-screen television was hung high in CotterDotCom's atrium. The atrium café, as usual, was busy. At eight in the evening most offices are the lonely province of security guards, cleaners and a handful of career climbers. Simon Cotter found that often he had to remind his staff, gently, to go home and help themselves to a life. He was there himself in the atrium that night, laughing with the others at Barson-Garland's introductory speech.

'Dear me,' he said, peering over the top of his sunglasses as the title sequence played. 'It seems that the net is in for a spanking, guys.'

'He talks,' said Albert Fendeman, who was sitting at the same table, 'as if everyone who has anything to do with the net comes from another planet. I mean, we've all got families too. Doesn't he realise that?'

'It's hard to imagine that *he* has a family, anyway,' observed an intense young girl standing by their table and looking up at the screen with distaste.

'Actually,' said Albert sheepishly, 'he's an old friend of *my* family.'

'Really?' Simon was intrigued. 'We should be polite about him then.'

'Christ no, I never *liked* him. He always spoke to me like a schoolmaster, even when I was young.'

'And you're so old now, of course,' said the girl, who was one of the best programmers in the country, but barely twenty herself.

'Sh!' hissed someone from another table. 'There's Brad Messiter.'

Barson-Garland was standing in front of a guest known to everyone at Cotters. Brad Messiter had founded the fastest growing free Internet Service Provider in the country and Ashley was preparing to roast him whole.

'You advertise during children's television programmes and in children's magazines. Your give-away CDs are available on sweetshop counters, packaged with cartoons and the faces of football stars. Yet your service offers no filters and no parental lock-outs . . .'

'Parents can buy fully functional gatekeeper packages which . . .' the hapless Messiter began, but Ashley swept on regardless.

'You'll get your chance to speak later. For the moment let's just set out what you do. You offer a full internet package, including unrestricted access to newsgroups of the most revolting kind. We're all familiar with commercial websites, many of which, it's true, are guarded by some kind of credit card security. But newsgroups offer pictures and movies to anyone. *Anyone*. Let me run by some of the groups a child on your service might come across without the need for anything other than a personal computer and infant curiosity. Alt.binary.pictures. bestiality, alt.binary.pictures.lolita, alt.binary. pictures.foreskins . . . and there are literally hundreds of others here that are too grotesque, too bizarre and too horrifying for me to mention on air. This is the nature of the business that has made you a millionaire many times over. True or not true, Mr Messiter?'

'There are thousands of magazines and photographs currently in the postal system . . .'

'True or not true, Mr Messiter?'

'Currently being processed by the Royal Mail, technically the property of the Queen, which you would find just as offensive and which . . .'

'True or not true, Mr Messiter?'

'True or not true!' chorused the studio audience. 'True or not true?'

'Yes, it's true, but as I say . . .'

'It's true!' Ashley whipped the microphone away and walked towards the camera. 'Mr Messiter's twisted logic would have us believe that Her Majesty the Queen is somehow a pornographer, which tells us all we need to know about Mr Messiter, I think. We'll be returning to him later, but meanwhile, let's follow our researcher, Jamie Ross. For six months now, in the guise of twelve-year-old Lucy, Jamie has been conducting a romantic relationship with a boy of thirteen called Tom. Innocent, charming, perfectly acceptable. Nothing more than a pen friendship. Tom has now suggested they meet. Our language experts have analysed the emails and messages that Tom has been sending Lucy and they have determined that they were composed by an educated adult. Jamie.'

The Cotter Atrium watched with barely suppressed giggles as an earnest reporter stood on the corner of Argyll Street and Marlborough Street talking in a hushed whisper. A small girl stood nervously beside him.

'Any moment now, I will be going into Wisenheimer's, a hamburger restaurant popular with young people, just fifty yards from London's famous Oxford Circus, for an assignation with "Tom". He will be expecting a small girl, so I have brought along my daughter, Zoë. In my rucksack I have a hidden camera and sound recorder. The police are standing by to make an arrest if it turns out, as we strongly suspect, that "Tom" is an adult, masquerading as a child. Here goes.'

A grainy but acceptable picture came on screen as the reporter, Jamie Ross, entered the restaurant and sat at a table, pointing his wide angled briefcase at the door. His daughter Zoë came in a second or two later and sat at another table.

'So far,' breathed Jamie into his radio mike. 'Nothing. Mostly young people here, tourists by the look of them, a few adults spread out at different tables. The ideal spot for this kind of rendezvous perhaps. Ah, what's this?'

A small nervous looking boy of twelve or thirteen had entered the restaurant, taken one look at Zoë, another at the table where Jamie sat with his camera bag and then sat down at an empty table.

'Well, perhaps, our experts were wrong,' the disappointment in Jamie's voice was palpable.

'Experts? Wrong?' The crowd gathered in the Cotter atrium were enjoying themselves hugely. 'Surely not?'

'Perhaps I should ask him what he's doing there . . .' Jamie picked up his camera bag and moved towards the young boy. 'Hello, there,' he said, placing the bag on the table between them. 'Your name isn't Tom by any chance?'

The boy made no verbal reply but stood up and pointed.

Instantly, from different tables, half a dozen men and women sprang forward and surrounded the astonished Jamie.

'You are under arrest,' said one, attaching handcuffs, 'on suspicion of luring a minor . . .'

'Wait a minute, I'm Jamie Ross from the BBC . . .'

'You do not have to say anything in your defence, but I must warn you that silence may be interpreted . . .'

The screen went blank for a second before cutting back to the studio and a rather flustered Ashley Barson-Garland.

'Well,' he said. 'It looks as though . . . that is to say . . .'

In the CDC atrium, Albert and the female coder were rolling around honking with laughter like seals.

'Sh!' said Cotter. 'Let's not miss the rest of it.'

'It seems that perhaps this was a case of two minds with but a single thought,' Ashley continued, drawing on all his reserves of aplomb, 'two hearts, ah, beating each to each.'

'*What?*' roared Albert, writhing with delight. 'Has he gone completely *tonto?*'

'Robert Browning,' said Simon. 'When the mind goes, reflex literary quotation takes over.'

'But none the less, a lesson to be drawn there. The world of the chat room clearly arouses enough parental concern to cause a great deal of worry. We will bring you, of course, news of Jamie Ross's release as soon as it comes.'

'Who's looking after Zoë?'

'Ah, well no doubt . . .' Ashley looked up at the bank of studio audience to identify the heckler. 'I'm sure she's . . .'

'Someone has just left a twelve-year-old girl alone in a West End burger joint. I can see it on the monitor above. She's just sitting there on her own.'

'I'm sure Jamie will inform the police right away . . .'

'Call that responsible?'

'Ah, Mr Messiter. It's you.'

'Too right it's me. Hoist with your own petard there, weren't you?'

'Mr Messiter seems very interested in the fate of unprotected children, ladies and gentlemen.' Ashley swiftly regained his composure. 'Yet his company continues to open the porn portals of the internet to all, without accepting responsibility. He even manages to blame the parents. It's their fault. If they only bought expensive and complex software to guard their children's access, then all would be well.'

'It isn't expensive, it's available free on . . .'

'Well, let me now introduce you to an expert in the field of internet security. From CotterDotCom, Cosima Kretschmer!'

The atrium fell silent and all eyes turned from the screen to Simon. He shrugged lightly. 'You're all free,' he said. 'If Cosima wants to speak and share her expertise on television, how could I possibly stand in her way?'

All heads turned back to the screen. It was rumoured that Cosima, whom Simon had brought back from the Geneva office, was more than just the head of the Secure Server Research Division. She and Simon had recently been photographed together coming out of the Ivy Restaurant. It seemed doubtful that she would consent to appear as a witness for Ashley Barson-Garland without Simon's express wish. Albert frowned as he watched her take the microphone. He could not believe that his mentor, his hero, his god, would lend support to anything that threatened the sanctity and autonomy of the net.

Simon was watching the screen with a look of bland benevolence.

'Fräulein Kretschmer, I'm sure only those who've holidayed on Mars for the last two years have failed to hear of CotterDotCom. You specialise in internet security, is that right?'

'That is quite correct.'

'I believe service providers can choose to make available all or only some newsgroups on their news servers, is that also correct?'

'Certainly.'

'So Mr Messiter's company, the largest free provider in the United Kingdom, isn't *obliged* to offer the full range of newsgroups. He could choose to filter out those which carry illegal child pornography, for example.'

'For sure.'

'Now, as you may know, I proposed a bill which would have allowed the monitoring of such obscene transactions and I was told by the so-called "internet community" that such a course was "impractical". Were they right?'

'Not at all. People may use proxy servers and firewalls, but it is usually possible to detect those who upload and download illegal materials.'

'It *is* possible? Do you think the government should take steps to implement the tracking of this kind of traffic?'

'No, I do not.'

Ashley flickered for a moment. 'Forgive me, Fräulein Kretschmer . . .'

'Cosima, please.'

'You told me earlier that you *did* believe in such monitoring.'

'Did I?'

'You know you did.'

'It is a complex matter. The question of civil liberties is important. I have been thinking more deeply on this subject lately.'

'Civil liberties? What about the rights of families to live free of fear and contamination. Do those count for nothing?'

A hearty round of applause interrupted the first part of Cosima's reply.

'Well, let us suppose,' she said, 'that in my research I came upon evidence of a person who had regularly used the internet for his own personal sexual gratification. Downloading illegal pornography and so forth. Do I have the right to expose such a person?'

'Of course you do. If their computer drives contain illegal material it's the same as possessing it in photographic form on paper. We all know that.'

'Ah but this person is clever. He looks at the pictures on screen, but does not store them. He deletes the memory cache once he has . . . once he has satisfied himself, you understand?'

Ashley's stern voice cut through a bubble of titters emanating from the back row of the audience. 'All this hypothetical speculation seems to me to miss the main point of our discussion,' he said. 'We are addressing . . .'

'It is at the absolute heart of our discussion,' Brad Messiter shouted from the back, unmiked, but loud enough to be heard. 'Tell us more about this hypothetical case, Cosima.'

'As a matter of fact,' said Cosima, who unlike Messiter had a radio microphone clipped to the lapel of her jacket, 'it is not hypothetical. I am talking about you, Mr Barson-Garland. *You*. You have logged up an average of sixteen hours a week accessing sites devoted to photographs of young teenage boys.'

A gasp ran round the studio as Ashley whipped round, his face white, to face Cosima. 'I should warn you that I am a lawyer,' he snarled. 'Such unsubstantiated accusations are highly actionable. You cannot have a shred of evidence to support such outrageous . . .'

'But I have,' said Cosima, pointing to a briefcase. 'I have tracked your internet use for many months now and watched you accessing web-cam sites, newsgroups and youth chat rooms.'

'I have . . . I have . . .' beads of sweat were beginning to appear on Ashley's brow. 'I have naturally researched all areas of the internet during the course of my campaign. It would be absurd to attempt to legislate against pornography without investigating it first.'

'But why only teenage boys? Why only sites with titles like "Studmuffins For You", "Twink Heaven", "Smooth Buns R Us" and "First Cum First Served" – why only those?'

Ashley felt he was drowning in a sea of laughter.

'It is perfectly clear to anyone of sense,' he hissed into

his microphone, 'that I have been made the victim of a very clever conspiracy to besmirch my name and belittle the national campaign I have set up on behalf of the family. You cannot possibly prove any one of these revolting allegations. You have only recorded the internet use on my part that suits you and deliberately chosen to ignore the thousands of other visits I may or may not have legitimately made in the name of research. These vicious and repulsive smears show how far the internet establishment is prepared to go . . .'

'I note,' Cosima continued remorselessly, 'that you always delete your client-side disk and internet cache. There will be no evidence at your home whatsoever.'

'Of course there won't be!' Ashley shrieked. 'There will be no evidence at my home because everything you have said is a farrago of lies, innuendo and twisted half truths. I don't know if your employer is aware of what you have been doing –'

'Your employer too, don't forget. You write a column for his newspaper –'

'Never mind that! If I discover that you have been snooping around me on Cotter company time, the legal consequences will be such as you cannot imagine. Let me assure you of that, Fräulein!'

In the atrium, two dozen mouths had dropped open and two dozen pairs of rounded eyes were staring at the giant plasma television. A scene, Simon supposed, that was reproduced in different numbers and configurations up and down the land. Albert peeked shyly once more at the face of his hero but could read nothing behind the mirrored lenses. Mild astonishment showed in the gentle uplift of one of his eybrows, that was all.

Albert's mother and father had watched the moon landing as children, Gordon in New York and Portia in London. Albert himself retained vague memories of O.J.'s white Bronco being followed by news helicopters as it wound along the freeways of Los Angeles, but *this* . . . this was a memory by which his generation would judge themselves for ever. Where were you when Cosima Kretschmer humiliated Ashley Barson-Garland on live television? I was watching television, derr-brain, the smart arses would reply, where were you?

Cosima Kretschmer appeared to be the only calm person in the studio. The director up in the gallery was deep in a telephone conversation with his channel controller who had a lawyer on the other line. 'Keep going,' the controller ordered. 'We're okay. It's up to Barson-Garland. He can hardly sue us for defamation on his own show.'

'It is my suggestion,' Cosima was saying, 'that you have consistently downloaded obscene and mostly illegal pictures of youths onto your computer. You have masturbated in front of these images and then deleted them.'

Several parents had clamped hands over the ears of their children, who writhed and wriggled in their attempts to work free.

'You have just earned yourself one terrifying court case!' Ashley yelled, pointing a finger at her and shaking with rage.

'That is your privilege. I have video pictures of you doing precisely that. *Yes*!' Cosima repeated as a sudden hush fell on the studio and all eyes turned to stare at Ashley. 'I have hours of videotape showing you masturbating in front of the screen in the study of your own house in London.'

'Such footage would be completely inadmissible in any court,' said Ashley, a terrible weight swelling in the pit of his stomach, '*if* it existed, that is. Which they do not. You are getting yourself further and further into trouble, young lady.'

'But we are not talking about *any* court. We are talking about *this* court,' Cosima continued remorselessly. 'Your court. You cannot have any objection to my showing my evidence here.' She pulled two cassettes from her briefcase. '"There are no steps that should not be taken in the name of the family, in the name of decency." Your own words. True or not, Mr Barson-Garland?'

Ashley stood frozen in the centre of the studio. Brad Messiter led a baying chorus of 'True or not? True or not?' The voices fused and swelled in his head. His mouth opened and closed, but his eyes followed the video cassettes that Cosima was brandishing above her head, never leaving them for a second.

'I have printouts of your diary too, Mr Barson-Garland,' Cosima's free hand dipped into her briefcase and brought out sheaves of paper. 'What extraordinary reading they make.'

Ashley screeched in rage and made a half lunge towards

her. At the last minute he veered away from her and ran from the studio, dropping his microphone on the floor. Blindly, he butted his way past security officers too startled and confused to know what to do. He tore down the corridors and into reception, barely noticing the cluster of BBC employees staring at the screens set into the wall. He pushed his way out of the glass doors and hurtled madly through the horse-shoe forecourt and out onto Wood Lane. He heard voices raised behind him but he charged through the security gate and into the street. Cabs were lined up on the rank and he hurled himself at the first, scrabbling at the door.

'All right mate, all right. Calm down.' The driver released his central locking switch and Ashley threw himself onto the seat.

'St James's!'

'I know you! You're that Barson-Garland bloke.'

'Never mind,' Ashley's breath came in huge gulping sobs. 'Duke Street, as fast as you can.'

'Righto. Shame that Bill of yours was never passed. It's about time those perverts were brought to book. Got kids myself.'

Ashley felt in his pocket and almost wept with relief when his fingers closed around his leather Smythson key wallet. He had left the keys in his dressing-room the previous week and had been forced to return to Television Centre at midnight to retrieve them. He had cursed himself at the time but had that not happened, he would never have decided to keep them in his pocket today. He looked out of the back window of the cab and saw a crowd streaming from the studio audience door at the side of the building.

'Had that Gary Glitter in here once,' said the cabby.

As Ashley had feared, a small crowd had already gathered in Mason's Yard. A handheld TV light focused on his front door and was turned towards the cab as it swung into the alley from Duke Street.

'Strewth, you've got a few fans, then,' said the cabby, shielding his eyes. 'Going to make you party leader are they?'

Ashley pushed a twenty pound note through the glass and opened the cab door, his keys ready. 'Keep the change.'

'Very generous, guv'nor. You've got my vote!'

'Mr Barson-Garland! Mr Barson-Garland!'

'I have no comment, no comment. No comment. No comment at all.'

He pushed his way through the press of people, head down, key outstretched towards the door.

'Is there any truth in these allegations?'

'No comment, I tell you! I have absolutely no comment.' He slammed the door on them and bolted it. As soon as he was alone, the tears began to flow.

The telephone upstairs in his study was ringing. He wrenched it from its socket and stood on the carpet, tears flowing down his cheeks. All around him were displayed the symbols of his success. The Romney portrait of a Sir William Barson that he had allowed people to believe was his ancestor stared down at him, hand on hip. His first editions of Gibbon, Carlyle and Burke gleamed on the shelves. And on the desk stood his computer.

It was a lie. All a lie. They had trapped him. For some evil, terrible reason they had trapped him into revealing himself. Video cameras in his study! It was inconceivable. Who would do such a thing? Inconceivable. Yet, they must have known. They could not have guessed that it was his practice to . . .

He woke his computer and input the first password. The diary files were also password protected, security within security. No one could have penetrated them. He double-clicked the most recent entry, made yesterday, when the world was still at his feet. The system demanded a second password, which he gave. The diary pages loaded themselves and he looked at them.

> Sad news about poor old Rufus Cade. By all accounts a 'drug hit', as these things are termed. I suppose it was inevitable. From schoolboy on, it was apparent that dear Rufus was destined for a life of dependency and decline. What Americans would call 'an addictive compulsive personality' or some such hogwash. I have not seen him since he called upon me some five years ago with an embarrassing request for money to 'invest' in a footling scheme to start up a model agency. I shall attend his funeral, I think and pray for the salvation of his soul. Grace will not be denied him.
>
> A gratifying review of the first programme in the

Telegraph this morning. It seems I am 'a natural performer combining ease of manner with a steely refusal to be diverted from the hard moral questions'. Look out, David Starkey!

Gratifying! Would he ever use that word again? Or any word like it? Wiping back his tears, Ashley scrolled down until he saw something that made his heart stop.

Red!

Impossible, but true.

The last paragraph of his last diary entry was in *red*. Ashley never messed about with coloured text. Never. The paragraph was in a different font too. A font he never used.

His eyes hardly dared drag themselves to the bottom of the screen. If he read the paragraph he would know for sure that it was not a mistake, not the result of some inadvertent series of mouse clicks on his own part. He did not want to know any such thing. But he had to read on.

Hypocrite, lecteur, mon semblable, mon frère! Not for the first time do I find myself reading your diary, Ashley Garland. You have not graduated far have you? From masturbating into school boaters to masturbating at pictures of schoolboys. What a pathetic failure of a man. All pretence, snobbery, intolerance, bluster, bigotry and show. With such a brain as yours you could have gone so far, Ashley Garland. With such a cold, constipated heart, however, you were always destined for disgrace, ruin and humiliation. I wonder how they will treat you in prison? You fake, you pervert, you canting hypocrite. My revenge on you is complete. May you rot for ever in the burning filth of your own corruption.'

The red text swam before Ashley's eyes. He pressed his hands to the side of his head and pushed inwards, as if forcing his brain to concentrate. Tears dropped onto the keyboard.

This was insanity. Wild madness of a kind that could not be explained. He had his enemies. He was not universally liked, he knew that. He had always known that. But such demented hatred?

A flashing folder icon on the computer desktop caught his eye. It was entitled 'Yummee!' and Ashley knew that he had never seen it before. He double-clicked the folder which showed itself to contain over two thousand files, all of them in picture and movie formats. He double-clicked one at random and his screen was filled with a video clip of such clarity and unspeakable, uncompromising physical detail that he caught his breath. The participants were all male and under age.

The doorbell rang.

Ashley closed the file instantly and dragged the whole folder to his desktop wastebasket.

The doorbell rang again.

Ashley emptied the wastebasket. A window came on screen.

Cannot delete without password

Ashley input his password and tried again.

Password incorrect

Ashley tried his secondary password.

Password incorrect. System shutting down . . .

Ashley stared unbelievingly at the screen as it went blank with a fizz and crackle of static.

The doorbell rang for a third time.

A flashing blue light was reflected on the wall behind the computer. Ashley rose, went to the window and looked down through the curtains. A battery of flashlights almost blinded him and he stepped back.

'Damn you all,' he sobbed, his whole body trembling. 'Damn you all.'

A picture arose in his mind of his mother and sister in Manchester. They would have been watching the programme. Perhaps with neighbours. There was a news camera down in the yard below him pointing up at his window. Yes, they would be watching now, white-faced and ashamed, hands over mouths. The neighbours would have crept away and dashed to their houses and television sets. Everyone from chambers, everyone in the Conservative Party would be watching. His wife, she was watching too and her father would be saying 'Told you so, something not quite top drawer about your Ashley. Thought so from the first.' Oliver Delft, he would have watched and already he would have scratched Ashley's name from his list of useful contacts. The news would have got round the Carlton Club and they would all be crowded into the television room, watching. Everybody would watch him being led away and everybody would watch his trial.

No, they would not. No one would watch him. No one.

The doorbell rang again and a distorted voice, amplified by a megaphone, called up from the street below.

'Mr Barson-Garland! My name is Superintendent Wallace. Please let us into the house. The yard will be cleared of cameras and press, you have my word.'

Ashley stumbled into the kitchen. His Sabatier knives gleamed invitingly. Those few friends that he had knew Ashley to be a fine cook. His knives, like everything else about him, were perfect. He pulled one from its wooden block and returned to his study, crying like a child.

All his life, he realised, he had felt like an antelope being chased by a lion. The hot stinking breath of fate had pursued him close but he had always found new spurts of speed, dazzling new zig-zags of energy and wit that had kept the beast away. Now he was finally being shaken in its jaws and he didn't care. Damn them, damn them all! It wasn't his fault. He had never chosen to be who he was. He had never chosen to be ugly, to be bald, to be 'not quite top drawer', to be attracted by youth, to be socially inept, to be despised by the arrogant ease and vanity of

Them. Them with their flops of silky hair and flops of silky charm. Damn them all!

He pushed the knife into his throat and twisted it round and round and round.

At the same time he heard the door downstairs being beaten open and saw, through the jets of blood pumping from his neck, that his computer had come to life. He imagined, and it must have been imagination, that he read these words crawling across the screen like tickertape from left to right in bright red letters.

Ned Maddstone sends you to hell

His mind had time to wonder why, in the delirium of his last moments on this mean earth, the name of Ned Maddstone should have come to him. Perhaps it was appropriate. Ned had been the archetype of Them. The very pattern-book of ease and flop-fringed assurance.

Ashley died cursing the name and the very thought of Ned Maddstone.

*

Simon Cotter locked his office door and descended the stairs three at a time, slapping his thigh as he went.

'Three!' he whispered.

Albert and the others were still crowded around the television. They turned expectantly as Simon approached.

'I couldn't raise him on the phone,' he said. 'He must

have disconnected himself. Oh look, the BBC is being coy, have you tried Sky News?'

Albert found the remote control and they all gazed up at the screen as live pictures played of a stretcher being rushed through the smashed front door of Barson-Garland's London town house.

Simon made a note to himself to call the editor of the *LEP* first thing. There was much to be attended to: an obituary, a new Voice of Reason – so many little things.

Oliver Delft took his pulse while running on the spot. Ninety-eight, not bad. He blew out five or six times and looked round the square, allowing his breathing to settle into a calmer rhythm. He did not like his wife to see him even slightly out of breath, so as a rule he would stay on the doorstep until he was able to go back into the house presenting the appearance of a man who has done no more than walk to the post-box and back.

Light was leaking into the sky from the east. Through the trees he could see that one or two of the Balkan embassies had their lights on. On a number of occasions in the past he had surprised his staff by warning them of impending crises, simply on the basis of his observations of ambassadorial windows, an irony that pleased him in this so-called digital age.

Oliver frowned suddenly. A car was parked in the bay next to his. A silver Lexus that did not bear diplomatic plates. He could see the broad silhouette of an enormously fat driver sitting at the wheel. He made a note of the number and fished for his latchkey.

The first sign that alerted him to something strange afoot in the house was the sound of the children's laughter. Oliver's brood were never merry at the breakfast table.

They slouched over their cereal, sulkily reading the packets or groaning for the radio to be turned off in favour of the television. The second sign of unusual goings on was the smell of bacon hanging in the hallway. Oliver was following a strict low fat diet and Julia had been a vegetarian all her life. The children, although the youngest was now thirteen, were still addicted to Coco Pops and Frosties.

Oliver heard a man's voice as he approached the kitchen. Bugger, he thought to himself. Uncle Bloody Jimmy.

Julia's brother Jimmy was a favourite with the children but, as so often with those that children take to, adults found him a complete bore. The time would fit, Oliver realised, glancing at his watch. Uncle Jimmy often 'dropped by' early in the morning, after his flight from America had landed and he had a few hours to fill before the business world woke up. At least his arrival cleared up the mystery of the Lexus and chauffeur parked outside. Oliver prepared a welcoming face and opened the kitchen door.

If he had been asked to compile a list of a thousand people he might expect to see sitting at his kitchen table performing magic tricks for the benefit of his family, the dot.com billionaire Simon Cotter would not have featured anywhere.

'*There* you are, darling!' said his wife.

Cotter looked up and smiled. 'Good morning, Sir Oliver. You must excuse me for barging in on your family like this. So early too. I was passing on my way to the airport and took a chance on your being in. Been for a run?'

Oliver, acutely aware of his tracksuit and headband and for no good reason embarrassed by them, nodded.

'It's a great pleasure to see you, Mr Cotter. If you'll let me shoot upstairs and change . . .'

'Come on, Simon. Where is it?'

India, the youngest, had grabbed Simon's hand and was feeling up his sleeve and tugging at his beard.

'Ah, now. Where would you *like* it to be? Would you like it to be under the sugar bowl, perhaps? In the toast rack? Inside the newspaper?'

'Under the sugar bowl.'

'Well, then. Have a look.'

'Bloody hell!'

Oliver was amazed to see that Rupert, back from Oxford and tiresomely sophisticated these days, was as wide-eyed and wriggling as the others.

'Another! Do another!'

By the time Oliver came downstairs again they were in the middle of a mind-reading trick. Even Oliver's mother, sitting slightly apart in her wheelchair, appeared to be enjoying herself, if the quantity of dribble sliding from the corners of her mouth could be regarded as a reliable index.

Julia, the children and Maria had all drawn shapes on pieces of paper and were clustered around Cotter, who put a finger dramatically to each temple and stared downwards with a great frown.

'The great Cottini must think. He must *theeeenk* . . .

aïeee . . . *no desme la lata*!' he muttered to himself. Oliver was surprised to see Maria giggle. She said something in Spanish and Cotter replied fluently.

'My spirit guide, he has advised me,' he announced, after turning his face in turn to each of the giggling, hot-faced children. 'Olivia, because she is *vairrry* clever and *vairrry* beautiful, she would be choosing a fine horse, yes? You have drawed a horse, I am fancying.'

Olivia unfolded her piece of paper to reveal a competently drawn horse.

'It's a pony, actually,' she said.

Cotter slapped his forehead. 'Ah, I am so stupid! Of course it is a pony. Not horse! *Pony*! Forgive me, child, my powers are weak in the mornings. Let me consider now, Hoolia. Hoolia will choose I think a napple. Yes. Of this I am quite sure. A napple. Half eaten.'

Julia opened her paper and the kitchen rocked with delighted laughter.

'Good. We make progress, yes? Now we come to Rupert. Rupert is most spiritual. He does not know this yet, but he is most spiritual person in room. He chooses I think a fireplace, which is for him a symbol of his heart, which burns greatly.'

'That is unbe-fucking-*lievable*!'

'*Rupert*!'

'Sorry, Mother, but how the hell?'

'Now, as for India. India is also great beauty, India is wise, India is cleverer than all her brothers and sisters combined together . . .'

Oliver exchanged a look with his wife. She beamed and he nodded back with a small smile.

'. . . so India, she would choose an object most deceiving, I think. What would be most deceiving, I must ask myself? *Nothing*. Nothing would be the most deceiving and wicked thing of all. Show me your paper, oh deceiving and wicked person.'

Blushing, India unfolded a blank piece of paper to tremendous applause.

'Finally, Señorita Maria. What shall we say she draws? Maria is a good woman. Maria is kind. Maria is holy. Maria will draw a chicken, I think, which is a holy creature of God, like herself.'

Dropping her paper and crossing herself, Maria babbled in Spanish, to which Cotter replied in a fluent stream. She kissed him and fluttered from the room, giggling.

'One more, please, one more!'

Cotter looked up at Oliver and smiled. 'I'm afraid I have to have a few words with your father now,' he said. '*Business*!' he whispered to them privately and gave a hollow groan.

The children groaned back and made him promise to visit again.

'We'll go up here,' Oliver led Simon upstairs. 'We shan't be disturbed.'

'Tremendous place,' Simon said looking round approvingly.

'It's my mother's, actually.'

'Ah.'

Oliver saw that Cotter was looking with interest at the stairlift. 'She had a series of strokes some years ago. Mind's all there but . . .'

'Very sad. And Maria looks after her?'

'That's right. Come in here.'

'Thank you. What a charming room. You have a wonderful family, Sir Oliver. Something rare these days.'

'Just Oliver, please. Well, I have to say you bring out the best in them. I'm sorry to repeat their badgering, but how the hell does that trick work?'

'Ah, well,' Simon tapped his sunglasses. 'I provided the paper they drew upon. Very dull chemistry, I'm afraid. Nothing more. Sort of trickery you MI6 boys used all the time in the old days, I expect. Promise not to tell them?'

'You have my word. But . . .'

'Yes?'

'What you said about India being cleverer than the others. It's true, but how could you possibly tell?'

'It's perfectly obvious. It's much easier to hide stupidity than brains. Surely you know that?'

'Well, you've certainly scored a hit. Please, sit down.'

'Thank you. You must be wondering why I'm here.'

Oliver, who had been biting his tongue with curiosity for the past fifteen minutes, shrugged amiably. 'It's a surprise, certainly. A pleasant one, I assure you.'

'Mm. I'm afraid my ways of doing business are a little unorthodox, as you may know.'

'New rules for a new industry.'

'Exactly. I'll be absolutely direct with you. As you may

know, CotterDotCom has had to dispense with the services of its head of internet security.'

'Cosima Kretschmer?'

'A grim affair. The woman is being treated by many as a kind of cyberhero, but as I have made clear, she acted entirely without the company's authority.'

'I understand that Barson-Garland's family is suing?'

'I have satisfied their lawyer that all Cosima's research was undertaken on her own time, not the company's. The action is now solely against her. She is in hiding somewhere. Germany, they believe. I fear that Mrs Garland will find it difficult to win so much as a penny from her. After all, it seems that the allegations were far from baseless. A sad business.'

'Hm . . . I have to confess it was quite the most riveting evening's television I have ever experienced.'

'You knew Barson-Garland quite well, I believe?'

Oliver studied his fingers and picked a sliver of skin from under a nail. 'Knew him? Yes, I knew him. I wouldn't say *well*, exactly.'

'Rumour has it that he was trying to recruit you as an ally for his Security Agency. That he'd promised you the job of heading it up, if it were ever to get off the ground.'

'Really? I –'

Oliver turned his head at the sound of a sudden creak on the stair. He strode quickly across the room and opened the door.

'Ah, Maria, how can we help?'

'I'm sorry disturbing you, Sir Oliver. I woss wunnering

if you or Señor Cotter like maybe some cop of coffee? Or some bisskiss? I have bake yesty some bisskiss. I come in.'

Oliver stood uncomfortably by the fireplace while Maria cleared away piles of art books and magazines from the coffee table to make space for her tray. Cotter chattered away to her in Spanish and she left the room, simpering like a schoolgirl.

'Lace on the tray!' said Oliver, closing the door. 'You've scored quite a hit there too. I seem to remember reading in some magazine or other that you are fluent in nine languages. Can that be true?'

'Thing of it is,' said Simon, helping himself to a biscuit, 'I spent so much time learning languages that I never learned to count, so I couldn't tell you how many I speak.'

Oliver smiled drily.

'You're probably wondering,' Simon went on, '– absolutely *delicious* biscuits by the way, simply melt in the mouth – how on earth I could know that Barson-Garland had been trying to seduce you.'

'That question had crossed my mind.'

'I haven't bugged the tables or bribed the Thursday waiters at Mark's Club, no need to worry about that. No, the fact is that dear old Barson-Garland was also flirting with *me*. Bit of a two-timing whore, that one.'

'I see.'

'He wasn't sure whether to go public or private, you see. His instincts were actually quite sound in that respect. Which way will the world go? Some think that governments should oversee the formation of a global internet police force. Many are afraid that this is exactly what will happen and scream about privacy and civil liberties. You are probably aware that the recent spate of viruses, worms, mail-bombs and portal attacks has led the international community to one inevitable and irrevocable conclusion. They can't do anything about it. Nothing will work. It's too expensive. It's too impractical. The legal ramifications of borders, copyright treaties and so on are complex and insoluble. The only answer is for private enterprise, at local corporate levels, to do its own policing, its own firewalling, its own vaccinating and prophylaxis. Only the private sector can cross the borders, only the private sector has the resources and the power to take the responsibility. The post of Head of Internet Security at CotterDotCom takes on a greater meaning than ever before. Frankly, even if Cosima had not gone mad I would still be offering you this position. That, if you had not guessed, is what I am doing. It's frankly the same job that Ashley Barson-Garland offered you, but it's bigger, it's real, it's now, it's free of political interference and it carries embarrassingly good pay. I do need an answer soon, however. I'm off to Africa later this morning and I'd love to know that you can start work as soon as you've cleared it with your people . . . in the meantime, I'm absolutely *dying* for a slash. You couldn't . . . ?'

'Oh, yes. Of course. Through there, second door on the right.'

'Do try one of those biscuits. So light. They can't do your diet the least bit of harm.'

Simon left the room and crossed the landing as directed. As he passed the stairs he noticed that the stairlift had moved from the bottom of the staircase to the top. A half open door caught Simon's eye and he pushed it open and went in.

Alone and immobile, Oliver Delft's mother sat on a wheelchair facing a window that overlooked the square. Simon came and stood beside her. Her eyes rolled up towards him. It seemed to Simon that her face was capable of showing some expression, for he thought he detected a gleam of surprised pleasure.

'Philippa Blackrow,' he whispered. 'How strange to meet you. I'm Ned Maddstone. Do you know that you are responsible for the destruction of my life? Do you know that because of you I spent twenty years imprisoned in an insane asylum? Twenty years because of you and your cunt of a son.'

Breath hissed and bubbled from Philippa's lungs and he could sense the strain in her as she tried to mobilise her sagging cheeks and drooping mouth into some shape that might move towards speech. Saliva ran from her lips and her clawed and wasted hands shook like dried leaves in a storm.

'I was to have delivered a letter to you. From your Fenian friends. Of all the people in the world, it was your son who intercepted it. That is how cruel fate can be. To protect you and to save his own worthless skin he hid me away to rot amongst the mad for ever. And now I have come back. I am much crueller than fate. I thought you should know that. Infinitely more cruel. They tell me that inside this lifeless carcass your mind is fully active. Now it has something to ponder on for the rest of its days. Goodbye.'

The last picture of Philippa that Simon took away with him was of a mother down whose withered cheeks tears were flowing. He did not see, as he flushed the lavatory and crossed the landing to return to Oliver, that her mouth was trying to force itself into a smile and he could not know that the tears dropping from her eyes were tears of joy.

Albert banged into the house and called out from the bottom of the stairs.

'Mum! Dad! Where are you?'

Only after he had yelled three times and heard no reply did he realise that Gordon and Portia would be out picking up his grandfather to bring him back for supper. That was the very reason for Albert leaving work so early, but the horrors of the tube journey had banished all such thoughts from his mind. He stormed angrily into the kitchen at the sound of the phone, swung his bag viciously onto the kitchen table, not caring if he cracked the screen of his laptop and pushed the phone off its hook, letting the receiver dangle down and bang against the wall. Java the cat wound around his ankles and he kicked him away.

'Shit,' he yelled. 'Shit on everything. Shit you all. Shit, shit, shit.'

Breathing heavily through his nostrils, he took the newspaper from his jacket, sat down at the table and read the article for the twelfth time. Java sat coldly in the corner, ignoring him with great dignity.

CAFÉ *UN*ETHICA

A coffee scandal was brewing in the world of 'ethical trading' this morning, when it was revealed exclusively to the *London Evening Press* that Gordon Fendeman, founder of Café Ethica and darling of New Labour and the eco-conscious chattering classes, had cheated an entire African community out of their land rights and destroyed the way of life of a whole people in order to start up his business. The so-called 'co-operatives' that Café Ethica claims to be supporting were actually, according to sources on the ground, bussed in from a tribe *two hundred miles* to the east of the plantation. Sources say that this was the result of a corrupt arrangement made between Fendeman (41) and the local government, which is composed entirely of the rival, majority tribe.

These disclosures will rock the rapidly expanding world of ethical commodities and cast fresh doubt on New Labour's business judgement. Only two weeks ago, the Prime Minister in a speech to the City referred to Fendeman's enterprise as a 'beacon of light that led the way to new ways of trading with the Third World', words which he must now be bitterly regretting.

Reports say that Fendeman, who is married to art historian Portia Fendeman, struck a deal in 1998 with the minority tribal leaders, who turned down a lucrative offer from a worldwide consortium in order to do business with Fendeman's new company. They were led to believe that a deal with Café Ethica would be

> in their best interests, offering profit sharing, improved working conditions and the promise of a secure future for their people. They were horrified to discover that the terms of this contract in fact allowed Fendeman to evict them from land they had owned for countless generations and replace them with workers from another part of the country. These displaced people now face a future of starvation, disease and homelessness in a country where their tribe has few enough rights. Fendeman's personal profits from the local government deal that kicked these people off their land and from the growing sales of Café Ethica products have been calculated to exceed one million pounds a year. *Comment, Page 12*

The 'comment' on page twelve was unspeakable, just unspeakable. Albert felt that his whole world was crashing down around him. It seemed impossible to separate the various strands of his despair.

His father. How could such a thing be written. How *dared* they? It must be lies. He knew his father too well to believe anything else. But it would hurt him so deeply. He was a proud man. Whatever the outcome, mud would stick.

His work: for five months, Albert had been toiling away in the field of Ethical Trading. He had broken new ground and achieved great things. He was proud of what he was doing and how it would help the world. Something like this, however deeply untrue it so manifestly was, would dwell in the mind of the public for ever. The consumer's hand would start to close around a product whose labelling contained the word 'ethical' and then draw back as if stung. 'Oh yes,' they would say to themselves. 'Wasn't there some nasty fuss about these types of companies? Better stick to Nescafé.' And all that good work would be undone.

Simon: The *London Evening Press* was *his* newspaper. He was a busy man, of course. Albert had never seen a man with such a capacity for work and detail. Only yesterday, in a wine bar, Albert had been boasting about him to his friends. He had used the very word 'detail' time and time again in describing Simon's awesome abilities. It was the quality that always marked out the great: their grasp on detail. And that was the problem. Albert could not imagine for a moment that Simon, however busy he was, could ever have been unaware of the *LEP*'s attack on Gordon. He *must* have known. But if he *had* known then how could he have *allowed* it? Not to warn Albert, not to take him aside and break the news. The same friends that Albert had talked to when raving on and on about him had been cynical. 'Believe me,' one of them had said. '*No one* makes that kind of money without being a complete son of a bitch deep down.' 'You're wrong, so wrong!' Albert had insisted. But a memory returned to him now of the strange sensation he had felt standing next to him while they watched the public destruction of Ashley Barson-Garland on television. There had been nothing in Simon's expression that Albert could pin down, but none the less he had been aware of a *feeling*. An *atmosphere*. Intense waves had radiated from Simon that Albert had tried to push to the back of his mind. It had been like smelling fear, or sexual desire, or guilt, yet it had been none of those things. It had been something else. And the rumours that had flown throughout the company. Cosima? Acting independently? Getaway! She couldn't take a pee without Cotter's say-so, let alone appear on TV. Albert had dismissed all that as office gossip. Maybe though, maybe there *was* something about Simon. If Albert inspected his feelings honestly, maybe . . . maybe what he had smelt that night had been *cruelty*.

Gordon was his father. Ethical Trading was his life. Simon was his god. Fathers are weak. Life is a betrayal. Gods are cruel. Albert had read enough and seen enough to know these as objective facts, but he had not expected to experience them quite so soon and all at once. All three had been taken away from him in a single blow of fate. One minute he had been cheerfully sitting on the tube, listening to music and skimming through the evening paper – he only *bought* that bloody paper because it was Simon's – and the next minute the triple pillars of his world had crumbled.

He rose from the table at the sound of the front door.

'Where is he? Where's my grandson?'

Albert folded up the newspaper and slipped it back into his pocket. 'I'm in the kitchen, Grandpa. Grabbing some food before you get it all.'

'Cheeky! The boy is so cheeky. Don't you love him?'

Albert adored his grandfather. He was a constant

reminder to him of his Jewishness and his heritage. It was hard to believe what his parents told him, that many years ago Grandpa had been a history lecturer and local politician. Rabidly left wing, Portia said, which was hard to imagine. Something had happened, Albert never quite got to the bottom of it, something to do with a wrongful arrest, but Peter had left academia and thrown himself into religion and the local synagogue. Theirs was a tight knit family, by definition. As the son of cousins, Albert had long endured the amusement of his friends at the circumstance of his grandfather also being his great-uncle and all the teasing suggestions of genetic weakness that went with it, but he loved his family and enjoyed the special closeness that came from not having two warring factions within it. No in-law jokes for the Fendemans.

He embraced his grandfather and saw, over his shoulder, that Portia and Gordon knew nothing.

'So, my darlings. What's to eat?'

'You'll see, Daddy, you'll see.' Portia laughed as she kissed her father and her son. 'You look worried, darling, what is it?'

'Nothing, Mum, nothing. Tough day at the office.'

Albert knew that it was not going to be a hard decision after all. Blood was thicker than worship. This was his family. They counted more than any hero. After all, there was Oxford. It wasn't too late. It was never too late.

'Hey, the phone's off the hook.'

'Leave it, Dad. No, leave it, really. It's Friday night. The sun has set. No work. No calls.'

Peter put a hand to his grandson's cheek. 'Love him! Couldn't you just eat him up? Am I right?'

Albert lit the candles and drew the curtains. He knew that soon enough the house would be under siege.

'Welcome aboard, Oliver. I know we've both made the right decision. If you like I'll walk you round the place, introduce you to a few people. How are you on heights?'

'Heights?'

'There's a fabulous office at the top of the building, one of the best views in London, but if you prefer, you can make your habitation a little closer to ground.'

'No, no. Heights are good.'

'Of course you're used to a view aren't you? As a matter of fact, you can see your old office from my window here. Would you like to wave to your successor?'

'Frankly no,' said Oliver. 'It's only when you've shaken the dust of public service from your shoes that you realise how much you always hated it. By the way, my children will kill me if I forget to pass on an invitation to dinner next week. Thursday, can you make it?'

'It would be a pleasure, please convey my grateful thanks. Now, let's amble, shall we? Ah, good morning, Albert. Let me introduce you to Sir Oliver Delft. Anti-virus, anti-worm, anti-hacker.'

'How do you do? Simon, I have to talk to you right now. It's *extremely* urgent.'

'Ah. Oliver, I'm so sorry, would you mind if I . . . ?'

'No, no. If it's all right with you, I'll wander on my own. I'd prefer it that way. I take it this pass allows me anywhere?'

'Absolutely anywhere. Introduce yourself as you go along, I broke the glad tidings to everyone by email this morning.'

'I will see you later then.'

'Albert, I have a very strong idea why you are here. Let me say –'

'How could you do it? *How*?'

'I'm the publisher, Albert, not the editor. I can't be seen to interfere in . . .'

'Oh bullshit, that's absolute *bullshit*. I'm not an idiot. And *this*, here, in today's *Times*, have you seen? They are claiming that my father bought LEP shares the day before you announced that you were buying it and that he was acting on inside information. That was *me*! The first day I came here you told me you were buying the paper and I . . . I happened to mention it to him. I didn't know it meant anything. And now they are painting him as some sort of crook. He's not. He's my father. He's a decent man. What are you doing to him?'

'Albert, calm down. I'm sure this will all come out right in the end.'

'Anyway, I – I came here to tell you that I'm leaving.'

'But Albert, that's absurd.'

'It's a matter of . . . of . . . *honour*. I can't possibly work for you. You're my enemy. It's family honour. We're going to clear his name if it takes every penny we have. I'm going to expose you for what you are. A wrecker of lives. An animal. I'll make your life hell. Goodbye.'

'Albert, this is nothing more than absurd posturing. Dry your eyes. Come back.'

Albert had been in his room for nine days. The pages were uploading. The world would soon know the kind of man Simon Cotter truly was. He had collected together every morsel of gossip, every hint, rumour and theory that had ever been whispered on the subject of his mortal enemy. More would come, that was the nature of the internet. It wouldn't matter if his subject was Mother Teresa, there would be people out there with scandal, conspiracy theories and reasons to hate. Albert had the advantage of knowing things. Nothing too terrible, but enough to make Cotter a figure of fun.

Albert watched the final page upload. He had chosen a free webserver in Australia. It made no difference really, but the site might as well be lodged as far away as possible. It gave the impression that Cotter's enemies were spread around the globe. When he got to Oxford next month he would continue his campaign. They might have taken Wafiq Said's money, but they'd never accept Cotter's, not once Albert had done his work. Simon Cotter. The arrogance of him. The vain casual arrogance.

'Albert! Let me in. Please . . .'

Why not? His mother should see that he hadn't just

been sulking like Achilles in his tent. He had been arming and preparing for battle.

'Okay, Mum. It's a bit of a mess I'm afraid.'

Albert got up from his chair and unlocked the door. Portia was standing with a tray in her hand.

'For goodness' sake! What have you been *doing* in there?'

'Yeah, I know. I've been busy. Hiya, Java.'

Portia trod gingerly in and stood in the middle of the room and swayed slightly as if she were about to lose her balance. 'Where on *earth* am I going to put this tray?

'Um . . . down there.' Albert kicked away a pile of CDs, photographs and underwear. 'Get *away* Java!'

Java had leapt onto the desk and was batting at the mouse, as cats will.

'Lunch,' said Portia firmly. 'In fact it's last night's supper and this morning's breakfast too. You absolutely *must* eat. I'm going to watch you. I don't care if I sound like the worst Jewish mother in the world. You simply *must* eat.'

'Yeah, yeah. Whatever. Look, Mum . . .'

'Don't you "whatever" me! I'm going to watch every sandwich going down your throat. And then sleep. You didn't go to bed at all last night, did you?'

'Okay, *okay* . . . only, look.' Albert grinned. 'You've arrived at a historic moment. The formal opening of the world's first anti-Cotter site. Watch this.'

Albert sat down at this computer again and his mouse started skating.

'See? www.ihatecotter.co.au. Here's the welcome page. "Welcome to my parlour." That's Cotter in the centre of this web, I've made him look like a spider. You move the mouse over the spider and he scuttles from one part of his web to the other. When you click, it tells you about each part, see? And you can look at different areas, like cupboards in the parlour? Here's a "Slap Cotter" page. When you click over his face, he gets slapped and it plays this sound. Hang on.'

The cartoon sound of a ringing slap came from the computer speakers followed by a treble 'ouch!'

'Pinched them from the Simpsons actually, but whatever. There's a gossip page. As people log on they can add their own stories. See? I've put in stuff like "he only drinks milk", "he dyes his hair". He's trying to buy into the establishment. He's been giving money to St Mark's in Oxford. To the MCC as well, so he can jump the queue and become a member, so I've got links to the official MCC and St Mark's sites so real members can campaign against him from within.'

'Darling, you can't do this. He'll sue.'

'Let him. Let him bloody sue. That would be brilliant. How would it look? Suing a seventeen-year-old whose father he has been smearing in his papers? I don't think so. Even if he got some sort of injunction or whatever, imagine what it would start. You know what the net is like. His name would be mud in days. He'd be the hate figure of all time. Share price would go frrfrfrfrffrfrrr . . . Check this out, this is a page of Conspiracy theories. Cosima Kretschmer, okay? This says how she was acting under orders to expose Barson-Garland. She was his girlfriend. That kind of stuff. Oh, and you'll *love* this. Here's a page of photos with him bald . . . you know like that kids' magnet man with the iron filings? You can give him beards and moustaches and different hair colours to see if he's actually a wanted criminal or something. You never know, someone may recognise him. That's the thing about Simon Bloody Cotter. Nobody knows who he is. Maybe he's a Nazi war criminal. Tell you what, let's make him Aryan blond . . .'

'Darling, he's a bit young to be . . .'

Portia broke off, very suddenly. Albert turned to look at her. She was staring at the screen, absolutely transfixed.

'You look like you've seen a ghost. Mum. What is it?'

Portia closed her eyes for a second.

'Mum?'

'Come on, let's see you eat those sandwiches, *right now*.'

'Yeah, yeah. But what do you think?'

Portia leant forward and kissed her son, amazed that she could speak so calmly. 'It's brilliant of course, darling. I can't begin to imagine how you could do such a thing.'

'Should I show it to Dad?'

'Not just at the minute, my love.'

'Is he . . . ? Where is he?'

'Here, in the dining-room. He's in good shape, don't worry. There's a board meeting next week. They want to give him a chance to explain. He's preparing his . . . his . . .'

'Defence?'

'Well, it's not quite like that. The board believes him completely.'

'I should bloody well hope so.' Now that Albert had started eating he found that he was extremely hungry. 'Top sandwiches, Mum.'

'But there's obviously a lot of pressure from shareholders.'

'He's never going to resign?'

'Well he thinks it may be in the best interests of the company. Its reputation and share price.'

'But that's like saying he's guilty! He *can't* resign!'

'Well, that's the point of the board meeting. To find a way of his stepping down that doesn't look like an admission of guilt. The whole board wants to help. Do you want me to make you some more?'

'These are fine. Thanks, Mum.'

'All right. I'm going out now. I shall –' Portia cleared her throat to hide the tremble in her voice '– I'll be back later and I expect to find you in bed, asleep. You understand?' She leant forward and kissed him, clenching her fists to cover the shaking. 'I do love you very much. You know that, don't you?'

Albert had turned back to his screen and he replied through a mouthful of chicken sandwich. 'Love you too, Mum. Love you too. Hey, look! I've already got an email from someone. Look at that, it's got an attachment. "I hate Cotter too." Wonder what it is.'

Albert double-clicked. Instantly the screen went black.

'What the *fuck*?'

A ribbon of bright red text chugged along the screen.

YOU WANT A DUEL? YOU'VE GOT IT.
ALL FILES INFECTED. GOODBYE.

'No . . . *no*!' Albert switched his computer off and started it again.

'Darling, what's happening?'

'It's him, it's *him*! He's sent me a fucking virus. I can't believe it. He's destroyed the whole system. Oh, Jesus.'

'But he can't have done . . .'

'He must be running a permanent search. He's found the Australian site and knows it's from me. *Shit*!'

'All right, Albert. Calm down.'

'I've still got my laptop. He can't touch that. I'll start again. Do it even better. Take it to a cybercafé. This is just the fucking beginning. Everyone's equal on the net.'

'Albert . . .'

'Can't talk, Mum. Work to do.'

Portia closed the door and walked slowly to the kitchen. The whole terrible truth had come crashing into her mind. Ashley and Rufus Cade. She should have made the connection before and been on her guard. Ashley and Rufus Cade. And Gordon next.

A noise like a farmer turning hay with a pitchfork came through the kitchen hatchway. Gordon was sitting at the dining-room table shuffling through a heap of faxes. Portia thought she had never seen him looking so energised and alive. She preferred not to remember the dread she sometimes saw in his eyes.

'We will fight on until my husband's name is cleared.'

How many times had she heard that over the years from the spouses of Aitken, Hamilton, Archer, Clinton, Nixon and countless others who had faced scandal while their wives 'stood by them'?

She knew that Gordon was not a wicked man. Like most people, he was a child anxious to be loved and like most men, a boy desperate to prove himself in the world. She could picture him doing so many bad things for so many good reasons. He had spent most of his life trying to catch up. A second choice husband living off the earnings of a wife who had married him out of pity and her own despair. At the start of their marriage everything had come from Hillary's money. Portia had been the brilliant young student with the doctorate and academic tenure, Gordon had been the American outsider who never quite managed to fit in. Ten years of bluff talk to friends had taken their toll on his pride.

'I'm in the financial adviser game at the moment.' He was selling endowment mortgages on commission. Somehow worse, in Portia's opinion, than double-glazing or herbal remedies.

'A franchise opportunity has opened up. Looking at that quite keenly. Quite keenly.' He considered managing a Seattle style coffee bar.

'Business consultancy, as matter of fact.' Nothing.

'Broking soft commodities.' Trading in coffee futures on the residue left by Hillary after she died. And losing it too.

And one last throw. The idea had come from Portia in

fact, though he chose not to remember it. She had heard a programme on the radio about the low world prices being fetched for tea and coffee, a subject Gordon had been kvetching about for years.

'Darling, I know it's tough for you that the prices are rock bottom. But what about the pickers?'

'Yes, well, obviously it's tough for them too.'

'Surely lots of people in the west would be prepared to pay extra for coffee and tea if they thought it would benefit the Third World?'

'That's a brilliant idea, Mum.'

'It seems to make sense.'

'Porsh, it doesn't quite work like that –'

'What about it, Dad?'

'I remember,' Portia had continued. 'Peter used to make us buy Nicaraguan coffee. To support the revolution and thumb a nose at America. You could buy it everywhere. Collett's bookshop, health stores, those sort of places. They used to advertise it in the *New Statesman*. Peter even put posters up in Hampstead library.'

'Sure, it sounds all very well in theory . . .'

'Why did you call Grandpa Peter?'

'Did I, darling? It's worth thinking about though, Gordon, don't you think?'

Finally he had achieved something. Success on his own terms.

Portia put her head through the hatch.

'Gordon, I've got to go out for an hour or so. Got everything you need?'

'Going fine, Porsh. Going fine. A lot of good evidence coming in from Africa, South America, Indonesia. It's looking good.'

Portia smiled and gave a thumbs up. She had long thought that there was a melancholy air of desolation that hung over dining-rooms that were seldom used for dining. Gordon had spread papers on that table before and never with any good result. The smell of furniture polish and candlewax reminded Portia of death. Dead flies had been candied and preserved in the lips of a half empty port decanter and cobwebs furred the dried flowers and fir cones in the fireplace. She remembered when the mirror over the sideboard had been draped with black cloth. Peter, Albert and Gordon, their neckties ripped, had sat Shiva for Hillary on low wooden stools, Albert's face so solemn and white that she had wanted to cover it in kisses and hug him close to her. Peter had stayed there the full seven days, mourning his wife and perhaps also the atheism and contempt for ritual of his only daughter. There was no hope to be had from dining-rooms. None at all.

Simon had enjoyed a busy morning on the telephone. He looked down at the To Do List on his Palm Pilot.

Letter to St Mark's ✔

John ✔

Floyd ✔

Drapers ✔

Estate Agents ✔

M'binda ✔
(Hotel?) ✔

Albert ✔

CE Shares ✔

DM ✔

As far as he could tell he was up to speed and on top of everything. He considered leaving early and visiting the nets at Lord's for a little cricket practice. A small part of him, looking at the checklist, had whispered the terrible word 'boredom' to him. Soon, it would all be over.

Simon swore at himself heartily in Russian. Then in Swedish. A man of his capacity would never be bored. The idea was absurd. He could be anything he wanted to be. Writer. Inventor. Translator. Statesman. Broadcaster. Philanthropist. Collector. Playboy. If he was never bored in a small room in a hospital on a remote island in the Kattegat, how could he imagine being bored when the whole world was his playground?

His desk phone rang and he pressed the monitor button.

'Mmhm?'

'I'm so sorry, Simon. I know you said no calls. There's a woman here. She says you'll definitely want to see her. I wouldn't pay any attention, only it's Albert's mother. I wasn't sure if maybe . . .'

'One moment.'

He pressed the monitor button again. His plans were so complete, so absolute, so thoroughly thought through. He had not expected this visit, but naturally he had considered it. He was ready.

'Very well, Lily. Show her in.'

Simon rose from his desk and moved round to the sitting area.

'Mrs Fendeman, do come in. Coffee? No, of course not. I'm sorry, that was . . . water, perhaps? Fruit juice?'

'A glass of water would be fine.'

'Would you, Lily? Thanks. Sit down, please, Mrs Fendeman. Tell me how I can help you.'

Portia sat down. She found it hard to raise her head and look into his eyes.

'I think you know what you can do, Mr Cotter. You can leave my family alone.'

Simon dropped into the armchair opposite. 'Oh dear,' he said. 'This is terribly difficult. Before you say anything else, let me tell you that I have absolutely no wish to hurt your son. He's a very fine, very intelligent boy. You should be proud of him.'

'I am proud of him. I don't need your endorsement.'

'Of course not.'

'I notice,' said Portia, 'that you did not say that you had no wish to hurt my husband.'

'Mrs Fendeman, it's very important that you try to understand the complex relationship that exists between a newspaper publisher and his editorial staff.'

'Oh please . . .'

'Ah, thank you, Lily. That's fine. Definitely no calls now, okay? Thanks, love.'

Simon watched her pour the water into a glass. She looked across at him and gave a sad half-smile.

'If I hadn't known when I came in, I would have known now,' she said.

'Excuse me?'

'That habit of jogging your knee up and down. I can see you as you were. A little lost boy.'

Simon stood up. He took a deep breath. 'Oh Portia,'

he said. 'Portia. I can't tell you what . . .' He started to pace up and down the room. 'I went to a lecture you gave last April. I have watched you in your kitchen, from the street. That same house in Plough Lane. I've read your books. I've seen your light in Albert's eyes. But to have you here. It's very . . .'

'There is no light in Albert's eyes. Not any more. You've put it out.'

Simon had no wish to be side-tracked down paths opened up by Portia. 'I suppose it was that page on his website, was it? I had a go too. Gave myself blond hair. Rather frightening. That's what told you, is it? Or did you know before?'

'I'm really not sure. I had only seen you on television and in magazines. There was *something* in my mind. A distrust. A worry, I suppose . . .'

'A *distrust*?' Simon came and sat down opposite her again. 'How can you say distrust?'

'An uncomfortable feeling. It should have been distrust. Please, Ned. I don't want to talk to you about anything but my family. My son.'

'He should have been *my* son!'

'But he isn't. Half of him is Gordon, half of him is me. None of him is you.'

'I know. I know. I thought . . . it crossed my mind . . . maybe you had lied about his age. Maybe he was actually two years older. Maybe he was conceived . . .'

'There go those knees again . . .'

Simon stood up. 'But I realise that he is Gordon's. What

you have to understand,' he started pacing again, 'is what happened to me. What they did to me.'

'Ashley, Gordon and Rufus. I know what they did to you.'

'You know? How could you possibly know? There isn't the slightest possibility you could know.'

'Gordon told me.'

Simon stopped and turned. 'He told you?' He resumed his pacing. 'Yes. I see. He told you. I suppose that makes sense. You realised who I am and you told him. He confessed all and sent you to me. It makes sense.'

'You may know many things, Mr Cotter, but . . .'

'Portia, please. You know my name. Use it.'

'You may know many things, Mr Cotter,' persisted Portia, 'you may speak many languages, run many businesses and control many lives, but you do not know the first thing about people. Gordon told me years ago. Years ago. Around the time Albert was born in fact. It had been preying on his mind like a tumour. He had watched me go into the hospital and talk to your father day after day after day and he knew that he was responsible. It burned him up. He loved me, you see. He never stopped trying to find you. I gave up long before he did.'

'That was certainly a clever way to win you. I never doubted his brains.'

'Well you should have done, he hasn't many. A good heart, but no brains. Look at the mess he's in.'

'Mess? Look at the mess that African tribe is in. A good heart?'

'Oh, for heaven's sake. You don't want a debate about moral responsibility do you? Do we prefer to treat Africans like children? When they hurt their own, must it always be *our fault*? Was he more wicked than the government that actually did the deed? More wicked because he's white and "should know better" than those poor helpless little piccaninnies? Yes, it was wrong of him. It's wrong of us every time we buy a doll made by children in sweat shops. Good, decent, high-minded, liberal men and women once stirred sugar into their coffee knowing it was picked by slaves. You're wearing leather shoes, one day such an act will be regarded as the height of immorality. We buy things, we live in the world, we're all involved, all messed up together in the same moral soup. For the love of God, how can you be so *arrogant*? Can't you extend a moment's sympathy to a man floundering in quicksand?'

'A quicksand of his own making.'

'That's what makes it so pitiful still. If it was not his fault he could be like you and wallow in the luxury of divine rage. If fate throws brickbats at you, it's easy. When they're your own and they bounce back at you, it's hopeless. It *is* his fault, so he . . . he pretends. You should see him . . . he's so lost. So completely helpless.' Portia was furious to hear her voice quavering and she knew that there were now visible tears in her eyes.

'I'm sorry, Portia. Truly sorry.'

'I don't want your pity, I want your promise. I suppose it's too late to do anything for Gordon's reputation, but Albert. Leave him alone. For God's sake leave him alone.'

'He's the one picking the fight,' said Simon. He was leaning against the opposite wall. 'If I know him, he'll be sitting in a cybercafé somewhere with a laptop, using an alias with a free account and not accepting any email for fear of more viruses. It's quite an intellectual challenge.'

'He's a child. You can let go.'

Simon considered the letter he had written to Oxford that morning. A letter that would certainly reverse the college's decision to accept Albert as an undergraduate.

'I'm sorry, Portia,' he said. 'Everything is in train.'

Portia looked at the space above his head. 'Everything thoroughly thought through, in fact.'

'One day you'll understand.'

'I can't pretend that I know everything that's happened to you. But I can see the result. Perhaps you should be thanking Gordon. You have almost boundless wealth and a mind that everyone assures me is terrifying in its breadth, knowledge and power. You seem to have everything that the world covets.'

'Not you, Portia. I don't have you. I don't have your children. I don't have a family history, a youth.'

'Whatever had been done to him, do you know how Ned would have reacted? If Gordon had cut his arm off, say, in a fit of rage? Ned would have blushed and stammered and said, "Gosh, that's all right. My fault, actually. Please don't worry yourself. Awfully sorry." That's how Ned would have dealt with whatever fate had thrown him. With a dazzling smile and an embarrassed shuffle of the feet.'

'I am Ned and that is not how I reacted.'

'I don't know who you are, Mr Cotter, but I can state with absolute assurance that you are not Ned Maddstone. I knew him well, you see.'

'You will understand. And soon.' Simon moved towards her. 'I am not responsible for what is happening. All this will soon be over and you will understand completely. We will have time to talk and remember. You will see that I am merely an instrument. An instrument of God.'

From the doorway Portia shuddered. 'Oh dear heavens,' she whispered. 'You poor man. I'm so sorry.'

Simon stood for while alone in the office, thinking. After a while he called Lily on the internal phone.

'That post I put out. It hasn't gone yet, has it?'

'Still here, Simon.'

'Bring it in would you? There's a love.'

He found that he still could not sit down without his knees jiggling up and down, so he leant against the window as he reread the letter to St Mark's. He laid it on the desk and smiled to himself. It could keep.

5

Albert and Portia had sat quietly in the kitchen for a quarter of an hour each smelling the residue of Gordon's fear, neither speaking of it. He had left the house for his board meeting at half past eight.

'Doesn't do to look overkeen,' he had said, cheerfully stuffing papers into his briefcase.

Mother and son were each proud of the other's hypocrisy. Albert had not imagined Portia capable of a phrase like 'Go get 'em, Tiger!' and she had not thought that the day would ever dawn when Albert would punch his father on the arm and say 'Attaboy, Dad!'

Gordon had swept out with a brisk nod of the head, as if to show that it was an ordinary day. On ordinary days, as Albert and Portia were all too well aware, he would have kissed them each and said, 'Time to cast some pearls before swine', 'Wish me luck' or even 'Yeugh! Another shitty day for our hero.'

While the coffee went cold in their cups and Java howled in vain for admission, Portia had told Albert everything she knew about Ned Maddstone.

'Why didn't you tell me this before?' he had wanted to know. 'Why didn't *Dad* tell me?'

'I expect we would have told you one day. It didn't

seem . . . necessary. But Dad doesn't know that Ned has come back. And there's no reason why he should either. I only realised myself the other day. None of us knows what happened to Ned after he disappeared. I don't suppose we ever shall. But your father worried about him terribly for years. Perhaps he still does. We don't speak about it.'

'Do you . . . do you still love Ned?'

'I love your father very much. And I love you.'

'And Grandpa.'

'And Grandpa, of course.'

'And Java?'

'Naturally Java.'

They had both laughed. Portia had squeezed Albert's hand in appreciation of his lightening her load and he had returned the pressure.

Sitting now in his bedroom with the laptop open and Java on his knees looking in vain for a mouse to swat, he awaited an email. His mother had never answered his question and he supposed that she did still love Simon, Ned . . . whatever.

The computer chimed, Albert jumped in his seat and Java leapt crossly from his lap. He saw the letter there in his Inbox.

Simon Cotter Re: Ned

There was no attachment. He didn't even care if Cotter knew a way of sending viruses by plain email. He moved his finger along the track-pad and double-clicked with his thumb.

on 10/10/00 09:20 am, Albert Fendeman at
aef@anon_anon_anon.co.tm wrote:

>Dear Mr Cotter
>
>My mother has explained things to me, but she
>has no idea I am writing to you.
>
>I am extremely sorry for any pain my father has
>caused you in the past.
>
>I understand why you are doing what you are
>doing and promise to leave you alone from now
>on.
>
>Thank you for the valuable experience I derived
>from working with you. I hope everything goes
>well for you and your company.
>
>Please do not stop the good work you are doing in
>the field of ethical trading.
>
>Yours
>
>Albert Fendeman

Albert

Thank you for your email. Start up your computer. Ignore the fact that the screen is blank. Press Alt-Control-Shift N, wait a few seconds and then press Shift-Delete. When prompted, key in the password 'Babe' (observe the upper case B). You should find all your files intact.

Enjoy your time at Oxford. If ever you find yourself looking for employment afterwards, you know where to come. A brilliant career awaits you. Live up to your mother's expectations.

Yours

Simon

PS: A splendid email address. My directory tells me that tm is Turkmenistan. A fine touch.

–

Simon Cotter simoncotter@cotdotcom.com

****

Any opinions expressed in the email are those of the individual and not necessarily the company. This email and any files transmitted with it are confidential and solely for the use of the intended recipient or entity to whom they are addressed. It may contain material protected by attorney-client privilege. If you are not the intended recipient or the person responsible for delivering to the intended recipient, be advised that you have received this email in error and that any use is strictly prohibited. If you have received this email in error please forward this email to housekeeping@cotdotcom.com

This footnote also confirms that although this email message has been
swept for the presence of computer viruses,
the
recipient is responsible for ensuring that the email and contents have
been swept and accepted by their own virus protection systems

****

Simon closed his laptop and placed it carefully on the seat beside him.

'Wait for me, John,' he said, as he opened the door. 'I shan't be long.'

'Very good, sir.'

Stepping from the car, Simon looked up at the tall building across the street in front of him. He stepped through the battery of cameras, neither looking into their lenses, nor avoiding them.

Half an hour earlier Gordon Fendeman had looked up at the same building in much the same way. He had made the mistake of trying to hold his briefcase up in front of his face as he ran the press gauntlet which only served to make him look simultaneously guilty and absurd.

He had left the house with a sensation in his stomach that he had not experienced for twenty years, since the days of lurking in terror of the police calling with news of Ned Maddstone and a warrant for Gordon's arrest.

His wife and son hadn't fooled him with their false joshing and cheery arm-punching at breakfast time. He had seen the dread in their eyes, clear as clear. They disbelieved him. They disbelieved him twice. First, they thought him guilty of a heinous betrayal of ethics and second they had no faith that he possessed the capacity to see this thing through. He had read that distrust in Portia's face. 'Don't make it worse, Gordon. Please, don't make it worse.'

The *contempt* they had for him. It was as though he had the letters F-A-I-L-U-R-E stamped across his forehead. 'Look at me, I'm a schmuck!' he wanted to shout at the other passengers in the elevator. 'I'm a piece of shit. Laugh at me, why don't you? Help yourself. Everybody else does.'

When he was upset, Gordon still thought to himself in American. It helped him feel more of a person. Maybe . . . maybe if his parents had not died so early he would have been a success. What kind of upbringing did he have in that Hampstead nuthouse, anyway? Damn it, he was *still* living there. That same dark, dreadful house. He should have moved Porsh and Albie to the States on his passport years ago. For the price of the Plough Lane house he could have bought a place in upstate New York. Ithaca maybe. Albie would've grown up American. Portia could've gotten a job at the University and Gordon could have *achieved* there. Americans didn't have that snobby look in their eyes. That English public school politeness that was like a knife in the guts. The murmuring 'Gosh, awfully sorry' and that oh-so self-deprecating smile. Self-deprecating, my ass. They knew who was boss, they knew who was in and who was out.

His family loved him, sure. But what kind of love was it that looked at you like you were a wounded deer? Too scared to say what they're thinking because they think you're too scared to hear it. That's not love, that's abuse. Abuse, nothing less.

He loved them too, he knew that. He wanted to provide for them, protect them, be loved and adored by them, but he never got the chance. No one had ever asked his advice on the simplest question. Even plumbers and electricians, when they came to the house. They always asked Portia to show them the ring main or the stop-cock, or whatever damned thing. These days they asked Albie. It was like some instinct they had. He could be standing there, in the middle of the room, master of the house, head of the family, but would they ask *him* if he wanted MDF or plywood? Jesus, the stink of failure he must give off.

His own son was earning more aged seventeen than he

had most years of his life. That fucking asshole Simon Cotter. His humiliation of Gordon would never end.

On the forty-third floor the board was waiting to meet him with all the usual hearty jokes and false civilities. Purvis Alloway came forward with a handshake and – sure sign of betrayal to come – the simultaneous hand on the shoulder.

'Probably best, Mr Chairman,' – how they loved the formality of titles – 'if I chair this meeting, since it's mostly about . . . you know . . .'

'Sure, sure . . .' Gordon waved the politeness aside. 'I was going to suggest the same thing myself.'

'Shall we be getting on?'

Gordon, breathing heavily felt sweat breaking out over his face as he sat at the opposite end from Alloway. He opened his briefcase and scooped out piles and piles of documents onto the table in front of him. An embarrassed silence fell and he knew that he had overdone the paperwork. Only crazed litigants and public health scare fanatics carry so much documentation about with them, he realised. He could feel pins of sweat beginning to push out from every pore on his face and he was breathing heavily as though he had taken the stairs.

He sat down, flushed while Alloway coughed and proceeded with business.

'Gentlemen, I call this extraordinary meeting to order. Under article nine we may dispense with minutes and proceed to the single item on the agenda papers before us. I have promised the press a statement by twelve noon, which I think gives us time to cover all our, ah, bases. Before we listen to Mr Fendeman would anybody care to make any opening comments?'

Everyone was gentle and tactful and kind. No one wished to cast the least doubt on Gordon's integrity. Several board members had wry and vinegary remarks to make on the subject of the British press and its irresponsibility.

Suzie, Gordon's secretary, sat on Alloway's left and took notes in shorthand.

'I don't believe, Mr Acting Chairman,' said one board member, 'that the *London Evening Press* even possesses an Africa correspondent.'

'That's right!' Gordon put in eagerly. 'I have a friend who works for the BBC World Service in Nairobi, and he deposes that at no time has a single British print journalist . . .' He broke off, realising that it was not his turn to speak. 'Well, I guess we'll come to that later.'

Others wished to remind the board that it was Gordon Fendeman's vision, Gordon Fendeman's sense of justice, Gordon Fendeman's idealism and sheer guts that had created this business in the first place. He had built it up from nothing, to a respectable shipper in speciality coffees and thence into a major quoted stock market player. A famous brand. The question of his share dealings in – ironically – the *London Evening Press*, was not a question for this board. If Gordon needed time to deal with his detractors, perhaps he could step down temporarily? The board member wished to emphasise the word 'temporarily', place it on the record and urge strongly for its inclusion in the press statement. When Gordon had cleared his name – and the board member for one never doubted that he would – then the way would be clear for him to be welcomed back to the chairman's office. How was that for a plan?

The 'hear hears' and pattings of the blotters came so fast and so unanimously that Gordon realised at once that this compromise had been prearranged behind his back.

'Before we come to a vote on that . . .' said Purvis Alloway. Gordon swallowed and drew in a breath ready to begin his great speech, 'I have a special request to put to the board. It is a little unorthodox perhaps, but since this is an extraordinary meeting called under extraordinary circumstances, I take it there will be no objection.'

Everyone looked at Purvis and this time Gordon knew that the surprise was not being sprung on him alone.

'I received this morning a letter from a lady staying at Hazlitt's Hotel,' Alloway continued. 'Her name is Princess M'binda and she claims to have information vital to the good name of this company. She is waiting in my office now. I think we should hear her.'

Gordon's mouth was very dry and he took a sip of water, knowing that every face was turned in his direction. Setting down the glass he looked up, feigned surprise at the sight of so many eyes upon him.

'Of course,' he said, 'why not? Show her in by all means.'

Alloway pressed the chairman's buzzer under the table and the door to the boardroom opened.

Everyone around the table rose awkwardly to their feet, Gordon last and most clumsily of all.

'Good morning, Your . . . ah . . . good morning, Princess,' Alloway was a little unsure of protocol and like the others had been thrown off guard by the extreme beauty of the girl who had come in and was now backed shyly against the wall. She was six foot tall and wrapped in vivid green, red and yellow cotton. The board members became suddenly and uncomfortably aware of the photographs on the wall which displayed similar girls in similar dress, girls with berry-filled baskets on their heads smiling toothily at the camera.

Alloway went to the side of the room to pull forward a chair which he placed to the right of his own and a little further back from the table. 'Please, madam, if you would be so good as to sit down.'

She stayed where she was, arms outstretched and palms flattened against the wall, her large eyes fixed on the window. Alloway understood at once.

'Is it the height, my dear? Would you like us to draw the curtains?'

The girl nodded and one board member attended to the blinds, while another switched on the lights. Immediately, the tension went out of her body and she dropped onto the chair with great elegance. Her eyes met Gordon's at the end of the table opposite and held them steadily.

Gordon's breath had been growing very shallow since the moment her name had been mentioned and his mouth was dry and clacky, but he knew that to take another drink of water would be to lose a psychological battle. He met the girl's gaze and she slowly dropped her eyes to her lap.

'Now then,' Alloway was looking at a letter on the table in front of him. 'You say that you have information vital to the interests of this company. Perhaps you would be good enough to tell us who you are and what information it is that you have for us?'

'I am the Princess M'binda of the Ankoza,' she began. 'We are a people of the hills. My father B'goli was their king . . .'

As she talked, and Suzie's pencil raced along her pad, Gordon was transported in his mind back to East Africa. He had been forced to go there because a shipment of futures on which he had invested the last of his – of Hillary's – money had been delayed, as he thought, in port. In fact, the beans were in store somewhere, close to rotting. It had been his fault. Some piece of paperwork, eight months before, had not been sent from London. Typical of his luck.

It had been sorted out at last, at great extra cost, and he had met a man in a bar who had told him about the Ankoza. 'They grew the plantation themselves from scratch, it's just coming into maturity now. Some Robusta but Arabica mostly. Top quality peaberries too. Good high air, but they don't know shit about selling coffee. They take it to market would you believe? Waste of damn good growing country. I'm trying to get my people to take an interest.'

Well, Gordon had found them first and charmed B'goli, their chief, into agreeing to accept him as their exclusive buyer for the produce of their soft lilac-coloured mountains. He had hurried back to civilisation to sell his original consignment, at a thundering loss, and used the cash to set up his own brokerage and to hire lawyers to hammer B'goli's agreement into an ironclad contract. He duly obtained B'goli's signature and word got about that there was a new player in town. A fortnight after he had registered his brokerage a man from the government came to see Gordon.

'Dear me. It cannot be that you are going into business with the Ankoza? But everybody knows how corrupt they are. They will cheat you and rob you. My people, on the other hand, the Kobali people, thoroughly reliable. How much easier to deal with them. The government is entirely Kobali. How much more quickly your coffee will go through port, how much more efficiently it will be handled if you deal only with Kobali! Trading with the Ankoza, it is doubtful that a single bean would reach the warehouses. No, no, my friend. Much better deal with us. What's this? The contract is not with the Ankoza . . . it is with the *land*. My dear fellow, this makes it so simple! The Ankoza do not *own* this land. No, no, no. I assure you they do not. I tell you what we shall do. We shall compensate you for all this extra work – a hundred thousand pounds English sterling – and we shall help you to remove those scoundrel Ankoza from the land they are illegally occupying.'

Not his fault. Not his fault. It was the man in the bar.

Someone would have got there if Gordon hadn't, it was inevitable. The Ankoza were always going to be kicked out. Not his fault. But M'binda . . .

The moment he had seen her, he had wanted her. He had asked that she be kept behind. She had wept inconsolably as her father and his family had been loaded onto lorries like potatoes and driven down the hill.

It was not rape though. If she said that it was rape, she was lying. She had been . . . if not compliant, certainly not non-compliant. She had been nothing. A lifeless doll.

Her word against his, that was the point. His word against hers. For the time being it was important to look surprised, outraged at everything she said, as if each fresh accusation came as a shock. He was somehow upset by the presence of Suzie in the room. She had never once looked up, but her pencil had never stopped moving and her lips moved imperceptibly as she scribbled. The whole story was down there in Pitman hieroglyphs and later today she would type it up into minutes. Gordon wanted to wrench the pad from her and rip it to pieces.

Nobody was looking at him now as M'binda finished her tale. That wasn't true. She was looking at him. No disgust in her eyes, no flash of vengeful hatred. She just looked with a cool and steady gaze that screwed his lungs into a ball.

'When I was allowed to leave I found my family living in iron sheds in a dusty village below the mountains. When the rains came the water from the mountains filled the village and the dust became mud. My mother and two of my brothers died from malaria. My father and my sisters, they died from cholera. That is my story. My father the king, he trusted Mr Fendeman very much and now he is dead and my people are starving, diseased and their hearts are broken from loss of home.'

Alloway leaned forward and patted her on the hand. 'Thank you, Your Highness. Thank you very much indeed.'

Gordon coughed involuntarily and tried to turn the cough into a laugh.

'Preposterous,' he spluttered, dabbing at his face with a handkerchief. 'I mean, gentlemen, please!' He looked them all in the eyes, each one in turn. 'I think . . . I *insist* that it is time I had my say. Firstly, I have to tell you that I have never seen this woman before in my life.' He used the word 'woman' because he was uncomfortably aware how young she looked. He knew that everyone around the table would have made their calculations and determined that five years ago, at the time Gordon was in Africa, she can have been no older than thirteen or fourteen. 'Secondly, what she says about the contract with King B'goli is a clever concoction of half truths. Yes, the deal was with the land, not with the people. But that is standard. You all know that. She paints a charming picture of naïve simplicity and honest dignity, but *poverty*? Excuse me. This lady has flown from Africa and is staying – where did you say, Purvis? – the Waldorf. The Waldorf Fucking Hotel, you should excuse my French. We should all be so poor, Princess. Most importantly of all. Where is the proof? Am I to be condemned on the say-so of a plausible actress, playing on your guilty heart strings. Christ almighty, I'm a married man. I have a family. Where is the proof? Without proof none of this is anything more than slander.'

'Perhaps I can help you there, gentlemen.'

Every head turned towards the doorway, the source of the interruption. Simon Cotter strode in, smiling and stood behind M'binda, a hand resting on the back of her chair.

Gordon blinked the sweat out of his eyes and tried to speak, but no words came.

Purvis Alloway had sprung to his feet 'I don't know who let you in – Mr Cotter is it not? – but this is a private board meeting and I must ask you to remove yourself. If you have any submissions to make, I suggest you make them formally, in writing, to the chairman.'

'I'm not in the habit, Mr Alloway,' said Simon smoothly, 'of writing to myself, formally or otherwise.'

'Excuse me?'

'As of ten o'clock this morning I became the majority shareholder in this company. I think that gives me every right to be here.'

A murmur of conversation broke out and one board member's hand inched towards his mobile phone. Alloway slapped the table.

'Gentlemen, please!' He turned back to Cotter.

'Is this really true?'

Simon passed a piece of paper. 'A record of the transaction from my broker. You may check with your own people, if you prefer.'

'No, no. This seems in order . . . really, Mr Cotter, we

had no idea of your intentions towards our company. You come at a difficult moment.'

'I could not help but overhear Mr Fendeman defending himself. He has a carrying voice, if I may say so.'

Gordon's face was grey and he was finding it difficult to control his breathing. He could feel the sweat around his collar and the cold drops ran from his armpits down the side of his body to his waist.

'I said I can help you,' continued Simon, 'and I can. Let me deal straight away with the subject of proof. I have here –' he laid three pieces of paper carefully on the table, '– sworn depositions, duly, as you will see from the seals, notarised. The first confirms Mr Fendeman's receipt of a hundred thousand pounds from the government. It is signed by the man who offered the bribe. The second contains the signature of another government official who testifies that Mr Fendeman insisted as part of the deal that the thirteen-year-old Princess M'binda be kept behind during the eviction of the Ankoza people. The third affidavit is signed by two drivers and a soldier, each of whom saw Mr Fendeman personally carry the Princess into a hut. The soldier, I'm afraid, who was young at the time, actually looked through a hole in the wall of the hut and witnessed the entire rape. At a moment's notice any or all of these people can be flown to the United Kingdom if Mr Fendeman wishes to contest their evidence.'

Despite the hammering in his chest and the buzzing in his ears, Gordon managed to speak. The sound was hoarse and barely above the level of a whisper but everybody in the room heard it and Suzie's pencil faithfully recorded the word.

'Why?'

Simon smiled. 'Why? *Simple justice*, Mr Fendeman. Simple justice.'

The sweat was running into his eyes but, with a jolt that wrenched at his lungs the realisation came upon him. He had only met him once, twenty years ago, but the image had never left him. It was an image that summed up everything Gordon hated about England and everything he hated about himself.

'It's *you*!' he croaked.

He had only one thought now. The window. The blinds were down, but if he ran fast enough and led with his shoulder he could do it. He could break free and do one last thing that Albie might admire.

He charged like a mad bull. He heard cries of 'Stop him!' from the table and out of the corner of his eye he saw Suzie's startled face look up from her pad at last.

He hit the window hard and, contemptible, useless prick that he was, failure from first to last, he bounced back like a squash-ball. As he crashed to the ground he felt his throat tighten in an iron stranglehold and a lightning-bolt of pain flashed and thumped down his left side. This was how he had watched his father die twenty years ago. The same roar of pain and clutching at the throat. Suzie, God bless her, was the first by his side, loosening his tie and raising his head. The others clustered behind her and at the back he saw the face looking down at him.

'Ned fucking Maddstone,' he said as he died. 'Fuck you for ever.'

Simon was out of the room before the last breath had left Gordon's body. Time was fleeting by and he was on a tight schedule. Hairdressers to see and miles to go before he slept.

'Two!' he whispered, tactfully closing the door behind him.

Oliver Delft had been sent to find a hacker in Knightsbridge. Not to arrest him, but to recruit him.

'Cosima picked up his trail and we've been watching him from a distance ever since. A good poacher who'll make an even better gamekeeper,' Cotter had told him. 'Very young, but quite brilliant.'

Oliver was having trouble finding the right address. There was 46, an ice-cream parlour and there was 47, a College of English. Of 46B there was no sign whatsoever. He stood at the door of the College and pondered the problem. It was undignified to be back in the world of legwork. He had taken the Cotter shilling gladly, but he should have known that there would be a price. In his world, Oliver had been supreme commander. The pay was atrocious and the bureaucratic constrictions suffocating. Was he now nothing more than a bird in a gilded cage?

As he stood examining the doorbells a hand fell on his shoulder from behind. Oliver dropped the shoulder and tried to turn, but the hand knew what it was doing and had anticipated his move. It gripped the shoulder harder.

'You come along with us, sir. Micky, car door. I shall read the gentleman his rights.'

If this was the private sector Oliver wanted nothing to

do with it. The two bent-nosed pluguglies either side of him were not officers of the law, for all their uniforms, plastic cuff-links and portentous language. Oliver had known a few in his time and he would have been prepared to bet that all this pair knew about police stations was the colour of tiles inside the cells. He sensed the strength and the violence in them, however, and was not prepared to argue just yet. If they were working for this hacker, then CDC had been seriously compromised. That kraut woman, his predecessor, was clearly incompetent, everyone at Cotter's had told him so. She had stumbled on something she did not understand. However. Delft trusted his wits and at the end of it all smelled the possibility of gain. When Delft follows you into a revolving door, he likes to say, he always comes out first.

They drove north in silence. The driver interested Oliver. He saw the eyes watching him from the mirror. Sixty-ish, more dignified than the yahoos in the back. *He* could be a copper easily. Something familiar about him? Probably not.

The car swept into a farmhouse driveway and again a little stab of déjà vu visited the pit of his stomach. A childhood holiday? Mysteriouser and mysteriouser.

Oliver was led into a bare kitchen and told to sit down.

'Don't move.'

'It isn't easy to sit down without moving.'

Ah, big mistake. An enormous fist crunched into the back of his neck. Oliver sat down. Sudden blows to the back of the neck, as to the nose, can cause the tear ducts to spring. Oliver blinked rapidly and widened his eyes to let them flow without reddening. He really was not going to be seen crying. That would be too ridiculous. He looked up at the ceiling, dilating his nostrils and sniffing, like a man who looks into the sun to make himself sneeze, while they removed his shoes and his tie. Did they imagine that he, Oliver Delft was the type to hang himself. Just when things were getting so interesting? The two barbarians left and he heard them lock the door behind them.

The tears subsided and he looked around. An Aga and a fridge. Was it a holiday? A dirty weekend years ago? He was *sure* now that he had been here before. It was an old-fashioned fridge, a squat Prestcold. Yet he could see lighter paint against the wall that suggested it had been put in to replace a taller, slimmer one. All very odd.

There was an *LEP* on the table. Today's early edition.

ABUSE IN SWEDISH HOSPITAL OF HELL

It wasn't the headline, it was the photograph inset halfway down that grabbed Oliver's attention.

Mallo!

Thank Christ he was out of the service. God bless Simon Cotter. Looked like there was going to be a stink.

Would Mallo talk? If he was being threatened with arrest he might. Idiot prick, the whole point of Mallo was that he followed the regulations. Diplomas on the wall, government inspections, everything nice and legal. What the hell had he done to bring down the wrath of the Swedish government?

Who was there left in the padded cells who might lead a nosy investigation back to the department? Well, there was that mad idealist from Porton Down of course, research chemist – what was his name? – Michaels, Francis Michaels. There was Babe Fraser if he was still alive, which was doubtful. The only time Oliver had seen him, as a junior on the trail of all the money that the son of a bitch had salted away, the great legend had been as potty as a prawn, brains fried to hell. That was when Oliver had found out about 'The Island of Dr Mallo'. No, there was no danger from Babe. Finally of course there was young Ned Maddstone. Oliver remembered him as a mental weakling. He'd have been ECT-ed into gaga-land years since.

The article didn't say much. Just that the conditions had been 'medieval' and that there had been allegations of physical and sexual abuse. Hardly worthy of the front page. If it had all taken place in Britain, Oliver could understand such a report appearing in an English paper, but why bother Londoners with such routine dross? Sexual abuse, he decided. The phrase sold millions of papers up and down the land. The law-abiding liked to read about it at their breakfast tables and on their trains. They tut-tutted in horror while deep inside their deepest, darkest fantasies were touched.

'Sorry to keep you waiting. I hope you haven't been uncomfortable. You've been crying I see, do borrow my handkerchief.'

'Simon?' Oliver stared. Cotter was removing his sunglasses. He had dyed his hair blond. No, he had *un*dyed his hair. The blond was streaked with grey.

'Simon?' said Ned. 'I know no Simon. Look again.'

Oliver looked again and saw that he was looking into the blue eyes of Ned Maddstone.

'Not *exactly* the same fridge,' he observed at length.

'No,' Ned admitted ruefully. 'But as close as I could get. Thought it might help you feel at home.'

'Oh it does, it does.' Oliver was holding himself together very well. 'You've been busy,' he remarked.

Ned looked around the kitchen. 'Thank you. I always say good design is all about taking away, not adding. You'll note that aside from the fridge there is no other furniture or fitments, for reasons you will discover later. The old place hadn't changed that much, as a matter of fact. Oh, there's the Aga of course. Same old one. Tch! Agas, eh? Where would we be without them?'

'No, no. I meant Ashley Barson-Garland and now poor old Gordon Fendeman. I should have made the connection.'

'People keep saying that to me. You mustn't blame yourself, it was a long time ago. But we mustn't say "poor old Gordon Fendeman", you know. He's happy now. Gone to a better place.'

'Quite the avenging angel, aren't you?'

'I do my best, Oliver, I do my best. As you will discover.'

'You escaped then, from the "Swedish Hospital of Hell"?' Oliver jerked his head towards the newspaper.

'Ah, I thought that might amuse you. All nonsense as a matter of fact, had the paper specially made up for your entertainment. You'll be pleased to know that dear Dr Mallo is still there. He's working for me now. I have some documents in my possession that he would prefer kept private between ourselves. He's a very reasonable man, as you know. He likes to describe himself as a rationalist. Pompous, but rather touching.'

'Am I to be lectured at? If that's your punishment, I might as well tell you here and now that I'm very good at switching off.'

'My dear old periwinkle, was I lecturing? How very graceless of me. Let me fetch you a glass of milk. No? I'm having one myself. Sure? Okay then. Fresh and creamy this time. Not UHT semi-skimmed. There are limits to authenticity, after all.'

Oliver was thinking rapidly. The plastic bracelets around his wrist were more than he could cope with on his own. The man behind the wheel he had now identified as Sergeant Floyd, the Drug Squad officer he had bribed to keep his mouth shut over Ned's arrest. He still had no idea who the other two men might be, but he had a nasty idea.

'Smart of you to escape. I have to confess I didn't mark you down as that sort.'

Ned sat down at the table opposite Oliver. 'You met Babe, I think. You were one of the squad that tried to beat it out of him when you found out that all that money was missing.'

'So Mr Memory himself put the jigsaw together for you did he? Thought it was rather beyond your limited capabilities.'

'His capabilities are now mine.'

'Oh I don't think so, old crocus. Babe was special.'

'Well,' said Ned, not allowing himself to be annoyed. 'We can agree on that at least. He even remembered your mother, you know? One glance at a file is all he ever had. Date of birth, everything.'

'Must have been fun for him to have a blank canvas on which to paint,' said Oliver. 'Dumb brick of a child, eager to learn. Taught you all those languages. Smattering of philosophy and mathematics. Arranged your escape too, I'll bet. You couldn't have managed that on your own. Too weak to make it over the wall himself. Am I to expect him to walk through the door at any minute? "Aha, you pampered Asiatic Jades, I've a thirst on me today." All that? My old boss used to do quite an impression of him.'

'Babe is dead. Yes, he did arrange the escape. Yes, he did teach me. Yes, I was a dumb brick. You can't expect me to rise to such obvious bait.'

'Above that, are you? All passion spent. What are you now? Nemesis? The Hammer of God? The Cold Hand of Fate?'

'Something like that,' said Ned. 'You will have plenty of time to decide what I am. You will be able to ponder too on what you are. Years you will have. There'll be Martin and Paul and Rolf and dear Dr Mallo to help you come to a decision. The best possible care. No one else,

I'm afraid. A small staff, but since there will be only one patient, I'm sure you won't feel badly served.'

'For fuck's sake . . .'

'The journey will be painful. But no more painful than was mine. My driver John, his two friends the Draper brothers and ex-Superintendent Floyd will take you over the water. My driver John – you'll remember him as Mr Gaine, he's put on a bit of weight, but you'll find he's lost none of his charm – will dislocate your shoulder which will cause quite shattering pain. It will unbalance your walk, which we can't have, so Rolf will dislocate the other one for you.'

'You're insane.'

'If I'm insane then so are you. Nothing will happen to you that did not happen to me. You are a grown man. I was a frightened child.'

'My family! I have a family. You've sat with my children.'

'I had a family, Oliver. The Fendemans had a family. When you had me recite the name of Peter Fendeman into a tape-recorder, did you consider Portia's family?'

'But her father is fine! He was released after a week. Special Forces had been a little rough when they arrested him, but he was soon released. He's alive, isn't he? He's happy? And *think* . . .' Oliver was clutching at straws now. 'Why did he name his daughter Portia? Remember Portia in *The Merchant of Venice*? "The quality of mercy is not strained, it droppeth like the gentle rain from heaven upon the place beneath. It is twice blessed. It blesses him that gives and him that receives."'

'How perfectly marvellous that you should mention Shakespeare's Portia. A happy coincidence, I was about to come to the one option left open to you if you really do wish to avoid a lifetime as a guest of Dr Mallo.'

'Yes? What? What is it?'

'There are, in case you have forgotten, *two* Portias in Shakespeare. One, as you rightly pointed out just now, in *The Merchant of Venice*. But have you forgotten the other Portia. The Portia in *Julius Caesar*?'

Oliver's head was dizzy. 'I don't understand.'

'She chooses to take her own life, if you recall, by swallowing hot coals. Always used to fascinate me as a child. How could it be done? Well, the Aga there is old-fashioned. The solid fuel type. There's no other means of self slaughter in the room, I'm afraid. I've checked thoroughly and I know something about how rooms are furnished to prevent suicide. The floor and walls are rubberised, nothing metal, stone or wooden here. You could bash your head against the Aga I suppose, but I doubt it would kill you and it would certainly annul our agreement. It's up to you. The plastic of your cuffs will melt against the stove very nicely. Agony, I should imagine, but it will work. You simply lift up the lid and help yourself. Basically, Oliver, it's up to you. Swallow fiery coals like Portia or face the rest of your life in an insane asylum. You have ten minutes to make up your mind.'

'You *are* mad.'

'So you keep saying. I don't understand how repeating it makes any difference. If it's untrue then you can hardly expect me to be swayed by insult. If it's *true* then I should have thought that it is even more useless to appeal to me. God have mercy on your soul either way, about sums it up. Nine minutes and forty-five seconds.'

The others were in the sitting-room, clustered around Mr Gaine, who was having difficulty with a crossword. Ned helped them finish it.

'That should be owl. "Tight as an –" Owl. You've put "eft", John.'

'Oh, well. Yeah. I reckoned, you know. An eft is a type of newt. Pissed as a newt, pissed as an eft.'

'Mm,' marvelling at Gaine's thought processes, Ned checked that everything was ready.

'Van warmed up? Good. The boat is ready. Everyone knows what they have to do.'

'Everything ready, sir,' said Floyd, smartly. 'When we arrive at Levington it should be dark enough to –'

The screams were like nothing anyone in the room had ever heard before. Mr Gaine and the Drapers had seen violence. Floyd had witnessed enough to last a lifetime, but this . . . this was something new. He started towards the kitchen, but Ned held his hand up to detain him.

'Give him a moment,' he said. 'This is his choice.'

The Drapers looked at each other with wide eyes. Gaine looked down at the carpet and Floyd stared at Ned. The screaming stopped.

'Now I think,' said Ned, who was the first to reach the kitchen door.

Delft's hair and clothes were on fire, blisters the size

of oranges had ballooned from his lips and his mouth was screaming. He had no tongue and no vocal chords with which to make a sound. He was hurling himself against the wall, clawing at his body.

He caught sight of Ned and lurched towards him. Ned smartly closed the door and bolted it. They heard the body bang against the rubber surface of the door.

'We'll give him another five minutes,' he said. 'He'll be done then.'

Floyd put a hand on Ned's chest. 'I'm sorry, Mr Cotter,' he said. 'I don't care how much you're paying me. Someone's got to go in there and put him out of his misery.'

Ned slipped aside and led the way back into the sitting-room. 'A word,' he said. He stood and faced them with his back to the fireplace. 'Now, let's just sort ourselves out shall we? Mr Floyd, you arranged the lease of this house?'

'You know I did, but what –?'

'You paid in cash. The same with the car and the van?'

'Of course.'

'No one knows you've been here. Once we've wiped all the prints, the place will be clean.'

'That's not the point, sir . . .'

'Oh but it is, Mr Floyd.' Ned took a small revolver from his pocket and shot Floyd through the throat. Moving round anticlockwise, he shot Gaine and the Drapers in the head. He dipped the end of the revolver in Gaine's cup of tea on the table by the sofa and it hissed pleasingly. Ned drank the tea and dropped down to Gaine's body. He pulled a set of car keys from the jacket, put them in his own pocket and moved to the kitchen.

Delft was lying on the floor writhing and twitching.

'One,' whispered Ned, administering a final kick to the charred ruin beneath him.

He drove the car as far as Peterborough, where he left it in the station car park, right next to the Lexus that he and Gaine had left there eight hours earlier. A busy day and still not over yet.

Ned was surprised that he was trembling, for he knew that he was calm. He had that true calm that can only come to those who have earned their night's repose. The peace that flows from true achievement.

Now he was ready to turn his mind to good things. The memory of Babe would be celebrated in every major city from Copenhagen to Canberra. Libraries, schools, hospitals. An international university. Research centres. Orphanages run on new, enlightened principles. The children of the world would be enriched in mind and body. Portia would be by his side. Together they would rule the greatest charitable empire on earth. All the good that would flow from them. Maybe, in some extraordinary way, everything that had happened to him had been part of a great plan. How dull his life would have been without this great cause that had lit him from within for so many years. The stars had guided him well. They had led him to this great point.

He looked across the street to the house. Through the darkness he saw that the lights were on in one room only.

Portia and Albert would be sitting in the kitchen, perhaps, talking quietly.

He rang the doorbell, but there was no reply. He rang again. A cat leapt down from the wall and rubbed itself against his ankles, mewing plaintively. Ned heard another plaintive sound from within, a low whining chant that he could not understand. He pushed against the door which swung open on its hinges. The cat jumped in ahead of him.

'Portia? Are you there? Portia, it's Ned.'

The chanting grew louder. Ned saw a light shining through the kitchen hatch and walked round into the dining-room.

'Portia, it's me. What are you doing here?'

A black cloth had been hung over the mirror above the sideboard and on a low stool sat Peter, his jacket and tie ripped. His eyes were cast down to the floor and he was chanting a Hebrew prayer.

'Peter? It's me. You remember me?'

Peter lifted his eyes. 'Ned. I remember you. It's Ned.'

'Where are Portia and Albert?'

'Gone. They are gone. My brother's son is dead, did you know?'

'Where? Where have they gone?'

'Who knows?'

Ned left the room and ran upstairs. Clothes trailed across the floor, wardrobes hung open, bottles of shampoo and tubes of toothpaste had fallen into the basin under the bathroom cabinet and the floor was littered with pill-bottles and combs and bars of soap. They had left in a hurry, in a terrible panic. Did they think they had something to fear from him? From *Ned*?

He rushed downstairs again. The old man's moaning was driving him crazy.

'Where did they go? They must have told you.'

Peter said nothing but continued to rock backwards and forwards, singing his prayers. Ned went into the kitchen to find some milk. The light of the fridge shone onto the table and that is where he saw the envelope.

Ned Maddstone

He remembered her handwriting! From all those years he remembered her handwriting. He held the envelope to his cheek.

'Now go,' Peter's voice came through the hatchway. 'Go and never come back. You've done enough. Go.'

He sat in the car and wept. Nothing for him. Just the old letters. Not even a note. She couldn't hide from him. His power would uncover her wherever she was in the world.

What then? Suppose he found her. What would he do then? Keep her prisoner? Force her to marry him? It was too late. It had always been too late.

Ned knew exactly what he had to do. He had to go home. It was so simple. So obvious. He must go home, away from the noise and terror of the world. Home, where it was either light and bright, or cosy and dark. Home, where they understood him. Home, where there was peace and ease and gentleness and love. Home, in every language that he spoke, it was the best and strongest word. Home. His Swedish island. Where his friends lived and where the ghost of Babe would come to him and teach him more.

*

He stood on the deck looking back towards England. He let the pieces of paper fly from his hand and dart like butterflies in the wake. They came from the last century, an age when lovers wrote letters to each other sealed up in envelopes. Sometimes they used coloured inks to show their love, or they perfumed their writing-paper with scent.

He slowly ripped the last of them, just glimpsing down at a halved sheet.

> I picture your hair flopping down as you write, which is enough to make me writhe and froth like a . . . like a . . . er, I'll come back to you on that one. I think of your legs under the table and a million trillion cells sparkle and fizz inside me. The way you cross a 't' makes me breathless. I hold the back of my envelope to my lips and think of you licking it and my head swims. I'm a dotty dippy dozy dreadful delirious romantic and I love you to heaven.

Ned let the wind whip it from his hand.